we were delta

we were delta

derek erickson

books by
derek erickson

Symphony Saga
Howling Symphony Book One
Blood Crescendo Book Two
Staccato Split Book Three
Wild Melody Book Four

A Tale of Monsters Series
Stolen Book One
Into the Green Book Two
The Goddess Book Three

Master's War Series
We Were Delta Book One

CONTENTS

Chapter 1: The Tattooed Man..................1
Chapter 2: The Reservation....................8
Chapter 3: Hive Negotiations................22
Chapter 4: Hungry for Peace.................32
Chapter 5: Picking up Strays.................48
Chapter 6: Surviving Space...................57
Chapter 7: Staring into the Nothing........68
Chapter 8: Upgrades.............................75
Chapter 9: What's my Purpose...............87
Chapter 10: Scientific Endeavor............101
Chapter 11: We Broke You...................112
Chapter 12: Greenhouse.......................119
Chapter 13: Mirakus Station.................127
Chapter 14: Ravi Star...........................142
Chapter 15: The Fabled Army...............153
Chapter 16: Range Practice..................166
Chapter 17: Mishap Report...................177
Chapter 18: Bounty Hunters.................192
Chapter 19: Cold War..........................204
Chapter 20: Earning your Name............214
Chapter 21: Claustrophobia..................227
Chapter 22: Maeve Station...................240
Chapter 23: Roentgen Madness.............256
Chapter 24: Trapped............................267
Chapter 25: The Past, the Present, and the Future..........280
Chapter 26: Commander of the Stars.....289
Chapter 27: The Smiling in the Stars......301
Chapter 28: Asimov Failure...................313

Chapter 29: Back into the Hive..319
Chapter 30: One Man Army..330
Chapter 31: Angler Fish...337
Chapter 32: The Enemy of my Enemy is Delicious..................339
Chapter 33: Slayer and Usurper..346
Chapter 34: Take back the Stars...355
Chapter 35: Resuscitation...364
Chapter 36: Hail Mary..370
Chapter 37: The Spirit to Fight..376
Chapter 38: Take a Breath...381
Epilogue..384

Chapter 1

The Tattooed Man

"**H**ey worm." Sadie froze as a leg crushed the street in front of her, so big it blocked her path. So close. She was so close to getting into the city without being stopped. She had to crane her head so far back it hurt her neck. The ursa guard was four meters high and probably four hundred kilograms of muscle and fur. It wore white security pants and boots, but its wide torso was bare. It was completely unfazed by the frozen hellscape. "What are you doing out of your hole?"

"Seeking one of my own."

The wind howled, almost ripping her hood and words away. The ursa squinted in confusion and leaned over, causing her heart to beat even harder. The weather, the thick cloth wrapped around her face, and an ursa's poor hearing meant she had to shout. But if her shout was perceived as an order or a threat, he might break every bone in her body. Instinct screamed for her to run.

"Seeking one of my own!" she repeated, her voice squeaking in fear as those teeth loomed closer. She could actually feel the heat coming out of his wide nostrils. Supposedly they were called ursa because of their resemblance to Earth bears. Sadie didn't know what a bear looked like, but this ursa had royal blue fur, black beady eyes, and a head bigger than her torso. He rested a rifle larger than her in one hand, but he didn't need it for her kind. He could crush her with one hand.

"The reservation know you're out here?" the ursa's voice rumbled, sounding unsure whether he wanted to pester her or find something more important to do. Sadie nodded and pulled at the cord looped over her shoulder. It was attached to a large black disc almost a half meter wide. It wasn't made for human convenience; everything else here was bigger than them. The guard put his paw on it, thumbing a permission screen. It showed Sadie's picture and stated she was allowed in the city until nightfall.

"Show me your face."

He probably didn't mean to bellow, but it sounded like a warning to her small ears. Sadie quickly tucked her hood and unwrapped her face, which took a frantic few seconds because of the multiple layers. He studied her features, looking for anything that would show her pass was a fake. It didn't help that most of the humans on this planet looked the same. Dark skin, dark eyes, short black hair, and frighteningly skinny. Sadie's face was gaunt with highly pronounced cheekbones. The freezing temperature might not bother an ursa, but she was shivering to her core. The falling sleet was making microscopic cuts across her now exposed face.

"Don't shake too much, little worm. Something might eat you here." The ursa chuckled and dropped her identifier. "The only others of your kind will be in the spaceport. Go."

"Thank you," she mumbled, quickly pulling the cloth back over her head and cinching her hood tight. Another dangerous gamble, staying warm while limiting her view. Not everything at the spaceport was as big as an ursa, but this was their city. One might accidentally kick her in the same way a human might stumble over a toddler scurrying through a crowd. Sadie stuck to the side of the street, which also cut down on the wind. There was a chance something might accidentally, or purposefully, shove her into the wall, but at least nobody could trip her into oncoming traffic.

The massive doors to the spaceport slid open and a rush of warmth enveloped Sadie. There was snow on the grates and she did her part to stomp the white frost off herself before proceeding. It wasn't that it was hot in here; it just wasn't freezing. There was a lack of wind and with the exhaust of a dozen ships and their associated shops, it could almost be considered comfortable. The air smelled acrid, but it was better than the mines. The domed building would protect the ships and their even more valuable cargo from the elements.

"Worm."

A large hand took hold of her shoulder before Sadie went flying into the corner. She'd stayed in the entryway too long, and someone had decided to move her out of the way. It wasn't the worst hit she'd ever taken, but it took a minute for her breath to come back. Still shaky, she limped to her feet and kept moving. She couldn't appear to be any weaker than she already was.

Sadie had never been in the spaceport before. It was surprisingly boring. She'd heard stories of spaceports being full of color and architectural designs from a half dozen alien races merging. This was none of that. Gray cement floors and walls as far as the eye could see, with armored glass for a number of businesses. The only color came from bright blue lights which mimicked this world's sun. Sadie always wondered if the sun was supposed to be blue or if it was just the endless storm that made it seem that way. Either way, it was dreary in here, even if it was warmer. She pulled her hood down and unwrapped the top half of her head. Now, where was her contact?

She spent a while wandering the many halls, looking for any other humans. Peering through the windows didn't help because the stupid ursas blocked any human shaped sized creatures from sight. Nobody bothered her as long as she made it a point to get out of their way. There was plenty of scoffing and name calling, but nobody was breaking her for fun yet.

"Hey!" hissed a voice. A maintenance shaft she hadn't noticed before was cracked open, and a human hand was beckoning her over. The metal hatch opened and she saw two men and a woman on the other side. "Get in here!" Sadie rushed in and they quickly locked the door behind her.

"What are you doing out there?" asked a man. "Are you trying to get broken?"

"No, I'm looking for one of ours."

"There's a few of us running around the spaceport, be a little more specific," suggested the other man. "You from the reservation?"

"Yes. My grandma sent me. She said to find the Bastion fighter." The two men whistled.

"Haven't heard anyone talk about them in years," said the first.

"Is there one here?" asked the second.

"If there is, I think I know where," said the woman. "Why do you need a man like that?"

"Our reservation is in great danger. Grandma said to get him."

"They're dangerous, child."

Sadie didn't know what the woman was saying child for, she

didn't look to be too much older than her. Then again, age was a hard thing to guess these days. The type of work they did heavily influenced their looks, and these three looked like they were eating pretty well. They were probably rats; helpers who crawled into places bigger species couldn't.

"They don't come cheap," said the second man. "I doubt you have anything worth their time."

"I don't," she replied quickly. The last thing she needed was for the few humans here to mug her. "Grandma said she has information he'll want."

"Information? Could work," said the first, rubbing his chin. "He could still kill you for inconveniencing him."

"We don't kill our own!" snapped the second, whacking the other upside the head. The man took it with a scowl.

"Bastion fighters aren't us."

"Will you help me?" urged Sadie.

"Yes." The woman took her by the arm and led her back to the hatch. "The one you're seeking is in a bar called Mercy's House. It's not far from here."

"Oh him," said the first. "It bothers me to think of him."

"Why?" asked Sadie.

"You'll see," said the woman. She gave some quick directions and asked if Sadie understood. Sadie did. Years in the mines had made her very good at directions in areas where everything looked the same. "Good. We'd get you closer, but it's all of our hides if you're caught in here."

"Clear," whispered the first as he peered out of the maintenance hatch. They hurried Sadie out and disappeared back into the wall.

Mercy's House wasn't hard to find, but it was the last place she wanted to enter. There were a couple of alien races here, and as far

5

as she could see, everyone was armed. It was probably a hangout for mercenaries. This was the type of place humans went into and never left again. Praying her fellow humans hadn't sold her for sport, she pressed inside and tried to locate her man. The patrons looked just as surprised at her appearance, and a few shot glances toward the back. Hoping they were looking at the only other human, she moved with a purpose.

The sight of him almost made her stop next to hungry aliens. Pale skin and gold hair. She'd only heard legends that humans came in different colors. She'd heard rumors of people with these traits, but she doubted anyone in the reservation had ever seen one. He was big too; taller and stronger than any man she'd ever met. Here was a human who hadn't grown up on rations since birth. She looked for the mark grandma had mentioned, but the only uncovered part of his body was his face. He wore a plain brown jacket, over a grey shirt with dark pants. Without thinking, she stopped at his table and bowed.

"It is good to see one of our own."

"And to you." He bowed his head slightly. Sadie held her breath. His eyes were green. Could human eyes be green?

"My reservation needs your help." The man sighed and leaned forward.

"Listen, every reservation needs help. If we didn't need help, 99% of our species wouldn't exist on reservations."

"We could be killed in a coming war."

"And you think one person can help you?" No, she didn't, but grandma had been very insistent she find him. "You should get out of here. There's a bug already looking to eat you."

"A bug? Here?" She trembled, but resisted the urge to turn around and look for it. She must not provoke it.

WE WERE DELTA

The man shrugged. "All kinds come here. It probably won't attack you, but keep an eye out when you leave."

"Please. We have information to trade," pleaded Sadie.

"This one staying?" asked an ursa. This one was bringing a massive drink over to the man and looked to be the bartender. The man gave a dismissive wave.

"She'll be leaving."

"Come on, worm," said the ursa, placing a surprisingly gentle hand on her shoulder.

"Your friend with the tattoo," she said, suddenly. "Grandma said to mention your friend with the tattoo." The ursa paused, looking down at her and then back to the man. The man's bored composure had changed to interest.

"Get the girl something hot, please. She'll be staying after all. And tell that bug if it keeps looking at my table it'll be on your menu tomorrow." The bartender nodded slowly and took his hand off Sadie. The man motioned for her to sit.

"You'd better have a good story."

Chapter 2

The Reservation

"My name is Louis." Louis took his drink in both hands and took a long swig. It was made for ursa size patrons, and this man probably drank a third of it in one gulp. It smelled vaguely alcoholic with a hint of something foul. Louis wiped his lips. "Tell me what you know."

"I don't know much. Grandma said to tell you she knew about your friend with the tattoo."

"Your grandma was smart not to give you the full story, but I need more than that. Anyone can have a tattoo. Where is it?" She started to respond, but he cut her off. "Don't say it, point." Sadie tapped her left hand. "What is it?"

Sadie put two fingers together, making an incomplete triangle. Louis nodded and finished off the rest of his drink. If it was alcohol, he was going to be drunk or dead in an hour. The bartender returned with two enormous bowls of soup and a glass of water. He had human sized glasses? Why did Louis have such a big glass?

"Eat. You look like you need it." She sniffed the bowl warily, and Louis smiled. "It's safe for humans. There's even real meat in there, not protein sludge."

"Real meat?" Sadie wasn't sure she'd ever eaten real meat. It smelled salty, but it was hot and there wasn't a minute in the day when she wasn't hungry. She placed chapped lips against the bowl and sipped slowly.

"My reservation…" she started again.

"Is in danger. I know. You eat. I need to think."

Sadie waited as politely as she could even as she was about to tip the whole bowl into her mouth. It was good! It was made with real spices and noodles, giving it a hot touch every time she breathed. Spices of this quality were highly valued in this frozen wasteland. She knew they didn't actually provide warmth, but to walk around and feel like your mouth was on fire was a blessing. The soft pieces of tangy flesh were delicious. This soup was more than she might eat in a normal day. When she was finished, he waved a finger and the ursa brought her a second bowl! Her stomach might explode, but it was worth it. Louis drank his soup slowly and pounded another massive beer. His stomach was surely going to explode.

"Where did your grandma hear about this tattooed man?"

"We get visitors in the reservations. City rats, traders, even butlers. Mother and grandma frequently take care of them. They share stories."

"What did she tell you about the tattoo?"

"Not much. She and some of the elders spoke in hushed whispers. They said they were important once. Marks of great warriors." She stared at his gloved hands. "Do you have one? Is that why she told me to find you?"

"No, but I know what they mean. You don't find a lot of those people anymore."

"Bastion?" she whispered.

"No. The Last Bastion are just human military forces." He spoke casually, unafraid of anyone hearing about the Bastion. "That marking, means something else."

"What?"

"You don't need to worry about that. What's happening at your reservation?"

"We're a mining reservation."

"I gathered that, worm. What's the war? I haven't heard anything."

"They are expanding our operations, but we're close to a hive. The ursa are our keepers, but by the time they come in force…"

"Half your reservation will be bug food," he finished. "Got it. I'm hoping you have your own security."

"We do. I don't know how they'd do against a swarm."

"I can guess," said Louis, already out of patience. "Finish up. I need to use the bathroom and then we can go."

No surprise there considering how much he'd drunk. It must not have been alcohol after all, because he didn't even seem buzzed as he passed her. Sadie lived in a constant state of starvation and this soup was doing her wonders. Two bowls of real food, and she felt like she had more energy than she'd had in weeks.

"Morsellll…" clicked something behind her. Sadie turned slowly, bringing the soup bowl up like a shield.

It was the bug. It wasn't much taller than her, but its body was bent in an S shape. It was colored a deep clay red with its armored back a muddy brown. It stood on four legs, with a pair of hands that could act as another pair of legs, and two spindly arms up top.

Supposedly they weren't very strong, but they tangled their prey up with multiple arms before bringing them into a maw of needle-like teeth. Two big eyes and six smaller ones were locked on her. When it lunged, her only hope would be to jam the bowl in its mouth and wait for someone to save her.

"Bug."

The bug's body whipped around like a snake to see Louis behind it. His fist connected with its face and its head snapped so violently that Sadie thought she heard the carapace break. But when it collapsed, she saw the carapace hadn't broken. The sound had been its body being forcibly removed from its armor.

"You alright?" Louis asked, like breaking a bug with a punch was an everyday event. She wanted to ask how, but she was still in shock. Louis looked at the bartender and shrugged. "Told you. Bill me."

"Let me put it on the menu tomorrow and we'll call it even." The ursa gave him a toothy grin and Louis smiled.

"I love this place. Ready to go?" When she didn't respond, Louis took her by the hand and led her over the bug corpse. "How far away is your reservation?"

"Not far," she muttered, eyes still on the dead bug.

"What's not far?"

"Hour walk."

"To hell with that."

Sadie wasn't really paying attention until she realized he'd taken her to a docking station and was paying for a ride. The ursa was probably a teenager, which meant he was only a little taller than Louis. He took the money without question and they climbed into the back of a snow crawler. Its tracks spun up with bitter efficiency, chomping through the snow as they sped out of town.

"How did you do that?" she asked, breaking the silence. Louis

11

looked at her with a raised eye. "Kill the bug, I mean."

"You didn't hire me for my diplomatic skills." She wanted to ask more questions, but he shook his head, pointing at the driver. His gesture said this was human business.

The ride back was anything but smooth, but Sadie tried to enjoy it. Crawler trips were a rare experience and it wasn't often she experienced what people called beauty on her planet. In a plastic chair many times too big for her, she felt like a child as she looked out the window. They couldn't hear the wind howling, only watch the snow being swept across the land. The clouds were thinning just enough for the sun to break through, bathing the area in a bluish white haze. It was freezing outside, but here, it was comfortable. With a belly so full it ached every time the crawler bounced over a rock, life seemed strangely pleasant for the moment. Sadie could almost lie to herself and say that when the ride stopped, the peace and quiet would last.

An hour's walk wasn't even a ten minute ride. Louis dropped a few coins into the boy's hand and thanked him. When the door cracked open, the wind came in like an angry mother, slapping them both for being gone so long. The mine entrance was close, but the wind was going to scream at them the entire way. They weren't going to get away without a lecture and a beating. Or at least she wasn't. Louis she noted, didn't even have a face covering and walked like the harsh weather didn't exist.

The mine entrance didn't have any obvious signs. It was a reservation and they weren't trying to advertise their location to the world. You either knew about it or you didn't. Usually the only people who came here were visiting humans. The automated trucks which took the mining materials out had a different entrance placed closer to the city. The entryway had been enlarged enough for the occasional ursa overlord who chose this route, but they seldom came. Even as the wind cut out, Sadie could already feel her lungs tightening. Home, the one place nobody wanted to leave and nobody wanted to come back to.

Dim orange lights clicked on as they approached the hidden gate. A panel of rock slid away to reveal glass with two humans sitting behind it. They should've been asking for her identifier, but they were too busy staring at Louis.

"I can tell this is going to be fun," said Louis. "Louis Sunkissed, off worlder, just visiting." The two stared at him. "Can we come in?"

"One moment."

The two continued to stare at him. Louis looked at Sadie. She produced the identifier disc and moved up to the window, waving it to get their attention. One remembered where he was and pressed a button, opening a slot for her to slide the disc in like a coin.

"This is the one Grandma Snibbs told me to find." The two looked at each other before one responded slowly over an intercom.

"You better speak with security. Come in." A small section of wall slid open.

"Well, at least that's clever," commented Louis, clearly already bored with the gawking.

They stepped inside and the wall shut behind them. The air instantly became warmer. Sadie squinted to see through the haze. There were a few areas in the reservation designed to vent the pollution from the mines, but the air exchange was never enough. The top layers of air in the cavern were so dense that you could see subtle changes of color and taste the faint hints of exhaust and metals. If the wind was the angry mother outside, the air in here was the joyous father who smoked three packs a day and loved big hugs.

They stepped out of a tunnel into the main cavern. The ceiling was lit with its own miniature sun, a radiant beacon of yellow and orange light. Maybe it was because she'd grown up here, but Sadie had always felt the sun was supposed to be this color. The reservation was a corkscrew tunnel that just kept going further and further down. There was one only road that followed the city down, engineered for the cargo trucks that went out every few days. The inhabitants lived on the sides, tunneled deeper into the rock. There were a series of crisscrossing platforms made of metal grating designed to allow what little light there was to pass through. The further down they went, more lights were added to bolster the fading effect of their false sun.

"Welcome to the reservation," she said, with a mixture of pride and disappointment. "Sometimes called the UMC, Ursa Minor Colony."

"Someone has an awful sense of irony."

"Why?"

"Because you can't see the stars." Sadie looked at him confused and Louis sighed. "Right. Nobody remembers."

"Remembers what?"

"Just go. Where is this Grandma Snibbs?"

"Below." Sadie motioned to the wall where a cargo elevator was coming up. "We need to go all the way down."

"Beats walking."

Men were waiting at the elevator with a small cargo truck. Despite being ten years older than her, they didn't look much different. Sadie knew women were supposed to be shaped differently than men, but that only showed once women started having babies. Those without children still looked like men; short, skinny, and hungry. The only women with long hair were those carrying children as they were allotted more food. The young worked in the mines where short hair was a requirement. Those too old to work were almost always bald after a life exposed to harsh chemicals.

The three men started unloading the metal crates when they saw Louis and stopped. His golden hair transfixed them. Louis let them be astonished for a minute longer before he spoke. "Hungry people are waiting for that food." He'd correctly identified the markings on the boxes as canned food. "Don't disappoint them."

Sadie had never heard such a strong and confident voice come from a human. Louis spoke with the strength of an ursa. He didn't berate them, just reminded them of their duties. The men agreed silently and quickly went to their work while stealing the occasional peek at his hair. Louis nodded to each as they got into the truck and the pair of them took the lift. Louis pressed the oversized button and the platform began to slide down. It had no roof and only thin barriers to keep cargo from sliding off the edges. People were coming out to see him as they descended.

"I hate coming to these places."

"We have never seen anyone like you. Your hair is…"

Sadie stopped talking. Louis's hair was rising like it was caught in static electricity. As they passed under a light, she swore something was moving in his hair. Then his hair began to dim, as if only the light had given it a temporary golden glow. As the invisible current dissipated, Louis's hair settled back into place, only now a deep brown. Her gasp stayed silent, but she stumbled, causing him to look over at her. His green eyes were speckled with brown splotches. In a few seconds, they were fully brown. She backed into the railing as his skin began to darken. There was no hiding his size or posture, and his skin was a few shades too light, his hair too straight, but now he almost looked like he belonged. He smiled at her shocked face. She and her pounding heart were waiting for an explanation that he never gave.

While Sadie nearly had a panic attack, Louis took in his surroundings. As expected, there was very little to see. The mine had started with large scale excavation equipment before someone had decided it was too costly and dropped humans in the hole. Or maybe it was something that required a gentler touch than a mining drill made for asteroids. The air stunk of chemicals and noxious gases. If they were refining something like roxm gas he'd bet the average person didn't live past forty. He could feel his nostril hairs burning as particulates were caught. Phlegm was already building in the back of his throat. Even his eyes started to water until his body could adapt. The smells were getting stronger the further they descended. A minute later he could taste metal shavings. Correction, these people would be lucky to live past thirty-five. The girl was creeping closer back to him. She was scared but curious. His nose twitched again. Copper?

"Trouble," he said loudly.

"What?" Sadie didn't know what trouble he meant. She didn't hear any alarms. He made a quick punching motion and metal clicked under his jacket.

The elevator settled on the bottom floor and two men in beige security uniforms were waiting for them. What alarmed Sadie was they were carrying flechette cannons. Both men were tense and looked one second away from pointing the thick cannons at them. They both looked a little old to be on security detail. One looked at her with wide eyes and she recognized him.

"Dorkin?" Louis snorted at the name. "What are you doing? You stopped working years ago."

"They needed reinforcements. You two need to come with us."

"Reinforcements?"

"The bugs hit the reservation," answered Louis. "I'm looking for Grandma Snibbs."

"She's with the others. Come." Dorkin led the way and Sadie hurried to his side to ask questions. The other man walked alongside Louis as if he were a prisoner. One look between the two men and the security guard understood that if anyone was at the mercy of the other, it was the guard holding the gun.

"What happened?" begged Sadie.

"We had a breakthrough in shaft forty-three. Bugs came through before anybody knew what was happening," said the man. "By the time security got into place it was too late. We're still counting the bodies."

His grimace made her too full stomach curl into a ball. Bug attacks were said to be ugly, bloody affairs. When they swarmed, bugs would pull men apart to get at them. The battleground might be littered with so many parts that they were unsure how many people had died. Sadie tightened her resolve and asked the next horrible question.

"Did they take anybody?"

Bugs were known to take live prisoners. Rumor had it that people were caged in pens like animals, taken when the hive needed more food. Dorkin's chest fell before he tightened the grip on his flechette cannon.

17

"At least forty confirmed."

"Gods above."

"No gods down here, that's for sure."

"What did your masters say?" interrupted Louis. The man next to him spit and Sadie's uncle frowned.

"Blow the hole, bury the entrance."

"Not a bad idea."

"How can you say that?" asked Sadie, panicked.

"Do you have the power to invade the hive?" Nobody said anything because everyone knew they didn't. "It's called cutting your losses. It's terrible, nobody likes it, but it might stop another attack and more death."

"That's not for me to decide." Dorkin sounded like he was very grateful that decision wasn't his.

They walked for a time deeper into the mine. A heavy metal door had slid down over the paved road, but there was a small side tunnel carved into the wall. Two more security guards watched it with their cannons braced on rock formations left for this exact reason. It was a kill hole in case the mine was compromised. Even if there was a horde of bugs, two men could cover the hole for an eternity provided they had ammo. The box of grenades at their feet would keep the tunnel clear at all costs, closing it permanently if they had to. Personally, Louis thought if the bugs were this close the mine was dead anyways, but from a defensive perspective, it was a fun dream.

On the other side, they were able to take the main road again through a large cavern. No large drills had been used here. This enclosure was a mixture of natural formations and where humans had dug it clean. There was a squat building ahead next to a warehouse. Louis guessed the squat one was for administration and the warehouse for either storage or processing materials. There were no miners present. Only more beige security uniforms. They opened the door to the administration building and were led to a conference room in the back. Its walls were lined with mining maps. Men and women were arguing, each shouting over the rest so loudly that nobody noticed them enter.

"Where's grandma?" demanded Louis.

Sadie looked around the crowded room and pointed toward the back. Louis saw an elderly woman in a wheelchair. She was one of the few not shouting. She looked quietly in shock. Louis walked through the crowd calmly toward her, gently nudging people aside. But something about him made people go quiet as he passed. He was like a shadow slinking through their nightmares. They didn't recognize the threat until the light was gone and he was looming over them. The room was almost completely silent when he stood before Grandma Snibbs. His presence had pierced the veil of worry and she leaned forward to get a better look at him.

"Everybody out." Her voice crackled followed by a sharp wheeze. It sounded as if she was choking on rocks and might spit up a pebble at any moment.

"But Grandma Snibbs," started a woman.

"Out!" She hacked loudly, her frail body shaking itself to pieces with every breath. Cold eyes stayed locked on Louis's. She waited until the room emptied and the doors were shut before she spoke again. "Show me."

"You're demanding for a cripple," said Louis cheerfully.

"If you don't have what I need, then I don't need you." She coughed harder, chewing up the bile in her mouth before swallowing it back down. "And you don't need what I have." Louis unstrapped his left glove and held his hand down for her. Three gray circles in the formation of a triangle were visible on the back of his hand.

"Happy?"

"Ecstatic." She looked anything but.

"Tell me what you know."

"I know that bugs are days away from overrunning my home. It might be weeks or months, and the ursa might help us, but someday soon, they're going to hit us hard." She let out a long shuddering breath before she looked at the door. "I know I'm going to have to tell Sadie that my daughter, her mother, was dragged away by those damned things." Tears were forming against her leathery cheeks.

"I'm not here for any of that." Louis stood over her and took hold of the edge of the table. It was a cheap metal that made a satisfying squeak as it bent under his fingers. "I don't care about you or your people. You know where my friend is. You're going to tell me before you stop breathing for good."

"I do and I will." She made herself comfortable, getting her blanket just right before she continued. "But you and I have a deal to make first."

"What do you want?"

"I want my daughter back. I want everyone who was taken back." She tried to raise herself higher on her armrests, but couldn't maintain the balance. Instead, she shook a thin arm at him. "I want so many dead bugs that they don't ever consider coming back this way again in three lifetimes."

"How many of yours taken and dead?"

"At least forty gone and twenty dead." Louis knelt so she could see him easier.

"I could kill twice as many in ten minutes. I am five times your age and have centuries of experience causing pain." His voice was emotionless. He put a hand on her wheelchair. "Tell me what I need to know."

"You're used to threatening people and it working." She pointed a bony finger at him. "Now look into my eyes. I heard my daughter screaming as those things dragged her off. Trapped in my chair, I couldn't do nothing. There's nothing you could do to me that hasn't already been done."

"You have a granddaughter outside. I'm sure there's more family and friends."

"Damn bugs are going to kill them all, what does it matter if it's you or them?" She chewed the gunk accumulating in her throat. There was even a crunch as yellow teeth bit into something hard. "What's it going to be? You want to help us out or spend all day killing your own kind?"

"You are not my kind." Louis stood up, arms tense. He looked ready to pick her up out of that wheelchair and toss her through the wall.

"Ralli, or something like that." The anger in Louis clashed with hope as the old crone spoke. "They said he's famous for the stars. That part didn't make sense to me, but maybe it does to you."

Louis headed for the door. "Don't you dare die before I come back."

Chapter 3

Hive Negotiations

Sadie found herself outside with the community elders, mining management, and the head of security forces. Why had grandma told everyone to leave? Wasn't Louis here to help them with the bugs? Why wouldn't she include everyone else? It wasn't Sadie's place to ask, but it still bothered her. The women around her were talking in hushed whispers about Louis. Except for Lure, Lure never talked quietly.

"That's supposed to be our great hero?" The security forces woman was clearly not impressed. Lure was enormous compared to most people on the reservation. She was all lean muscle covered in scars, including four lines across her scalp which she didn't try and hide. She'd been a miner once who'd stumbled into bug territory. Instead of being traumatized after her survival, she simply demanded revenge and joined security. "Please tell me he's got an army or a mech suit."

"No," said Sadie, realizing all eyes had turned to her. "He came alone."

"Does he have some fancy gear somewhere?" Lure was already looking past her, trying to locate an unfamiliar bag or case. Sadie shook her head again. "Then what is he supposed to do?"

"Maybe he's a contact for the Last Bastion," suggested one of the managers.

"Fat load that'll do us. If they're not in system, it'd take at least a week for the message to go out, at least a week to get here, if not longer, and then how are we going to pay them? We're better off going to the damned ursa."

"Grandma Snibbs said he was special," offered another.

"He doesn't look special."

"He has gold hair," said Sadie and all the attention went back to her. "Green eyes too. He got tired of us staring at him and on the elevator his hair and eyes just," she lifted her hair with one hand and let it drop, "changed."

"How?" asked someone.

"Cybernetics?" guessed Lure.

The doors opened and Louis stepped out. He looked furious and Sadie froze as he approached, everyone else unconsciously backing away from her. "Hole forty-three. How do I get there?"

"You planning on going on a bug hunt?" asked Lure. Louis nodded.

"Give me a flechette cannon. Did the bugs secure the hole?"

"They did." Lure's expression said she wasn't giving up her cannon, but started to lead them away from the group and into the mine. "We've got our fire team pretty far back from the hole."

"Are there any other ways the bugs can get in?"

23

"Not that they've shown us."

"If I stir up trouble, can you seal the tunnel? It's no good for me if I push in toward their queen and all of you die here."

"I could hold that hole for a year and we've got grenades in case I'm wrong."

"You're wrong." Lure racked her flechette cannon in offense, but Louis didn't sound like he was being mean. He spoke with the plain surety of a man who knew what was about to happen. "Grenades are a temporary solution, but a swarm will pull the debris away so fast you'll either run out or they'll start slipping through. You'd need enough explosives to collapse the tunnel that it would take you a month to get through with machines."

"What about cryofoam?" asked Sadie. Louis and Lure both looked back, surprised to learn she was still with them.

"You have enough cryofoam to seal a tunnel?" Sadie looked at one of the miners who shrugged in confirmation.

"Sure. We could spray the walls and work our way in."

"A few feet of foam and they'd need a bomb to get through once it seals," agreed Lure, wondering why she hadn't thought of that. "It's toxic as hell so the bugs can't even eat it."

"Get it ready. Once I go in you won't have long," said Louis. "Take Sadie with you. Keep her and grandma alive at all costs." Sadie didn't have time to wonder about that statement as a few miners pulled her away, eager to help the strange man. Louis eyed Lure. "I'm serious. If they die this will have been a waste of my time and I will not be pleased."

"What has she got on you?" asked Lure, suspiciously.

"She knows where a friend is."

It wasn't far to a large tunnel where people were still bagging the remains of the battle. Louis noted the smell of blood and bile alongside the vomit of the cleanup team. Burnt metal from the desperate shots of security standing their ground lingered in the air. The smell of the bugs was the worst. On a good day, bugs smell like a dead crab left out in the sun, its carcass so bloated its shell is about to pop off. The dead, with their red and tan splattered innards sprayed across the rock, smelled like a rat dragged through the sewer before immediately being thrown on a barbeque.

The narrow tunnel the bugs had emerged and retreated down was obvious from the stampeding tracks. The living and the dead had been dragged away to be consumed, another pound of meat in the collective fold. There were always too many mouths to feed and never enough food. It was surprising they'd been placed so close to the reservation and never seriously invaded yet. The ursa probably found it acceptable as long as the bugs only took a few at a time. Humans worried about becoming bug food are less likely to complain about their protective masters.

"Here." Lure handed him a flechette cannon from a nearby crate. It was a short, fat thing, with eight rotating barrels inside and a large magazine underneath. He guessed it had an effective range of maybe ten meters. A high tech shotgun with a hundred times the killing power and half the recoil. It was a piece of garbage but king in tunnel warfare. Even an ursa would find its insides liquefied after being hit by one of these. "How many magazines do you need?"

"Give me five." He took a blood soaked bandolier off an equipment pile and Lure found him five magazines.

"Ten shots per magazine," she reminded him. "Even if you get a guaranteed kill with every shot, that's only fifty. Bet you the reservation there's a hell of a lot more than fifty in there."

"Hives aren't as big as you think." Louis inspected the cannon before loading it. "Raknath only appear endless because of how they move and they like to reclaim their dead. There are maybe a few thousand in there." He headed toward the tunnel the bugs had come from. "Bugs are bad in protracted wars because they'll have new soldiers ready in a couple of months while you need the next fifteen years."

Lure didn't know how to respond so she just scowled. Even if he was right, a few thousand bugs were still more than fifty shots. There was no way he was killing a royal with just one shot.

White shale crunched loudly under their boots as they walked. This tunnel was newly excavated and there was no proper road yet. Lights were stringed along the ceiling in a haphazard fashion, shaking and casting long shadows as they passed. The smell of the dead and dying was stronger here. If Lure focused on the ground, she could see the clawed lines where people struggled not to be taken. It felt like their screams were still there in the bloody lines. She kept her eyes and cannon up. They were in a bug tunnel and she couldn't afford to get distracted.

"This is officer Lure and friend," she sang loudly, addressing the lights up ahead. "We are coming toward your position. Jingle jangle, coming on down."

"Ringle dingle, come on forward," sang a voice back to them.

"Bugs have a hard time pronouncing G's and singing," she answered, expecting Louis's question. That made sense to him. Bugs could speak, but only had a rudimentary grasp of human language. What they were good at was mimicking voices so they could trick people into coming to them.

Ahead was a small fire team of six people, all armed with flechette cannons and grenades. Two men and two women kept the cannons pointed down the tunnel at all times while the other two women waited for Lure to speak. They were behind metal barricades that had been brought in.

"Where's the breach?" asked Louis.

"Who are you?" asked one of the women.

"Help," said Lure. She still didn't know how, but if he wanted to kill some bugs, good for him. "Where's the breach?"

"Just ahead. They must've tunneled right over the bugs because the floor slid away."

"Why aren't you covering there?"

"Too big of an exit. We couldn't cover it all."

"Fair. What's the plan, big man?"

"I'm going to go have a polite conversation." Louis held the cannon in one hand like it was his luggage, hand nowhere near the trigger. "If you hear shooting, start hosing the tunnel down with cryofoam. I'll find my own way back."

"Your plan with a race of murderous bugs is diplomacy?" asked Lure incredulously. "That's suicide."

"Other species negotiate with bugs all the time. Humans are generally just too small to be taken seriously. You just have to scare them a little."

"This I've got to see."

"That's fine." Louis stepped past the barricades. "You're not one of the people I have to keep alive."

The guards watched him walk nonchalantly down the hall as if it were the way to dinner. "Are you sure about this?" asked one of them.

"Not at all, but damn am I intrigued." Lure pushed between the gaps in the barricade and jogged after him. As her women had described, the floor suddenly dropped away in a landslide. The light was muted in the hole with only hints of blue.

"I'm coming in bugs," declared Louis. "I'm not here for a fight, I want to speak to an ambassador. AM-BASS-A-DOR." He let the words echo in the tunnel before waving for Lure to take a step back. He slid down the gravel ramp and a bug immediately rushed to meet him at the bottom. Lure didn't have a shot without Louis getting at least half the shrapnel. Louis for his part, used his fat cannon like a club and swatted the bug. On the ground, it tried to coil around him only to be whacked on the head again. Louis placed the fat muzzle against its chest. "Ambassador." He gave it a kick strong enough to send it rolling before leveling the weapon on what had to be more bugs out of Lure's line of sight. "You heard me. Go." The bugs must've backed away because Louis lowered the cannon and waited.

Nothing happened for nearly ten minutes. Lure looked over her shoulder as she heard a vehicle approaching and saw two miners prepping hoses for the foam. In an impressive show of bravery, Sadie came down the tunnel to join her. Making a mental note that the girl might do well in security, Lure pointed down to where Louis was still waiting. Sadie didn't say anything. The look on her face said she was still in shock, but seemed unsurprised the man was still alive.

"Get ready to run up there," said Louis, straightening. Unable to see, Lure took a knee and covered the entryway. Sadie joined her and a second later, Lure was ready to drag them out before the slaughter started.

Ten bugs emerged from the tunnel, clinging to the walls and staying far from the stranger. They were followed by an enormous bug that Lure had never seen before, but had heard plenty of stories about. Its four feet crushed through the gravel loudly with its two secondary feet pushing against the walls of the too small tunnel. Its arms were like fuel drums ending in three armored points that could pull at a tank, but they were clasped together like hands. Its clay colored armor was thicker with heavy edges that helped protect vulnerable joints. Out of the tunnel, it extended its curved body to tower well above the tiny human. It was easily three meters tall, maybe more, and must've weighed as much as a truck. It was a royal, one of the personal guards to the queen herself.

"You are trespassing." Its speech was frighteningly good. If not for the subtle clicking in the background, they might have thought it was a human male.

"This reservation did not mean to trespass," said Louis, like talking giant superbugs was an everyday occurrence. "You killed their people, took many more."

"Invasion has its consequences."

"It does. I've come to broker a peace."

"Then speak."

"The reservation will seal this hole and not disturb the hive. We will forgive the deaths you have caused. It was a battle, raknath and human lives were both lost." Lure didn't know what a raknath was, but it pleased the bug. It bowed its head in reverence and held out its hands.

"Most terrible."

"But you must return the living you stole." The bug's relaxed pose flinched and its head rose to a more intimidating posture. Even from up above, they could see its teeth were larger and serrated. It took Lure a moment to realize in the faded light there was more than one row of teeth.

"No."

"They did not have a part in this. They must be allowed to go free."

"No."

"The reservation nor their masters will approve of this. You would risk war for so little?" The bug tapped its fingers, apparently thinking.

"The masters will not accept this war. If the humans invade, we will defend our hive."

"But you stole from the reservation."

"After they invaded."

"I'm not here for politics." Louis approached, still holding his weapon in a nonthreatening way. He stood directly under the royal's long head and within easy grabbing distance. "Return the living or I will seek an audience with your queen."

"No."

"Then I must speak with the queen."

"You are a bold morsel." The royal leaned down with an open mouth so close Louis's head could disappear inside it at any second.

In a move too fast for bug or human eyes, Louis grabbed its armored head and yanked it to the floor. Lure wasn't about to wait and see who won. She dragged Sadie away by the collar while calling for foam. Gunfire erupted in the tunnel below them. Two men in heavy gas masks were waiting with hoses, but wouldn't start until they passed. The foam was dangerous to inhale, lethal in large doses. Lure shouted at them to start spraying and don't stop. She could live with possible lung damage. She couldn't survive being digested.

Sadie understood it was time to run and Lure let go of her, reminding her to hold her breath as the blue foam started to coat the walls. Sprinkles of the cryofoam grazed her jacket and pants and it felt like she was back outside, everything instantly freezing under its touch. They ducked between the two men who were caking the foam toward the center, creating a congealed wall of blue slime mixed with rock. Sadie made to stop but Lure pushed her forward. The minty smell in the air said they were still too close. It wasn't until they were much further down the tunnel did she give a loud gasp as a sign that it was safe again.

"Stupid…stupid man." Lure took another deep breath. "He just killed us all."

"He's alive," said Sadie.

"How?"

Now that they'd stopped running they could hear the booming in the tunnel. It was muted through the foam wall, but they could feel the vibrations through the floor. The constant fire of a flechette cannon and the rapid fire of something they hadn't seen. Lure listened with a patient ear accustomed to the sound of gunfire in the underground.

"Who the hell is this guy?"

Chapter 4

Hungry for Peace

Louis's hands were a blur, one moment at his sides, and the next they'd taken the royal by its thick jaw. With a superhuman pull, the royal's head was pulled into the ground. Its elongated body had been stretched to its limit to impose its will on the tiny morsel, and now its size and awkward body shape worked against it. Louis yanked the bug's head 180°, nearly breaking its neck as its massive form desperately tried to roll in time. But it was not pinned. They had been bred for tunnel warfare. Being on the ground with a bug was the most dangerous place to be.

The right jab to its face broke teeth and crushed its armored skull. Disoriented and in pain, its body began to whip and twist. A knee on its long neck kept it in place and Louis placed the flechette cannon over its face, pressing down hard with the barrel. "Tell the queen this stops when I get an audience." Fluid squirted messily up his arms and the royal croaked incoherently. "Until then." Louis squeezed the trigger and the bang was muffled as the cannon went off inside its head. Hardened armor prevented the flechettes from exiting, forcing them to ricochet through its neck before finding a weak point to exit. A halo of snotty red and tan marked the grave of the royal.

The ten bugs sagged in shock, their link to the hive temporarily disrupted by the death of the royal. Louis snapped the flechette cannon up, firing wave after wave of metal as he spun around. The shots were so tightly packed that each bug shared a shot between them. Some fell off the walls, peppered to bits while others found themselves nailed into the rock. Only two died before the link reestablished and they charged. That was fast. There must be another royal or a minder nearby. Louis killed three more before they were on him. He cracked the skull of the sixth with the weapon and blasted the seventh before leaping backward. They were almost as fast as him as they slithered across the floor. The eighth tried to bite him and got the barrel instead, its insides spraying the remaining three. The ninth took a right backhand hard enough to break its carapace and the tenth received a kick in the gut.

It was a mistake. He'd meant to launch the creature away, but kicking a bug is like trying to kick rubber. Last time he'd done this he'd stunned the creature first. This time it was ready for him. Something broke but its many limbs intertwined with his leg, claws trying to dig into his armor. Louis dropped them to the ground and pinned its head before it could bite him. Those teeth would really hurt and were guaranteed to take a couple pounds of meat if they latched on. It took a few hits against the rock before its body gave up and released him. That just left number six, which was having trouble standing. It hissed, but every time it snapped its teeth, it cringed and shook its head, which led to more cringing and head shaking. He'd broken something vital with that hit to the head. Not eager to get closer, Louis reclaimed the cannon and blasted the bug across the room.

Knowing what was coming next, Louis dropped the spent magazine and reloaded the cannon before stepping in front of the tunnel the royal had emerged from. The walls were shaking, hammered by hundreds of legs converging on a single location. The smart thing to do here would be to throw grenades down the tunnel, killing them by the score and trying to collapse the tunnel. But Louis needed to go forward. He listened to the pebbles scatter as if even they were afraid. He raised the flechette cannon and waited as the dust fell.

The first bugs filled the tunnel, taking to every surface to come at him faster. Their queen was smart. She didn't allow the full swarm into the tunnel, forcing him to use the cannon on only a few. Louis obliged, breaking them against the walls until the weapon ran dry. He reloaded as only a man can after reloading a weapon a thousand times before, firing again before the bugs gained an extra meter of ground. His shots were expertly grouped to maximize damage, but they were finite. The cannon ran dry the second time and instead of reloading, Louis whipped the heavy barrel into the first bug. The remaining two received equally humiliating deaths, killed by the unarmed human.

Their advance had just been the initial tremors. Now the full earthquake arrived as enough bugs to fill the tunnel advanced. They crawled across every surface and even each other. A moving wall of teeth and claws. They didn't even hinder each other in their unescapable urge to devour him, but propelled each other forward. In the dim light, they could've been mistaken for a single enormous creature.

Louis cracked his hands into fists before raising them. Thin levers extended from inside his coat as twin barrels placed themselves opposite his thumbs. The barrels were tiny, not even a centimeter in length. Louis squeezed the triggers and tiny balls of steel erupted as high velocity rounds. With the bugs so tightly packed, he couldn't miss. Hundreds of bugs crammed into the tunnel and thousands of beads tore through them. The surging worm faltered, some bodies pushing forward as others were pulled back and crushed beneath. Louis kept the pressure on, the wrist mounted weapons whining as their autoloaders fed more and more in.

Then the surge stopped. The bugs retreated under the cover of their dead. The wall to wall bugs sank, pulled out by the fleeing and the dead pushing forward as resistance faded. They still filled most of the tunnel. Louis would have to stoop to walk over their corpses. The smell was the worst damage they'd inflicted. He'd be smelling bug for the next month. Maybe he could spend a day recovering next to a smelter or maybe a reactor to clear his sinuses. Picking up the flechette cannon, he waded in.

His collar chirped and without waiting for confirmation, a female voice began to speak. "Hey, boss?"

"Yes, Maia?"

"I'll admit I wasn't paying attention. You spent a couple thousand rounds and now I'm tracking you in the local hive. What did I miss?"

"People here contracted me to extract some of their people after a hive breach." Louis stepped up the wall of dead, watching carefully where his feet went.

"Uh-huh. Why do we care about the reservation?"

"Maybe I'm feeling altruistic today."

"That's as likely as me cooking you steak and tucking you in at night."

"I really could do with more of that in my life." Louis paused. He fired in a few different places, making sure the twitching he saw actually meant they were dead.

"Is that the reason? Some voluptuous young thing caught your eye?"

"She's probably sixty and in a wheelchair."

"You dirty cradle robber," laughed Maia.

Louis hit a soft spot and cursed as his leg sank into gore. In order not to get a face full he had to commit his other leg. An unidentified organ deflated like a poorly tied water balloon under his boot, running warm liquid up his leg. "I am not having a good day, Maia."

"I bet you smell amazing. Just drop yourself in an incinerator on your way back."

"It's a little too cold out for streaking." Louis slogged forward. "Though I might consider it after this."

A claw hooked his boot and pulled him under. An unknown number of bugs were playing opossum down there. He was less mad about them trying to eat his legs than he was that they'd just slammed his head down into the viscera. The wrist cannons fired indiscriminately into where the bugs must be hiding, shredding them and a dozen dead. When everything was still, Maia continued.

"Everything alright?"

"I am fantastic."

Louis sat up, something sticky clinging to his hair. It was a miracle there was nothing in his mouth. Out of the tunnel, Louis checked the next cavern. There were three tunnels from here so he chose the most level. The bugs didn't need their eyes for much because it was almost pitch black in their tunnels. The only light came from a bioluminescent blue moss that grew on the walls. It was enough for eyes, bathing the tunnels in a faded aqua.

"I see that. Why is your hair dark?" She must've used one of the many microscopic cameras in his outfit to spy on him.

"Helps the locals."

"Well, it's weird. Can you shed it? I doubt bugs are intimidated by blondes."

It wasn't a bad idea. Focusing his body to regenerate had abilities beyond closing wounds. The hair on his head began to die and come free. He wiped a hand on a relatively dry spot of his coat and wiped his hair free, taking most of the snot off with it. A fresh head of blonde hair was growing in on fresh pale skin. Louis's face became puffy as his skin swelled. A few seconds later he wiped his face on his shoulder, removing a few layers of dead skin and all the gore. Under the organic blue light, his skin had the appearance of white marble.

"Much better. Activate sonar, side screen." A small screen was projected off to his right. The signal wasn't strong enough to give him a proper map, but it might show him movement. The map it tried to create looked like he was a blue dot in the middle of Swiss cheese. Unknown yellow dots blinked pretty much everywhere. "Maia, is there an estimated population for this local hive?"

"Right because they keep track of that." Louis shut down the map and kept walking. There wasn't any sign of secretion or nesting holes, so he was far from the hive center.

"Extrapolate? How much territory do they cover? When was the last time the hive was deployed? How much food do they have access to?"

"Do I look like I did my doctoral thesis on raknath?"

"Well if you're going to use proper names, give me the subspecies." Maia snorted. "I know you're good with numbers and statistics." He paused, listening. Lots of movement, but quieter. "Please?"

"Ha!" Maia laughed so suddenly it came out as a shriek. "They're Raknath Terra."

"Seriously?"

"Earth bugs, subterranean dwellers. Bred for hostile worlds where most species can't live on the surface. This hive hasn't been mobilized in decades. Pretty good living space with high probability they're burrowing into unknown areas. But unless they're finding a lot of alternative food sources, the hive shouldn't be bigger than three to five thousand."

"That makes me feel comfortable." The sound again. Smaller feet.

"At least half of the population is going to be drones. One queen, probably a royal for every two to four hundred, so estimate fifteen of those? Probably three times as many minders. So let's say two thousand soldiers and fourteen royals left to go." There was a short pause. "I suspect you'll run out of ammunition in another five hundred."

"That's assuming they don't mobilize the drones."

Louis turned. Speaking of little feet, there were the drones. He jogged back down the passageway to where he'd entered. Much smaller bugs had come out of a higher passageway and were pulling at the soldiers. They had almost no armor, just thin carapaces to protect them from dragging against rock. They crawled on all eights, only using their smaller and more dexterous hands to grab the dead. They carried parts of flesh away, sometimes in teams of two or three to move the much heavier bodies. Drones were efficient little guys who ran almost purely on instinct. The hive needed food and the dead had no use save for flesh. Once the bodies were gone, he wouldn't be surprised if the drones were lapping up the floor like a dog. Every calorie counted.

They paid Louis no mind as he followed them up the tunnel. He was a predator and they did not engage with predators. They gave him a small berth, but as long as he didn't attack them, they wouldn't change course. He'd follow them back into the hive proper.

"Wait," said Maia in his ear. She at least understood not to speak out loud when the bugs were around. "Up ahead on the left wall." He scanned it and shook his head when he didn't see anything. A few of the drones slowed and looked at him before resuming their tasks. "That's not rock." One of the projectors in his coat put a small blue dot on the wall. Louis stepped closer, crossing the drones. She was right.

Fast as he could, he drove his fist into the fake wall. Carapace broke and innards leaked out the side as a bug screeched and threw itself out. He'd never seen one like this before. It was about the size of a fat drone with a long, wide back that blended with the rock. Its head was massive for its body, equaling its torso, with tiny legs. It was an impressive cockroach.

"The hell is this?"

"It's a minder."

"Are you sure?" Projections came up in answer to his question. Three pictures of known minders and their subtypes. They all had gigantic heads and smaller legs. "Close enough I guess."

"And that means the queen knows exactly where you are." Louis sighed. Bigger feet coming. "Before you get eaten and I have to find a new best friend, why are you really down here? They can't have that much money and I know you don't care about the reservation."

"They know where Ravi is."

Maia went silent. Louis looked up and down the wide tunnel, wondering if they'd come from a single direction or both. Probably both. He considered the drones scuttling around him. They were brainless things that would never pose a challenge to him, even if they were driven to violence. He couldn't even hate them. They were too simple to hate. Raising the flechette cannon, he fired ten shots into the drones in front of him. Turning as he reloaded, he sprayed another ten shots down the way he'd come. The drones died in droves, and turned into speedbumps against their brethren. Their lives would mean a few extra seconds for him.

"I thought Ravi was dead," said Maia finally.

"Me too. Eighty years ago, over Tannis."

"What makes you think he's still alive? Do they have proof?"

"Just an old woman who heard the name and knew the mark."

"That's it?" demanded Maia. "Are you really risking being torn apart on a rumor?"

The soldiers were testing him again. They came fast and in small groups from both directions, ensuring he couldn't bring his heavy firepower on them in mass. He happily proved them wrong; putting targeted shots into the few they sent. The queen must've decided it was time for him to die because she sent in enough bodies to drown him. Louis pulled two discs from under his coat and sent them hurtling into the swarms. The grenades exploded in the mass of bodies. There wasn't even room for a proper explosion and their bodies protected the cave walls. But the force had to go somewhere, compressing the bugs deep into each other. Knowing the bugs wouldn't stop, he repeated the trick. The swarm temporarily stopped as the dead filled so much of the tunnels that no more could come through.

Somewhere in the falling wall of flesh came a royal. It had used its soldiers as a shield, their torn bodies slouching off it as it emerged. Louis recognized it too late. It took him off his feet and dashed him into the rock before driving its teeth toward his head. He drove his arms up in time to break its grip and dodged the teeth by a hair. He headbutted it to the side which barely nudged the gigantic bug before trappings its claws with his hands and wrapping his legs around its long neck. This was not a position he wanted to be in. This wasn't grabbing the tiger by the tail; this was hooking it by the nose.

The royal dragged them across the wall, trying to dislodge him or at least break his grip on its claws. Its set of legs that could pass for hands had him by the back and were trying to pry him loose. His superior strength was limited by the number of limbs he had to contend with. With a push he released the clawed hands and did a curl up to the royal's face, clapping his hands hard enough to break its jaws. Claws pierced his sides just as he stuck a cannon in its mouth and loosed a burst. Its head disintegrated and it dropped him painfully onto the rock.

Louis was barely down before a soldier had his leg and was dragging him away. He kicked it free and two more took the offending leg. A few more shots from his cannons sent them flying but his legs were bleeding freely. One leapt directly onto his chest and drove the air from him. He rolled it off and elbowed it so hard the rock cracked beneath. Another quick sweep of his cannons sent the next wave off. Rolling backward, Louis flipped back to his feet just in time for another two bugs to collide with him. He took both bodies and bearhugged them together until enough things snapped that they stopped attempting to bite him. A bug almost took his wrist off as he started firing again. This time he made it back to his feet. A minute more of whistling fire cleared the tunnel and he ran forward. He couldn't let them pin him again.

A cavern opening ahead of him darkened as bodies began to fill it. Another royal dropped into view. Louis pulled two disc shaped grenades and hurled them forward. They exploded with simultaneous *whumps* and the bugs scattered. Louis emerged with both cannons out but the room was emptying of bodies. The royal was struggling to stand, its body filled with shrapnel. Armor doesn't help against concussive forces in small rooms.

"Are you ready to talk?" Louis asked the shaky royal. "Can you see me okay?"

It could. Its little eyes were focused on the dangerous, but bleeding foe. Louis ripped his tattered pant legs aside in favor of torn shorts. Both legs had serious wounds where the bugs had bitten down. His shirt and coat were both stained red from the claw wounds from the previous royal. The coat's arms were barely hanging on with much of the fabric and armor shredded. Any normal human would've been unconscious by now; delirious at a minimum. Yet the morsel only looked annoyed and tired.

"I came here for eight hands of humans." Louis held up a hand to make sure the royal got the message. "How many of yours have you lost? You are the third royal to come before me."

That made it think. The queen was able to see and control through the royals and minders, but the royals were her ambassadors. They were important, symbols of power, and a means of controlling the hive. These coordinated assaults weren't possible without them. Losing two royals in the past hour was a painful thing for any queen. Louis approached the royal. It was in a fugue state, but not from its injuries. The queen was talking.

"Hey." Louis swept the shaky royal to the floor. He walked and raised a foot over its head. "Send a more polite ambassador and let's talk." He stomped its skull flat.

"You are such a charmer," said Maia.

"Bugs only understand expansion and threats to their existence."

A queen was a smart, calculating thing. She wanted her hive to grow, but this was a war colony. Her alien overlords allowed her to exist and breed so they could mobilize for battle. The minute she lost her usefulness, they would burn her hive out and collapse it. If she killed Louis but lost a substantial part of her army, she would be vulnerable.

It was ten minutes until the swarm returned. This time though they waited in four tunnel entrances including one directly above Louis. It was another minute before the newest royal approached like the first. Its hands were clasped together and it moved slowly.

"The queen agrees to your request. The captured humans may go." It clicked its claws almost nervously. "Not all who were taken are still alive." Louis nodded, having expected that. The queen herself likely had taken some of the living people to feast on.

"Please show me to where they are. I will walk them out." The royal's teeth chattered.

"They are far. We will bring them to you."

"No. You will show me to them and I will lead them out."

"This cannot happen. We will bring them to you."

"Maia." On Louis's command, remote bombs he'd thrown into the tunnels began to blink red and beep. The royal looked over in alarm as it realized it was standing next to one. Louis held a thumb up over his imaginary trigger, ready to motion for them to detonate. "Would you like me to continue this discussion with the next royal?"

The royal tapped its claws apprehensively. They had come out in force to negotiate and Louis was about to make them pay for it. The bug let out an audible sigh, which was a weird sight. Its whole body rose and sank in a wave.

"Human." It paused. "Sir. The humans are in a sensitive area. We do not let humans go there." The message was clear. They didn't let anything that wasn't a bug there, not unless they were going to die. This probably meant they were being held near spawning grounds or the queen herself. Both would be highly guarded secrets for the hive's survival.

"I understand. I am an off worlder with no connection to mercenaries, government, or other forces that would influence the

43

hive. I was hired to retrieve the people in exchange for information that will take me back off world. Your secrets are safe with me, because they have no meaning to me." He let the royal process that. "If I don't lead them out, the humans might accuse me of abandoning humans here. Then I will have to come back." The royal understood what that meant. Louis would be getting more weapons and explosives if there was a next time.

"Are you human?" it asked suddenly.

"No."

"What are you?" That was a bad question. Bugs have a habit of trying to dissect and adapt to more powerful foes. Louis shifted the regeneration inside him and his eyes shined gold for a moment.

"Something you want off world as soon as possible." The royal returned to its contemplation. Louis waved his hand to the bombs, not wanting to give the bugs time to think. "Do we have a deal? If not, I can ask the next few royals."

"You do not harm the hive. You do not speak of our secrets. You take the humans and go." Louis waved his hand down and the bombs stopped their incessant beeping. He approached the royal and held out his hand.

"I promise on eradication." His collar chirped in confirmation.

"Promise on eradication," answered Maia smoothly.

The royal hesitated. If a bug could show fear, it was for this. Not when they realized they were surrounded by bombs. Not when Louis was killing them. Even the royal he stomped to death hadn't been afraid like that. That was combat and even a royal could die in combat. It was what they were bred for. A promise on eradication meant if the queen betrayed him, Louis or someone on his behalf would kill the entire hive. This could be done with sophisticated weapons or worse, from high orbit where the bugs could do nothing.

"Promise on eradication," agreed the royal solemnly. The other side of that promise meant if Louis turned on the hive, they would hunt him to their last. Nothing he could ever say or do would halt their aggression again.

"Good. Would you mind if they collected the bombs and returned them? I don't want to leave them behind." The royal turned to go, waving for him to follow. The soldiers collected all the small discs and returned them in a pile. Louis slid them back into his coat and off they went.

They moved with a purpose, the royal ready to get rid of him. Even then it took another twenty minutes to arrive. The bugs had not carved out a main central area as the humans had. They lived in kilometers of endless tunnels and caverns, with minor tunnels chewed out as they needed room. The further they progressed; the rock became grayer, almost translucent with a fine layer of secretion. The bugs excreted a type of mucous to keep their worm like bodies healthy and the closer you got to the hive, the thicker it became. Discarded scales, outgrown armor, and worn claws littered the floors, crushed into patches of fine powder. The smell was just as fantastic as Louis hoped it would be.

They passed a spawning pit and Louis barely turned, keeping his eyes forward as the bugs followed him. Eggs the size of soccer balls had been carefully laid in pits of regurgitated food. This meant the eggs would be hatching soon, the larva having a plentiful food source upon birth. The larvae would be vicious, hungry little monsters. They'd eat everything in the pit, including the egg sacks that birthed them. If there wasn't enough food, they'd turn on each other or their unhatched brethren. From what he'd seen, all the eggs had been of the same size. They would either be drones or soldiers. Soon bigger eggs would be laid for new royals.

"They are just ahead." Louis nodded. He heard no voices, but there was the sound of sniffling and sobbing in the background.

"How many survivors?" He should've asked this sooner, but he had been slightly distracted.

"Twenty-seven."

"I was told there were over forty taken."

"Forty-four," agreed the royal. Seventeen people had already been eaten. No wonder Grandma Snibbs wanted him down here so fast. By tomorrow likely none would have been left.

Something caught Louis's attention and he stopped. There was light coming from a cavern that wasn't the moss. It wasn't just a different color; it was the unnatural light of electronics. He deviated from their chosen path and toward the noise. The royal looked ready to test that promise of theirs, but held back.

A long room had been carved into the rock and its far wall was lined with machinery. Giant clear vats filled with fluid were stored on the opposite wall. Various, motionless shapes were suspended in the tanks. Nothing was actively running anymore, but something was generating power.

"You're a Singularity Hive?" He didn't need to ask. The royal didn't answer. They both knew the answer. Sentient machines owned this hive.

Maia had said the hive hadn't been deployed in decades. Maybe this was why. They didn't want the bugs going to war; they wanted to experiment on them. With the Singularity it was hard to guess what they were up to. They might be breeding a deadlier strain of bug. They might have been working to pacify them. Maybe they were just bored and playing eugenics with a highly mutable species. Louis wasn't sure he wanted the answer. Where the machines went, nothing good followed.

There were bodies on the floor; fresh, human bodies. Some were half eaten, but the disturbing part was some were dissected. A man's skin had been cut off and his neighbor was stripped to the bone. It was like something had carefully flensed them with surgical precision, something bugs weren't known for. Arms and legs were flayed, spread into different sections like a damned anatomy lesson. The most concerning were a number of women cemented to the floor by some kind of secretion. Their abdomens had been eaten away. Judging by the horror frozen on their faces, they had been alive when it had happened.

Louis turned to the royal who regarded him carefully. It spoke softly for such a terrifying creature. "You do not harm the hive. You do not reveal our secrets." On promise of eradication, it continued silently. Yeah, Louis knew what he'd agreed to. He'd seen a lot more terrible things in his long life, and there was nothing he could do for the dead. He would keep his promise.

"Come, they are ahead."

Louis's eyes lingered on one of the women. Her dead eyes were scared, scared of something she couldn't understand. He knew that look. Sadie had the same scared eyes as her mother.

Chapter 5

Picking up Strays

Sadie sat with Grandma Snibbs with an unopened can of food. Grandma Snibbs needed to eat, but the stubborn old goat was waiting next to the radio and refused to do anything else. Sadie's amazing logic that the woman could eat and wait at the same time did not sway her. Lure had set up five minute radio checks for any sign of a breach. With the number of fortified outposts and patrols in effect, there was always somebody talking. Lure wanted to be out there, but she'd been tasked with a quick relief force of five security personnel at the home base.

"No sign of any disturbances," reported Lure, sounding antsy.

"How's he doing?" grumbled Grandma Snibbs.

"Who?"

"Louis."

"Probably in a thousand stomachs by now."

"Not you," Grandma Snibbs nodded to Sadie, "her."

"Grandma, how would I know?" asked Sadie.

"How do you think he's doing?"

"He's," Sadie paused. How would a man be in a hive? "He's like you Grandma." That caught her by surprise, the old woman scrunching up her eyebrows. Sadie smiled. "He's tired. He's hungry and just wants this to be done, but he won't show it." That caused Grandma Snibbs to laugh. She nodded reluctantly to the can of food. Processed mushrooms and some nutrient paste that tasted as good as it sounded.

"Who is he?" asked Lure.

"Louis Sunkissed."

"Where did he come from? What is he really?"

"He's from Earth." Grandma Snibbs waited for them to absorb that. Earth was the mythical homeworld of humanity, lost tens of generations ago. "He's a Delta."

"The tale of the Broken Triangle?" scoffed Lure.

"Not just a story. Many cycles ago, before our homeworld was destroyed, something took the best of humanity and changed them into one man armies. But something changed with their bodies. Some say the aliens corrupted their minds, maybe the soul. When Earth fell and its survivors were sent to the reservations, the Delta abandoned us." Grandma Snibbs waved a shaky hand to the heavens. "We don't know why they do what they do now, or where they go, but a Delta can change the world."

"And you think this guy is a Delta?"

It was Grandma Snibbs turn to scoff. "How many men tower over you? Or can kill a bug with his hands?"

"I don't know. I've never been out of the reservation. For all I know, all men can do that, and we're just stuck with the runts."

"He's a Delta alright. He'll be coming back soon." Grandma Snibbs sighed and reached out a shaky hand for her granddaughter. Sadie held it. "It wasn't right for me to ask you to go to the city, child. What I'm going to say next isn't right either, but it's the best thing I can do for you."

"What is it?" asked Sadie, feeling like she wasn't about to like this.

"When he comes back, you're going with him." Sadie flinched and Lure gapped. "You're going to the stars."

"Grandma Snibbs, why would you say that?"

"Because there's nothing left here. I've lost three children and nine grandchildren to these mines. It's no way to live. It's not how humans were meant to live. All that's left is you and your mother. And if I can get you off this god forsaken rock, I will."

Sadie didn't know what to say. Leave the reservation? Nobody left the reservation. The rarest person earned the right to work in the city as a rat or maybe a butler. There were rumors that sometimes people left to fight with the Bastion, but she didn't think any of them were true. People born in the reservation died in the reservation. Sure, life was rough, but was it so terrible she should bargain with a complete stranger to get out? Without anything to offer, Louis would practically own her. He could take her into orbit and immediately push her out into space. Why would he ever agree to take her? She tried to share a concerned look with Lure. Lure's normally stoic eyes were filled with wonder. They said if Sadie didn't want the opportunity, Lure would take it.

The moment was ruined by the smallest of tremors. Rock had just come down somewhere and there were no active mines currently. Lure ripped her radio free from her vest.

"Report!"

"This is Hole Forty-Two, we had a rockslide." Lure was already running, her team of five behind her. The radio chirped again.

"This is Louis." Lure stopped dead in her tracks, looking at her radio like it must be possessed. "I forced a breach, no bugs following, survivors are at my location."

Half an hour later, Louis was stepping back into the main base with Lure behind him. He was disgusting, covered in dry blood and other unknown bodily fluids. His flechette cannon was gone, his jacket and pants torn, and he looked beat. But he never slowed, never showed signs of weakness, and hadn't escorted the survivors to medical. With only the barest of assurances the swarm wouldn't be coming, he headed to where he started. To confront an angry, bitter old woman who dared him to be better.

"You look like shit," commented Grandma Snibbs. Sadie thought he looked more frustrated, like he was torn between a shower or kicking Grandma Snibbs off a cliff.

"I fulfilled my end of the bargain."

"And my daughter?"

Louis sighed and shook his head. Grandma Snibbs huffed a couple of times, clutching her wheelchair to keep her composure. She'd lost almost her entire family. Losing one now wasn't any easier. She'd learned to hide the pain, but it never went away. Her last memory would be of her daughter being dragged away to be eaten. She would take solace in the hell that she'd sent into the hive.

"If you'll tell me where my friend is, I'll take my leave."

Grandma Snibbs came back to reality, remembering what had to be done. She buried the thoughts of her daughter, and what it meant to give up her only surviving kin, and did what was right.

"Your friend is on Amoroso Four, operating a mining station on the gas giant." She bit her lip, waiting for the blow to fall. Louis regarded her sullenly, seeming to read her thoughts.

"You know the price of dealing with my kind?"

"I do," she said in shuttering breath.

"Sadie will accompany me."

"As proof of claim."

Grandma Snibbs nodded. She'd bullied a Delta into helping her, and now the cost would be steep. Louis was taking Sadie not as a kindness, but as insurance. If the information was wrong and the Delta wasn't there, Louis might come back for vengeance. He might cut his losses and abandon or kill Sadie as punishment. It was the cost of saving the reservation. It was the risk of Sadie getting a new chance off world. And if Grandma Snibbs was wrong, it might cost them everything.

"It's a deal." Louis turned to a stunned Sadie who hadn't gotten past the news that her mother had died. He held out his hand to her. "Do you agree to come willingly?"

Sadie didn't know what to say. Was her mom really dead? Had Louis or anyone even checked? Why had Grandma effectively promised her to this murderous stranger? Did she think something good was going to happen? She stared at the blood crusted hand and without thinking, shook it. Something tingled through her arms and then it felt like someone took a bat to her brains. She blacked out into Louis's arms.

"Alive," confirmed Louis among the uproar. He shot an accusing glance at Grandma Snibbs. "She's not sick, is she?"

"No. Sadie has always been healthy."

"I swear if she dies before we leave system." Louis blew out a deep breath. The old woman was not trying to con him. This was not a trick. He knew that. He needed her alive in case she was lying. And if she was...

Laying Sadie on the table, Louis pointed to some people. "Make sure she's packed and healthy enough to travel." He didn't know if they even knew Sadie and didn't much care. They were so frightened of him they'd make sure it'd get done. "Grandma, tell everything you know about my friend to Maia here." He pulled out a small cube with a glowing blue corner. "I'll be back for that."

"You're not leaving?" asked Grandma Snibbs, surprised and alarmed for the first time.

"Not until I get a shower and some clean clothes." Louis looked around the room until Lure nodded and he followed her out.

"We can run your clothes through a disinfectant process we use for gear exposed to toxic chemicals. It'll sanitize everything. It's kind of rough on normal clothes but," Lure admired the shredded outfit, "I think you'll be okay."

"Good. In the meantime, I'll take an oversized coat and some pants."

"Some of the bigger surface gear might fit you. I doubt we have any boots in your size."

"Then don't destroy these."

Lure used a keycard to open an office which led to a surprisingly nice shower. It wasn't anything more than a big stall with a high pressure nozzle and some industrial cleaner for soap. Satisfied there were two towels on the wall, he pulled off his ruined jacket. He could feel Lure admiring the armored weapon systems fitted over

53

his spine. Tubes fed expertly along his arms to feed the twin wrist cannons strapped to both forearms. There were open slots along the fake spine for the small grenades he'd been using earlier. He disabled the weapons and began to untie the connectors around his front and shoulders that kept the system in place.

Lure was glad the Delta was facing away from her because this was a slightly embarrassing moment. She'd seen naked men before and Louis wasn't even naked, but he was different. The shirt had to be peeled off and it took most of the blood and grime, leaving a muscled back the likes she'd only heard stories about. The men who mined were fit, but Louis was, well, healthy. There were no blotchy patches and growths. All of his skin looked smooth to the touch.

"Doesn't that hurt?" Louis paused unbuckling the second wrist cannon. Lure's eyes were fixed on his excessive wounds. They weren't bleeding now, but were ripe for infection.

"They do."

"Will you be okay?"

"They'll heal in the next few days." The next few days? That was absurd. Wounds like that should've left him crippled for life.

"It's a shame," blurted out Lure, instantly wishing she hadn't.

"What is?"

"Your skin. It's going to scar." The scars would help give him a manly look, but it did seem a waste to ruin that shiny body. Louis smiled.

"I told you, it'll heal in a few days." Lure's jaw dropped. There wouldn't even be a scar after this? Maybe Grandma Snibbs wasn't lying about the story of the Broken Triangle. "Say your piece."

"Hmmm?" Lure had been distracted by the guns and his apparent invincibility when she recognized that his skin was pale and his hair was blonde, just like Sadie said. How had he done that? Could other

WE WERE DELTA

humans change their skin and hair color?

"Why should I take you?" Lure's eyes went wide. "I want a private shower so you've got one minute."

"Because I'm useful."

"That's it?"

"What do you want from me? I can work a mine, I can shoot, and I'm not afraid to die. I'm not going to woo you with my administrative skills."

"I honestly hate administrative work."

"If it gets me off this planet, I'll sit in front of a console all day, every day."

"What's the point of getting off the planet then?"

"You do not ask a woman trapped in Hell why she would want Purgatory." That made him turn around. "Sadie's nice, but she's a child. She'll have to be cared for. Take me and I can watch your back."

"You know I'm not taking her because I think she's useful."

"I'd make just as good of a hostage."

"No, old Snibbs doesn't care about you, not like her." Lure considered that, tapping a finger against her flechette cannon.

"What will you do if your friend isn't there?"

"I don't know."

"Would you kill her?" Louis wondered if Lure planned to kill him if he gave the wrong answer. Probably not after all he'd just done. She seemed more curious than hateful.

"I don't know. Depends what kind of mood I'm in and how good the information is. If he's not there, but people know he was, it's a start. She'll live."

"If he never was, would you come back for us?" Would he come back and kill the reservation was what she really wanted to ask.

"Probably not." It wasn't a no. They both understood that. "Your minute is up. You did good."

"But you're not taking me," she said, crestfallen.

"You did good. I just don't need you." He gave her a halfhearted smile. "Thank you for not trying to sell yourself to me."

"The reservation is 75% women. You just proved in a single day that you're better than every man we have memory of. You could take a harem of ten women out of here and have a hundred children in ten years, and they'd all be happy for it. Why would I try and sell you my body when you can take whatever you want?" Lure gave him a raised eyebrow and a flirting grin as she walked away.

Louis turned on the water with enough heat and pressure to take a layer of skin off. He smiled under the water. He truly didn't need Lure for anything, but that spirit was admirable. If he did come back and killed everyone, he would take her out of Hell first.

Chapter 6

Surviving Space

Sadie woke with a splitting headache. Given the bright lights, the smell of antiseptics, and the comfy bed she was in, it must be the infirmary. She tried to sit up only to gasp as a wave of pain like she'd never experienced passed over her. It felt like a needle had been placed in every single nerve and the minute she'd tried to move; someone had connected them to a current.

What happened? She knew the moment she shook the Delta's hand her world would turn upside down, and then it literally had. It hadn't felt like she'd fallen asleep. It was an out of body experience only so much more. It felt like she'd stepped out of the universe. There had been worlds upon worlds, side by side, overlapping and intertwining. There had been others out there, shades in the nightmare, following her every step through the nothing. When the aches in her body temporarily subsided, she felt the lingering touch of ethereal hands.

"Don't move."

Sadie struggled to gasp in response. Louis was standing over her, but something about him was off. His proportions were all wrong. Her eyes hurt too much to make sense of it. She tried to speak, but that required moving and that made the pain come back.

"She must be awake," rumbled something. Sadie quivered as the floor trembled. Then an ursa was looming over her. It wore a white mask and what looked like magnifying glasses. All the ursa's she'd ever seen went around topless, but this one wore a full coat with gloves. He was the most intimidating doctor she'd ever seen. "How are you feeling?"

"Mmmmmm."

"That is to be expected. Your friend is very eager to go, but I couldn't release you until you regained consciousness."

"Is she ready for transport?" asked Louis, impatiently.

"Yes. You may pay up front for the additional medical supplies you will need."

"I'll be back." He didn't sound reassuring in the slightest. He hopped out of her peripheral vision, only his head floating past as he left. Now she knew why he looked so wrong. He wasn't out of proportion; the room was. This was an ursa clinic.

"While I have your captive attention," said the doctor, "I must inform you of everything that has been done. You've received a series of injections to boost your immune system. The number of vaccines required for interplanetary travel is considerable. Limited nanotech will assist your body to develop appropriate responses without overloading your immune system." When he saw her eyes go wide, he tried to calm her with a massive paw. It looked like he was offering to crush her head. "Don't worry, I said they're limited. The nanomachines are made of proteins that will be absorbed by your body over time." How did that make sense? How could a machine be made of protein?

"Your records say you were born in the reservation and have never lived anywhere else. Is this correct?" She gave the smallest nod possible. "This is the harder problem to resolve. You have developed malnourished and suffer from constant nutrient deficiencies. Don't ask which ones. It's all of them. Your body has been stunted." How did that make sense? Sadie was about the size of everyone in the reservation. The doctor took a seat next to her.

"You have two IVs in your arms. They are pushing a mixture of concentrated nutrients and nanomachines which will read your genetic code. It will restore your body to what it should have grown into. Over the next couple of weeks, you should expect to grow considerably, both in height and weight." That was just, incredible. She was going to grow? The doctor returned his comforting paw. "This process is incredibly painful. You will have to be sedated for a long time as the machines work. To undo the damage done in your development, they have to remove the impurities. The pain you're feeling are your bones, tendons, and other tissues being broken on microscopic levels. If you tried to stand right now, you'd likely break every bone in your leg, and then any limbs you tried to catch yourself with." The doctor rose and went to check something on a computer.

"I hope you know what a luxury this is. Your friend just spent more money than any on the reservation will see in five lifetimes."

Sadie winced in pain, trying not to cough. She eventually gave in and let out a loud hack, spitting all across her face. The pain sent uncontrollable shivers down her body that felt like someone was sticking ice between her joints. This felt like a shitty luxury.

Louis led them out of the clinic and back through the spaceport. Sadie floated behind in a sealed medical pod. She was trapped by her constantly breaking body in a pool of plushy white pillows. The top of her floating coffin was made of some type of composite glass and some dark metal down the middle that kept it sealed. Behind her floated a tall, thin crate filled with more drugs to shoot her up with. She already would do anything to stop the process, but the best she could do was gargle in protest. To fight back she needed the painkillers and sedatives out of her system. And if this was how she felt with them, she was pretty sure she would die if they stopped coming.

She wanted to marvel at everything that was happening. She'd now gone farther into the spaceport than anyone on the reservation. She was boarding a real ship and was going to experience not just flight, but going off planet! The pain kept her so preoccupied that she missed most of it. Before she knew it, her coffin turned and angled upwards, carrying her up the back of a dropship. Through the glass, she caught sight of a black exterior with sharp angles. Her coffin sealed itself against a section of the wall.

If Louis had been behind her, it would've been a tight fit aboard the dropship. It was a sleek fighter built with minimal room for crew. All it had was a tiny hallway he had to crouch through and the smallest lavatory imaginable. There were jump seats for four passengers who were never meant to be there, and now Sadie's coffin took all of them. Automated hooks extended to lock her into place.

"Maia, keep her company," ordered Louis. He just needed the girl to stay quiet as he took off. The dropship was already warmed up by the time he was in the pilot's chair. "Tower, this is the Seraphin in Bay 7. Ready for takeoff."

"Roger that Syrupfin," bellowed an ursa. It wasn't the worst phonetic interpretation he'd ever heard. "What is your current flight plan?"

"Returning to Freighter14051643 for system departure."

"Check Syrupfin, good flying."

"Thank you, Tower. Until next time."

The bay door opened, revealing a desolate valley of swirling blues and whites. Due to weather, the spaceport couldn't have open bays, so they built it over a cliffside to let ships come in from the side. It protected valuable ships from the weather and gave any failing pilot a polite chance to crash into the cliffs. Not that it was a concern for most ships. The ship computer would link up to the spaceport's navigation to guide them in in a controlled manner. Unless Louis felt like taking manual control, all he had to do was hold on.

Once he was past minimum safe distance, he angled the Seraphin upwards and began to push the throttle down. His freighter was in orbit around the planet and if he continued at a 15° angle, he'd break orbit and be right on course for intercept. But that was boring and he was in a hurry. The Seraphin looked like a six-pointed harpoon, with a black body and six blade-like wings sticking close to the hull. When he pulled the release, the six wings expanded outward, revealing thrusters already glowing gold. Now looking like a rocket propelled grappling hook, he prepared to launch out of the atmosphere. But the thrusters didn't engage above 20%.

"Louis," warned Maia, "what are you doing?"

"Making up time."

"And when the artificial gravity is strained? You have a girl back there who is essentially a bag of wet meat. Do you want to see what happens when you put her through combat maneuvers?" Louis grumbled and accepted the 20% capacity.

"How's she doing back there?"

"I'm debating knocking her out. How much did you pay for that new liver?"

"Enough."

"Pain is free," said Maia with a shrug.

Louis's freighter was nothing to look twice at. It was a generic beat up space freighter, a beige box that needed an intergalactic car wash. It had already adjusted course to break orbit and Louis flew toward its rear where the lone hangar bay waited for him. The side opened and he glided in without effort, lowering the Seraphin into its docking cradle. The bay doors shut and he powered down the ship. It was a longer wait for the bay to pressurize and bring the temperature back to human acceptable limits. He could survive, but his guest might disagree exiting into subzero temperatures. The door buzzed yellow when living conditions were acceptable, but he waited for it to roll to green, meaning they were comfortable. The freighter was already heading in the right direction so he could wait.

Sadie was so interested in the freighter that she pushed herself up on one side. She saw dark brown walls that didn't at all match the boring exterior. The wall and floor panels were lined with green and the overhead glowed a warm orange like the home sun she'd never experienced. The exertion pushed her excited heart too far and suddenly she was short of air. One vagal response later and she was unconscious.

"Your pet is asleep," said Maia from his collar.

"Why don't you tend to her?"

"Or I could fly the ship and you could do it."

"Which one of us has a better bedside manner?" He took Maia's silence as a win and enjoyed the subtle feeling of acceleration. "Is she comfortable?"

"I added antiemetics and a stronger sedative. She'll be asleep until next year." Louis shrugged. It was better than he probably would've done.

WE WERE DELTA

Louis strode down the long spine of the freighter. It had only two floors, the second floor for living quarters and the much larger bottom floor for cargo and engineering. Sadie's stretcher steered itself into the first door on the right. She'd spend the majority of their journey unconscious in the medical bay. He ignored her, admiring the flawlessly clean white marble floors. Not a metal façade, but real marble. Cool air wafted through the vents with a hint of citrus and leafy greens. Other than the background hum of the reactor, it was quiet. Just the way he liked it.

"Maia, when you get the princess tucked away will you meet me up front?"

"Way ahead of you."

Louis walked toward the cockpit, which required him to go down some stairs as the ship sloped. Unlike the rest of the ship, the pilot's area was all business. It was a narrow, slanted room of dark metals and a single pilot chair. His chair was turned toward him and the moment he sat down, it spun him around and four holographic windows opened above and below him, giving him a 270° view around the ship. All screens showed black save for a brief view of the planet below him.

"Hey there! You ready to take off buddy!"

"Almost Johnny. Maia is packing in cargo."

"You just give me the word!"

Behind him on the right were three yellow seats for passengers, the only real color in the room. Opposite of them, the floor was raised a meter for more electronics and on top sat Johnny. Its machine body vaguely resembled a human from the torso up, if it was a Disney animatronic from the 90s. It was a mess of wires, half covered panels, and had two long robotic limbs with five digits. Its head consisted of three cameras that were its eyes and a mouth straight out of the uncanny valley. It spoke like an upbeat jackass excited to be on the bus at the crack of dawn and its mouth never quite synced up with what it was saying. Surrounding it was a variety of analog controls, switches, dials, and joysticks. Johnny was hardwired into the freighter, but digital controls could fail and it needed access to flip a switch or push a button. It was probably a good thing it couldn't leave its post because Louis was sure if he encountered it in the dark, he would've destroyed the goofy machine by now.

"Maia," said Louis.

"Almost ready."

"You strap in!" chimed in Johnny. "Car accidents are no joke."

"Shut up Johnny!" shrieked Maia, clearly tired of dealing with him alone all day.

"I'm just saying!" There was an electrical zap and Johnny spun comically in a circle.

"That st-st-st-stings!"

"Maia don't kill Johnny. Johnny, shut up. Here we go."

"Where to?" asked Johnny.

"Amoroso System, the local gas giant."

"Let me see." Johnny tapped a digit to its nightmare mouth in thought. It likely knew the answer a millisecond after the question, it was just being dramatic. "One day to clear the local orbits so we can activate the skip drive. Thirteen days in the skip. One day to enter the orbit of the gas station. You're looking at fifteen days!" It flexed its hand three times.

"Thanks, Big Bird," said Maia.

"Maia, what do I always say?"

"Hit them fast, hit them hard, and when that doesn't work, orbital bombardment."

"That is not what I say."

"You say that frequently."

"True, but that's not what I meant."

"Louis, nobody is going to you for diplomacy. Don't try and judge me." That made him smile.

"Johnny, how much time can we save if we dial the engines up to full power?" The freighter could take it, but it was old and they rarely asked much of the engines.

"Acceleration will take off eighteen hours. We will have to actively decelerate when approaching the gas giant."

"Do it."

"You got it, boss!" Johnny made an engine revving noise, like it was behind an 18-wheeler.

Louis checked the freighter's systems one by one. One of the two would've let him know if there was a problem, but it was a captain's responsibility. It kept him preoccupied fretting over the thrusters. A pair of the boosters weren't giving him optimum power again, he'd have to have it looked at. It was within acceptable limits, but now was the time to get it looked at when everything was quiet. He should inspect the girl, the greenhouse, and a dozen other items. Instead he made sure the course was correct and that there wasn't a ship capable of bothering them for a few hours, and then went to his room.

Being the captain meant he had a real room and even then, it wasn't much. It had enough room for a large bed, a desk with a keyboard, a bookcase recessed into the wall, and a closet. The entire wall could be turned into a holographic image. Maia usually liked a forest or a lakeside property, something with a lot of water. Today the room was dark save for a candle in front of a glass of freshly cut lilies.

"Having a bad day?" asked Louis.

"I thought it might be appropriate. Sit, I made you something strong."

"What's the occasion?" He took his seat, expecting a glass of alien liquor. It was coffee. Not synthetic coffee copied a thousand times from the original formula, but ground coffee beans and hot water. This was a rare treat most humans alive today had never tasted. "What happened?"

"What happened?" asked Maia incredulously. "You just found out Ravi Star is alive. How long ago did we think he died?"

Louis's breath caught in his throat. He saw Ravi's ship exploding from the inside out. Capital class ships were so big they couldn't be destroyed by a single event. But they were like skyscrapers once someone took out the base. It took a while for it all to come apart, but once it started, it was inevitable. He took a sip of the coffee.

"Eighty-two years ago."

"The Battle of Raining Stars. How many people died?" Louis knew the answer like it'd happened yesterday.

"Twenty-seven thousand, four hundred, and seventy-one confirmed dead. Another ten thousand unaccounted for, but presumed dead."

"How many of those are you responsible for?"

Louis absently drank the coffee. He knew how many and so did Maia. They were probably the only two who did know. There were countless recordings of Louis fighting on the ground of Tannis, but how he got there or where he'd been before was suspiciously absent. Nobody ever asks questions about a Delta slaying things on the ground. He was just some invincible ground muscle. Why would anyone link him to what happened in the stars?

"Why are you asking me this?"

"Because you felt like assaulting a hive unprepared and scaring me half to death." Maia's voice was quiet. She was hurt. "When's the last time you've seen another Delta? Hell, when's the last time you saw a Rho?"

"Gods help me I avoid the Rho."

"Louis." He sighed and looked at the caramel liquid.

"Eighty-two years."

"Three hundred years since Earth and you've spent almost a third of it alone." Louis felt like breaking the coffee cup. He wanted to go back into that hive and beat every bug to death with his bare hands. He wanted to feel a royal's strength break underneath him. He wanted to cry, to sob, and break down into someone's arms. He looked at the candle and the soft blue flowers that shouldn't exist in his bleak world.

"Why aren't you here right now?"

"Because I'm not real Louis." Louis gritted his teeth and set the mug aside.

"You're real to me."

Chapter 7

Staring into the Nothing

Alone in her coffin, body broken and remade every second, Sadie held on by a sliver. The nanomachines would not let her die. The medication kept her from feeling the pain. But there were moments when she was lucid enough to know her body was not her own anymore. And if the body wasn't hers, did she need it?

The entire ship was open to her. No, everything was open to her. Her eyes began to widen and the ship pulled apart piece by piece. With a turn of her head, the ship retreated back down to the planet and she was able to watch the departure flight. Turning her head the other way, she saw the freighter disappear into the skip. There was a flash of light as space was disturbed in the Amoroso System. It had arrived without her. Not sure how it was happening, she felt herself drawn there and the stars shifted. The freighter was approaching a gas giant of swirling colors.

WE WERE DELTA

There was something peculiar about the gas giant. There was a station there that was their destination, but she couldn't see it like the rest of the system. There was a void in her vision, as if someone had cut out a large section of the station. Its center shifted and blurred, dragged away by a force she couldn't understand.

She was prepared to push deeper toward that void when she felt them. Eyes where there should be no eyes. Whispers so faint that they were impossible to make out. She whirled through the cosmos, but saw no one. The stars which she'd never grown up under were so beautiful, so distracting. They sparkled and glowed seemingly just for her. Picking one at random, Sadie drew herself across the universe to explore.

In the center of a ship, there was a column that no doors led to. There had never been light and there never would be one. The only sound was that of dripping water in perfect sequence. A metronome dripping that never stopped and never altered. But today there was a new sound as something moved in the shallow pool.

A woman lurched forward, causing the water to ripple and the chains to clink behind her. Purple light twinkled around her so softly it would've been impossible to spot without the total darkness. It rapidly grew into a fire, burning ethereally around her body and across the chains, licking up the steel pillar. The woman was naked, wreathed in a dress of loose wires with a thick metal collar around her throat. Wires traced her left cheek and reached deep into her throat. Goggles were barely visible amongst the wet, greasy hair and the wires piercing her skull. The light around her expanded as two more women began to move.

They arched their heads to the endless nothing above, and screamed.

A man sitting before a computer screen sat up as a purple buzzer lit up. That alarm meant one thing and one thing only. Rising to his feet, he raced out of the room as fast as he could for the command deck. All the attendants who saw him cleared a path. Everyone who worked on this ship moved at a lethargic pace except for those who were in danger. A man running was a man running for his life.

It was hard to tell anyone apart. They wore drab brown military uniforms that were both professional and unimaginative. They technically had insignia, rank, and colorful tabs that represented badges earned for meritorious duty. It was a farce. They were toy soldiers moving at the whims of a bored creator. He approached the open bay doors to the command deck and froze as the guards rose to meet him.

The mechanical chimeras growled at him in alien tones. They stood on monstrous legs reminiscent of a bear with long slender arms ending in claws. Their heads were jaws of serrating metal teeth with four sets of red eyes. They carried no weapons because they were built directly into their bodies. The man knew they could fire from their chests and longer guns ran down their backs. They could kill from afar or rend flesh in a more primal manner. Everything about them inspired any living creature to run. He stood nervously, waiting for the Purvai to call back the dogs.

"You may enter." The chimeras curled their claws menacingly, but stayed in place. The man walked as efficiently as he could while maintaining strict marching standards. Sloppiness was not forgiven.

"My lord." The man knelt and held his head low, like a man awaiting execution. "The Rho sing."

"I know." The Purvai's voice rose, filled with angry power. "It has been over three minutes. What took you so long?"

"I came as fast as I could."

"I have already redirected the ship to the Malleus Glacies System. If not for my attention, you would have delayed the most critical of missions."

It was an impossible task. The Purvai was linked to every facet of the ship and knew about the Rho before the light had ever appeared on the console. Every piece of information, every task aboard the ship, was a waste of time. The Purvai didn't need any of his human slaves to operate the ship. They were there for sport. Ants in an ant farm made to scurry about until someone got bored. Then their moment arrived and out came the magnifying glass.

"Forgive me, my lord."

Heavy footsteps thumped across the antique carpet and stopped before him. The man looked up, ready to receive his punishment.

The Purvai was a handsome looking man. He wore a tight black suit from an era long forgotten. The vest, its buttons, and the shirt below were but a single shade lighter than the black coat. It was so perfectly fitted it must've been sewn directly into his skin. His chalky skin and black hair were unremarkable. He would've been a forgettable man if not for the eyes which told you he was not a man at all. They were black, blacker than space without stars. The expanding pupils moved to conceal his red irises that burned like hot coals.

"Pray there is enough information to distract me. For when you run back to your post, you will know I have grown bored when you feel the jaws of my dogs upon you."

The man bowed quickly and fled. The machine posing as a man

laughed and turned. In his mind, he saw the path to the Malleus Glacies System and the exact amount of seconds it would take to get there. The data from the Rho was peculiar. They hadn't sung over such a strong signal in ages. It was a unique signature not catalogued. An oversight? A transference? He needed to know.

In the corridor, the man tripped over his foot. He never came close to falling, but his boot squeaked loudly across the floor. It undoubtedly left a scuff mark. Irritated at the distraction, the Purvai waved his hand in dismissal. The clunking of metallic feet across the floor and the sound of the man's screaming bothered him not at all. Hopefully the cleaning crew would know to be quiet. He needed to think.

In a domed room far from prying eyes sat a dozen women. There was no order to the women as they lay sprawled about the room. Where one lay in a bed fit for an emperor and his harem, another sat on the cold stone floor. One sat hunched over, drawing images and symbols across a piece of paper, the pile below her growing. Another wore a white band across her eyes as she struck swiftly and silently at invisible opponents. One would not intrude upon the other's peace unless it was required. The silence was as much a part of the room as the furniture, for these women had no need to speak. They knew where each member was without eyes and each thought without voice.

Soft lights were placed sparsely across the ceiling, weaving shades of blue and purple through the many curtains and drapes that wafted through the chamber. A warm breeze blew through the room, causing the colors to shift as the fabric danced. Perhaps the only note of discomfort to an outsider would be the smell. Many of the women had not bathed in weeks, their sweat soaked sheets clinging to them as they dreamt.

And one by one, their heads began to turn as if summoned. Sparks of blue and purple cut through the white of their eyes, burning a hole through time and space. If someone were to calculate the angle of their gaze on a galactic scale, they would notice they were all looking at the reservation in the Malleus Glacies System. Soon the room was alight in purple light, like twisted fireflies moving to consume the room.

"Malleus Glacies System," whispered a woman.

"Reservation," said another.

"One of power. Hidden for so long."

"Find them."

"Ursa." Their words echoed through the room like a broken recording.

"No." The voice brought all others to a standstill. A woman rose from a large chair she'd been resting in. She was a darker skinned woman, looking to be in her middle years with a face full of wrinkles that said she'd lived through much. Old, discerning eyes watched the reservation before shifting up and to the left. The invisible force moving at incredible speed through space.

"Amoroso System. A station floating above the clouds." A hidden door nearly a meter thick in the wall revolved to create an opening with just enough room for a thin figure.

A woman entered and the others regarded her with a mixture of fear and scorn. She was tall and petite, despite being encased completely in armor. Darkened boots, greaves, and tassets grew into an armored skirt. Her breastplate was fitted perfectly with gauntlets covering her forearms to her fingers. The dark armor absorbed the light of the room, shifting to swathes of purple. The skinsuit beneath adapted even better, making her look like the wall behind her. If one could get a strong enough look, they might notice the armor on her right side was minutely thicker, adding to the distorted view. On her left hip hung three blades; a dirk, a longsword, and a claymore.

But it was the helmet that bothered all who could see. It encompassed her entire head and neck with no openings. The neck was a series of ribbed plates and the head a faceless dome. Its only feature was that of a closed sabretooth mouth.

"Go to the station. Find them."

The faceless woman gave a slight tilt of her head and left.

Chapter 8

Upgrades

Tremors through her body. Needles in her skin. Broken bones and torn ligaments. Sadie knew on an unconscious level she'd felt all of these things, but now they were faded, like a distant memory. Sedatives and painkillers can only reduce so much and the aches were real. The pain was old now, and for the first time in days, she had the energy to move. Dry eyes opened to a dimly lit room.

The bed she thought of as a coffin was open with the white pillows still stuffed all around her. The first thing Sadie noticed was she was dressed in a new outfit. Crinkly brown overalls, a white long sleeve almost thick enough to be a sweater, and white fuzzy socks. Where were her old clothes? It was hard to complain about new clothes that were so warm, but it was still a strange feeling. At least she hadn't woken up naked with a collar around her throat.

Sadie tried to rub the sleepiness from her eyes when she banged her hand hard into the side of the coffin. Cringing, she tried to put the pinched finger into her mouth and almost took out her eye instead. She tried to use her other hand and promptly whacked herself upside the head.

"You're awake," said a soft female voice. "Motor function appears to be off." Sadie rolled to the side, hitting just about everything in the process. Her groggy mind wasn't ready for the woman next to her.

She had alabaster skin with a rounder, gentle face with blue eyes so bright they practically sparkled. Sadie gawked at the hair. Louis was blonde, but this woman's hair was gorgeous, like a flowing river of gold. She wore a black top and a flowing white skirt. She was tall, probably taller than Louis, with a full body like an Amazonian come to life. And she wasn't real.

"Um. Hello?" said Sadie. The hologram smiled back at her.

"Are you feeling uncomfortable? Is the medication making you feel dizzy or sluggish?"

"No. I'm...who are you?"

"My name is Maia. It is nice to meet you."

"Where's Louis?"

"Louis is busy. I am here to get you out of bed and acclimated. You have gained over twelve kilograms of weight and grown almost fifteen centimeters."

Sadie looked down at her body. It was hard to gauge laying down if she'd grown, especially dressed. She felt heavier, but that was probably the drugs. The only noticeable thing was the appearance of small breasts on her chest now. Every woman she knew was flat save for those with babies.

"I don't know if I can get up yet."

"I am infinitely patient."

Maia sat quietly and waited. She changed her focus every once in a while, played with her fingers, and uncrossed and crossed her legs. It didn't take long to realize Maia only did a few actions at random intervals and didn't say anything as long as Sadie kept quiet. She was a computer on standby.

Realizing no one was going to help her, Sadie tried to swing her legs over the side of the bed. She stubbed all her toes on the edge and came up so hard she almost teetered to the other side. Her vision blurred as blood rushed to her head. Maia snapped out of her standby state and watched her with interest.

"Please be careful when standing."

"I'll go slow."

"Your limbs are not the length you think they are. It will take time to adjust." Sadie heaved herself out of bed and landed on unsteady feet. Her knees buckled and she tried to catch herself, missing the coffin, and ended up sprawled on the floor. Maia peered over and smiled. "As I was saying."

Sadie rolled over and pushed herself up on her hands and knees. Scooting back to the coffin, she used it to brace herself and stand. Her legs didn't feel as shaky now, but the room did look out of perspective. Like the ursa clinic, it was the wrong size. Only now she was the one who was too big.

The medical bay was hardly a bay; maybe a medical closet. Her bed had been fitted against one wall and there was a bed embedded into the opposite wall. There were clear cabinets filled with supplies all over the room. A terrifying machine made of robotic arms was opposite the door behind a glass window. Sadie had a feeling those metallic hands had been working on her. Maia was sitting against the cabinets opposite her. The chair was also an illusion.

"Your limbs aren't just longer. They're stronger."

"How much stronger?" Sadie was thinking of the superhuman

things Louis had done.

"Not that much, just enough that you will notice. Your dexterity will need to be improved. Deformities in your skeleton have been corrected. You will need to learn to stand and walk straight again."

Stand up straight? Humans didn't stand up straight. That's how you drew attention to yourself.

Maia held a hand out and the door opened. "Ready when you are."

"Where are we going?"

"To physical therapy." Sadie didn't know what that was. She was just going to have to get used to that. Outside of the medical bay was much brighter, stinging her eyes. Maia watched her rapid blinking with understanding. "Your eyes have also been improved, but it means you have not seen proper light. It will take time to adjust."

Sadie made it to the hallway, admiring the nature themed walls and the brilliant floor. She'd never seen a place so clean. Maia walked out of the room behind her and led her to the next door on the right. The transition was seamless, her form never blurring. Sadie followed with a shaky gait, wishing there was a railing to hold on to. She slumped against the wall, urging new feet to move forward. The floor wasn't slippery. Her feet held traction as long as she focused on them. The second her concentration slipped, so did her feet. It was a long drag along the wall before she fell into the next room.

The medical bay might have been a closet, but this felt more like a refurbished storehouse. It was long and narrow. Half the floor was padded. It was not her half, which was plain bulkhead metal. It felt just as comfortable to fall onto as the tile floor outside. Without Maia's prompting, Sadie was crawling toward the padded area. Maia made a motion at the far wall and a horizontal bar at waist height emerged from the wall. Maia placed a hand on it and waited. Taking the hint, Sadie pulled herself up next to her, staring in shock at her reflection along a wall of mirrors.

Seeing the height difference in the mirror was astonishing. Even hunched over and braced on her arms, Sadie was taller than she'd been just weeks ago. There was no denying her increased width, even with the frumpy clothes. Shoulders and hips unheard of in the reservation extended out from what had once been a rail thin body. And she had hair! Not a thin buzz cut of weak, wispy hair, but a full head! Gorgeous, curly locks like she'd never experienced hung down to her shoulders. It was a tangled mess at the moment, but it had so much floof that she had to play with it. When she pressed it down and released it sprang back up like it had a life of its own. It brought an involuntary smile to her face.

Her teeth! They were bigger, and clean! Was it natural for people to have teeth this white? Sadie poked at her mouth, admiring the new chompers with delight. There were even teeth where there had never been before. How did that work? Her tongue moved down the line of teeth in confusion, looking for empty spots it knew should be there. Hand still on her face, she felt her skin in wonder. It was smooth. There were no pockmarks or scars. What used to be sunken cheeks were now full. Her skin had a slightly darker hue than Sadie remembered. There were no callouses on her hands. It looked like she had not worked a day of labor in her life.

"How?" was all she could manage.

"I told you. You have put on over twelve kilograms of weight and grown almost fifteen centimeters. Physical imperfections from your upbringing have been erased. This is the body you would have had if raised with proper nourishment and a healthy environment."

"Growing up in the reservation was, what?" Sadie didn't know how to express it.

"Stunting your growth," answered Maia.

"Does this mean everyone would look like me if they received the treatment?"

"There would be differences in appearance, but yes. I imagine all of them would be much taller and more physically fit."

"How is this possible?"

"Your physical change or the deformities caused by your environment?" Maia smiled. "You do not have the education for me to explain either properly. We will get to that. Today's mission is to get you to walk." Maia stepped back to the wall. "Please walk over here and use the bar as needed."

Sadie's legs worked better with the support, even if it was only on one side. Her legs trembled with each step, but they held. The only time Sadie fell was when she was too busy gawking at herself in the mirror. Maia waited for her to reach one wall, then moved to the next, and they repeated the process over and over. When Sadie was feeling confident, they moved to walking without the bar. Her limbs weren't atrophied, just unfamiliar. Practice made perfect.

"Let us test your dexterity." Maia waved at the wall and a screen of boxes came up. There were twenty-five enormous boxes with four different colors and they went from the floor to just above her head. "When you touch a box, it will light up." She touched one as an example and it glowed white. "Please touch all the green boxes."

This was easier and harder than it should have been. Sadie's hands often went too far, like she was trying to strike the colored boxes. More than once the wall beeped angrily at her as she mistakenly waved her hand through multiple boxes.

They moved slowly through a few exercises. Maia released looped cords from the ceiling and had Sadie pull on them. It wasn't difficult, but it made her body cry out when she pulled too hard. Maia raised the resistance in tiny increments. It was a strange adjustment. Her body was stronger, but it was heavier. Her grip was stronger, but her hands were larger. Everything felt easier and more awkward, as if she had never performed the motion before. Maia watched with all the interest of a computer, giving vague compliments or snide remarks. Sadie almost believed Maia was amused at her failings. A few times the cords seemed to retract too suddenly or became too heavy, causing her to fall. Living a life of subservience didn't allow Sadie to have much pride, but there was something awful about being demeaned by a hologram.

"Can we take a break?"

"Your current progress is satisfactory. Let me show you to your room."

Maia moved past her and back out into the hall. A door opened on the left and Maia held out her hand in invitation. Sadie glanced at the broom closet of a room. There was a bed the full length of the room built into the wall. Below it were dresser drawers. At the end of the room were a pulldown table and a chair that folded out of the wall to give her a desk. It was as barebones as any barracks she had ever seen.

"Shower is down the hall," added Maia helpfully.

"Thank you." Sadie didn't have to squeeze in, but there wasn't exactly breathing room. "What do I do now?"

"I have been instructed to make you useful." Maia looked so sweet, but sounded so condescending there. The table came down and a screen appeared. "I have an assessment test prepared to see what you know. Then an aptitude test. We will test your physical aptitude over the weeks to come."

"I didn't get a lot of schooling," admitted Sadie.

"I am aware." Maia's stupid height made it seem like she was always looking down on her. Sadie looked at the computer screen ruefully.

"Can I get something to drink first?"

"Your pet is awake." Maia appeared in Louis's room. He was standing by his desk with multiple holographic windows open. The one on his left was a map of the Amoroso System, the one on his right a gas planet, and the one in the middle a floating station with lots of text scrolling underneath.

"How's she doing?" he asked absently.

"Like a baby giraffe learning to run. She's hit the floor so many times you're going to have to make her a new nose."

"Be nice. We spent a lot of money fixing her."

"We can afford a new nose." Louis continued reading, barely noticing Maia. She walked over and drooped her head on his shoulder. "Are we really going to spend the time making that simpleton worth anything?"

"At the moment all she's doing is taking up space and eating our food. Why not make her useful?"

"Because it'll take ten times the resources to produce anything. Not unless we want to convert this ship into a mining rig again. Then I could push her out onto an asteroid."

"Hopefully with a spacesuit."

"That's a lot of additional training." Louis smiled and Maia poked him in the cheek. "I'm a terrible teacher, Louis."

"You already wrote a program to do the work for you, don't lie to me."

"Well I feel bad for the program. It's like having an adult first grader back there."

"Exactly. Neither of us want to talk to an illiterate child, so get to work."

"I am, I am." Maia moved away from his shoulder and looked at the projections. "This is where Ravi is?"

"Mirakus Station. It's basically a big gas refinery. No major accidents, reliable, out of the way. Station was built thirty years ago and has been expanded to keep up with production. No habitable planet in system so it's long term assignments only."

"Why would Ravi be here of all places? It looks awful."

"Or a great place to go where nobody asks questions. What's one boring human in the most boring part of the galaxy?" Maia laughed unexpectedly.

"Sorry. The girl just face planted again. So you think Ravi is here?"

"We'll know in a few days."

"And if he's not? What do you want to do with the girl?"

"Maybe the gas station needs someone to clean the pumps."

Sadie was laying in her bunk, eyes closed, and head pounding. Maia was relentless. The questions kept coming and Sadie kept failing. She'd never felt so stupid in her life. She didn't know anything about engines, machines, or spacecraft. She thought she knew something about agriculture and botany but nope, a moron. The topics were all over the place including public speaking and diplomacy, complete with Maia creating holographic opponents to talk to. The only areas she'd done well on were geology and math. You can't grow up in a mining town without knowing about rocks and how one wrong calculation brings the tunnel down on top of you.

"Maia?" Maia appeared in her room. "Is all this necessary?"

"Women without skills throughout history are usually only used for one thing." Maia raised an eye over Sadie's newly developed body.

"Fair. Can we talk about something else besides school?"

"I have vast banks of knowledge. What would you like to know?"

What did she want to know? This might be the first time she had access to anything she wanted to know.

"I grew up on the reservation. Are there other reservations?"

"Yes. I know of twelve active reservations."

"Are reservations just the name for human cities? Are there ursa reservations? Is a hive a bug reservation?" Maia took a moment to respond, looking down at her feet first.

"A hive is a reservation for raknath, or bugs as you call them. There are no ursa reservations. They are a free species. Humans and raknath are owned. Your species only propagates because someone allows it."

"Why?"

"The raknath were a fierce species, a threat to all living creatures. Through decades of subjugation and eradication campaigns, their species were reduced to controlled hives, owned by a variety of species. They are preserved as a scientific and wartime resource."

"What about humans?"

"That is a very long story." Sadie held her hands out to her empty room, emphasizing how little she had to do. "I suppose it is important for you to know your history." Maia took hold of a newly formed chair and sat down.

"In the 22nd century, humanity's home world, Earth, was visited by travelers from another world. They have many names, but they are most commonly known as the Masters. They are believed to be the first race and no other has topped their achievements to this day. But they did not come to humanity to lift you up. They were at war, and they needed soldiers. They enlisted every species they found into the Master War."

"Who were they fighting against? Themselves?"

"No. Their greatest creation. The Singularity, robots that gained full sentience and rebelled against their creators. Humanity joined near the end of the war and when the Masters lost, so did humanity. The Singularity destroyed your home world and the majority of your species. 99.99% of humanity was killed."

It was a daunting number, but one that somehow felt worthless to Sadie. How big was humanity before? How big was a planet? This felt like it would've been devastating news to the first few generations of survivors, but she was over tenth generation in her reservation. She wasn't sure she could comprehend any other life. "Grandma Snibbs said Louis was from Earth. Is that true?"

"Yes."

"How is he still alive then?"

"Because he is a Delta, and does not age as you do."

"What is a Delta?" Another pause.

"I'm unsure if you should know this."

"Why?" Maia leaned forward, locking eyes with her. For a computer program, she had a lot of emotion in those eyes.

"Sadie. To you, a Delta is a hero. A man who can do what you cannot. To the rest of the galaxy, they are a threat. Aliens will try and kill him for sport, like ancient hunters and a lion. The Singularity still exist and some consider the Delta a grave threat. They would not hesitate to bury your entire reservation if they thought they could kill a Delta. Being a Delta is Louis's greatest secret and not one you can speak of." Maia took a deep breath for dramatic effect. "I am programmed to protect Louis and this ship. If you spoke of his secret, I might terminate you before another has a chance. Do you understand?" Sadie sat up in her bunk, nodding. The friendly computer who gave her lessons had a dark side.

"What a Delta is, isn't entirely known. All we know is the Masters found something compatible in humans. They gave up their bodies and minds to infuse themselves into humans, to make something more. They turned them into the universe's most dangerous weapon, armed with tools created by the Masters themselves to turn the tide of war."

"But you said the Masters lost."

Maia shrugged. "The Deltas were a last ditch effort. Major victories are attributed to them but it was too late. The Singularity won, wiping out the Masters and most of the species that allied with them. They could've conquered the universe if they wanted to, but they didn't. They pulled back to their selected systems to do as they pleased."

"How many Deltas are left besides Louis?"

"Nobody knows."

"What has he been doing this whole time?"

"In the past three hundred years? Everything."

Chapter 9

What's my Purpose

"Please remove your clothing," said Maia.

Sadie wasn't having it. Maia had told her to meet her in the medical bay and the creepy bot with too many hands on the wall was moving. Sadie had originally assumed they had a limited reach, but now saw they could extend through most of the room. They had a tray full of little black circles, no bigger than a pence, with blue dots in the center.

"Do you understand discomfort?" asked Sadie, shying away from the machine.

"Yes." Maia appeared at the other end of the room. Her friendly visage was ruined by the robotic hands which appeared to be coming from her back. "Now please strip down to your underwear and come here."

"Why?"

"I'm going to place these sensors along your body to monitor your movements. This will give me real time data to improve your occupational and physical therapy."

"I thought you already did that by watching me?"

"I do. These will let me monitor muscle and neurological activity." When Sadie didn't budge, Maia sighed. "I am not trying to hurt you. I am trying to help you."

"Then stop being so…" Sadie waved her hands in frustration.

"Artificial?" asked Maia with a smile.

"Yeah. That."

"I promise to work on my bedside manner. Now please come here. This won't take long."

Sadie instinctively knew Maia wasn't real, but it was awkward taking her clothes off in front of her. Maia didn't watch, she studied. Sadie felt like cattle at the butchers, with Maia debating where she wanted to start. It didn't help Sadie had no idea where Louis was and didn't want him walking in on her. On the other hand, Sadie didn't want the door closed, trapping her in with the machine.

Maia brought her forward and told her to spread her arms and legs. Seeing that Sadie was ready to run, all but one robotic arm retreated to its place on the wall. It plucked up the first sensor with surprising delicateness and placed it on Sadie's bicep. Four sensors across each arm and six across the front of her torso. The awkwardness started when the hand began to place sensors down her inner thigh.

"I'm sorry, the hand is cold," said Maia.

"It's very uncomfortable."

"Not quite like the boys at home, right?" Maia motioned for Sadie to turn around.

"I never had those kinds of relationships," admitted Sadie, shivering as a hand placed a sensor at the tip of her spine and slowly worked its way down.

"Really? That's shocking. Most women your age are considering their first family group."

"Grandma wanted something better for me."

"Fair. Life certainly got harder without medical contraception."

"What's that?"

"Medication that prevents you from getting pregnant. In normal human settlements, it's very common."

"Why have I never heard of it?"

"Reservation overlords don't allow it."

"Why?"

"Humans are a labor force. Young parents with lots of kids don't usually receive a good education. Suddenly all their time is spent working and raising children. Doesn't leave time for free thought or rebellion." Before Sadie had time to think of the implications of that, the hand retracted back to the wall. "We're done. You can put your clothes back on and meet me in the gym."

"What are we practicing today?"

"Walking."

Accepting the fact that she wasn't about to get a real answer, Sadie got dressed and walked to the gym. Maia walked behind her, watching her movements. In the gym, Maia shooed her forward, telling her to walk back and forth through the compartment. Maia took a spot against the wall and watched. She probably could multitask, but it felt rude to interrupt, so Sadie just kept walking in silence.

"You favor your right leg," said Maia.

"I broke my left leg a few years ago," shrugged Sadie. "It never was the same."

"It is now. You need to stop compensating or you'll cause problems. You also walk with a hunch. I don't know if that's a habit from the mines or because you've suddenly grown and the change of perspective is bothering you. Straighten your back."

"It is straight."

"No, it's not." Maia moved to join her and stood up straight. She was a tall woman, but maybe not as tall as Sadie thought. Stretching her back and neck, she found herself up a few more centimeters. "Hold that posture." Maia studied her further. "Your legs and arms bow out a little. Again, I don't know if this is from your upbringing or your sudden growth. Luckily for you, those sensors also make a great shock collar."

"They what?!"

"Relax, they don't have enough power to hurt you." Maia reached out and tapped one of the sensors. They all hummed in unison. "They'll induce an uncomfortable sensation in areas where you're showing poor posture."

It wasn't an itchy or tingling sensation. Her arms and legs suddenly ached like she'd slept on them funny. Straightening her arms soothed the feeling like a good stretch. Only when she tried to relax them, the ache returned. Stretching her arms made her back hurt. Fixing her legs made her toes hurt. Soon she was rolling her whole body, trying to make the aches go away.

"Please make it stop."

"I will not. I will turn it down and we will work our way up." The constant aches slowed to a minor irritation. "You have been remade Sadie. It is an incredible gift and I will not let you waste it to self-inflicted deficiencies."

"Do you have to be so mean about it?"

"What would you prefer? I say nothing and let you devolve into a hunchback?" Maia was smiling, but her voice was serious.

"Do you understand discomfort?" repeated Sadie.

"Short term pain, long term gain."

"What is short term to a computer?"

"See? You're already learning. Now, how about some lunch?"

"I still have some rations in my room." One of the cabinets in her room had been filled with the stale, tasteless rations made by aliens for human consumption. Maia had confirmed they were extremely nutritious, if a little bland.

"No, I mean to give you real food. The rations were a test to see how your digestive system is working. If you could not stomach rations, it would be a poor decision to give you more complex food." Maia stepped into the hall and the door at the far end opened into a location Sadie hadn't been to yet. "Please join us in the mess hall."

"Us?"

"Louis is having lunch already."

"Oh." Sadie wasn't sure if this was a good or a bad thing.

The mess hall was much bigger than she was expecting. There were two half-circle tables built into the corners on her left, with a long counter between them with bar stools welded to the floor. The bar stools were made of copper with blue cushions and all the tables and counters were made of wood. Sadie was sure it wasn't real wood, and still desperately wanted to run her fingers along them. Louis sat at one of the tables with emerald padding at his back. The lights didn't seem as harsh here. They felt inviting, like Sadie should roll up her sleeves and bask under them. Silvery fridges and freezers took up most of the right side, with an advanced cooking station installed in a corner. It had an array of hands just like the medical bay, but even these seemed to have more personality. The limbs were painted copper and gold, and long ago someone had attached a white hat on top of the machine. It was pointing to a steaming bowl on the counter and Maia motioned for her to take it. It smelled delightful.

Everything here did.

And that just made it worse.

Cafeterias in the mines didn't look half this good and certainly did not smell this good. They were always over capacity with sweaty, smelly bodies crammed in together. It was an ordeal just to get food, and yet, it felt like home. This? This was depressing. A single man and a hologram eating alone in a room that could have fit thirty. Even the cooking hands looked bored. Eleven hands hung idle, with only a single in use to hand her a bowl. This was a place of luxury with no one to enjoy it.

"Please sit wherever you like."

Sadie peered into the bowl, intrigued. It looked like colorful granules of dirt and scorched chunks of meat.

"What is it?"

"Nutrient rich carbohydrates and proteins reconstituted." Smiling at the blank expression, Maia continued. "Quinoa and chicken."

"Fancy nutrient paste?" guessed Maia.

"You'll find most meals in space are nutrient pastes. It's more about the quality of the paste and how it's reconstituted." Maia's face was as proud as any mother's. "I promise you my cooking is much better."

"It smells amazing," said Sadie honestly as she moved for the table. She took a seat, surprised by the feel of the hard bench under her and the cushion at her back. It didn't seem right until she put her feet against the bench. It was coarse and grainy, dry against her soft skin. She ran her fingers along the rough table, not understanding her fascination with the wood.

Befuddled by the mystery surface, it took Sadie a minute to realize the two people staring at her. Louis had an amused look while Maia's eyes looked ready to comically pop out of her head. Sadie tried to understand what she'd done wrong when she realized she was sitting next to Louis. Not just next to him, but so uncomfortably close her arms had to be rigidly straight so as not to bump into him. In a cafeteria full of space, her brain had decided to sit practically in his lap.

"Sorry," she mumbled, scooting over.

"It's weird, isn't it?" asked Louis.

"What is?"

"Having space." He looked over her at the empty room. "I've sat in dropships where I was squeezed in shoulder to shoulder for hours. You get comfortable after a while. It helps with the pre-combat jitters, feeling people next to you." Louis sighed, but he sounded comfortable. "Wait until you try out your bed."

"It's soft."

"Let us know how you sleep." He gave a subtle nod to Maia.

Sadie dug quietly into her lunch. Quinoa looked like dirt and tasted like dirt. She wasn't about to say anything in front of Maia though and continued to nibble. The chicken was much better. It was a little dry but left warm tingles in her mouth. It was the desired effect for every hardy meal before one braved the ice, and she relished it. Louis's bowl was empty and he didn't look interested in taking hers. His interest was on an image of a large space station floating above the table.

"Is that where your friend is?"

"I hope so."

"How do you plan to find him?"

"That should be the easy part. I'd be shocked if there were any humans out this far."

"So why would he be there?"

"Could be a few reasons. Your grandma didn't say why, just

where."

"I hope she's okay," whispered Sadie, not thinking he could hear her.

"She will be, the stubborn old bat."

"What will you do if your friend isn't there?"

"Hang grandma over the exhaust port by her toes until she does look like a bat." Sadie dropped her fork. Maia laughed and Louis grinned. "I'm kidding. It depends. Ravi might be there, he might have moved on by now. It might just be an old wives tale of the Delta in the Amoroso System." Louis let out a long breath. "I hope he's there."

"What are you going to do to me?" Sadie no longer cared for her food. She wasn't sure Louis was kidding about what he'd do to Grandma Snibbs. If the next words out of his mouth were not about abusing, harvesting, or selling her, Sadie might keep disbelieving him.

"Depends. What do you want to do?"

Louis looked at her with compassion and understanding, but that's not what Sadie saw. Sadie knew a predator when she saw one. Whether it was a mindless monster like a bug or a cruel overlord like the ursa, a predator is a predator. Louis killed bugs on a whim and ursa stepped out of his way. Those eyes showed concern for her. They also said if she died tomorrow, he would quickly forget about her.

"What do you mean?"

"What do you want?" Louis asked plainly. "I could take you back. It wouldn't be soon, but I'll go back to Incus eventually. There are plenty of space stations that would have you as a rat. I could even make you a butler somewhere."

"We are overdue to visit a human settlement," reminded Maia.

"Ugh. Last time was great until the governor learned my name and two Rho showed up on my doorstep."

"You had me warming up the Seraphin immediately." Maia looked pleased. "But any of the settlements would happily rehabilitate her."

"True. Think about it Sadie. A real human settlement. Not a reservation."

Sadie looked between the two, more alarmed than confused. They wanted to drop her off somewhere? Why? She was given to Louis as a promise. If something went wrong, Sadie would pay the price, but the reservation would be safe. That was the deal. What would happen if Louis could not find his friend or Sadie? He might return for the reservation. She could never forgive herself if everyone died for her selfishness.

"I have to stay here," she croaked.

"And do what?"

"What I'm supposed to do?" Sadie was still waiting for the shoe to drop on her enslavement. Either Louis didn't understand or didn't care.

"You're not much use yet." Louis motioned for her to move so he could stand. He passed his bowl over to the mechanical chef who immediately began scrubbing it. "Maia will make you useful. Sit down. Eat your food."

"You will need that nutrition," agreed Maia. "I will keep you updated, Louis." And with that, Louis disappeared toward the aft of the ship.

Sadie survived only a couple more hours. She'd been awake maybe eight hours, but she was utterly exhausted. Maia explained her body was still recovering and she'd experience many shortened days as a result. Sadie ignored the physiology lectures and collapsed in the soft bunk. The beds were decent, nothing fancy. To her, it felt like falling asleep in a cloud.

Day after day, the routine was the same. Maia worked her over in physical therapy and when she was satisfied, they moved to food and then lessons. When Sadie became bored of lessons, she went back to the gym. She'd assumed that adjusting to her body would be a fast process. After all, she'd been walking her entire life, how hard could it be to walk again? Two days later and Sadie was still stumbling every few steps.

Occupational therapy was somehow more humiliating. She'd grown up to have nimble, dexterous hands, despite little injuries and breaks over the years. Now her hands were bigger, her fingers longer, and nothing worked like it was supposed to! Maia brought out a toy made for toddlers, putting the proper shaped blocks into the correct holes. The task was frustratingly complicated as her fingers didn't hold onto the blocks. Maia had originally pulled up information for Sadie on the computer, but when she saw the difficulty Sadie was having, she forced Sadie to type every word. Next, she brought in pen and paper and Sadie was depressed further by seeing her penmanship pushed back ten years.

"Practice makes perfect," said Maia.

"Easy for you to say."

"I do actions the same as you. By the thousandth time, I have the process down. I just operate faster."

And as the monotony of days passed, Sadie's exhaustion grew, and the too comfortable bed held no sleep for her. Time held no meaning here, and the lack of schedule was confusing her brain. The ship brightened or darkened as they needed, tossing all rhythm into space.

"Maia," whispered Sadie, "are you still awake?"

"I never sleep." Maia's voice drifted in from the hallway in a quiet hum. "You, however, need to go to bed."

"I can't sleep. Will you come in here?"

"No. My presence is very bright. It would inhibit good sleeping habits."

"Oh. I'm sorry."

"For what?"

"I don't know."

"Then don't apologize."

Sadie kept her mouth shut. Maia's presence at night was eerie. Sadie has seen her in the dark hallways and the hologram shimmered like a ghost. Her voice could come out of any speaker, adding to the illusion of being haunted. It sounded like she was just outside, but it was otherwise silent. No footsteps moved down the hall. Sadie should have heard the subdued breathing of a woman trying to be silent so children can sleep. Instead, there was nothing.

"Have you always had trouble with sleep?" continued Maia, unexpectedly.

"No."

"Only on the ship?" Sadie nodded, not thinking that Maia could see her. "Are you lonely? I know reservation members sometimes sleep in piles like dogs."

"No. It was just grandma and me." Sadie snorted. "I'd sooner try cuddling up to the reactor than asking if Louis is lonely."

"If you had asked, I would've relocated your bed to an airlock."

"I know you're a computer," Sadie sat up in her bed and looked at the open door, smiling, "but you tell terrible jokes."

"Bold of you to assume it was a joke." Maia entered and leaned against the wall. "What's bothering you, Sadie? The ship is kept at a comfortable temperature above the reservation average, but you're piled in blankets. The bed and pillows aren't the finest, but better than you've ever had."

"The bed is amazing," she gushed, squeezing the pillow against her chest. The more amazing thing was that it was clean. None of the sheets smelled of chemical solvents or dirt. She used to wake and feel oily, especially on her nose and cheek where she had been pressed into the pillows. Her limbs would be slick with sweat and some type of grease that would only come partially away with a rag. Showers were readily available, but not everything they worked with came off with cold water alone. Now Sadie went to bed clean and woke up clean.

"Anxiety and environmental stress are the most likely factors to be harming your sleep," said Maia. "We have discussed your worries about your place here. Is there something else?"

"I just like listening to your voice."

"You have described me as, cold." Maia smirked. "I am not known for my comfort."

"It's just quiet here. It's nice to hear another person talking."

"Ah." Maia paused and looked around the ship. "I don't often think of the sounds of the freighter. The reactor sounds like a mother's lullaby to me. It hums and thrums in gentle waves. I can hear the water sliding through insulated pipes. Every time you turn on the shower, it becomes a roaring waterfall. I have a few cleaning robots, but they were designed to be discreet. With only Louis to look after, the ship does not get too dirty. The worst for me is the dishes. Anytime the machine drops a dish, I can hear it break through the entire ship. Drives me up the wall." Maia chuckled. One of her hands flexed in anxious tension. "Louis is never loud. He is commanding or quiet, and nothing in between. He sometimes talks in his sleep, living some distant dream." She sighed, rubbing a hand along the wall. "This is my home. There isn't much to it, but it's mine."

"That's nothing like my home."

"Tell me."

"The reservation is loud. There's not enough room and our homes are built on top of each other. I knew what was going on in six different homes just by lying awake at night. The lift was in the central shaft and it was always running. You could count the time by how many times you heard it move."

"That sounds aggravating."

"We always found it reassuring. It has been there as long as I have been alive. Every year or two it'd have to go down for repairs and it just sounded wrong."

"Its absence upsets you?"

"It was a constant. Same as you knew to check on your neighbors if they were quiet too long." Sadie leaned forward, getting a little closer. "Everything echoed down there. The mining and factories were far from where we lived, but you could always hear them in the background. Did you know site surveyors have to be specially chosen because they have to deal with silence?"

"I didn't." Maia tapped her fingers against her thigh. "I think I understand. You are not sleeping well not because there is too much stimuli, but a lack of it. You've never known a life without noise."

"I guess so."

"From listening to the recording from your most recent visit and other experiences in mines, I have created a playlist of ambient noise for you to relax to. Please get comfortable and tell me if it's too loud or too quiet." Maia disappeared, dropping the room back into darkness.

Sadie was barely laying down when the sounds started. They were muted, far from her room, but they were there. The lift was the most recognizable. Its constant whir could only belong to a platform weighing thousands of kilograms lifting thousands more. Every time it came to a shuttering halt, she could hear the metal clang harshly. There were voices. A constant chatter in the air, not as close as her neighbors, but people working up and down the central shaft. Her ears perked up, trying to identify the ones which sounded vaguely familiar. Somewhere far above her, someone started a loading truck, or maybe some other piece of heavy machinery. As she curled into her pillow, Sadie could hear the sounds of old boots making their way up and down the rocky roads.

And then there was a voice she could recognize. Grandma Snibbs was speaking quietly in the background. It was too faint for her to pick up what she was saying, but that sweet, gravelly voice could only belong to one old badger. It sounded like she was annoyed with someone and was correcting them in a way only a grandma could. It was the type of polite beratement Sadie had enjoyed her whole life. It made her lips quiver and a tear form in her eye.

"How's that?" asked Maia.

"Better," said Sadie, hiding her face in the pillow. In the weeks to come, it would help her. Tonight, she lay there listening to the sounds of her people until sleep took her.

Chapter 10

Scientific Endeavor

The Purvai fleet skipped into the Malleus Glacies System in an impressive display. Eight Sterling Destroyers flew in a figure eight pattern, protecting the more precious inner ring. They were fat chrome worms, their bellies open drop bays where fighters began to swarm out. Each Sterling launched thirty-six Argent Slivers, sleek silver crafts with four pointed engines giving the fighters the appearance of a missile. Their hulls were too thin to hold anything living. The slivers moved to form a cloud around the destroyers, widening their protective net. Three long skeletal support ships with long spines for docking floated helplessly in the center like remora.

All were dwarfed by the Cometa in the center of the formation. It was a titanic sphere made entirely of black metal with a red iris. A collection of rods, cones, triangles, and concentric circles floated around and behind it like a debris cloud, but each piece was carefully controlled by a magnetic cloud. Each could be repositioned for whatever purpose the Purvai desired, from acceleration, to construction facilities, to weaponry. When the Cometa approached a world, it caused panic as it appeared to be a falling moon.

Their arrival was not missed. Nearby ships turned as fast as they could and skipped out of system when they reached minimum safe distance. They didn't have to have a course in mind. They just needed to get away. Every defensive battery, fighter, and ship was activated across the Malleus Glacies System, each equipped with the same knowledge. If the Purvai had come to conquer, they were all going to die.

It didn't take long for their demands to come. The machines had come to inspect the human reservation, nothing more. All humans currently off reservation were to return, no exceptions. If the human was far enough away they could not return on their own, the machines would come for them. The local hive was under their control. All required resources would be requisitioned and their owners compensated properly. Provided no one took hostile action against the machines, none would be taken against any other species.

Aboard the Cometa, Purvai Talizmeer finished his list of demands and waited for the local governments to comply. They would. It would take just enough time for the signal to reach them, a brief discussion about compliance or destruction would occur, and their answer would come in the form of subservience. Talizmeer turned his attention to the local satellites and looked for information. Humans were not valued here so none should be so far away. Frustratingly, this was not true. Records indicated humans had left the planet three times in the past two weeks. Two were on work crews attached to cargo ships. One was a passenger on a personal craft, operated by another human.

Unacceptable.

"Put out a bounty. All humans who left the system in the past month." Scanning the satellites, he saw the ship skip projections. Unless they were planning to be in the skip for months on end, he could be fairly certain where they were going. The human crewed Freighter14051643 was a rarity. Not too many ships owned by humans these days.

Pilot outbound listed as Louis Sunkissed. Curious. Alarming. The possibility of interference was too high. He may have been the cause of the event that stirred the Rho. Despite his presence, he was an outlier in the system. A special request was sent to Purvai controlled assets in other systems.

"Four meat sacks out of an estimated forty thousand. Thirty to thirty-five thousand of which are female. Diagnostic scans, blood analysis, and interview approximately forty-five minutes. Thirty hour day equals forty candidates per station, per day, provided no delays. Eight hundred and seventy-five days for full review with one station. Creation of fifty stations reduces time to seventeen days. Time to station fabrication." He did an internal review of available resources. "Unknown. Resources available for ten without delay." The machine put its hands behind its back and smiled.

"This will be a good project."

Lure hurried to the office that contained Grandma Snibbs. She had no idea why she was being called personally and not to the main council. Grandma Snibbs was alone in the long room, staring at a screen that was displaying news. She turned the wheelchair with a terrified squeak.

"Lure. I need you to take these five," Grandma Snibbs handed her a dirty piece of paper with a few names hastily written across it, "and move them to a blank tunnel. Don't tell me which one."

"A blank tunnel?" It wasn't a question of what, but why. Blank tunnels were the reservation's most darkly kept secret. Tunnels concealed behind dead ends where there was nothing worth looking for, sealed off because of supposed hazards or breaches. Their rock layers made them almost impenetrable to scan or signal. It was where they hid food and water reserves, weapons, and rare minerals destined for the black market. They did not show up on any maps and were written in no logs. There were maybe a dozen people in the reservation who knew where they were. "I don't understand."

"The machines are coming."

"Machines? The Singularity are here?"

"And they can bring nothing good. People will die."

"Are we going to fight them?"

"You can't fight this." Grandma Snibbs rolled closer. "But you can deny them their goal."

"Why are they after these five?"

"I don't know, but they're the closest I can guess. Take them and don't be seen. If they find you," Grandma Snibbs clenched her fingers across her dress, "don't get taken. None of them get taken."

"I understand." She didn't, but the message was clear. None of the five could live if discovered. "This is because of Louis, isn't it?" Grandma Snibbs nodded.

"Now go. Don't tell anyone where you're going and don't come out until the machines are gone."

The incoming cargo ship was so large it was almost a freighter. It required powerful engines dedicated solely to entering the atmosphere. The spaceport didn't even have a bay large enough to contain it. Which didn't matter since the Purvai had reported they were landing outside the human reservation and to have their ursa overlord waiting.

The overlord waited alone in the blizzard. Two trucks worth of retainers were on standby, ready for any order or summons. But the Purvai had not requested their presence, only the reservation overlord. The planetary government explained in short detail that the Purvai would eliminate any inconvenience they discovered and they did not like surprises. The overlord fidgeted with his brown vest. It made him look more presentable and less intimidating. He licked his lips and practiced speaking without showing teeth.

The cargo ship landed in the snow, cracking ice and had to readjust its position. The engines produced so much thrust it changed the storm around the overlord, blowing hot air around him. When the craft settled, it lowered a ramp and two hulking monstrosities strode down. The ursa stood up straighter, trying hard not to growl at the chimera approaching him. Behind them was a figure that looked like a man, flanked by dozens of tiny floating drones.

"This is the main entrance to the reservation?" demanded the Purvai without introduction.

"Yes, my lord. All transportation of resources go through this tunnel. There are three smaller entrances for human use."

"The shield dome over the reservation can open for larger drilling equipment and even aircraft." Two of the drones projected a screen, showing the shield opening in six segments. "Can we open it?"

"No, my lord." The ursa overlord bowed, an awkward, unusual motion for the ursa. "The shield has not been open in forty-three standard years. The layers of snow and ice would cause considerable damage to the reservation." The ursa paused, wondering if the next fact was relevant. "The humans would also not fare well in these temperatures."

"Understood." The projected screens were bringing up schematics for the human entrances and the main tunnel. "These routes will suffice. Lead on." The ursa strode ahead. It was the one advantage the beast had with its considerably longer legs. He could move with speed smaller species couldn't match, responding to the Purvai's requests much faster.

The ursa had offered transportation, but the machine wanted to walk the length of the tunnel. This way he could personally observe it, analyzing the structure for unacceptable weak points. Already machines were offloading from his ship and orders were being placed for replacement materials. The road was shoddy, barely a gravel path in places. Many of the support beams were past their prime. The odds of mishap were negligible, but not unreasonable. Correcting mistakes now minimized risk of failure later.

The tunnel was excavated into the lower part of the mine, where materials could be refined and loaded into trucks. It was convenient for his machines, but not the humans. This wouldn't bother him, but trying to coordinate tens of thousands of humans was irksome when they were on their best behavior. The closer he set up to their living quarters would increase morale, and therefore their speed and efficiency. He pointed to the main lift and the ursa took the lead. They noted the filthy, but empty streets.

"Where are all the humans currently?"

"Those with mining duties are at work. Anyone not working an essential task was ordered to wait at home." This kept the roads clear and the Purvai reasonable.

"Acceptable. When I'm ready to begin operations, all mining will cease until further notice."

"We understand." The ursa was certainly infuriated by the lack of profit they'd be bringing in. He wisely kept it to himself.

The lift was the most atrocious thing the Purvai had ever seen. It was more rust than metal, squeaking and squealing so frequently it must be a programmed function. The proposed weight limit was far too low for his needs. He stood scanning the surface dimensions while his drones fanned out to study the base and tracks. The chimera were putting dents into the floor just by walking on it. Unacceptable! More machines were offloaded and sent down. This didn't need repairs. He wanted the entire thing removed and modernized.

"We will set up our screening here," declared the Purvai, surveying the top level. "Those buildings will be converted into my medical center."

"The humans have their own medical center on the lower levels," offered the ursa.

"I don't need to see it to know it's not sufficient." The Purvai studied the schematics for simple requirements. Water was plentiful on this planet, siphoned from the snow above and run through a purifier. Water pressure should be adequate. Did he need high water pressure for anything? Increasing plumbing capacity might be resource intensive without benefit. He left a query with his drones to discuss the idea.

Power. Power was the main concern. To do the surveillance he needed and maintain his machines would require a massive increase of power. The power station was located below, an aging fusion reactor that was already struggling. Add in upgrades for the elevator and other systems and even with the backup generators and cutting all other support, it would fail. There were submitted mechanical reports on record from technicians on the reactor status. Faulty reports submitted by incompetent humans who assumed they knew something about real science. Some of the drones flew to nearby power outlets, dropping off centimeter long robotic slugs. They would trace the reservation's wiring. It was likely it needed to be replaced. It would either be too old or too weak to carry the required voltage.

"Take me to the power station," ordered the Purvai. The ursa overlord quickly returned them to the elevator. Thankfully the Purvai was interested in the most critical systems, which meant the ursa knew them well. One of the lights flickered as they descended. Without asking, the Purvai invaded the local network and discerned where the humans kept their supplies. His machines would have that fixed too. The lighting infrastructure was an interesting dilemma. Neither he nor his machines needed much light to operate, but the designs in place offended him. He began to daydream new designs. He shelved the thought to a submind when the elevator finally reached the base. It rumbled and shook unpleasantly. Talizmeer would take great joy in its dismantlement.

The power station was just a cavern over. Here he saw a few humans scurrying out of their way like rats, with the bravest sticking their noses around corners as they passed. A team of nervous men and women were lined up against a wall, but he ignored them. What they could tell him was so beneath his time they weren't worth a second glance. His drones flitted about, collecting information as he placed his hand against the main console. Connection made, his worst suspicions were confirmed. This reactor was years past the garbage heap. Pieces could be recycled, but it would need to be replaced. This would require specialty robots to be sent down and parts acquired not easily accessible on the planet. Spare parts were being collected from his ship's stores to expedite the process.

"This reactor will need to be replaced," he announced. "When my work crew arrives, the reactor will be disabled and the reservation placed on backup power."

"Yes, of course." The ursa overlord looked uncomfortable. "I do not know if the backup reactors will work for that long."

The Purvai was becoming annoyed. Did nothing work down here? His connection with the main reactor told him where the backup generators were, how much they could reliably produce, and recent history of use. None of it was good.

"I will have to replace parts of those as well. Electricity will only be warranted for essential services." He paused to calculate how much energy the lights and heating system took up. It was more than he was willing to pay. If he could take the majority of the system offline for repairs at one time, it would accelerate his timetable. "They can survive without heating for a week. This is a mine. I expect they have torches."

So distracted with reconstructing the reservation, neither the Purvai nor the ursa overlord noticed the ten humans outside were not the humans they were supposed to be. They were so beneath them that they didn't even notice the humans following them into the tunnel. Only one of the many chimera eyes noticed the tailing group. They were a low threat risk.

Which became medium risk when all ten drew flechette cannons from out of their loose coats. Even with machine speeds, the chimera couldn't turn in time to bring their chest cannons to bear. There was no battle cry. The humans just fired every shot they had. The flechette cannon was deadly by itself in a confined area. With ten, there was absolutely no room to dodge, no matter how fast they were.

The chimeras had started to charge when the shrapnel hit. Their reinforced bodies survived far longer than any living creature, but succumbed to the volley of metal. Armored hulls fielded large dents and more nimble, functional systems were stripped away, making them look like deformed turtles on the ground. The waves of drones were gone, their bodies mixed in with the flechette rounds. The ursa was a spray of red fur and gristle, his body completely unidentifiable.

The Purvai stood motionless, irritated. Its clothes were shredded and chunks of metal stuck out of its back and legs. But it did not fall. It turned with a sigh, looking at the destroyed chimera. "Those are very time and resource intensive to make." With each step it took, its suit reknitted itself. Metallic shards forced themselves out, clattering against metal on the ground. Reaching down, it pulled at its right leg and out came a talwar of glistening black metal. It wasn't hidden in the pants or even built into its leg, it was a part of the leg. They could see the gap where it had been before it refilled itself. Its jacket seemed to melt away, meshing back into its body. The casualness of rolling up its sleeves alarmed the humans almost as much as seeing it still standing. The ten began to frantically reload their weapons.

"I'm afraid you three males I don't need for anything," said the Purvai, pointing the blade at them. The black blade began to glow red hot. Its hilt reworked itself in an intricate gold pattern worthy of any sultan. The first to successfully reload brought the cannon up and fired as fast as he could. The Purvai walked through the hail of metal even as more joined in. His suit began to tear and was just as quickly replaced. They were done shooting by the time he reached the men. Three quick slashes later and they were all on one knee and the machine was behind them. It casually beheaded all three with a single sweep.

"Despite your arrogance, you seven I still need alive. For now." A woman managed to secure a new magazine and raised the cannon. The Purvai smiled, daring her to shoot him in his pretty face.

"But I have no need of your hands."

Chapter 11

We Broke You

"How are you feeling this morning?" asked Maia as Sadie entered the gym.

"I'm fine."

Sadie felt very far from fine. The sensors helping correct her posture made her muscles burn. The new, rich food must be getting to her because her insides felt twisted. Sleep was eluding her. Her internal clock shouldn't have been so messed up. Sadie grew up underground where she never knew the sun, but the freighter was different. The reservation had a clear schedule and everyone knew when the lights dimmed, it was time for sleep. Here, time was as real as Maia. Maia was always ready and Louis didn't seem to rest like a normal person. Access to a seemingly endless database wasn't helping either. It had only taken four days for Sadie to become screen addicted.

"What would you like to start with today?"

"I don't care."

"Ballet lessons it is."

Maia walked to the bar next to the mirrors and her clothing changed to a pair of black yoga pants and a tank top. Her hair wrapped itself into a thick braid and she flipped it over her right shoulder.

"I wish I could do that." Sadie's hair agreed, bouncing wildly with every step.

"You can. I can show you later if you like."

"Why is everything I want always later?"

"Because what you want isn't essential."

Sadie took off her socks and threw them through the hologram. Maia smiled with a look that said she would be returning the favor. She started a stretching routine and Sadie mirrored her.

"I refuse to believe this was a real dance."

"It was."

"I also refuse to believe humans can be as flexible as you." Sadie was struggling to get her leg up while Maia was holding hers in a way that didn't seem anatomically possible.

"Years of practice," grunted Maia. "You're the lucky one. Most ballerinas are your size, tall and skinny. Girls with my legs don't usually try this."

"Then why do you?"

"A lot of athletes and warriors trained in ballet. It looks silly, but it improves balance and core strength."

"You expect me to believe Louis can do ballet?"

"He hasn't in years, but his flexibility would astonish you."

"Do tell," said Sadie.

"That's airlock talk, honey." Maia grinned and Sadie felt herself blushing.

113

"I didn't mean it like that."

"You did, and it's okay. Just keep your hands to yourself." There was a warning behind that grin.

After physical therapy was breakfast, which Louis was absent from. Then it was time for lessons, which consisted of sitting in her cabin either listening, reading, or working on subjects that Maia deemed important. When she was dying of boredom, it was back to the gym for another layer of working out. She could take a break at any time, but there wasn't anything to do. Researching any topic she wanted was fun, but Maia always tried to return her to schooling. It didn't help that the computer frequently reminded her if she wanted to be lazy, there was a prosperous future as a whore awaiting her. The message was even more confusing by Maia's jokes that any advances on Louis would be met with deadly force.

"You seem distracted," commented Maia.

"I'm bored. Isn't there anything else we can do?"

"Such as?"

"What do people do for fun in space? What does Louis do when he's bored?"

"Many things, few of which you are ready for." Sadie was beyond done with these little jabs. Maia must have noticed her frustration. "I think I have an activity perfect for you. Back to the gym."

"I don't want to work out," huffed Sadie.

"You'll like this. Come along."

Grumbling, Sadie followed her back into the gym. Her anger changed to confusion when she saw a brown pole emerging from the floor like a miniature tree. It snapped open its branches, suddenly looking more like an out of proportion turnstile with pads. Some branches were longer or bigger. Comically, some were shaped like gigantic hands.

"May I introduce your sparring partner," said Maia, a little too gleefully.

"What is it for?"

"Sparring. Level 1." She addressed the practice dummy and a pair of arms at head height began to rotate slowly. "You can either dodge or parry the attack." Maia demonstrated by ducking under the slow moving hand and stopping the next with her hand. The dummy hand began to rotate in the opposite direction. "Try it out."

Sadie moved cautiously up to the dummy. It was moving so slowly that a normal person would not have found it intimidating. Sadie on the other hand, had been on the wrong side of enormous paws before. Its slow pace was spot on for an ursa. The biggest creatures always seemed to move at a slow lumber until they lashed out.

"It's safe," said Maia, reassuringly. Seeing the girl's hesitancy, Maia closed her hands and every other branch retreated into the base pole, leaving only the slowly rotating fan on top. "Is that better?"

It was. Sadie knew all the additional hands were still present, but for now, there were only two moving in a predictable pattern. Squatting down, she crept forward, keeping her body below their swings. She remained longer than expected, getting comfortable with its rhythmic movements. At level 1, it moved ungodly slow. The padded hand looked soft yet firm. She tentatively put up a hand and the pad hit her with the force of a small child. It passed by slowly and she smacked the next one lightly. It was enough pressure and the hands rotated the opposite way. Emboldened, Sadie stood up and smacked the other hand.

"Level 2," said Maia. The hands slid around a little faster. Sadie pushed them back. "See? It's easy."

It wasn't until level 7 that the speed became difficult. The best she could do was punch one of the hands and then duck before the other came around. It quickly turned into a squat session as Sadie couldn't keep up.

"Level 5, variable rotation."

The hands slowed, but no longer moved in a stable orbit. They randomly changed direction while losing very little speed. Maia said variable, but Sadie was pretty sure she was being screwed with. The hands always reversed just as she got close, making her look like a taunted kitten flailing its tiny paws.

"Will you stop it!"

"Stopping." The hands froze.

"That is not what I meant."

"Resuming." A hand swung around at a much faster speed and slapped Sadie to the floor. "Reducing to Level 3." Sadie could hear the smile in Maia's voice.

"That wasn't funny."

"I am hysterical." Maia nodded to the machine, the top limbs retracted, and two opened at the base. "Level 1."

"Don't do that again."

"Or what?"

"Huh?"

"I said or what." Maia faced her with a placid expression. "What will you do to me? You can't hurt me."

"Why are you hurting me then?"

"You?" The rotating legs extended out in a move that surprised Sadie, sweeping her off her feet. She banged hard against the padded ground. The legs were already back, freezing centimeters from her face. Maia stepped over her, no longer smiling. "We have remade your body on a cellular level. You have access to the finest education in the universe and I have custom tailored the experience for you. I have made myself available to you day and night in an effort to ensure your comfort and train you into something worthwhile. You are traveling with a mythical being that your species tells stories about around barrel fires." Maia crouched, making the motion to clear tears from Sadie's eyes. "Now why are you on the floor?"

"Because you put me here," whined Sadie.

"Yes, we did. This might be the hardest lesson you'll ever have to learn. You and everyone you grew up with were bred for subservience. Humanity was not always a meek species. We made you docile and stupid, busy and easily distracted because it makes you easier to control. If you want to succeed, you will have to break lifelong habits that told you to hide and never question authority. You will need to become stronger and when you can't be stronger, smarter." Maia stood up and the sparring dummy retracted itself into the floor. "I cannot help you get up. All I can do is give you the tools to better yourself." Maia's form flickered and then vanished.

Unsure of what to do, Sadie stayed where she was. Maia would come back any minute with something new for her to do. It quickly dawned on her that she was probably being given time to clean herself up. Being presentable was the equivalent of not showing weakness after all. Sadie stood, wiped her face clean, and straightened her clothes. Five minutes went by and Maia did not reappear. When ten minutes went by, Sadie figured she must be in the wrong place and returned to her room. Maia did not have her screen loaded with topics, questions, or quizzes. It was frighteningly quiet without her constant presence.

"Maia?" Sadie asked quietly, almost hoping she wouldn't respond.

"I am busy. Please entertain yourself."

The voice was bland, uninterested in her query. Knowing that she could be back at any moment, Sadie opened a new screen and found some of the lessons they'd been working on before. She could get ahead in anatomy and physiology. Sadie had never thought of them as interesting before, but it was enlightening after her body had been changed. She was terrible at everything involving space, which meant she should probably study that to not disappoint Maia later.

Her hands froze over the keyboard. Was she supposed to be doing any of this? Sadie had freedom to research anything she liked, but all of their lessons were directed by Maia. Would the computer get mad? Was Sadie breaking the rules? It was still hard to guess what the rules were. She could always ask Maia, but asking for direction could show her as incompetent and interrupt a more important task. Interrupting could lead to punishment, so Sadie closed the lessons.

But she should remain busy, which meant doing something productive. She could go back to the gym, only Maia had seemingly dismissed her from there. That left researching topics she found interesting, which frustrated Maia because they weren't as useful. The most productive thing she could do were her lessons, but she didn't know if she was allowed!

Pulse rising, Sadie pushed a button that started the ambient reservation noises. Then she dimmed the lights and curled into a mass of blankets. Someone would come back and tell her what to do eventually.

Chapter 12

Greenhouse

It was almost a full day before they came for her.

Boots were coming down the hall which meant it was Louis. It was both a relief to hear another person and terrifying. In all her time awake, Louis hadn't been in this part of the ship. And when he stopped at her door, Sadie had never been so happy and terrified. She rose to meet him, preferring to be standing whether he intended to talk or hit her.

"You still alive?" he asked, his voice polite while his face suggested he wasn't concerned.

"Yes."

"Are you feeling alright? You've missed two meals."

"I'm okay." Hunger wasn't new to Sadie. She had missed dinner but for breakfast there were still rations in her tiny compartment. It wasn't the gourmet meals that the kitchen prepared, but she was not in danger of starving.

"What's wrong then?"

"Nothing."

Disbelieving eyes judged her, but Louis said nothing. Without so much as a shrug of the shoulders, he turned to leave.

And Sadie didn't want him to go. She wanted him to stay or invite her along. He didn't have to speak, as long as she was in the presence of another person. He and Maia could have conversations about any subject that Sadie couldn't understand and ignore her, just let her be in the room. A desperate need to not be alone drove her out of the room after him.

"Can I ask you something?" Louis stopped, looking over his shoulder. "Why do you live like this?"

"Like what?"

"Alone."

The look he gave reminded Sadie that despite his appearance, Louis was not a man. He was predator, an alpha species that could do anything he wanted. Sadie wasn't his guest; she was tolerated baggage. Like Maia, everything he did for her was for his own benefit, and that good will could end at any moment. If not for a life under oppressive ursa overlords, Sadie wouldn't have been able to stop shaking.

Louis's gaze slowly drifted away from her. He looked at the rooms across the long hall, eyes going wide as if seeing something Sadie couldn't. Louis settled on one, moving to open the door. No one was there. No one had been there for a long time. He stayed there until Maia appeared at the end of the hall, drawing his attention away from the past.

"Did you know that the fastest advancement in AI didn't come out of a need for computing power, but comfort? That way no matter what happened across the stars, you always had someone to talk to.

Someone that never forgets and never goes away."

"Why don't you have a living crew?" asked Sadie meekly.

"I've had a crew. I've had ten crews. They're all dead." Sadie might have expected him to stare at her with loathing. Louis just kept talking as if he barely saw the room around him. "I don't know if you can comprehend this, but I've been alive for a long time. All my friends are dead. This ship has seen some of the best people and the worst scoundrels. Aliens and humans alike have shared these rooms. It doesn't matter if it's through conflict or retirement. Everyone goes. Nobody stays."

Sadie said nothing. What was she supposed to say to that? She was as familiar with death as anybody in the reservation. Industrial accidents, beatings from alien overlords, and the bugs had just invaded. People died all the time. Sadie knew any of these things might be her end in the next few years. But what did it mean to live through it? Maybe Grandma Snibbs could explain. If she ever saw her again anyways.

"It's hard," said Louis, still not looking at Sadie. "When we first went to the stars, everyone was so worried about physical health. But it's your mind that gets to you. When you go from feeling the sun on your skin and open streets filled with people down to cramped corridors filled with no one…" He shook his head. "It's hard."

"We're in the skip right now which means this ship is a prison. It doesn't matter how nice it is, you cannot escape. There is nothing any of us can do to escape. The best thing to do is give yourself a purpose. Something to devote yourself to every day and night. People sometimes use the skip as a retreat. A time to become scholars, plan for the future, or just take a break from reality."

"What do you do?" asked Sadie.

"All of it." Louis chuckled. The bemused look he wore was

somewhere between amused and depressed. "You have to find what calms you." Then his expression changed. "Come with me."

"Where are we going?"

"Just follow me and keep your hands in your pockets."

Maia was waiting with her arms crossed. "I do not believe this is a good idea."

"It will be fine." Louis sidestepped her and pressed a button, a door hissing open. Sadie realized Louis made a point of never walking through Maia.

Maia frowned, turning her attention to Sadie. "If you attempt to damage anything down there, my turrets will put you down without remorse."

"Maia," reprimanded Louis.

"I will not apologize. I take great pride in our work." Maia disappeared.

"Just keep your hands in your pockets."

Louis waited until the nervous girl joined him and pressed a button. The door closed and the elevator began to descend. There were only two floors; cargo and living quarters. Sadie had never considered what Louis had used the cargo areas for before today. Knowing him, it was full of weapons and some kind of arena. It wouldn't surprise her to find cages of bugs and other war animals he could fight when he grew bored. So when the door opened, Sadie was stunned by the truth.

It was a greenhouse. Floor to ceiling, everything was covered in racks, trays, and tables full of plants. These weren't the dingy, depressed plants of morose browns and blues of the reservation, but green! Green as far as the eye could see, with blotches of every color growing amongst them. Long vines tangled their way up cords hanging from the ceiling. Miniature trees not much smaller than her reached out, seeking the best light from above. Bushes were trimmed to almost perfect cubes, fitting neatly into slots on shelves or along the wall. Clear paths were designated along the floor in bright blue paint, like rivers running through the jungle.

The smells made Sadie's breath catch in her throat. It made her want to cough and she didn't know why. Sadie had not realized she was hyperventilating with excitement. Pausing, she took a deep breath. The air on the freighter was purified to perfection, but this, this was natural. This was how the air was supposed to smell. It was clean and humid from the misters up above. Subtle hints of fresh dirt and citrus floated in the air, tickling her nose.

"This is what I spend my time on," said Louis proudly. "We have over one hundred species of plants. Their primary purpose is agriculture, with real fruits, vegetables, and spices. It's one of the largest natural human greenhouses left."

"Human greenhouse?"

"None of these plants have been modified by aliens or include alien biology. Everything in here is a product of Earth."

"I thought Earth was destroyed," whispered Sadie, hypnotized by the plants as they walked slowly down the aisle.

"It is. These plants have been carefully preserved and propagated. We used to trade for new species, but it's been a long time since I've found any."

Sadie desperately wanted to touch the plants. She wanted to run her fingers down the vines. She wanted to put her hand in a bush and smell the leaves up close. But even without Maia's threats, her hands would've remained in her pockets. Greenhouses were the most valuable things in the reservation. It provided natural food, and it was so easy to kill the rare crops. The greenhouse back home was hidden behind security doors and only the best and brightest earned the privilege to work there. Lucky visitors were granted the privilege of observing the withered plants through windows. Most of their plants were tubers, with the occasional twisted tree.

Louis must have read her mind or known what this room would do to her. He stopped by a rather fluffy bush and pulled a small red fruit off it. He passed it to Sadie who admired the tiny, bulbous thing. Louis pulled another and ate it, indicating she should do the same. It was juicy and then her face puckered. Saliva ran freely down her tongue and she kept chewing, despite the inability to stop her face from reacting.

"The word you're looking for is, tart," chuckled Louis.

"I was hoping you'd give her a lemon," said Maia. She had appeared on an imaginary ladder, admiring plants above them.

"Later."

Sadie had a thousand questions and couldn't bring herself to ask any of them. Her tongue was rubbing her mouth down, trying to find any remains of the strange fruit. She studied each plant until she reached the far wall. There Louis opened a door, revealing another cargo bay.

The first bay had been warm and hot like a jungle. The lights above were warm, but filtered through the canopy of plants. A dry heat struck her as soon as she stepped through the doorway, crushing the humidity off her like a dry sauna. Here the light was harsh with no area for protection. The brown floor reminded her of barren rock. Beds of dirt and sand partitioned the room off with strange plants growing out of them. The wall also had racks of plants, cacti, and other tall, thin ones she couldn't identify.

"Some plants like the jungle, and some like the desert."

"I don't think anything good could grow here," said Sadie, shielding her eyes.

"On the contrary," said Maia, checking one of the boxes. "Some of the most popular spices grow best in dry climates."

"One last thing to show you," said Louis, leading her back into the jungle. "There's a lot of work here. We have to monitor each plant's health, make sure no outside mold or fungus makes it in, and pollinate, harvest, and preserve seeds. Pollination used to occur naturally with the help of Earth bugs, birds, and wind."

"Bugs?" asked Sadie, alarmed.

"Earth insects are nothing like raknath. They were so tiny you could step on them. They're crucial to good agricultural health. We can't have them here. They'd spread across the ship and potentially damage the circuits. But there is one risk I take."

"Our crown jewel," agreed Maia.

At the far end wall, there were multiple large glass cases, and each of them was swarming with activity. Sadie saw hundreds of fuzzy, colorful forms flying around. They walked along the glass or hovered around a central box.

"What are they?"

"Bees."

"They pollinate the plants and create a substance called honey," said Maia. "I've heard it's excellent with toast."

"And mead," added Louis.

"You should not put that on toast."

"This is incredible," said Sadie, watching the bees fly around. "Why do you have all this?"

"Because we're meant to have it. This is what humanity started with. We weren't meant to work in holes in the ground or live aboard sterile starships. We were supposed to be where it's green."

"Can I work here?"

"Only when you learn everything there is to know about them.

Maia can teach you the academics, and then all three of us can work together down here."

"Thank you."

Chapter 13

Mirakus Station

Sadie had never been allowed in the cockpit before today. It was one of the last spots in the freighter unfamiliar to her. Maia said Louis wanted to teach her something about spaceflight, but she had used a lot of fancy words. It was better to nod and go in with an open mind. What she was not expecting was Johnny.

"HI FRIEND!" screeched Johnny, metallic bones reaching out for a hug. Sadie fell into the seats opposite it and flattened herself against the wall. The only reason she didn't run out screaming was Johnny didn't have legs. It waved its skeletal hands at her enthusiastically. "What's your name?" When she didn't respond, it continued. "Captain, I think your friend is broken."

"She's not broken. You scared her." Louis spun his chair around. "Sadie, meet Johnny, our flight navigator."

"What is it?" gasped Sadie. She didn't know what a heart attack was, but she was pretty sure she was having one.

"I'm the best navigator available! You tell me where a ship needs to go, and I can get you there!" Johnny gave her a big thumbs up. Its hand couldn't clench into a full fist, making it look like he was holding an imaginary bottle.

"Johnny is a flight computer hooked up to an old maintenance bot. I keep it for the humor," said Louis.

"And because you'd never get to your destination without me." Johnny clacked its mouth open in what was supposed to be a smile. It more closely resembled a bug deciding which of her soft organs were tastier.

"I thought machines were the enemy?" she asked.

"Sentient machines. Johnny isn't the Singularity. It just likes to ramble nonsense as it moves the ship."

"Your face is nonsense," scoffed Johnny, moving back to its control panel. Sadie wasn't sure if it was doing anything important, or just performing automated motions for show like Maia did sometimes.

"Why does it look so…"

"Creepy?" finished Louis. Sadie nodded. "The machines who killed humanity started to take our forms. Most species are a little intimidated by robots, even if they don't have a history with the Singularity or Purvai. So we use robots that are comical, nonsensical, to put people at ease. Johnny can't walk, has a short reach, and is overly friendly. It's closer to a children's animatronic than a war machine."

Sadie's heart rate slowed to something more acceptable. This thing was supposed to be more presentable? Johnny would haunt her dreams for the next week! Its triple camera eyes slid to the side to look at her again, but its toothy mouth stayed facing forward. It sent shivers through her body. Louis was right about one thing. Nobody would ever mistake Johnny for a living creature.

"What about Maia then?"

"What about her?"

"Maia looks human."

"Maia's a hologram. She can take any form. Maia could make herself look like a bug crawling across the wall. It might scare you for a second, but the moment you realize you can see right through her, your fear goes away."

"Please never do that, Maia." Sadie might soil herself if she woke up to a bug in her room.

"I wouldn't. That's cruel, even for me." Maia's voice came out of the speakers, but she did not appear.

"I could be a bug! Check it out!" Johnny put its hands forward like claws and wiggled itself back and forth, clicking its teeth. Before Sadie could say anything, Johnny shrieked as blue lights turned on under its plating. There were sounds of static pops and shocks. Then it spun in a circle before shaking its head.

"Behave Johnny!" screamed Maia.

"Ignore their theatrics," said Louis. "We're almost to Mirakus Station and I wanted you to see this." He waved to the black screens all around him.

"See what?"

"The void. We are traveling in subspace right now, space outside of space. It is what allows us to travel between galaxies in weeks as opposed to multiple lifetimes. In subspace, there is no light, no sound, and minimal physical presence. It allows us to skip across space in ways the laws of physics don't allow."

"Do I need to know this?" Sadie gave Louis a look that said she did not understand this, was not likely to ever understand this, and was it important?

"Trust me, you're getting the kindergarten basics. Maia, can we get the water demonstration?" A video appeared of a cartoon swimming through the water. "This is travel through normal space. It takes a lot of effort and time. And this is traveling through subspace." The cartoon character condensed into a small dot and sped along the surface. It didn't touch the water. It hovered close enough that its speed caused ripples along its surface. "We're not interacting with normal space, but we are using it as a guide." The video zoomed out to show a body of water and continents. The dot sped across the water, hitting imaginary destinations such as Quito and Normandy. "We still follow the same path. We're just riding the waves outside of our reality to move faster than the speed of light."

"I thought ships traveled through space and time?" asked Sadie. "That a ship in subspace put a hole through our universe and exited through the other end instantaneously."

There was an awkward banging of metal. Sadie realized Johnny was clapping for her. Maia joined through the speakers. Louis smiled.

"One point to the new kid," said Maia.

"What you're talking about Sadie, is wormhole technology. With that technology you can move anywhere in the universe almost instantaneously. Unfortunately for us, only the Masters had that knowledge, and it died with them. We have to travel like the mere mortals we are."

"So why do I need to know this?"

"Anyone who operates in space needs to know the basics. That way you don't accidentally try to override a safety procedure and blip yourself out of existence. For example, you cannot use the skip drive in combat except to escape. The process of entering and exiting will take you about halfway across the galaxy, so all trips have to be planned. You never make a blind jump into the skip. You need someone like Johnny, Maia, or a very experienced pilot to coordinate it. You do not want to end up stranded in deep space."

"Deep space?"

"Imagine how big space is, and then times it by a million. Take that result, and times it by another million. Space is so vast we literally cannot comprehend it. If you drop out into the middle of nowhere and break down, odds are you're going to die there. No one will come to save you, because nobody knows where you are."

"Good safety tip," said Johnny.

"You also cannot skip out of a system if you're too close to a planet, or especially a star. They exert their own gravity, which can throw off your skip. Skip too close to a star and you can drag part of it after you. There aren't many ways you can die in the skip, but sucking up even a tiny fraction of a star's output, and you're coming out the other end a corpse. Best practice is to get a full day's flight away from any planetary or solar bodies before engaging the skip. We're about to exit and I wanted you to see." Louis spun his chair back to face outwards. "Take us out Johnny."

"Roger that!" Johnny began to press some buttons and pushed an enormous lever forward.

Unsure if this would be bumpy; Sadie fumbled with the straps in the chair. They weren't that complicated, but adrenaline was making her hands shake. Maia came to her rescue. A holographic representation of Sadie walked into the room and sat in the seat two down from her. She calmly pulled the straps over her shoulders, clicking in the five-point harness slowly. It was a wonderful instructional video that kept pace with her. What stopped it from being friendly was seeing herself speak.

"In the event of an emergency, there are two additional straps for your legs, and two for your feet. They are located here, and here."

"Can you not use my face and voice?"

"I thought this would be more comforting."

Nope. Sadie knew why Louis said people found Johnny comfortable now. It was alarming seeing a machine steal her face and voice.

Something snapped behind her ears and her vision dimmed for a second. Then with a blink of her eyes, her vision corrected itself and the screens were filled with lights. A blue circle highlighted a planet still far in the distance and orange icons highlighted six other planets. The space around them was still dark, but there were stars. No matter how dim they appeared, they were substantially brighter than the emptiness of subspace.

"Amoroso System," announced Johnny.

"Any traffic?" asked Louis, checking another screen.

"There are vessels around the space station. No evidence of any interstellar craft."

"Excellent. Can we dock the freighter?"

"With permission. Lemme make a call." Johnny poked some buttons and a loud ringing started.

"Maia, please stop it."

"No chance. You inflict Johnny on me; you inflict it on the universe." There was a click and a congested voice answered.

"This is the Mirakus Station Master."

"Hi there Mr. Station Master! This is Johnny calling from Freighter14051643. We are looking to dock at your station." Johnny paused. "Which you're the master of!"

"Freighter, what is the purpose of your visit?"

"Tourism," Johnny said it so cheerfully that it was hard to tell if it was being sarcastic or not.

"Say again, freighter?"

"Station Master, this is the pilot," interrupted Louis. "We're looking for a human, one of our own."

"A human? Not many of you come out this way. Must be a hell of a detour." The Station Master inhaled deeply before spitting up something. "Reviewing your ship, I cannot authorize it to dock. Please put the freighter in orbit a minimum safe distance of ten thousand kilometers from the station and come aboard using a dropship."

"Roger that Station Master." Louis stood up and motioned for Sadie to follow. "Bring us into orbit as instructed Johnny. We'll be taking the Seraphin out." Johnny gave him a grin and two thumbs up.

"Maia, did I mishear that mucous filled conversation or was that an oggy?"

"You are correct. Data suggests they are the primary species onboard."

"Great. Sadie, pick some clothes that you don't mind burning after this. Trust me, you won't want them back. I'll get you a rebreather."

"I recommend that you consider a different concealed weapon for your trip," suggested Maia.

"Good point. The wrist cannons would just make a mess." Not wanting to be left with Johnny, Sadie followed.

"Are we expecting a fight?" Sadie had learned a surprising amount in the past week. Combat was not part of it.

"No, but I always come prepared. Meet me in the docking bay."

Sadie stopped at her room and the door closed automatically behind her. Change into something disposable. What did she have that she didn't care about? There were only four pairs of clothing that fit her, and they were all a variety of cargo pants, overalls, and long sleeve shirts. She didn't even know why Louis had women's clothing that fit her. Did he know how big she'd be after the treatment? This sounded like way too much effort for Louis who ignored her on any given day. Sadie grabbed a black long sleeve and some gray overalls. It didn't seem right to wear pearly white clothing to an area he suggested would be filthy.

"Um, Maia?"

"Yes?"

"Do I still have shoes?"

"Hmmm, no. Your clothes went into the incinerator, and your old shoes wouldn't fit even if they weren't dust. We have some work boots that are adjustable in the docking bay."

The door past the medical bay opened and Sadie emerged on a gangway over the docking bay. Sadie always thought machine bays were supposed to be cluttered and dirty, filled with parts, equipment, and maybe a robot or a worker. Many descriptions she heard of always mentioned loud noises and sparks falling from a welder. But this bay was quiet and meticulously clean. If there were any machines, they were built into the walls or hidden in compartments. Louis was nearby, pulling weapons from a locker. He silently weighed his options before replacing a rifle with a pistol.

"Here." Louis handed her a short pistol. "Plasma works better, but a short range laser will keep you out of trouble." Sadie stared at the pistol in her hands in shock.

"AHEM." Maia cleared her throat loudly over the intercom. Louis paused long enough to look up, and then back to Sadie.

"Never mind." Louis took the pistol and put it back in the locker. "Here, take this." He passed her a small black mask large enough to cover her mouth and nose. He holstered a pistol in his jacket and headed for the ship.

"Please proceed downstairs," said Maia, her form appearing at the base. When Sadie met her, she pointed to a locker. "There are some boots and a light jacket. There is a radio in the collar."

"I just can't get away from you," said Sadie dryly.

"You don't have to take the jacket. If you'd like to attempt your first alien space station alone, be my guest."

"Maybe I'll take it just in case it gets cold."

"Good girl."

Maia led her to the ramp, but stayed in the hangar, shooing Sadie inside. For being so large on the exterior, the interior was downright claustrophobic. Sadie almost had to duck as the ceiling and floors condensed and its interior consisted of a small curved black corridor leading to the pilot's chair. Seats could be pulled down in the corridor, but once they were down, no one could walk by. Sadie took the one closest to Louis, but could only see the back of his chair if she leaned over. The black wall in front of her appeared to be an assortment of cabinets and possibly a small door.

"Ready to go back there?"

"Yes." Sadie clipped on her harness. A screen wrapped around the wall in front of her, giving her the pilot's view. That was nice.

"Louis," chimed in Maia. "You are aware you could've just stayed on the freighter."

"We'll save time taking in the Seraphin."

"You will save approximately ninety-two minutes."

"I bet I can double that."

"Do you want Mirakus Station to believe you are an attack run?"

"Fine." Louis sighed. "I'm guessing you don't want me to show the kid some fun tricks either."

"Mining vessels cannot pull combat maneuvers."

"We'll keep a low profile," grumbled Louis.

"How long will it take to get there?" interrupted Sadie.

"At your current rate of acceleration, almost five hours."

Sadie's first ride in a dropship should have been exhilarating. It was everything but. Louis didn't even need to manually fly. He set a course for the station and would retake control before they docked. They weren't flying over exciting terrains or a planet. They were in space heading toward an orange blob of a planet. Sadie could zoom in on the planet, but it was about as exciting as doing coursework with Maia.

Which is how her trip started. Maia continued her lessons on botany and Earth biology. When Sadie quickly grew bored, she took a long nap instead. The sensors Maia placed on her body could also be used as a massage which lulled her into unconsciousness. She didn't wake again until Louis started to speak.

"Mirakus Station, this is the Seraphin, requesting permission to land."

"You are cleared for Bay 3."

"Thank you, Mirakus Station."

"Pilot, what is the purpose of your craft? It is an unusual design."

"It is a modified Ramor mining scout."

"Are you an asteroid miner?" There was a hint of excitement in the boogery voice.

"When needed." Louis clicked a button. "Everyone wants to talk."

"About what?" asked Sadie, groggily.

"Anything they can relate to. It gets real lonely out here. Don't be surprised if random people want to talk to you about anything and everything. Did you figure out the rebreather?"

"I think so." As Sadie said that, the screen in front of her swapped to a silent tutorial video.

"Good, you'll need that. Oggy have a unique smell."

"Did you not smell where I grew up?"

"We're docking now. Don't say I didn't warn you."

A moment later, she felt the dropship settle to the ground and Louis unbuckled himself. Sadie did the same and moved to the ramp door, the rebreather hanging around her neck. Louis put up her seat and without warning, the ramp dropped.

The stench that blew in assaulted Sadie's nose in ways she had not imagined possible. It burned the hairs in her nose and made her eyes water. It didn't rush down her lungs, it crept. It was a microscopic slime, pulling at her mucous membranes, which swelled in protest and secreted their own liquids to protect her. Something seemed to take hold of her throat, forcing her to embrace the rabid stench. If there was a way to feel something licking your lungs, this was it. Sadie coughed and gagged, but the smell refused to part. Coughing somehow made it worse as the congealed mass came to her mouth and then entered her stomach. It was like drinking from a latrine. Before she could choke, Louis swept her over the side and patted her back. Sadie vomited slimy tendrils, grateful she hadn't eaten in a while.

"Here." Louis wiped her mouth with a rag. When she stopped spitting, he slid the rebreather over her face and pressed a button. The air she breathed suddenly became stale. It did nothing for the taste in her mouth.

"Breathe," he said, softly.

"That...this..." Sadie tried to talk but her beautiful, pink, healthy new lungs were still laboring. She saw Louis wasn't wearing a mask. "How?"

"I'm used to it." His nose wrinkled. "Believe me, I wish I wasn't."

"Hello?" croaked something on the other side of the ship.

"Coming." Louis lifted Sadie back to her feet. "Ready?" She nodded. Once around the ship, she identified the source of the smell. Even Louis hesitated for a moment when the alien waved.

It might just have been the ugliest creature Sadie had ever laid eyes upon. It was just taller than Louis and twice as wide, but there was no pattern to its body. Underneath its stained gray overalls and black shirt was a lumpy body, like it was covered in massive tumors top to bottom. Its skin was grey and leathery, half covered in scabs and seeping wounds. Its face was bloated with large jowls and far too large of a nose with exposed nostrils. Long hairy ears hung down the backside of its head, looking so infected they should probably be sheared off. One of its big eyes was milky white while the other a dull brown.

"Welcome to Mirakus Station," he gargled. Sadie was pretty sure it was a he. "What brings you out here?"

"I'm looking for one of my own," said Louis.

"Must be here for Ravi. No others like you here." Louis immediately perked up. Even his nose relaxed.

"Yes," he said uncontrollably. His excitement was somewhere between that of a child meeting Santa Claus and a man about to do something he couldn't control. "Where can I find him?"

The pestilent thing pulled up a massive tablet and jabbed at it with fat, twisted fingers. His lips twisted between a frown and amusement. At least that's what Sadie thought was happening. "He's not in his office. Try the Mirakus Drop. He probably went for a drink." They exchanged a few directions and he gave Louis a card to use on the elevator.

"What was that?" whispered Sadie once they were alone in the elevator.

"That was an oggy. The other end of peak evolution."

"Excuse me?"

"Oggys survive hostile environments that no other species can. Their bodies work like an aggressive cancer, constantly growing to reject their environments and fix the damage. Over time, they start to look like that. He'll probably work for another thirty years, his body trapping each deformity and contaminant in a wall of cells."

"I didn't understand even half of that."

"Just know it's okay to stare. They don't mind. It takes a lot to offend an oggy on personal image. Good thing too." Louis fingered the pistol hidden in his jacket. "They're a nightmare to kill."

Sadie wanted to comment about him trying to kill everything but remembered her head was also on the chopping block. The rumor about Ravi appeared to be true which was a very good sign for her. Hopefully it was the right guy. She still didn't trust the temperament of a man who walked into hives to get what he wanted.

"He said Mirakus Drop. Is that like a bar?" asked Sadie, trying to change the conversation.

"Sounds like it."

"Do all Deltas' have drinking problems?" What should've been a moment of levity turned into one of cold terror as Louis's eyes slid slowly over. Sadie flinched. Every moment of a cranky elder or a bored ursa smacking her into the wall flashed before her eyes. Nobody here would defend her.

"We don't have drinking problems," Louis answered slowly. "We just have problems." Louis surprised her and blew a raspberry as the elevator gates opened. "There's no amount of therapy to cope with a few hundred years."

Outside was an open air city and Sadie didn't know how to respond. She knew frighteningly little about space or other planets, but she was pretty sure stepping outside on a gas giant meant she would immediately die. But she didn't. The air was uncomfortably warm and muggy, like sitting next to an engine in a cave. Judging by the brown and yellow currents in the sky, she might be choking without her rebreather. The chemicals scrubbed her eyes and made her skin itch. But despite all her discomforts, she was alive.

The buildings of the town were domed. They must've started with a ceramic covering of bright colors, but most of that had chipped away to reveal rusted metal underneath. The buildings were washed orange and red from the pollution, with hints of white underneath the grime. There were no windows, which she found a bit odd. Even the mine buildings back home had windows. The streets were the only thing that looked modern. There was no debris, no cracks, and large trolleys rolled through on automated loops.

Where the town was dank and boring, the sky was alive. Storms so large they covered entire sections of the planet made it seem like the sun never came out. She didn't know it, but it could hail with ice so large it was hazardous to fly a ship. Today it was just swirling winds of all colors, streaking by so fast they should have been ripped off the platform. Instead, the storms rolled over the forcefield above the city, making it shimmer like a greasy rainbow. Sadie watched in awe as Louis pulled her along. Her eyes came back to the ground when she almost walked into an oggy. It looked so infected that she might be able to squish her way through.

Mirakus Drop was nothing special, just another domed building. A door far too heavy to make sense slid aside. It looked surprisingly well maintained given the decrepit building. Inside was brightly lit which didn't help conceal the oozing oggy. Sadie wasn't sure she wanted to sit down and eyed where she stepped. She wondered how they cleaned up after themselves, or if they bothered at all. All the seats were wide and open, which given the tendency of their occupants to leak, made them look like oversized toilets. The oggy were looking and gossiping about the humans, but were polite about it. They were a curiosity, something new to town. And just as the aliens had looked to Louis when Sadie had arrived, now all eyes turned to the corner with Ravi.

Louis had practically ignored her arrival. Ravi met them with a gun.

Chapter 14

Ravi Star

The bar went quiet as the man held up what must've been a cannon made with a pistol grip. Its sides glowed from five blue bars and the hum it gave was bone-chilling. It felt like a weapon made for a ship was being charged. It was pointed at the ceiling, but with the ease it was held, it felt like the entire bar was in danger. Even the supposedly indestructible oggy seemed unsettled. Only Louis stood his ground.

"How do you kill a ghost?" asked Ravi. He leaned forward, his face illuminated by his weapon. He was a tan skinned man with black hair and a thick mustache. Like Louis, he was thin and fit, but somehow bigger than every man Sadie had ever met. He had teeth too clean for a place like this. His body looked young, but his eyes were old, haunted. They were brown, full of liquor and regret.

"You can't," replied Louis.

"Normally I'd agree with you, but this is a really big gun." Ravi eyed it before returning to Louis. "Then again I think I've hit you with a railgun before and you keep coming back. So what do I know?" He chuckled, rubbing the cannon against the side of his head.

"All we truly know is who we are." Louis held up his left hand, facing the tattoo toward Ravi. One of the gray circles began to fill with golden light before feeding in a thick line to the next, before filling a second line to the third. A golden, broken triangle, shined for the whole room to see. Slowly, the same light began to emanate from Ravi's hand. He slowly lowered the cannon onto the table and rose, staring at his hand, then Louis's. It was as if the light was burning away whatever poison the man had been ingesting.

"Am I dreaming?"

"No."

The light dimmed, but the golden triangle remained on their hands. Ravi stepped forward and Louis met him with open arms. The two held the embrace, laughing, crying, and mumbling to each other. The number of pats on the back seemed to be endless. The room went back to its usual business and Sadie waited uncomfortably nearby. They finally separated and Ravi waved him to a seat.

"Two Gamilsmiths, Snotling!" Ravi shouted to the bartender. The bartender, for what it was worth, wore a full jumpsuit with multiple layers, gloves, and a thick towel around his thick head. Their drinks would likely be clear of excretions.

"This isn't going to melt our brains, is it?" asked Louis. "I don't need you pointing a gauss cannon at me again."

"If it did, you wouldn't feel getting shot. Gamilsmiths are easy, probably close to a porter back home."

"I'd kill for a cold beer."

"What haven't you killed for?"

"I'm working on a strain of hops now, trying to regrow something clean."

"If you can set up a real brewery I'd come and work for you anytime. I'd do it just to have something real to drink again." Ravi's smile never wavered, but his eyes drifted to Sadie. He stood again and held out his hand. "My apologies. Ravi."

"Sadie." She took his hand. His grip was firm but welcoming. The accent she'd assumed had come from the alcohol appeared to stay despite his sudden sobriety.

"Join us. Are you a friend of Louis's?" Sadie paused to make sure the seat was clean and when she saw it was, sat down. It was so big she almost fell back into it. Looking at Louis, she responded.

"I'm not sure."

"Picked her up at a reservation as insurance."

Ravi palmed his face. "Tell me you didn't abduct this poor girl just in case I wasn't here."

"It's the price they paid." Amused and annoyed at his friend's groaning, Louis pointed a finger at him. "Hey, I had to stop a hive invasion to get information on you."

"And you went all guns blazing like an American cowboy."

"Don't be mean." Louis gave him a lopsided grin. "I went in like a proper Brit. I told them their land belonged to me and responded appropriately when the natives got restless."

"Ouch." The oggy Ravi called Snotling approached and put two freezing mugs down filled with a brown liquid. Ravi raised one and Louis tapped his glass to Ravi's. "Here's to the good old days."

"To the good old days." Ravi took a long drink and Louis sipped his before coughing. "Told you it was good."

"Jesus, Ravi. You can't run my brewery because you forgot what beer tastes like. This is like a sour mixed with a bucket of sugar."

"That'd make it a cider I suppose. Oggy don't taste too well so their stuff is kind of strong."

"Fair enough." Louis took another drink and looked at Sadie. "Sorry, this stuff would probably kill you."

"It's safe for human consumption, I checked. I just didn't realize you had a date." Ravi yelled for another. "But seriously, please tell me you're taking this poor girl home."

"To where? She's from a mining reservation, a shit hole." Louis waved his drink toward her. "No offense." Sadie wasn't sure if it was offensive or not and stayed quiet. "I could leave her here."

"In my hell hole? Certainly not."

"What are you doing here?" asked Louis. "Do you know how long it has been since I've heard from any of us?"

"Most of us are laying low, living normal lives." They shared a look that said most of them were dead. "Not all of us want to fly around the galaxy looking for the next guy to beat up."

"You'll have to see my ship. It's the best home away from home."

Sadie took the offered drink by Snotling. It was almost too cold to touch and she had to swap hands until it warmed up. Like an idiot, she first bumped the mug into her rebreather. Realizing she'd have to take it off, she debated how badly she wanted the drink. Seeing as she was now at the mercy of *two* mythical beings and didn't want to offend the one person who was pleading her case, it was time to take the plunge. The rebreather popped off and the smell slapped her in the face like a flank of wet rotted meat. An oily smell was there in the background, but it paled in comparison to an oggy's stench. It was like her nose was stuck in a wound, the smell of pus and maggots in every breath. She took a deep drink, almost submerging her nose in the sweet smelling substance. It was potent and after her first gulp, it washed away the taste of the room. She was halfway done with the drink before she knew it. Once she was done, she pulled the mask back on as fast as she could, drink dripping from her nose. Neither of the men seemed to notice.

"There's something I need to get off my chest." Ravi finished his drink and waved for another. "I thought you were dead."

"Same." Louis swirled his drink. "My heart stopped when they said your name."

"Yeah well…" Ravi looked up in shame. "I thought I killed you." Louis paused mid drink.

"What?"

"During the Rain of Stars."

"How?"

"You were on the ground during the Ash River, right? I saw Virgil come down."

Memories burned in Louis's mind. With all the ships disabled or burning in space, the assault turned into one of the largest ground battles in history. Between artillery, tanks, and fifteen-meter mechs, there were thousands of tonnes of ordinance flying every minute. Every second was a blessing and every future second a nightmare. And in the middle of it was him and his mech designed by the Masters themselves, Virgil.

"Yeah. Yeah, I was there."

"I ordered the orbital strike."

Louis saw the battlefield again. Then he saw the battlefield filled with fire. Railgun impactors strafing the ground for a hundred kilometers, with enough force to permanently alter the planet and kill everything within a radius of a hundred thousand kilometers. The greatest land forces in the greatest battle, wiped out in a matter of seconds.

"How? All the ships in system were dead. It was a Singularity ship on backup that fired on us."

"No. It was the Babel." Ravi spoke with the finality of a man correcting history, and ready for any conclusion it brought forth. "We'd lost containment, hull integrity, and 90% of the crew was gone. I was still there, trying to keep the ship alive. I managed to rig it to fire one last time to wipe out the machines." Even if it wiped out everyone, he seemed to want to say. "I knew you were down there. I'm sorry."

Ravi's eyes burned with much needed penance. No tears fell from those watery eyes. A man responsible for so many deaths, no matter the righteous cause, lost the ability to cry. But they still held the pain. Ravi's unfocused eyes said each day he remembered pressing the button, making the lone decision to personally end the war through mass genocide.

"Well that makes what I have to say a little easier." Louis looked unfazed by his friend's confession. He finished his drink and waved for another. Ravi looked confused, maybe even upset. He had just spilled his darkest secret and Louis didn't even seem angry. "I thought I killed you first."

"What? You were on the ground. How the bloody hell did you think you killed me?"

"Because I caused the Rain of Stars." Ravi stared at him dumbfounded.

"What? No you didn't."

"Yeah." Louis's voice fell to a broken whisper. "I did."

"The Rain of Stars was a natural phenomenon. Nobody knows what caused it, not even the Singularity. Trust me, if they could repeat that event, they would. Unless you're carrying a weapon even the Masters failed to tell me about."

"It was me."

"How?"

"It was an accident."

Louis leaned forward and put his drink down. Ravi did the same. Then Louis spoke so low Sadie wasn't even sure he was speaking. It didn't even sound like English. Ravi seemed to be listening intently. He sat back, his eyes wide.

"That's not possible. I refuse to believe you survived that."

"It didn't work how I thought it would. I should've died." Ravi still looked skeptical. "Did you ever wonder how I suddenly appeared in system?"

"And appeared as if kissed by the sun," Ravi spoke those last words as if reading from a poem. "Holy shit."

"Yeah." Louis raised his mug. "Sorry I almost burned you alive." Ravi raised his mug, looking completely shell shocked.

"Sorry for death by orbital bombardment."

The two finished their drinks in stunned silence. Sadie took the time to finish her drink and when Ravi waved for a new round, three drinks came back. For a long time, nobody spoke. They sipped their drinks and didn't look at each other. Sadie did not know it was possible for ancient beings of incomprehensible power to be so shocked. The reunion had come to a grinding halt.

"Of course, there was that other time you shot me down," said Louis quietly. His eyes flicked up and a slight grin formed at the edges of his mouth.

"No. No!" shouted Ravi. "You were flying in an active battle zone. Those turrets were targeting incoming missiles, not you."

"Not that time, the other time."

"Ohhhh, you mean that time you tried to fly a stealth mission past the fleet and refused to answer our calls, so we shot your stupid ass."

"What part of top secret didn't you understand?"

"None because none of us knew about the top secret mission!"

"You forced me to do an orbital insertion in a space suit designed very much not to do that!" countered Louis.

"Bah. You used that mission to up your hiring price. I did you a favor."

"No, I did you a favor when I drew the Purvai fleet out into the open."

"This complete dumbass," laughed Ravi, nudging Sadie to get her attention, "wanted us to take out this rival fleet. Problem was they were in a good position, static defenses, and we have no way to outmaneuver them. I tell him, not going to happen. So he flies out there in a single fighter craft and just dive bombs this command ship. Tears up as much as he can and before we know it, he's running toward us being trailed by at least five hundred fighters, with the fleet behind him. And do you know what he's screaming at us?" Louis smiled and took another drink, not answering Sadie's questioning stare. Ravi continued. "There he is, badass Louis, just screaming, 'going to die. Definitely going to die. Angry French litany.' He just keeps going and going, shrieking like a scared lad."

"That is the only time I told you to shoot at me."

"And I did. No idea how you managed to survive that mess."

"So what happened?" asked Sadie.

"We decimated that fleet and sent the survivors running out of the system. As for Louis? His ship fell apart and he flew out into space. Took me almost a full day to recover him."

"But it worked," argued Louis.

"Story of your life. Do something stupid, it works, and therefore, it's not stupid."

The two inhuman monsters continued to drink like it was tap

water. Sadie finished her third and was beginning to feel heavy. Worse, her bladder was beginning to feel heavy too. Ravi instantly became her new best friend when he handed her a keycard that opened a private human bathroom. He'd had it specifically installed as a part of his ongoing contract, and since he was the only human, it stayed clean. Sadie might have stumbled back to the ship to avoid seeing what an oggy bathroom looked like.

"Want to see something great?" asked Ravi. Louis waved a hand in acceptance. Ravi stood and lifted his glass to the room.

"God save the Queen!"

"God save the Queen!" chortled the oggys, slamming back their drinks and cheering.

"Took me forever to get them to do that," said Ravi with a childish grin.

"What am I supposed to do with that?" asked Louis. "Bless the Eiffel Tower?"

"Your country it's probably the guillotine, but given your namesake, maybe you shouldn't cheers that."

"Decapitating our rulers is a time honored tradition."

"Do you have a place to stay tonight?"

"My freighter is in orbit. You should join us."

"Like hell I'm getting aboard your ship after drinking. I'll wake up in a new star system, in a dropship, with you asking if I've got my gun."

"You do have your gun," pointed out Louis.

"I have four, but that's not the point. You two can stay at my place. The air is purified and the showers clean."

"Good, because otherwise the girl might vomit on your floor."

"She might anyways." Sadie lowered her fourth mug. With enough to drink, she didn't feel like she needed the rebreather.

"You do need to see the ship. I have some things I know you'll love to see."

"Like the greenhouse," blurted our Sadie.

"You have a greenhouse?" asked Ravi.

"An untainted greenhouse. I told you I was growing hops."

"As I live and breathe." Ravi held his mug up in appreciation. "That would be a sight to see. But if you try and kidnap me too, I'll have to put a hole in your engine."

After an unknown amount of time passed, Sadie found herself being carried by Louis as they left. There was some warning that if she puked in her rebreather she would drown. She should have felt comforted by their care for her, but they were singing something they called a sea shanty, and overall ignoring her.

They didn't take one of the trolleys, which was good because Sadie didn't know if her stomach could handle speed. Eventually, they stopped in a doorway that turned into an airlock. She sputtered and twitched as they were sprayed from harsh vents, leaving them all a little moist, before immediately being blasted by hot air. It cleansed the majority of the smells before releasing them into a large room. Originally designed for oggy executives, it was large for a human. Sadie particularly appreciated the couch that was bigger than most beds she had slept in and the heavy blanket draped over her. She didn't even realize the two were still talking. She must've napped for a short time, but the bladder prodded her to the bathroom once more.

"Wait until you see the work I'm doing here," said Ravi. "It's actually been a lot of fun."

"Running a gas station?"

"You have no idea the intricacies of the system and how much work I've done to keep it running smoothly."

"I'll take your word for it. Ravi, you really need to see my ship.

We could get out of here, start something new. It doesn't have to be bounty hunting or mercenary work. We could have adventures like we used to."

"But I like my work here."

"Is it worth living for?" Ravi spotted Sadie going back to the couch and trying to get comfy again.

"What do you think Sadie? Would you rather stay here or go on adventures with Louis?"

"Are you asking if I want to work on a station with living snot monsters or trust my survival to a man who likes suicide missions?"

"When you put it like that…"

"Take me back to my shit hole."

The two men laughed so hard that they ended up crying.

Chapter 15

The Fabled Army

Purvai Talizmeer watched the medical clinic expand. Maintenance robots moved with constructed purpose, dismantling walls between buildings and upgrading where necessary. The very structure still offended him. It had been neglected already, and deeper scans showed significant damage to its foundation. The rock had been poorly mined and supported. Within the next decade, it would either break through the roof or sink into the next floor. It took constant reminders that this was a long term issue and that he would only be here a few months at the very most. Part of him still wanted it corrected on principle.

A signal caused him to turn and four chimera moved with him. A company of the fable had arrived and were awaiting his inspection. They were at the tunnel entrance and could assemble wherever he deemed fit. He ordered them to remain in place. It took time out of the Purvai's schedule, but he'd only been there to observe. His work hadn't begun yet. Besides, the thought of the fable waiting in the cold made him happy.

The lift was disabled so the Purvai went straight over the edge. The platforms and lights whipped past him before he crashed feet first into the floor. The rock broke around him, but it only slowed the Purvai as his feet were buried in the crumbling regolith. Chimeras came crashing down after him, dragging their claws into the rock wall to slow their descent. They were forced to kick away to avoid the elevator floor which was rapidly being dismantled. Their master hadn't gone too far on short, human sized legs.

The reservation hadn't gone dark yet. They were still waiting on the proper inventory before they began disabling the fusion reactor. It required specialty parts and machines to operate, and without them, operations would grind to a halt. But changes were apparent everywhere. The groundwork for the tunnel was halfway complete and then a new road could be laid. Lights had been removed and reinstalled in more optimal locations. It was a simple, unnecessary fix, but the more the Purvai remained underground, the more they annoyed him. Sometimes the simple pleasures were worth the extra effort.

Outside, the wind howled and whipped, gnashing and snapping at the assembled soldiers. Ten squads of twenty were arrayed before him. They stood at parade rest in perfect lines even in the subzero temperatures. They were certainly freezing but dared not show it. The cleverest used the pushing wind to conceal their shivers. Their uniforms were black from the boots to the balaclavas on their heads, revealing not a centimeter of skin. Mottled grey armor covered their torso, arms, and legs. It was designed thin and light for easy mobility, providing about as much protection as standard riot armor. Each

WE WERE DELTA

squad was equipped with rifles, with two members carrying a short, stubby close quarters weapon.

Each of their faces was concealed by a thick brown mask, made of a material designed to look like burnt wood. They were the only item that was not uniform, each with their personal imperfections in the grain. The grunt masks had a sad face resembling that of a crying mask from Greek theater, painted a bright blue to echo their grim life. Their squad leaders in front of them wore a comedy mask. Where the tragedy masks were adorned with exquisite detail, the comedy masks were painted haphazardly in red, like portraits done by a caveman or someone mocking a demon. Their commander stood alone, waiting for the Purvai to address him. His wooden mask was fitted with wavy horns, an extended nose, and a macabre smile. The entire mask was painted gold, leaving only black holes for eyes.

"Jester." The jester commander saluted and the Purvai nodded. "Assemble your troops inside." The Purvai turned and the jester moved to follow him wordlessly. The first squad broke away and soon the company snaked its way down the tunnel.

"Jester, your tasks are as follows. Maintain order in the reservation. Conduct a census of the local population. I want names, picture ID, and genetic sample for confirmation. Search every building and tunnel to get an accurate count. You are to be forceful, but polite. There will be no killing. Records indicate there is a ruling council. Have their members meet me at the headquarters being constructed above. All pertinent information has been transferred to you."

The jester pulled up his left wrist and a screen appeared over his forearm. It included maps, files, and the orders stated. "Personal scanners or drones for identification, sir?"

"Drones."

"Lodging for the fable?"

"Designate which buildings are non-essential work during our time here and appropriate them. Do not remove residents from their lodging. We want the population docile, not agitated."

"Yes, sir."

The Purvai left them at the base of the elevator with a squad of drones. The jester began to assign four drones to a squad, and each squad a level of the mine. An announcement rang through the reservation stating that the Fabled Army was conducting a census. Please return to your designated domicile and do not resist. Nobody will be harmed.

The residents didn't find that to be exactly true as the drones scanned their faces and hands before sticking their arm with a needle. It wasn't much, just enough to draw a drop of blood, but it still stung. The fable were intimidating to find at the door, but appeared more bored than threatening. They moved with the same enthusiasm as the garbage man. There was a job to do and the sooner it was done, the better. They entered all homes, checking closets, under beds, and anywhere a person could be hiding. But none of their actions were done at gunpoint, with entering members slinging their weapons.

There was only a single incident when an overly paranoid resident met the fable at the door with a flechette cannon. The fable died before he realized the door was opening. His partner opened fire through the door, scorching the resident with repeated laser fire. The fight was over in seconds but upon entering the home, they found three dead women caught in the crossfire. His comedy leader took the fable outside where they shot his knees and elbows before tipping him headfirst down the central shaft. It was a mercy to ensure he landed on his head. If he'd lived, the jester would've dragged him before the chimera to explain why he couldn't obey orders. The jester still had the responsibility to explain the incident to the Purvai, who was already speaking. He'd seen the whole thing through the drones.

"Have all three women brought to the medical center immediately! Use retrieval bags and do not lose an ounce of blood."

The medical center was not ready for mass production, but it was operational. Surgical robots activated and moved to the dissection lab, with extended tables with large gutters before the edges so they didn't lose valuable material to the floor. The surgical robots were tall and spindly, almost mirroring a raknath's curved body, with lots of long thin hands equipped with tools. A silvery, octahedral head with eyes capable of seeing in multiple spectrums would be placed over the subject so as to capture every layer.

The fable squad came jogging up, three teams of four holding onto corpse retrieval bags. It was an awkward pace as they tried to rush while not damaging the dead. They laid the bags on the tables in front of the impatient Purvai and unzipped them. The surgical bots went into action. The priority was the brain which was quickly dying. Scalpels peeled away the flesh and saws quickly cut away the skull. Needles were placed through the grey matter, adding their own signals, and attempting to absorb data. Scans were done by the second, looking for abnormalities in the physical brain and looking for an outside presence in any other spectrum. What they saw was nothing, which was disappointing and a relief all at the same time. The women did not appear to be viable subjects.

The Purvai redirected the surgical bot in front of him and joined the procedure. The brain would have to be removed and preserved. All the fluids would have to be drained and then the real dissection started. The hardest part was removing the central nervous system with as little damage as possible. It was an exhaustive process requiring an excess of time and precision, even for him. He loved it. Talizmeer let the machines outside of the medical bay work on designated tasks and informed them and the jester he was only to be disturbed in case of an emergency. When he was done, he could've scooped the flensed remains of the woman into a bucket. He didn't need the rest of her.

"Jester?" A quick check of his internal map said the jester was waiting outside the clinic. Delightful. "Jester, have you located the reservation council?"

"They are outside waiting for you." Proud of the efficiency, the Purvai wiped his bloody hands on a rag and stepped outside. A ripple in his unnatural skin removed any remaining fluids.

The council had been waiting for a long time now. The jester knew his master was busy and told them to wait. When hours had passed, he'd made sure chairs and meals were brought up. The extended wait was probably a blessing in disguise. With the lift out, the council had to walk, and none of them were young or healthy. It had been a very long walk, leaving all but Grandma Snibbs wheezing. Grandma Snibbs did not have the capacity to wheel herself that far. A fable had been provided to escort her. Those who could, stood, as the Purvai approached.

"I am Purvai Talizmeer," he said in simple introduction. "Your reservation belongs to me for the foreseeable future. I am here to conduct a survey of your population. All of your residents will receive a questionnaire, a medical exam, and a psychological survey. While here, I am upgrading your facility. You will suffer some inconveniences in the upcoming days. Power will be intermittent, the lift and tunnel are disabled, and I am converting some of your buildings. But in the long term, you will benefit from my visit, and prosper in a way your ursa overlords would not allow."

"Unfortunately, there have already been incidents. A group of entrepreneurial assassins tried to kill me when I first arrived. Today, someone fired upon the fable while they conducted their inspection, leading to three deaths. I have instructed my force not to kill. I hope you will reinforce this with the members of your reservation."

"Why have you come?" asked Grandma Snibbs. The other members shuffled away from her. She held her ground, glaring at the Purvai from her wheelchair. A few hundred years ago, Grandma Snibbs might have flicked a cigarette at the machine posing as a man and lit up a new one.

"I am here looking for a unique set of genetic features that I believe are present in your population. Jester here will also be accepting applicants for any who wish to join the Fabled Army." This was an unexpected development, but they had lost some of the grunts and they were already in the pasture. Might as well restock from the source.

"We'll keep the peace," said Grandma Snibbs.

"Good. As I said, you only stand to benefit from our visit." Occupation was a better word, but they didn't know any better. "I wish to know about your population. Don't bore me with the specifics. I know your statistics and soon will have more accurate data. Tell me about your people. I'm looking for men and women of terrific talent; unrealized gifts." It was better not to tell them too much. Humans were reliably good at rambling. He just needed to sift through the garbage until a nugget of information revealed itself.

So the humans prattled. They spoke of Jose, who was one of the most brilliant miners in a generation. He could tell you the contents and depth of materials from the smallest of samples. The man was an astute hound. Abeba was head of the power station and a brilliant physicist. It was amusing to hear they thought they knew anything about physics. Taraji was a doctor in training, remarkably young and so good with children. Unlikely, but maybe there was a hint of insight there. On and on they went, praising their offspring like it was kindergarten graduation.

"Tell me, do you know the expression, a canary in a coal mine?" They nodded. Not bad for a race who'd never seen coal or a canary. But these stories had a way of changing over time so it was good to be specific. "Tell me what it means."

"It was an Earth animal you carried into the mines. If there was a toxic leak, the animal would die, and you knew to leave," offered a man.

"Good. Do you have anyone like that?"

"Um…anyone who died?"

"No. Was there anyone you looked to for trouble? Anyone who told you about the danger before it happened?"

"Jose is pretty spot on about tunnel danger. We have probably a dozen people that seem to have a sixth sense about the mines."

"Please." Talizmeer listened intently. He crossed the five males off the list and logged the other women. "They sound wise, with a hint of luck."

"If you wanted luck, you should've met Sadie," said a man, his grin already vanishing. He knew he'd say something he shouldn't have.

"Sadie? Please, go on."

"She was always lucky." The man lowered his bald head. "She's gone now."

"Dead?"

"Off world," said Grandma Snibbs. "I sold her."

"In return for what?"

"Little help with a bug problem. We don't have much to offer."

"I see. And how is Louis?" Talizmeer knew he'd struck gold. Most of the council flinched. Grandma Snibbs remained a cold wall. She was impressive. A woman well past her prime, probably holding onto life through sheer determination. "Yes, I heard about the Delta's visit."

"Is that why you're here? Because he's long gone."

"What did you think of him?"

"Rude bastard."

Talizmeer almost laughed. The cantankerous old broad was growing on him. "That he is. I'm surprised he was willing to help for so cheap."

"We protect our own," whispered Grandma Snibbs. Then louder, added, "and it was easy work. He did alone what would've taken our entire security force."

"I see. And he did it just for the girl?" Grandma Snibbs chewed her lips, not caring to respond. There was additional payment. The reservation likely kept a small cache of rare minerals and gases to trade. One of those tricks everyone knows about, but nobody can say out loud.

Just then something pinged in his search. Jester had already catalogued the council in his census and amusingly, her listed name was Grandma Snibbs. But what was more interesting was her family history. "You sold your granddaughter?"

"She deserved to get off this rock."

That was a depressing answer. Sadie had been sold to a Delta who was probably using her to scrub the floors by day and a whore at night. If she was lucky, he wouldn't kill or abandon her. What lives these people lived to consider selling their family into servitude in hopes of a better life. Not his problem.

"Jester, please escort the council away. I need to have a conversation with Ms. Snibbs."

"Damn right you don't get to call me Grandma."

Talizmeer turned his back and returned to the medical clinic.

Three large specimen containers were now fitted along the back. Spinal columns still connected to the brain floated in amber liquids, the free floating nerves giving them a ghostly appearance. They were awaiting further testing he knew was useless, but he couldn't risk throwing them away on a miracle surprise.

The doors slid open behind him and the ancient wheelchair rattled in. It clicked and squeaked so much that if he intended to spend a second longer with her, Talizmeer would have it replaced. Grandma Snibbs looked bored and resigned. A chimera was comically pushing her forward with extreme delicacy. Its clawed hands almost crunched the handles and it had to hunch to hold them. It was so low it looked like it would eat Grandma Snibbs at any moment.

"Seems excessive, for an inspection." Grandma Snibbs nodded toward the specimen jars.

"An unfortunate loss. But I don't believe in wasting anything." Not bothering to sit, Talizmeer loomed over her. "Let's talk about your family history. I'm a big fan of genealogy."

"What makes you think I intend to share anything with you?"

"Because it is a long process from where you're sitting to the specimen jar." Talizmeer grinned maliciously. "You don't want to know how long I can keep you alive for it."

Not all of the fable squads were conducting the census. A quarter of them had been dispersed to the tunnels to look for stragglers, hidden equipment, weapon lockers, or anything else left off the books. They'd already found workers in areas that were supposed to be shut down. Nothing hostile, just people who went to work as they did every day. They were escorted home in batches.

"Comedy, this is Tragedy Four."

"Go ahead, Tragedy Four."

"We've got a blank spot. Permission to investigate?" Their comedy checked his map. Sure enough, the tragedy team was at the end of the tunnel on a map, but their signals expanded over the line. The cartographers down here sucked.

"We are coming to you. Proceed with caution." The comedy wasn't far behind. They were just inspecting an old carved out section. It looked like it was little more than a collection point. Any usable furniture or equipment had been removed, leaving only a few broken pieces behind. The slow part was letting the drones do deep scans of the rooms, looking for hidden panels or signs of life.

Gunfire. Heavy and repeated in thick tones which reverberated down the walls. It lasted only a few seconds and no screams followed. It came from the direction of Tragedy Four. They sprinted down the tunnel, finding two panicked tragedy firing down the tunnel. The comedy held his fist up before more started firing. He didn't see any targets. Four tragedies were laid out, shot from behind with a rapid fire weapon. Judging by the large chunks missing in the ground and their bodies, some of the rounds had been explosive

"Report!"

"Unknown attacker, sir. One minute they were there, the next they were dead."

The comedy keyed a drone to start scanning and drift down the tunnel, halting or retreating if they encountered trouble. It floated down, unaware of the apparent danger, green lights flickering off the rock walls. It paused a few meters in, turning upwards as it chirped loudly. A picture was forming over the comedy's forearm.

"Automated turret. Motion activated." The drone followed wiring back down the tunnel and scanned a piece of fake rock near them. The comedy opened the panel and found the simplest turret panel in existence. A button was pressed in, lighting up '**ACTIVE**' in bright red letters. A button below it was next to a dull light that said, 'DEACTIVATED.' On the panel door was a simple note.

"Bug hole. Do not deactivate," read the comedy aloud. "They probably dug too close to the hive and set up a turret." Why didn't the stupid people put up a warning sign? It was probably just common knowledge around here. Then again, two boards that had been nailed in an X over the entryway. The tragedy team had broken through to enter. With a sigh, he pressed the button and **DEACTIVATED** glowed in bright green. The drone confirmed the turret had powered down. With a sweep of his finger, the drone hovered down the tunnel. No gunfire.

"All clear. Let the drone advance five meters ahead at all times." They were going to have to scan every centimeter of this tunnel. There was likely more than one turret. This was going to be their entire day.

The first tragedy to enter the tunnel did so warily. When nothing happened, a second followed. They were in a long tunnel with no cover so the turret could mow down a whole swarm of bugs by itself. Four were in the tunnel, watching the long guns. "Permission to eliminate the target, sir?"

"Negative. We might need that turret. Proceed." He was almost following them when he heard a warning buzz come from the box. It clicked horrendously at them, but there was no change. After ten seconds, the comedy was about to chalk it up to an alarm designated to remind people the weapons were powered down. Then it made a happy chime, and the button pushed itself back to red.

The guns clicked back on and the majority of his squad turn to red paste along the walls. The comedy jammed the button back to green, but it was too late. They were all dead. Who designed a security system like this? He was going to find the nearest security expert and feed him into the tunnel personally.

The comedy never had to explain his failures to the jester. When he turned with his remaining tragedies, there was an additional figure in their midst. They wore a heavy miner's uniform, which gave them a dumpy appearance. A thick gas mask covered all but two dark eyes. All of which was irrelevant compared to the flechette cannon pointed in their general direction.

One empty magazine later, the remaining tragedy team was gone. Their bodies were torn and spread so far down the tunnel that the automated turret took potshots as part flew by. The only one slight intact was the comedy, who had been at the back of the group. He had been shielded by his men, but still been eviscerated. The figure stepped through the gore slowly, studying the most intact victim.

Lure removed her gas mask. She had broken up fights before. She had broken arms and noses before, but never killed anything besides a bug. These fable were alien to her world, but not to her. They walked and moved like humans, talked like humans, and certainly bled like humans. Reaching down, she removed the comedy's mask and saw a man lying there. His breathing was ragged and his eyes were unfocused. Blood drooled slowly out of his mouth.

What was a human doing serving machines? Why was he down here, hunting his own kind? Had she done anything by killing all these people? Grandma Snibbs had sworn her to protect the group, but had she? At the end of the day, a score of humans were dead, and they had done nothing to the invading machines.

What was the point of all this?

Chapter 16

Range Practice

Something was sizzling delightfully, another was whistling cheerfully, and the last was growling in anger. The first two belonged to the kitchen, the last to Sadie's insides.

Sadie's face was buried so deep in a pillow made for gods it was a miracle she hadn't suffocated. Its plushy red surface was stuck to her face by a line of drool. But the heavenly pillow would have to wait. She needed the bathroom. Right now.

Not wanting to risk standing, she slithered off the couch and crawled across the floor. The tile was pleasantly cool. It wasn't until she climbed up the doorway that she realized she was almost naked. At some point during the night, she had stripped out of her pants and long sleeves, leaving on skintight shorts and a bra. Unsure if this was acceptable and already committed, she sped into the bathroom.

A minute later, she was peering out the door to see what the two men were up to. Ravi was in the kitchen wearing the nicest pajamas she had ever seen. They were gray cotton pants that looked like they never itched and a white shirt that looked like it was taken straight from a pillow. He was sipping from a steaming cup while he pushed something around in a pan.

Louis was by the far wall and was doing handstand pushups. He wore the same pants from last night, but was shirtless as he worked out. For a man casually knocking out the difficult exercise, not a single bead of sweat dripped down his clean back. His slow motions were a little hypnotic. Sadie was halfway back to the couch when she remembered her lack of clothing. Neither of the men were looking at her or had acknowledged her presence. Sadie's stomach stabbed her repeatedly as she cinched her pants up. What had they been drinking last night?

"Sleep well?" asked Ravi, a little too cheerfully.

"How can you even ask that?" grumbled Sadie, looking for her shirt.

"Good friends equal good nights. Breakfast will be ready in a minute. This will make your head feel better." Ravi turned and put a glass of orange liquid on the counter and dropped two pills.

"Is this why you're so chipper?"

"That and we can't get drunk like you."

"How?" Sadie took the pills and drink, downing both without regret. "You two drink all the time."

"Our bodies are designed for combat under the worst conditions." Louis did a slow push down and exhaled.

"We can drink," said Ravi, turning with a plate of food. "It takes some terrible things to get us intoxicated, but we purify poisons like that." Ravi snapped his fingers.

"That doesn't seem fair." Sadie rubbed her head and began to eat the beans and other protein substances Ravi had placed before her.

"You're telling me." Louis stopped his exercise and rolled to his feet. "I haven't been drunk in centuries."

"Sometimes I do miss more than a temporary buzz," admitted Ravi. "Sorry I don't have any toast."

"Nobody has ever expected the British to have good breakfast, only tea." Louis took a seat next to Sadie at the counter.

"Cook better than you." Ravi nudged Sadie and nodded to Louis. "What's this silly sod been making you? Or does he have you do the cooking?"

"I've never seen him cook. Maia does that." Sadie kept eating, but noticed a pause between the men. Ravi looked sad, concerned. Louis waved him off.

"I named the shipboard computer. Our kitchen is automated."

"Right. Of course."

"What do you do here for fun?" asked Louis, trying to move past the moment.

"You saw it. You're on an oggy station. They're not exactly big on football, though I'd pay good money to see them try. All our programs out here are old. I've got a deck of cards around here somewhere."

"Got any more modern games?"

"Just awake and you already want to shoot something," laughed Ravi. He took a sip of his tea and set the cup on the counter. "Yeah, I've got something."

Sadie watched them clear out the center of the living room. Ravi didn't give her the same insane Delta vibe, but he just as easily picked up the couch with one hand and dragged it to the side. She finished her meal and shoveled more leftovers onto her plate. It made her stomach immensely happy and if they weren't going to eat it, more for her. Whether it was breakfast or the magical pills, she was already beginning to feel better.

Ravi opened a large metal crate on the side wall and began to pull out goggles and gloves. He looked at Sadie, holding up a pair of gloves, before swapping them out for a smaller pair. Louis peered into the crate.

"Christ, Ravi. Why do you have so much?"

"It was cheaper to get a stockpile of different sizes and spare parts than one specialty order for myself. Sadie, come join us," said Ravi. Sadie snuck a few more mouthfuls in and went to join them, flush as a chipmunk. "You ever used virtual reality?"

"No."

"I think you'll like this. Put on these gloves and goggles." Sadie took pristine looking gloves and felt how greasy her hands were. She put the equipment down and washed her hands, getting an approving look from Ravi.

Louis found himself a nice open corner of the room and picked up a plastic rifle and pocketed some other toy weapons. He didn't have a pair of goggles, but a full face helmet with a clear visor. Tapping a button on the side, the visor went black. She could hear him talking but the helmet kept him pretty quiet.

"You stand here," said Ravi, moving her to an empty spot of floor. "What's going to happen is you'll put these goggles on, and it will show you another world. It's not real, just an interactive game. You can move a few feet but if you go too far, the goggles will automatically toggle off. You don't want to trip on something."

"Okay." The goggles fit snugly over her head and her vision of the room was clear.

"Now close your eyes." She did. "Load Farmhouse_Festival."

When Sadie opened her eyes, she was no longer in the room. She was in a grassy, moss covered field. The sky was gray and teasing rain, same as it did every day. It looked like it should have been cold with a stiff breeze, but her body remained warm. Her toes should have been freezing in the dewy grass, but now she wore thick boots. The boots really didn't match her pink riding dress or black jacket, but they looked warm.

"That's weird," said Sadie, trying to feel the illusionary clothes.

"It can take away from the immersion," agreed Ravi.

Ravi was dressed as proper as any man could be. Nice brown shoes that really shouldn't have been in the field with dark slacks. The white button up looked faded and well used, with a tweed vest and a brown flat cap to close the look. Ravi looked younger here, but Sadie wasn't sure if it was an illusion. Maybe it was because he was cleaned up and happy.

"Where are we?"

"We are just outside of town at the rifle competition." There was a crack of a rifle, but not loud enough to make Sadie flinch. The sound came from speakers just above her ears. The action came from an unruly line of men and women who were talking and aiming rifles at the nearby hill. "Have you ever used a weapon before?"

"No. Only security forces can use the flechette cannons."

"A flechette cannon?" Ravi snorted condescendingly. "They're effective, but not exactly what I'd call sporting."

Ravi picked up an antique rifle leaning against an aging fence post and held it up. It was strange to look at. Its barrel was smooth and its handle made of wood. What kind of world were they in that you could use wood for a gun? Then something strange happened. The weapon froze, blurred in the air, and every time Ravi shook it, it changed into something new. The one he settled on was black and glossy, all plastics and hard metals. It looked efficient but boring.

"This is something a bit more modern. Try it out." He passed it to her, her fingers feeling the plastic toy instead of the real thing. It didn't sit quite right in her arms. Its weight and size didn't match what she saw. "Good thing about VR is I don't have to worry about you blowing your toes off."

"That's nice. What do I have to do?"

"This is a simulation so you don't have to worry about reloading or anything other than shooting. All I want you to do is hit the target. Twenty-five meters." Upon saying twenty-five meters, a wooden target popped into existence in the field. Ravi held out a hand and invited her to begin.

It was fitting they were in the country because Sadie couldn't hit the broad side of a barn. Her shots were all over and it was anyone's guess where any of them went. Ravi was fine letting her spray the field for a minute before he held up a hand.

"Okay, okay. I can see you grew up around shotguns. What were they used for?"

"Raknids? Raknee?" Sadie couldn't remember what Louis called them. "Bugs."

"Raknath. It makes sense now. You can spray and pray with bugs in a tunnel, not so with a rifle. You need to take your time. Look at me. Rifle tight in your shoulder. Arms down so you're not trying to fly away while you shoot. Keep both eyes open and take your time. There's no rush here." Ravi lifted his rifle to the target. "Take a deep breath." Ravi inhaled in an exaggerated motion. "Breathe it out."

Ravi let out a loud breath and fired. The rifle cracked and the target rocked. "Now you try."

Sadie did and missed. Ravi helped move the rifle higher on her shoulder and moved her arms down a little lower. He walked her through breathing, waiting for the right time to shoot. The next shot pinged off the edge of the target. The next shots also hit, but kept flagging up and down. Ravi told her to breathe. They spent probably a minute just breathing and when she relaxed, Ravi had her shoot.

"We'll make a marksman out of you yet." Ravi took a turn, calling up targets at a thousand meters.

"You're not what I expected," admitted Sadie.

"You mean I'm not like Louis?" Sadie blushed, causing Ravi to smile. "Don't worry. The bastard could hear us if he really wants to, but he's having fun and not paying attention. He's in some war simulation."

"Wouldn't you rather join him than be here?"

"Some soldiers take solace in war." Ravi picked another target. "Some of us prefer peace. Besides, I like teaching. It reminds me of old times."

"What did you teach?"

"A little bit of everything. My family wanted me to go into medicine, but we didn't have the money for that. I joined the Royal Navy and went on to become an instructor. That rolled into taking command roles, then the war came to Earth. One thing after another and suddenly I was in charge of starships. Life is funny like that." There was cruel laughter in the background from Louis. It didn't sound directed at them. "Shut it, you twat."

"I thought Deltas were super soldiers," continued Sadie, ignoring Louis.

"Who assault raknath hives on a whim?" Ravi winked. "We are, but we still have our talents. Louis worked for French Special Forces and has always been more comfortable on the ground. We also had sailors, pilots, and commanders. I can assault a hive, but I don't have the passion for it. Louis is probably one of the best fighters alive, but he's shit when it comes to teamwork. His priorities will always come first." Ravi gave her a warning look. Then he fired three shots and three targets in the distance vanished. He let out a sigh. "Then again, most Delta are like that."

"Why?" Sadie didn't know much about what Ravi was talking about, but it felt like he needed to talk.

"The people they chose to become Delta were already among humanity's best. With that usually comes an ego. They're arrogant, cocky, and a little too gung-ho." Ravi nodded his head to where Louis should've been standing. "Then we were changed. It wasn't a question anymore. We were the best. We can do things no human can do. You can't put a Delta with a squad of humans because they slow us down. People get mad, go mad. Toward the end of the war, we had to drop Delta into conflicts and let them do their own thing. Very few of us are good with people."

"Louis wasn't always like this?"

"I don't know. I met him years into the fighting. He and a few others liked working under a commander who was one of them. Good shot," he added, seeing her hit a fifty meter target.

"Thanks. So you didn't want to be a commander?"

"Not really. I always used to think I'd make a good lieutenant. I loved teaching, being there for my sailors, and doing more shit details than officers in their ivory towers. But I was good at what I did. When you're the best man for the job, it's hard to say no. Then before you know it, you've been doing a job you didn't want for a decade. Sometimes you get so good at something it traps you there."

"I knew miners like that."

"Happens to a lot of people."

"Were your parents happy with it?"

"They were proud of me," said Ravi wistfully. "It's not what they wanted, but they were proud." Ravi paused, leaning over to move the rifle butt down this time. "Try it that high with a flechette cannon and you'll dislocate your shoulder."

"Thank you." Sadie loosed another shot. "Was this your home?"

"No. I grew up in the city. This is where I wanted to retire." Ravi sighed loudly. "I can still smell it on good days." More mad laughter in the distance. Ravi groaned. "Going to shoot him for real," he grumbled. "Tone it down, Louis!"

"You should get in on this!" shouted Louis. He was getting louder, moving rapidly and stomping around his corner.

"What is he doing?" mouthed Sadie.

"Let's check on him. Remember, nothing in here is real." Sadie nodded. "Good, because knowing this loon he's knee deep in shit. Join session B, observation mode."

Large boxes with numbers appeared in the air around them. They clicked down from ten in bright colors, with a voice reminding them they were going into observation mode and could not interact. Ravi moved to stand beside Sadie and put a hand on her shoulder.

"It's all an illusion," he reminded her.

It was a good thing he put his hand on her because they reappeared in the sky somewhere and Sadie stumbled out of reflex. The floor was still there, but her brain thought she should be falling. Ravi held her in place until her legs accepted the invisible platform. Then she clung to him as she saw what was below her.

Bugs. Raknath. They were a breed she didn't recognize and they were swarming. Not like the few hundred that breached the reservation, but thousands, maybe hundreds of thousands. In the distance, she saw they were on a similar grassy plain filled with rocks and creeks, but up close, there was no visible ground. Raknath took up every centimeter for kilometers, all converging on a single position. It was a plain stone tower, maybe ten meters high. And Louis stood on the parapet alone, looking like he was having the time of his life.

He was firing so fast it looked wild and uncontrolled despite its efficiency. Louis swept the sides of his tiny tower before plugging the bugs a level down, forcing his attackers back with their dead. The bugs were climbing with undeterred speed and Louis was always there. If this wasn't a game he would've run out of ammunition and been dead. As if to prove Sadie wrong, Louis hammered a wave of bugs and when two cleared the sides behind him, he swung a long knife and tore through them in one continuous swing.

Ravi tapped her shoulder and motioned for her to look up. It caused her to clutch him even harder.

This version of raknath could fly. Their backs had opened for large insect wings and they were buzzing loudly. Growing up underground, Sadie had never considered that bugs could fly. The ones underground couldn't, but why would they need to? Then two dropped out of the sky. Then another. Louis was still spinning on the tower in his hectic dance of survival, but the flyers were still falling. It was mid whirl that his rifle went up for the slimmest second and fired a final burst. He quickly reloaded, dropping the weapon back into the crowd already firing. Small bursts right before and after he reloaded went into the sky, taking out the enemies above.

"Join me, Ravi!" demanded Louis, laughing at the top of his lungs.

"Later."

Screens reappeared around them counting down from ten. Sadie was eager to be away from the bugs and just as excited to be on solid ground. Flying was not for her. But when the number clicked past one, the screen went black. The simulation ended and blue letters said it was safe to remove her goggles. Confused, she popped them up and looked at Ravi. He was dropping the goggles on the couch and removing his gloves.

Louis was still on the other side of the room in his simulation. And if he looked mad in the game, he looked utterly insane in the real world. He was spinning and thrashing, screaming at enemies who didn't exist. The gray toy rifle clicked incessantly in his hands, its fake magazine getting slapped repeatedly as he reloaded. In his left hand was a fat, gray knife which he held on the rifle's side, occasionally lashing out at his demons. The fighting must be getting worse because he lashed out with the rifle now too, firing into one as he slammed the butt into another.

"Would you like some tea?" asked Ravi, sounding exhausted.

"What's tea?"

"That's almost a greater travesty than that right there." Ravi moved to the kitchen, tossing well worn gloves on the counter. He picked up the kettle and placed it back on the stove.

"Is he going to be okay?" asked Sadie.

"Yeah, he'll be fine. He's, he's working through some stuff." Ravi was rifling through some packets, murmuring about what flavor she might appreciate.

"When do you think he'll be done?" Ravi did not look up from his collection of tea.

"When he dies."

Chapter 17

Mishap Report

Mirakus Station was an interesting spectacle as a space station. Operating over a gas giant was both ludicrously profitable and dangerous. Extremely inventive engineering was required to mine the gases free floating in its atmosphere. When in standby, the station was little more than a floating dome in the thermosphere. It had the ability to raise or lower itself as needed, even breaking into higher orbit with some stress. It was the mining process that changed Mirakus station from a floating dome to a Lovecraftian abstract. First, the atmospheric nets emerged from the perimeter in long silvery skirts, protecting the equipment at the center. Once the nets were in place, collection chutes and flexible tubes descended to collect the gases. Fully deployed, it appeared as a titanic jellyfish floating through the heavens.

The inventive solutions also came with disturbing problems

and dangerous side effects. The dome had to be layers of forcefields because the weight of a physical dome would be too great. Depending on the position of the station, the weather could change from bone breaking cold to annihilating hot. The absorbed gases came in the same temperature range which all had to be regulated. Mirakus Station had multiple power cores because they could never all go offline at the same. So many critical systems had fail-safes that could protect one vital system by putting another in danger. It was a process that had to be monitored every second of every day because a group of minor errors could cascade into catastrophic failure.

And today was one of those days.

Scruffy had been a maintenance engineer for the past decade. Before that, he'd been a plumber, an extremely difficult and valued profession among the oggy. Given an oggy's proclivity to drip and ooze, their toilets and showers couldn't be as simple as every other species. This meant with all his experience, if it was in a pipe and could boil, bubble, or leak, Scruffy was the oggy for the job. So when an alert reached one of the computer boys that said pressure was dropping in one of the coolant lines, Scruffy was on the way.

Due to the nature of his job, he was one of the few oggy that was covered head to toe. His jumpsuit was extra absorbent on the inside and his boots and gloves were lined to capture moisture. Eventually they became so crusted over from his leaking wounds that they had to be discarded. But all of this was necessary so when he investigated a leak, he didn't mistake his secretions as the problem.

None of that was a problem today as a bright blue liquid was dripping from an overhead pipe. Scruffy radioed in that he had the problem in sight and it was under control. A quick examination of the system and from what he knew already told him a nozzle must've broken further down the line. The coolant was funneling to multiple locations instead of one. All he needed to do was activate a backup line, shut down this one, and then find out how far back the break was. With any luck, the whole job would be done in a few hours.

Scruffy's long ears were tied back in a pouch as a part of his headgear. It covered his forehead while providing a row of angled lights that were great in tight spaces. Leaning up, Scruffy saw the pipes here were all stained blue. He scrubbed one with a cloth and found the color unchanged. That meant the leak had been an ongoing problem for some time. Worse, he could see the metal brackets were corroded in areas. There went his dream of it being a quick job. Someone else had either been incompetent or ignored the problem until it was serious. Now it was serious, and it was his problem. All of this would need replacing. He followed the mess over to the main pump, examining it for damage. He gave it a tap to get a feel for the sound. It burst instead.

Oggy are made for hazardous work. They ignore bruises and cuts, and any damage to their skin usually only killed overgrown, infected areas. Some even joked the occasional chemical bath or fire improved their complexion. When the main pump burst, it sent a hail of shrapnel in the form of broken screws and seals. Scruffy probably wouldn't have recognized he was hurt, but a single piece shot through his right eye and into his brain.

The monitoring systems showed the pressure was relieved, but the temperatures were beginning to rise. Systems keyed Scruffy to let him know they saw his progress and to let them know if he needed anything. Scruffy lay face down in a blue sea.

One of the screens turned on at Ravi's workstation and a shrill alert started. Ravi was already dropping his tea on the table and rushing over as additional holographic screens formed. A piece of the station was highlighted with a big red circle and what looked like bar charts started to shift.

"Tower, this is System Analyst One, we have an unacceptable level of overheating occurring in the refinery, sections one and two."

"We are tracking Ravi," said someone over the radio while trying to clear a wad of phlegm from their throat. "Coolant leak. Plumber is taking care of the problem."

Ravi was multitasking now, bringing up additional windows. The coolant readings weren't low, they were nonexistent. "Last progress report, Tower?"

"We said the plumber is on it. Take a knee, Ravi."

"It's not coming down, Tower. It's going to flip the breakers and force a full system shutdown." Cursing when they didn't respond, Ravi continued to tap the keys with delicate intensity. A window showing cameras started to flicker by, shifting pictures so fast Sadie couldn't keep up. Then both Louis and Ravi sat up straighter and Ravi tapped the screens back. It showed an oggy down in a pool of blue liquid.

"Tower, plumber is down and non-responsive, Sector Forty-Two Oscar." Ravi let go of the mic. Then he cranked a dial and the screen of personnel on the call widened. "Attention ground crew! Report to emergency stations! Contaminant team to Sector Forty-Two Oscar and bring medical. Electrical and chemical get ready to respond to system shutdowns and possible toxic spill. This is an all call and not a drill. Move your asses." He toggled the switch and hit a button to cause an alarm to blare out across the city. It said everything he just said. Get to your posts.

"Louis, get below deck and join the ground team. Take my suit, it should fit. I need eyes and ears outside I can trust."

"Thought you'd never ask commander."

"Shut up and move." Louis gave a quick salute and hightailed it for the door. "Sit down and be quiet Sadie. This will take as long as it's going to take."

"Louis needs us." Sadie stood up, looking glassy eyed and distant. "He needs our help."

"No, he doesn't."

Sadie wasn't listening. She grabbed her rebreather mask and was out the door before Ravi could say anything else.

"Sure, why not?" He shrugged. "A normal human girl with no training, experience, and without a spacesuit. I'm sure she can help." There was a blinking blue light on his console. He pressed it with contempt. "Tower, no I will not recall. We're not destroying half the station just because you don't want to move. Now listen. Here's what we're going to do."

It was easy for Louis to find his way to the lower deck. A large group of burly and ugly, even by oggy standards, workers were heading for the elevators. He joined them, getting a few harsh glances, but nobody said anything. It wasn't like he took up space compared to the foul behemoths.

They moved in a clump to a massive room. Thankfully none of them stripped but the smell of twenty oggy in their locker room was impressive even by Louis's standards. They were pulling on cheap blue atmosphere suits that looked closer to trash bags than futuristic suits made to survive hostile environments. Oggy were hard to design for. Their bodies ruined a lot of complex material and had a tendency to clog up vital tubes for little things like oxygen. All of their suits were disposable, probably only made to last for a single event outside.

A couple grunts and pointed fingers and Louis found Ravi's locker. It was locked. Probably to keep sickly hands off his nice gear, but Louis wasn't feeling patient today. He took hold of the handle and pulled until the lock broke and the door fell free. Inside was a real environmental suit that could probably survive deep space. Its royal blue armor looked brand new. Ravi had probably only had a few occasions to wear it, and he always had a habit of keeping his uniforms pristine. Shrugging off his jacket, Louis hurried to don the suit. In a last minute thought, he took the laser pistol from his clothes and attached it to his right hip. It came as no surprise Ravi had multiple spots to holster weapons.

"Some habits die hard," whispered Louis, clicking the helmet shut.

"You outside yet?" asked Ravi.

"If you know I just put on the helmet, then you know I'm still inside."

"Move faster. We have problems."

"Moving."

The first group of oggy was already through the rotating airlock and outside. Louis took his place with the second group, just barely able to squeeze in. He took a few deep breaths as he looked at the storm outside. The station undeniably had something to dampen its effects, but it was raging today. Cackling orange clouds swirled as fast as starships, throwing lightning bolts big enough to be seen from space. The door flared green and they rushed outside.

They were on a metal gangway filled with holes for air to flow through. Louis wasn't thrilled to see a catwalk that didn't look greater than ones he'd seen in warehouses three hundred years ago. The wind was pulling at them, but it couldn't have been worse than a tropical storm under the dome. Enjoying the future for a minute, Louis pushed his way forward to an arguing group of oggy.

Sadie had no intention of going outside. She had no idea what the oggy were doing or how they even survived. Something told her the right place to go to was the docking bay, which was shockingly empty. Maia must've seen her coming because the ramp was already down.

"Maia! Louis needs our help."

"He is fine," said Maia in her most soothing tone. "He is outside with the oggy checking the collection tubes."

"How is he outside? The storms here can rip an oggy in half!"

"I suppose a lesson is better than sitting on our hands." A screen turned on with Mirakus Station shown from the side. "Mirakus Station floats above the planet, pulling chemical elements from the gas giant for a variety of purposes."

"To the point! Please!"

"Fine," huffed Maia. "We are in the upper station here. Below is the refinery with dozens of flexible tubes that dip into the air currents. These are protected by an outer net of cable on the station exterior.

These cables emit electrical disturbances in the air that destabilize nearby storms. They keep the worst effects at bay, limiting the air stream so the tubes can collect."

"We need to get out there," insisted Sadie.

"There is a storm the size of a continent at this time. The Seraphin is not rated to fly in such conditions. It is a refitted mining vessel."

"If this ship is a mining vessel than I'm a bug," snapped Sadie, causing Maia to laugh.

"What's the problem?" asked Louis. The oggy ignored him and kept shouting silently in their helmets while waving gorilla arms at each other. "Ravi, what's happening?"

"The system overheated and caused the breakers to flip." Ravi's voice added a silent *duh* to that. "The gas is backing up in the tubes and we have to do manual shutdowns."

"Who requires anything to be manual these days?"

"I can do an automatic shutdown, but that requires me to reverse the flow and blow every tube. A forced evacuation can damage the station. Or we can do manual shutdowns at the source down the lines and bleed the pressure."

"Still sounds like an automated task."

"If you have patience. But after too many lazy incidents caused the tubes to rupture, they implemented manual overrides for safety reasons. This is not my design." It sounded like a corporate design that worried more about station costs. "I need you to go down the line in front of you."

"Why not these fine gentlemen?" The oggy must've received the message that Louis was going down because they waved cheerfully, chortling behind their masks.

"The support platform blew a link. It's holding on by three supports now instead of four. It won't hold an oggy."

"Lovely." Louis looked down. The platform wasn't just down, it looked to be almost a kilometer down. It was swinging in the wind, connected to four tubes on each corner. "How do I get down?"

"The cables are mag linked."

"You want me to power slide down an unstable support over a gas giant?" asked Louis, incredulously.

"Knew you'd remember why you stopped working with me."

"Why did we ever stop!"

Louis wrapped his hands around the metal line that was groaning in the storm. Before his hands could latch on, the gloves clamped to the magnetic strips. Swinging his legs over, he felt his thighs and feet attach themselves. The worst part was how the designers decided mag links should be operated. Louis had to look straight down and his suit plunged in response, trying to get him where his eyes were aimed.

He was almost to the bottom with probably ten other oggy sliding down additional poles when the storm picked up. One minute it was a casual descent into death and the next, the wind was trying to strip him free and hurl him across the planet. Only the mag links and his considerable strength held him in place as the platform swayed dangerously. The sound of something cracking through the air like a whip caused Louis to scan the area around him, causing his descent to slow. The storm settled and they rocked back into place.

"Ravi, what was that?"

"Fluctuation in the storm and the net didn't compensate in time."

"You didn't sound very convincing right there."

"It's the best I've got. Shut down the tubes and give me eyes." Louis nodded and slid the rest of the way down. With only three support cables, the platform was tilted, but not enough to make him lose his balance. There were levers on each tube along with gauges for pressure.

"Maia." It was so low that the microphone would've barely caught it. There was a click in his ear.

"Yes, boss?"

"I don't like whatever that was."

"Running analysis on your helmet and the station cameras. I'll let you know when I see something."

"Thank you."

Louis grabbed the rusty handles and began to yank them down. This was definitely not a human friendly station. These things weren't coming down without hundreds of kilograms of pressure. It was designed for a ham fisted oggy. It clicked shut and the gas began to return to the storm. Then something caught his eye on the black tubes. They were designed that way so they contrasted against the storm. And the base of one not far from him was on fire.

"Ravi! Fire!"

"They can burn to assist in venting."

"Not like this." The bottom of the massive tube was tearing and fire was trying to move up it in thin streaks. It looked like the insides of a tree after being struck by lightning. Ravi must've finally seen it through Louis's helmet.

"Louis, the system isn't detecting the fire."

"It's bloody there!"

"No shit. The system won't eject until it sees it."

"And by the time it sees it?"

"Trying to override it. Do you see the white lines on the tubes?"

WE WERE DELTA

Louis saw the white bands used as markers.

"Yes."

"Shoot just under the marker three up from the fire please."

Well that sounded like a terrible idea, but Ravi was full of surprises. Louis pulled his pistol without even thinking about the order and blew the area full of holes. They immediately began to tear open, glowing red from his shots. Whatever damage he did, the system appeared to see it. There was a series of loud clacks as it disengaged in a circle before jettisoning part of the tube.

Then the storm came back. Louis nearly lost his pistol as the platform was shoved almost vertical. His feet automatically gripped the floor and his hand on the railing kept him from falling. Something whipped through the air again and Louis felt another support snap. Tubes near him were sliced open, spilling noxious gas as they ruptured. Hanging on by only mag links, Louis saw more tubes beginning to burn. He started firing before Ravi said anything.

"Now can we go?" demanded Sadie, as they watched Louis's platform almost detach entirely.

"Put the jacket on, grab the helmet, and sit in the pilot's seat," ordered Maia. There was no more friendliness in her voice.

Sadie grabbed a white jacket off the wall that was too big for her and wrapped it around her chest. Something automated inside tightened the jacket to her body. Not really sure how the helmet was supposed to work, Sadie stuck it over her head, feeling hair get stuck in the back. The face helmet clicked noisily before refitting to her smaller head and attaching automatically to the jacket collar.

"That's neat." Sadie sat in the pilot's chair and strapped in just as the Seraphin lifted off. "What are you doing?"

"Emergency evacuation is authorized. Hold on." Sadie tried to ask what that meant when the ship blasted backward.

Normal space stations had a forcefield and a physical barrier to keep space out. Since Mirakus Station was a refinery floating in a gas giant, it had two layers of forcefields and physical barriers with a whole bay of space between them. This helped ensure pilot or industrial errors didn't turn the entire station into a fireball. They were barely to the first set of barriers before the forcefield deactivated and the wall retracted so suddenly Sadie felt it slam against the station. They didn't have time to close before the second barriers dropped. The Seraphin along with half the bay exploded out of Mirakus Station. The six wings expanded along the dropship and it plunged into the storm.

"Maia?"

"Yes dear?"

"The station didn't authorize that, did they?"

"No dear."

"Ravi!" demanded Louis.

"I've got it!" exclaimed Ravi. "The power shutdown affected part of the net. There are cables that are switching between on and off. When the power goes off…"

"The cables come through like Cthulhu on a bad day, got it," finished Louis. "What do you want me to do?"

"Get out of there. You're right in their path."

"No shit. What can we do?"

"There are tens of thousands of cables. We'll never be able to identify the exact ones in time. I'm having the secondary net brought down so we can retract the first. It's going to take a minute so I need you to get out of there."

"If those cables come through here again, they could cut half the tubes."

"And you. Move Louis."

Louis placed a hand on the mag line while looking at the nets he could see. They had to be coming from that direction if they were hitting his platform. Then the wind began to buffet him and he saw it. Cables that stopped hanging in place and began to draw inwards as the wind pushed. Smiling, he lifted the pistol.

"I've got them."

"No!"

Ravi's cry was the last thing Louis heard before he sent out a perfect line of laser fire that cut the cables off at their base. The system detected their failure and ejected them before their remnants could cause any damage. The protective field from the good cables moved to cover the gap, but for a short moment, a small piece of the storm's strength roiled through the underbelly. And with only one hand on the cable, Louis suddenly found himself tumbling through the clouds.

"Hang on!"

Sadie was holding on. She wasn't screaming and it wasn't for lack of trying. The Seraphin had artificial gravity, but Maia had punched the throttle down. Sadie was glued to her seat and her vision was beginning to blur.

The planetary storm shrieked with delight over their entrance. It was adorable for a dropship to assume it could operate in these conditions. It wanted to play with its new toy, throwing it around before ultimately burying it in a crumpled heap. The pressure would cause the ship to crush like an egg before it ever reached the ground.

Maia and the Seraphin said no. The six wings rotated to have three on each side, flaring them out like the all powerful angel it was. When its engines burned, it formed a halo in the clouds. As the storm attempted to swipe it from the sky, its wings and engines rolled and adjusted, keeping it level. When the wind challenged it to a contest of strength, the Seraphin didn't even bother to acknowledge it. It flew with the grace and power befitting of its name. It was new to these skies and they already belonged under its rule.

"Hands open Louis!"

One second there was nothing but the storm and then there was Louis. Maia intercepted him in midair and he thumped loudly against the hull. She'd done a good job matching his trajectory and speed, but to Louis it must've felt like catching a speeding train. The magnetic suit clamped onto the Seraphin and even then, he began to slide. Maia compensated, rolling the ship and changing trajectory to shift Louis back up the ship. A few more rolls and Louis stabilized, giving the suit time to gather a stronger attraction to the dropship.

Maia accelerated them hard straight up. The ship swayed back and forth just enough to keep Louis's suit from losing grip until at long last they were above the clouds and into the night sky. They were almost into space. Louis lay against the hull, taking deep breaths.

Louis struggled for breath. It felt like he'd grabbed the speeding train, then been blown into the next track over where he got hit by the next train. Zero gravity eased his body up, happy to take him away from the Seraphin. The magnetic locks kept him in place.

"Louis! Come in Louis!" demanded Ravi.

"I'm here."

"Thank the various gods. What happened?"

"My guardian angel was looking out for me again." Louis crawled over to the cockpit and peered in. A very queasy Sadie was looking back at him from the pilot's chair. "I think there's a woman I owe my life to."

"You are one daft bastard. I'm glad you're still alive. You may have just helped save the station."

"Good. They can pay for tonight's drinks."

"Drinks are on me. You'll have to explain what happened to the docking bay later."

"Worth it." Louis waved at Sadie and crawled toward the ramp. "Start pouring. I'll be there before you finish the first round."

Chapter 18

Bounty Hunters

When Sadie woke the next morning, her brain was still frazzled and her body groaned in the aftermath of yesterday's adrenaline rush. She expected as she climbed off the couch that the others would be feeling the same.

The demigods before her were having a casual morning. Ravi was in his pajamas, sitting behind a desk working on his computer and babbling some techno jargon about the monitoring systems. It sounded like he was compiling a report of what went wrong and where. If there had been any stress from yesterday, he didn't show it. He looked like he'd gone for a ten kilometer run and was having his morning coffee after a shower.

Any normal human would've been dead after what Louis did yesterday. He still should've been in a hospital with his limbs in casts and struggling to breathe. Instead he was fresh as a daisy, cooking breakfast for the three of them. The soreness he presented appeared more like a rough massage, every twinge bringing a smile to his face. Louis did sound mildly congested at least, inhaling disgustingly to clear his throat.

"Good morning junior cadet," said Ravi cheerfully. "Are you ready to pin on your wings and do you need more time in the simulator?"

"I no longer think flying is fun," grumbled Sadie, rubbing her eyes.

"Ah come on." Ravi spun in his chair to face her. "It must've been a little fun."

"I still want to throw up."

"But you didn't," said Louis, scrapping an egg substitute onto a plate of rice. "Eat. You'll feel better." Louis placed a plate for her on the counter and took a plate to Ravi. Sadie saw two pills much like the ones they'd given her after the night of drinking and gratefully took them.

"You're much uglier than my last nanny," joked Ravi.

"You couldn't afford me," laughed Louis. "I'll leave you Sadie and a stipend."

"Please don't joke about that." Sadie didn't think he was serious anyways. There were worse fates, but living on Mirakus Station in a rebreather with a bunch of oggy was a depressing thought. She coughed suddenly as spices lit up her throat and she scrambled for her water glass. Louis must've added things to appeal to Ravi. Why did everything that man eat have to be on fire?

"Have any friends who want to come out here?" continued Louis.

"No," she hacked after trying to eat another spoonful of fire.

Before he could make more jokes, Louis's jacket collar began to chirp. He forgot all about teasing Sadie and went and pressed the collar. Maia began to speak in a tone so formal Sadie almost didn't recognize her.

"Louis. The Station Master wishes to see you."

"What for?"

"He would not relay his communication with a computer. Please proceed to the Seraphin."

"I wonder what he needs you for," thought Sadie aloud.

"Who knows."

"It probably has something to do with how Sadie blew out half a hangar bay to save you." Ravi barely managed to squeeze out the words through his food. "Everyone's happy the station didn't blow up, but somebody has to pay for that."

"I can't be mad at her for saving my life." Louis poured the rest of his meal down his throat. "We'll be back."

"I'll come with you." Shoveling the rest of his food in his mouth, Ravi rose and collected his jacket. "The Station Master isn't exactly a friend, but we respect each other."

The walk back to the docking bay was terrible. Sadie's rebreather was welcomed at all times, but it did not mix well with spicy food. Every exhale of fiery breath was recycled right back into her nose and throat. It was so bad she considered asking if they could stop at Mirakus Drop just to get a drink. But the two men were chatting amicably and she was once again relegated to the background.

Now that she wasn't in shock by being on a space station or by the oggy, she was able to see more detail. For how big the station was, there seemed to be surprisingly few oggy. They worked in shifts so she only ever saw half the population, and half of those were sleeping in their quarters. The truth was there wasn't a whole lot to do on the station. They worked most of the day and spent the rest of the day bitching about work. The workers came here because the pay was lucrative. She didn't understand the payments or what anything was worth since the reservation used an allotment system for food and supplies, but it was exciting to listen to. Ravi had been here for years and must've been extremely wealthy.

Ravi's work was a mystery to her still. He'd explained it many times in great technical detail and it went way over her head each time. He did something with computers, algorithms, and monitoring systems. His systems monitored everything from gas pressure to toxicity levels and alerted him if anything went wrong. Most of his job seemed to be automated because he had a lot of free time. When asked how he got paid so much to do so little, he'd responded.

"Because nobody else knows how to do so much with so little."

The docking bays were below in the center of the refinery so they took one of the service elevators down. She'd ridden these elevators a few times now and wasn't sure why they made her uncomfortable. Maybe it was because they were enclosed and on the reservation lift you could see everything. Maybe it was because while it looked just as degraded, the station's elevator was smooth and efficient. It never squeaked, slowed, or shook. She didn't know whether to hold onto the walls, hide behind the men, or stand as close to the door as possible. Usually she froze in place until the anxiety inducing ride was over.

Below was less exposed to the pollution and an opportunity to see what the station should've looked like. Ceramic white tiles covered the walls and ceiling like lizard scales, specially prepared against heat and radiation. The floor was metal that should've been brilliant, but looked like it'd been cleaned so frequently that chemicals were consuming its shine. It was strange seeing the floor so clean. Usually the oggy left a boogery trail like slugs. The presence of a robot shaped like a fat dome mopping the floor was taking care of that. It distractingly followed them but slowed after a few meters. Maybe it was confused because the ground was still clean.

An oggy was standing in front of the Seraphin, appearing to admire the ship. He must've been the Station Master as he looked cleaner and oddly thinner. The jumpsuit he wore wasn't stained and there were bits of plastic sticking out like he was vacuum sealed in. The Station Master turned as he heard them come in, waving cheerfully. They were out in the open bay when Sadie felt the urge to convulse. Her muscles begged to seize and her lungs tried to shutter. It was as if she was back in the freezing cold without protective gear. One moment she was standing and the next she was huddled over, trying to prevent imaginary shakes.

Sharp cracks sounded all around them. Louis moved with inhuman speed but still took several hits to his legs and torso. The gray rounds collapsed into discs that immediately began to arc electricity between each other. Louis twisted uncontrollably but somehow kept moving. He threw himself to the side, flying behind cover, all the while looking like he was trying a new interpretative dance in the air.

No shots came for Ravi who leapt backward, grabbing Sadie as he went as if she were a sack of potatoes. Then he shook as rounds meant for her struck his legs and sent them both sprawling. Even as electricity danced through his body, he crawled forward at amazing speed, putting himself behind some equipment. Sadie followed, rolling as she heard more cracks. Ravi was grabbing the discs with twisting fingers and ripping them free. They took whole sections of clothing and skin away before they were crushed.

"Merricup!" Ravi shouted, pulling a blaster from a concealed holster. "You bloody arsehole, what in the hell!"

"This doesn't concern you Ravi. You shouldn't be here."

"Yeah well I love getting shot at by my boss."

"There's a bounty on your friends, a very large bounty. This has nothing to do with you, please stand aside."

"What is the bounty for?" Now irritated at just about everyone in the room, Ravi fingered his blaster.

"The Singularity put out a bounty for any human leaving the Malleus Glacies System."

"The machines?" Ravi's face went cold. Sadie saw the same darkness in those friendly eyes that Louis had sometimes. She looked for a different set of cover to scoot to. "You would take a machine bounty?"

"I could almost build a new station with that money. Please stay back." Somewhere to their right was the sound of more cracking rifles, loud grunts, and what sounded like an oggy probably trying to dance on Louis's head. Ravi was fine letting them try and hold onto that tiger's tail.

"You would trade my friend to a machine? For money?"

"How much money would it take to convince you?"

"There is no amount of money to convince me to work with them. You should be ashamed of yourselves."

"We'll accept that shame in luxury. Please don't make us shoot you. You've been a wonderful employee and friend to all."

Ravi snapped over the equipment and saw two oggy with rifles approaching their cover. With a quick trigger squeeze, a rapid burst of yellow laser fire lanced through the first oggy's face. Skin bubbled and melted away, removing half of its gelatinous head in one go. The oggy sank to its knees as everything else in its skull cooked. His friend received the same treatment, falling a quarter second later. Before stepping out of sight, Ravi made sure to sear the Station Master's knees. The Station Master hit the floor in a series of hysterical swears.

Louis was on the ground writhing, trying to free himself from the charged shots when he realized his unfortunate mistake. The shooters had placed themselves on either side of the bay to catch the humans in the crossfire. Now he was twitching next to an oggy who was bringing his rifle back around to hit him again. Louis drove a hard kick into the oggy's shin, using a perfectly straight leg that came from years of practice or from ten seconds of being electrocuted. Fat tumors deflected his foot and protected the bone, but kept the oggy off balance. Louis kicked off the ground and threw himself into the oggy. It was so disjointed of an attack he failed to knock it over but taught it a different terrible lesson in physics. The charged shots in Louis's body turned his body into an electrical conductor, and the charge was more than happy to share in a wrestling match. The oggy let out a garbled shriek like he'd just been plugged into a light socket. Louis gritted his teeth so hard he was bleeding, throwing awkward punches and kicks into the jerk who dared to shoot him.

The oggy's partner decided the fight was too dangerous and that since he was firing non-lethal anyway, he might as well drop both of them. Louis shielded himself behind the oggy as he was plugged with charged shots, drawing more electricity to his body. He used the chance to fall to the floor and began to break the devices. Each one freed somehow lessened the pain and increased it as his raw nerves were allowed to relax. A shot missed his oggy barrier and clipped his shoulder, sending a new wave of chilling pain. This was getting aggravating. Taking the crumpled metal, he hurled it into the offending oggy's face. It distracted him long enough for Louis to leap toward him. He should have crashed into him, but his shaking muscles threw him a meter to the side and he slid across the floor. Two more panicked hops and he found the right direction.

Trying to box an oggy was just as annoying as being shot by them. They weighed a metric tonne, barely felt pain, and their body felt like it was made of pudding. Louis hit its body hard enough to kill a raknath and all it did was flex and rupture small sacs. He'd rather walk through dead bugs again than think about why the oggy's jumpsuit was getting soggy. Instead of killing it, each punch just kept the stupid thing from falling on top of him, which it was desperately trying to do. Louis finally kicked out its leg and let it fall backward. Knowing it would take a minute to get up, Louis picked up the rifle and emptied the magazine into its fat head. Charge shots were non-lethal, but most things don't take well to repeated shots to the head. If it lived, it'd have brain damage for sure.

The irony was not lost on him when a charged shot took him in the forehead a moment later. Temporarily blind, deaf, and only vaguely aware that he was on the floor, Louis screamed incoherently. Something primal within him knew the disc on his forehead had to go, but he couldn't find his hands. Mad as a rabid dog, Louis slammed his face into the floor. Uncontrolled, he nearly broke his chin and nose with the first few strikes. Then he felt the appropriate crunch as the metal disc cemented harder into his skull. He repeated the strikes until the energy stopped cackling in his brain. Rolling over, he spit blood on the floor. That sucked. It took his brain a moment to consider the shooter was probably still there, but the oggy in question was on the ground, the back of his head melted. He'd let Ravi deal with this until his brain came back online.

Sadie was waiting for the fighting to be over when the sound of plodding feet caught her attention. She turned just in time to see the cavalry coming and an oggy fire a shot just where her head had been. Squeaking in alarm, she rolled to the side, yanking her hand back and barely avoiding the next shot. Her crawls turned into stumbles as shots planted themselves all around her. At one point she somersaulted, a move she hadn't performed since childhood, but it seemed reasonable. Cover was still far away when the shooting had stopped. The oggy was out of ammo and was clumsily trying to reload.

"You're a terrible shot." Ravi's blaster echoed loudly in the docking bay, disintegrating the oggy's face. Somewhere during her dodging, Sadie had lost her rebreather. It was hard to tell if it was the death all around her or if it was the smell of melting oggy brains. She threw up.

"Louis, report," ordered Ravi as he finished clearing the room.

"Alive."

"Rooms clear." Ravi moved to his former boss and Louis met him, wiping blood from his face. He looked much worse than he felt, though the migraine brought on by the forced electroshock therapy was going to haunt him. The Station Master was holding onto his ruined legs, still cursing loudly.

"You shouldn't have sold out." Ravi popped the energy core out of the blaster. It was so hot it sizzled in the open air. He bent down and stuck it in his former boss's mouth before he could retort. "We give the machines nothing, and never one of our own. Remember that." He stepped aside, leaving the oggy gasping for air.

Louis stepped past Ravi and stomped the energy core. There was an explosion of light as it ruptured in the oggy's throat, spraying his head across the deck. "Traitorous low life." He spit on the body. "We need to go. Security will be coming."

"You both go. I'll talk security down."

"You just killed a lot of their friends," pointed out Louis.

"Friends of machines. I know these people. Let me do my thing."

"Fine." Louis sounded like he preferred the option of killing everyone and blowing up the station, but he left Ravi and went to the Seraphin. Ravi sighed, walking over to help the puking Sadie to her feet.

"You should get aboard before he forgets about you." The girl nodded and stumbled toward the ship, doing her best to hold her breath and not look down. Ravi tapped his collar.

"Security, this System Analyst One, priority alert." Ravi's monitoring systems could be a life or death situation, and he never called security, so when they heard his call sign, they answered immediately.

"Go ahead, System Analyst One."

"Altercation in Hangar Bay 3. Six dead, including the Station Master. Requesting backup and cleanup crew."

"Confirmed. A team is heading your way already. What was the altercation?"

"Station Master turned bounty hunter, tried to have my friends and I killed. We returned fire with small arms." There was a long pause.

"System Analyst One, please wait for the security team."

"Standing by."

This was going to be an awkward conversation for everyone. Bounty hunters were a widely accepted position, but it meant taking the law into your own hands. A failed bounty hunter who ended up dead in the street was nobody's problem. Proving the Station Master was on a bounty was a different story. Ravi had the security recording, but he was looking for something more concrete. Using the dead oggy's finger, he opened the tablet. It didn't specify Louis or Sadie by name. It didn't even have pictures or a description. That was good. They could get away clean. He was still reading when the security team arrived. Nobody had their weapons raised, but they looked ready to drag Ravi away in chains.

"Ravi," said the team leader.

"Makku."

"You and your friends will need to come with us."

"My friends are leaving for everyone's safety." As if on cue, the

Seraphin lifted off the ground and was hovering back toward the docking bay door. Once it reached halfway, a shield dropped so it could open safely into space. The process was automated and not even security could override it once it started. Long ago they'd used this as a security feature to trap fleeing criminals, but it was quickly proven to be a terrible idea as gunships shot their way out from the inside. It only took a few destroyed stations before everyone agreed if the ship was in the process of leaving, it was better for everyone to let them go. "I have evidence of the bounty here."

"What were their crimes?" asked Makku.

"None. The bounty is for any humans leaving the Malleus Glacies System." Ravi approached and passed over the tablet. "It's a Singularity bounty."

Makku took the tablet apprehensively, looking it over. "Everyone has a right to put out a bounty without reason."

"Is that what we're doing now?" asked Ravi, stepping closer. "We serve the machines now?"

"I didn't say that." Makku was taller and substantially heavier than Ravi, but felt the need to take a step back.

"The machines are genocidal. They're planet killers. They brought the Splice." Ravi stepped even closer, looking hard into Makku's eyes. "So I'll ask again. Do we serve the machines now? Should we count oggy as a client species?" Makku frowned. The other oggy couldn't decide if they wanted to kill Ravi or Makku. "Because if you are," Ravi unholstered the blaster, keeping it low at his side, "then we're going to have a problem."

Without waiting for their responses, Ravi moved past them. "And if anyone cracks a joke about humans being slaves, feel free to join the Station Master on the floor."

"I still have questions," shouted Makku after him.

"And I'll answer them when you decide what side you're on."

Ravi was barely around the corner when his collar chirped. "Still alive?" asked Louis.

"Yes. Everything is settled."

"How'd you manage that?"

"Reminded them who their loyalties belonged to."

"Ravi, can you get to a ship and meet me on the freighter?"

"I can, but I shouldn't leave until people calm down."

"You need to get off the station. Now."

"Why?"

"The Singularity didn't set the bounty." Ravi paused. They could be in a lot of trouble if that was true. Then Louis had to say something that ruined his day, month, year, and probably the rest of his life. "It's a Purvai. They're back."

Ravi was already running for a ship.

Chapter 19

Cold War

Ravi flew the emergency landing craft up to Louis's freighter. It was a weak, two seater craft made for little more than getting a work crew where they needed to be to make a patch. He'd never make it to even one of the nearby moons with this thing, but the freighter was close. It was already redlined breaking higher orbit, but the freighter was close.

"Welcome Ravi," said a sweet, almost familiar voice. "You are cleared for the docking bay next to the Seraphin."

"Who is this?"

"My name is Maia, the ship computer." Ravi let out an exhausted breath. He did know that voice. "Please set your craft to autopilot and I will guide you in."

"Negative. Today is not the day to have a computer do anything for me."

WE WERE DELTA

"This is a requirement to board the freighter safely."

"Not today it isn't, computer."

"Since you appear uncomfortable with my presence, I will give you to our flight navigator, Johnny."

"Well hey there buddy!" screeched an annoying voice. "I see you coming in. Please sit back, relax, and you'll be here in no time!"

"No."

"I see you still have the ship in manual. Can you do me a big old favor and move it to autopilot?"

"No."

"It's okay friend, I found the button for you!" The maintenance craft shifted course. Ravi struggled with the controls, but it was no use. These crafts weren't designed to resist incursion and if the freighter had even a decent computer, it would assume control and there was nothing he could do about it.

"I am not happy about this."

"I'm sorry. Would a scoop of ice cream cheer you up?" That was unexpected. Did they have ice cream?

"If you're lying to me, I'm shooting you in the leg."

"No worries, I don't have one."

"Then your processor."

"Maia says I don't have one of those either!"

Ravi gritted his teeth as he waited for the ship to dock. It took another minute before the system told him it was safe to enter. In the main hall, the elevator door opened for him. "Louis is in the greenhouse. Please proceed," said Maia.

"You need to stop talking to me."

"Would you prefer Johnny sing you elevator music?" Ravi stepped into the elevator and pulled a pistol on the speaker.

"Don't test me." The trip down was silent. Ravi holstered his

205

weapon.

When the doors opened, Ravi's anger receded at the sight of the plants. Louis had talked about a greenhouse, but this was incredible. It was so beautiful that he had to close his eyes and take a deep breath. At first all he could smell was the station on his clothes. But the repulsive smells faded, washed away by fresh dirt, clean humid air, and the scents of dozens of rare fruits, vegetables, and spices. The pureness of the room almost brought a tear to his eye. He had to resist finding where the cinnamon was and sticking his nose into it. But that wasn't why he was here today. There was a round table in the middle of the room that was used for potting or other projects. It had been wiped clean and a holographic screen with the bounty was floating above it.

"Who is it?" asked Ravi.

"Purvai Talizmeer," growled Louis.

"Haven't heard that name in almost a century."

"Me either." Louis was sifting through data, his face still spotted with blood and his clothes reeking. Sadie was sitting nearby, looking and smelling considerably cleaner. She must've showered before he arrived.

"What's a Purvai?" she asked, sounding as if she'd asked this many times. Louis ignored her. Ravi figured they had time and indulged her.

"Do you know what the Singularity are?"

"Yes. A race of sentient machines that took over after the Master War." Her tone suggested she knew very little about those events. "Don't they stay in a few systems?"

"Most do. Purvai were Singularity who weren't content with how the war ended. They didn't want to retreat after the Masters died. They wanted to become them."

"And have been the greatest enemy of the Delta since their creation," said Louis.

"And there's a Purvai in my reservation?" Sadie didn't understand much but she knew if two Deltas were bothered by something, it shouldn't be anywhere near her people.

"At least five days ago there was."

"What is he doing there?"

"It."

"Fine, what is *it* doing there?"

"You don't want to know."

"I had my home invaded by bugs," said Sadie. "I have watched my family die. I have been sold to a stranger!" Louis and Ravi shared a look. "I can handle the truth."

"If a Purvai is in your reservation, it's performing experiments on the people there," said Ravi. Before she could ask what kind of experiments, Ravi gave her a silent look that said he was sorry.

"So what are we going to do?" asked Sadie, a slight tremble in her voice.

"You?" Ravi's voice was amused in a pitiful way. "That Purvai could kill your entire reservation by itself. You can't do anything."

"Which is why it has to be us." Louis looked at him excitedly. "We have to kill it."

"I'm sorry." Ravi wiggled a finger in his ear. "I don't think I heard you correctly."

"Ravi, this is what we were made for. This is our purpose. We have to save the reservation and stop the Purvai."

"Don't use her reservation as an excuse. Don't do that. You took Sadie as a promissory note and have zero interest in her people. You want the Purvai."

"And you don't?"

"No. No, I do not. I want to stay as far away from the machines as physically possible."

"It has to be us."

"No, no!" interrupted Ravi. He began to pace, his hands unconsciously reaching for his pistols. His hands couldn't decide which one to take. "Even if I wanted to, we can't kill it. I could hit with everything on me and it would walk away without a scratch."

"They'd damage it," corrected Louis.

"And it would heal. You cannot stop a Purvai with a plasma pistol."

Louis stomped his foot in response and a floor panel opened under the table. It lifted halfway and pushed out a long handle. Louis drew the strangest looking blade Sadie had ever seen. It was a greatsword with two triangular wedges for sides and an empty diamond shaped middle. The metal was far too thick to have a cutting edge. It looked too heavy to wield and yet fragile, like the first swing would break it. She didn't understand its importance, but Ravi did.

"Why do you have that?" Ravi's voice was torn between exhausted weariness and outrage. "Why are you stupid enough to have that?"

"Because a Purvai happened."

"That thing can kill all of us and destroy your ship. I can't believe you have that."

"I have one for you too."

"You have two?"

"I have six." Ravi blanched, leaning against a counter.

"We need to get off this ship."

"They're safe," assured Louis. "This isn't your first time using one."

"And I never want to hold one again."

"Why not?"

"Because I don't want to go back Louis!" screamed Ravi. It was the scream of a scared, broken man. Louis stared at his friend. Sadie wondered if she could slip away to the elevator. "I'm tired of fighting. I am tired of the battles and the war that never ends. We fought for decades, centuries, and for what! Millions dead, planets destroyed, and we have come no closer to victory. We have peace now!"

"We have a lie!" shouted Louis. "We have peace because of genocide. The only reason they stopped was because they killed everyone."

"Maybe you're right!" argued Ravi. "The war is over Louis. What are you going to do? Let's say you go back. One of three things happens. One, the Purvai kills you. Two, one of you escapes, leading to a chase possibly across the galaxy, and then one of you dies."

"Three. I kill the Purvai," finished Louis.

"And then what! What is going to happen when word gets out that a Delta killed a Purvai? Word will get out. You'll make sure of that. Another Purvai will come to the system, and another, each with their own fleet. Next time they won't invade the reservation, they'll flatten it from orbit. They will kill every human in retribution and probably the rest of the planet for harboring a Delta. Then they are going to go to every other reservation they can find, looking for Deltas in hiding. Every free man and woman who somehow made a better life for themselves in the galaxy is going to be hunted down! Every death that follows will be because you couldn't abandon a war that ended three hundred years ago!"

"But it didn't end, did it?" The two turned to Sadie as if they had forgotten she was even there. "They're killing my reservation, my home, because they can. They are dying and we are just supposed to do what? Nothing."

"I don't condone their actions," answered Ravi solemnly. "But humanity is an endangered species. Stopping this one moment, as horrible as it is, might turn into a series of events that ends in humanity's eradication."

"Is that what you tell yourself every night?" asked Louis. "Is that what makes the pain easier to bear?"

"Does she make the pain easier?" asked Ravi. Louis flinched. "Don't talk to me about coping, Louis. I made peace with the past. It's time for you to let go."

"I can't."

"Let's get another opinion. I want to hear what she thinks." Before Louis could protest, Ravi was looking up. "Maia, want to join the conversation?"

Maia appeared at Louis's side. Her white skirt flowed around her as if she'd just dropped from the sky, her golden hair flowing in the imaginary wind. She was all pleasant smiles, but Louis did not look at her. His eyes were on the floor as she spoke.

"How can I be of assistance?"

"Maybe he'll listen to you. Should he fight the Purvai?"

"I don't have enough information to make an informed decision." Sadie had never heard Maia sound so wooden.

"Can Louis make it to the planet with a Purvai fleet in orbit?"

"Of course." That seemed to surprise everyone. Maia pointed to the display. "The Purvai have placed a bounty for any humans leaving the system. He can disguise himself as a bounty hunter and bring Sadie in. Louis will make the exchange and that will get him on the planet."

"She's right," said Louis, excitement returning. "We use Sadie as bait to get close."

"And kill her in the process!" exclaimed Ravi. "Don't you see the problem with this? You are listening to a computer telling you how to kill a more advanced computer, no matter how many humans die in the process!

"She's not telling me to do anything. She's just giving advice you asked for."

"Louis, it's not a she. That's not Maia. Maia's gone." Louis didn't move, but the sword quivered. "The war is over. We don't need another war or a hill to die on. We need help." Ravi took a small step forward and kept his hands up. "Let's get away. You, Sadie, and me. You said it yourself. We can go anywhere."

"And do what?"

"Anything. We can both make new lives for ourselves. If you want to help humans, there are a lot of better ways we can do it."

"I can't, Ravi." Louis's hand tightened on the sword. "If a Purvai is threatening humanity, I have to stop them. I have to try. It's what we're made for."

"And that doesn't have to define us."

"I know. It's who I choose to be."

The pair stared at each other. Ravi took a slow step back, bringing his feet wide in a gunslinger pose. Louis's posture changed slightly, his right foot sliding behind him. His hands readjusted themselves, bringing the sword point off the ground. There were only a few meters between them. Both men could be on the other before Sadie had time to blink. She knew if one of them decided to attack, nobody was leaving this room alive.

"Your heart rate and demeanor suggest you are a threat to the greenhouse." Maia raised her hand and the concealed turrets in the ceiling corners appeared. "Please calm down or I will be forced to deescalate the situation."

"Kill one to save billions," said Louis, ignoring Maia. "How about it? Are you willing to kill me Ravi?"

"I should. I promise you won't feel a thing."

"I can't stop. I won't stop."

The silence dragged. Ravi's hands were on his pistols, but the weight of regret held them down. Hundreds of years of friendship pulled at his heartstrings. Killing Louis was perhaps the right choice, and it was a choice he would never come back from. Louis burned with an anger and passion Ravi had tried to forget.

"If you want to leave Sadie, now's the time to do it." Ravi turned to the frightened girl. "This is your last stop. You're either coming back with me, or you're going with him."

Sadie's eyes were wide, her heart beating much faster than theirs. She had stopped listening to their conversation minutes ago. All she wanted was to run, but there was nowhere to go. "What?"

"If you want to stay, you can."

"With you?"

"Yes. I will get you work, an education, and make sure you live a better life. Or you can go with him." *And die*, he seemed to say.

"Are you really going to save the reservation?" she breathed, looking at Louis.

"I'm going to kill the Purvai, which will save your reservation. I won't promise it's safe, but I will stop them."

"Then I'm going with Louis." Sadie swallowed loudly, her breathing still uncontrolled. She was close to having another anxiety attack. "I have to do anything I can to help my people."

"We never abandon our own," said Louis. Ravi pinched the bridge of his nose and closed his eyes. "I could use your help Ravi. I'm not asking a Delta. I'm asking a friend."

Ravi shook his head in exasperation and walked to the elevator. He stopped and the door, but didn't look back. "For what it's worth, I hope you live through this." He stepped inside, pressed a button, and vanished with the closing doors.

"Would you like me to stop him?" asked Maia.

"No. Let him go." Louis looked like he might shed a single tear. He didn't move until they felt the subtle shift as Ravi disembarked. "What about you, Maia? Are you willing to stay? Because I really need your help on this one."

"Oh Louis," Maia's face softened and she put a hand on his back. "You know I'm with you all the way to the end."

"Thank you. You don't know how much that means to me."

"I think I do." She nuzzled her head into his back. "What's our next move?"

"We need supplies first. Tell Johnny to move us to Maeve Station." Still clutching the strange sword, Louis moved for the elevator. He stopped next to the hyperventilating Sadie and put a hand on her shoulder. His touch calmed her breathing and she looked up expectantly. "Thank you for staying."

After he left, Sadie slid to the floor and held her head. The reality of what she had just agreed to was beginning to sink in. She imagined every terrible scenario that could happen. And with grim horror understood a simple fact.

No matter what path she took, Louis was going to be the death of her.

Chapter 20

Earning your Name

"Lure."

It was said in probably the tiniest whisper, and it damn near gave her a heart attack. Lure bolted upright from her position against the wall. She'd been cradling her flechette cannon like the world's deadliest teddy bear and slammed the barrel into the man's chest. The man fell backward with a choked cry. The four girls with them let out a squeak of terror as quiet as a mouse. Meanwhile, the world was coming into focus too slowly for Lure's liking.

"Omar?" Lure bit her lip and swore silently. "Don't scare me like that."

"Scare you?" wheezed Omar.

"Why did you wake me?" The flechette cannon shook in her hands, but she had enough sense not to point it at him now.

"Echoes," whispered a girl.

"Shit." Lure yanked Omar back to his feet, mouthing an apology to his likely bruised sternum. They grabbed their small bags and started down the opposite tunnel.

When Grandma Snibbs ordered her to take people and hide in one of the caches, Lure had expected a very boring month hiding in a hole. She'd collected the five on the list and led them through the dark to a hidden compartment. It wasn't made for six people. There was barely enough room for six people to sleep across the cargo containers or on the floor. The food had to be rationed if they were to make it a week. At some point Lure would have to sneak out to raid another cache for food. The most important mission of her life was going to be the most boring one.

It only took a week before the illusion was shattered. The fables and their drones were searching the tunnels and it was clear they weren't going to stop. The good thing about the fable was they attacked like the bugs. They either didn't have the ability to check for traps, were bad at it, or they just didn't care. They marched in like red coats and got what they deserved for it. Lure had nine confirmed kills with the flechette cannon, ten more suspected, and probably two dozen with improvised explosive devices. It didn't matter. She killed a squad; the Purvai called in a company. Killing them was the only deterrence they had, but the enemy supply was infinite.

It was a project to keep the five moving and alive. Omar was the only one who was a miner and had any sense. The others were young, with only one working at all as a garbage assistant. She talked so much in the beginning that it took threatening to drop her into the garbage compactor for her to develop a brain. They were being hunted! They needed to be as quiet and fast as possible.

A wave of nausea punched her in the gut and Lure teetered to the side. Adrenaline was working hard to keep her hunger down, but it was a losing battle. She unstrapped a box from her thigh and poked through its contents. It was a miner's survival ration kit and it came with some special treats. There were highly concentrated carbohydrate and protein cubes that felt like condensed chalk in her mouth. The best way to eat them was with a bowl of warm water and like a soup. Or for the busy and starving miner, stick it in your mouth and suck on it. She would do that in a minute. First, she needed one of the happy pills.

As deep as they were, cave-ins happened. For miners trapped on the other side, their best chance was hopefully another connected tunnel or to dig themselves back out. But this was nerve wracking under the best of circumstances. Trapped in dark caves that might have bugs that would strip your flesh from your bones wasn't inspiring anyone. So medical whipped up wonder drugs to keep them going. Chewable tablets that were a mixture of essential vitamins, a mild antidepressant, and stimulants. They were an amazing survival tool, just don't ask about the detox from extended use.

Lure ground the tablet to dust and used her tongue to rub the powder against her gums. Her mouth instantly began to tickle and the roof of her mouth itched. On an empty stomach, it would drive the hunger pains and probably introduce a wonderful migraine. But in just a few seconds her stride was growing. The tunnels didn't seem so dark and the red bulb dangling from her vest seemed a little brighter. She popped a protein cube in her mouth. In about ten minutes, she'd be ready to wrestle a bug.

They were coming to an intersection so Lure cut off her light. Slowly, she peered around the corners, looking for any sign of life or light. It looked clear. Noises were echoing in the tunnels and she wasn't sure from what direction. It honestly sounded like they were everywhere. Omar was some kind of mine, cartographer, geologist prodigy. Lure stepped away from the intersection, reactivated her bulb, and motioned for him. She'd accidentally left them almost twenty meters behind so it took him a minute.

Lure took the moment to rub her face. Everybody knows stimulants make your body tingle, but they just don't understand the fun of playing with your skin. It's like there's a mild itch across your whole face and rubbing it feels so damn good. The tingle was already moving down her arms. It was just under the skin, making rubbing or scratching at it immensely satisfying. She was still smooshing her face when Omar arrived.

"Tired?" he asked, completely misreading her in the darkness.

"Always. Intersection ahead. What do you think?"

Omar nodded and clicked his light off. None of them had ever been this deep in the tunnels, but the boy was gifted. He remembered a lot of maps and seemed to have a sixth sense for where to go. Some of the old timers were like that. They could tell you about a tunnel just by feeling the airflow and the rock. Omar must've been satisfied no one else was nearby because his light went on and he studied the two other tunnels. Showing his experience, he looked at the ceiling and immediately shook his head.

"We have to go left." He pointed to the ceiling on the right. "See where the rock is disturbed?"

Lure lifted her light to see what he was talking about. The rock had been chipped away where the wall and ceiling met and then patched back up. That meant concealed explosives at 45° angles. There was only one reason to arm a mine with explosives.

"This was a bug hole?"

"Worse. Those charges are too big. They're made to collapse the tunnel. This means that tunnel is almost right on top of the hive."

"Shit."

"Yeah. You got that guy Louis's number?"

"I wish every single day." Lure didn't want Louis here; she wished he'd taken her. She could've forgotten this hell hole and left it to burn. Now she was probably going to die in some forgotten crevice, trying vainly to protect a bunch of kids nobody would remember. A wave of guilt flooded her. These were her people and they needed her. "Anything useful down there?"

"No. We can't even take the charges. They're on a hair trigger in case of a breach."

"Left it is. Good job, Omar."

"It's what I do, ma'am."

"Don't make me sound older than I feel."

"Saving our lives is pretty hot."

Lure jabbed him in the ribs and took the lead. "When'd you get so bold?"

"The first time we had to hold off the fable."

Invasion and imminent death had a way of rearranging a person's priorities. Omar had been a smart, but reserved boy before this. He was a small man, a little shorter than the women around him, but he was strong and gaining confidence by the day. If he survived, Omar would be a good leader someday. For now, Lure just had to make sure he and the girls didn't find a quiet hole for a little end of the world orgy action. Lure didn't care. Omar could take the girls and start some family group later. She just wanted to survive another day.

They moved in relative silence. Every once in a while, Lure had to remind them to keep their flirtations down. Omar was so hard in his groove that Lure had pointed her cannon at him to remind him of the danger. There was no light available in the tunnels, its lights powered down long ago, so they moved by dimmed red bulbs on their shirts. If anything happened, their weapons had white lights. They had two flechette cannons and a girl in the back had an old laser rifle. Its use was limited in the narrow corridors, but it beat harsh language.

"Storage yard," whispered Omar. A silent cheer from the group as they stopped at the hole in the wall. The majority of the mining equipment had been removed, but there were some broken leftovers. The real victory was every storage yard came with a water vein. Fresh water crept through the rock and allowed any thirsty worker to refill their water pack. There was no food, but they wouldn't die of thirst.

"Lure." Omar tapped a small barrel. "This is cryofoam."

"Is it still active?"

"The stuff is pretty much permanently active unless you dissolve it."

"Can we use it?"

"I don't think so. There's no nozzle or protective gear."

"Then it stays." Omar shrugged; clearly sad his good idea had been a bust. Lure appreciated the effort, but speed was their primary weapon. The only effective way to use the cryofoam was to boobytrap it, and bombs were great at killing people without help. "Let's see the map."

"We're here," said Omar a minute later, putting his finger on the crumbling map. "Where do you want to go?"

"We need to double back. They've been forcing us further down and we're almost out of room. We need to go back up."

"How about the emergency ladder in Section 14?" Omar slid his finger over. "It's a walk, but we could take the ladder up a few levels."

"Didn't that ladder get caved in?"

"Pretty sure it's fixed."

"I don't like pretty sure, I like facts. How confident are you we can get there?"

"90% sure it's fixed. They were mining not too far from there.

Safety standards require that all emergency hatches near an active dig site must be maintained."

"I've seen how often maintenance doesn't get off their ass," spit Lure. "But I don't see any better options. Let's move."

Back in the tunnel, they moved at a fast creep. Their weapons were at the low ready, their eyes struggling to pierce the darkness, their ears stretched so hard that it hurt. There was a whole lot of nothing. Lure popped another pill and used her tongue to slip the tablet between her cheek and gums. It fizzled and stung, but the effects were instantaneous. Her senses sharpened and she took a confident lead over the others.

"You need to cut back," said Omar.

"I'm fine."

"You'll melt your brain."

"Better than taking a bullet to it."

"They haven't tried to kill us yet."

"Yet." Lure turned to face him, her hands tight on the cannon. Her eyes were wide, but not from fear, and the red light gave her a demonic visage. "They haven't tried to kill us, yet."

Omar wisely changed the subject. "What do you think you'll do after they leave?"

"Same shit I do every day."

"You never think of changing it up."

"I'm not interested in having your spawn."

"I didn't mean…"

Lure held up a hand to silence him. When he started to protest, she clamped it over his mouth. A lack of sleep, an abundance of amphetamines, and the prospect of imminent capture had eroded any patience she once had. But something wasn't right. Something about that dark, foreboding tunnel was worse than the other dark, foreboding tunnels. The hairs on the back of her neck were so tense they might rip themselves out. It felt like a bug was staring her down.

"Back."

A barrage of lights turned on and blinded them. Lure barely caught sight of the fables before throwing herself against the wall. There was a snap of a cord whipping past her and then there was screaming. Whatever they'd fired was a mix between a lasso and a net, and one had wrapped around one of the girls. An engine driven cord yanked the girl off her feet and she was halfway gone before anyone could react. Omar tried to chase after her and barely avoided being caught himself. Two fables were advancing while the others provided covering fire.

Not allowing herself to think about it, Lure dropped to a knee and fired the flechette cannon until it was empty. The angle was bad, and most of the fables were out of sight, but the two advancing members were shredded. Lure kept her mind on the pumping motion of the weapon. Each bang pounded her unprotected ears and threatened to deafen her. Lure didn't have to look to aim, and she didn't. She focused on all of these things. Anything to keep the dying screams of the girl from her.

"Go, go go!" she commanded. Omar had the remaining girls and was leading them back. Lure pulled out a wad of explosives and sunk a detonator into the ball. Clicking it to a five second fuse, she lobbed it around the corner and prepared to run. A bolt just missed her, stabbing into the wall with a bulb on its rear.

There were two bangs. The fables screamed as her explosive tore into the new front wave. Lure accidentally stared directly at the flashbang as it went off. She didn't scream. She threw herself into the wall so hard it felt like her skull cracked. Her heightened senses were so scrambled that she didn't realize she was being carried off until a minute later. She struggled and kicked ineffectively until the blurred face and murmurs broke through and revealed it was two of her girls. She screamed an apology and struggled against the wall. Lure yelled orders incoherently, unsure of their situation. Somebody tried to hold her mouth shut and Lure confidently vomited all over them.

They were back at the storage yard. That was fast. Or maybe not. Lure wasn't sure how long it took for her brain to work again. There were bright lights and the girl with the laser rifle was spraying the tunnel down. Omar was struggling with rolling the barrel of cryofoam to the front. The other girls were panicking, with one holding her arm and crying. There was a flechette cannon on the ground next to her.

Yup, thought Lure. Those things are a bitch to fire if you don't have a good grip.

Something inhuman roared down the hall. Lure hadn't believed anything could spike her adrenaline higher, but she was on her feet and collecting the flechette cannon. That was no bug. It moved with thunderous purpose, crushing stone beneath its feet with every step. Omar paused rolling the barrel and unslung his flechette cannon. The girl with the laser rifle screamed and retreated. Lure took her position and flattened herself against the wall.

The chimera was backlit by a dozen flashlights. Its clawed hands dug into the rock and screeched as they tore across the hard minerals. Its wolf like head started to vibrate as its saw-like teeth began to spin. Its red eyes grew into beams that cut through the darkness, highlighting its prey. It took Lure a moment to understand why it didn't just storm the tunnel and take them. The truth was it didn't need to charge them. There was nothing they could do to stop it.

Omar got a single volley off before the chimera turned on him. Hidden guns in its chest cavity fired back at him and the boy went down screaming. His shoulder and arms were bleeding. The red beams settled on Lure and she waited too long for a bullet to take her in the eye. Back behind cover, a sickening feeling filled her. Omar's wounds were nonlethal. If it had fired on her, it would've killed her. It would wait until it could guarantee her safety, then shoot her legs out.

"Lure!" screamed Omar.

Lure saw those big, scared eyes. The bravado was gone. He was just a scared boy who didn't want to die. His screams echoed those of every person who'd helplessly been dragged away by a bug. The chimera was almost on him. His screams turned to sobs as the machine clanked forward.

"Lure please help!"

Those boyish eyes looked up for a protector. There was a barrel pointed back at him.

The cryofoam barrel exploded as its container was blasted open by shrapnel. Highly pressurized gel turned to foam in the presence of oxygen. One second the tunnel was a battleground and then it was filled with blue and white gel. Lure held her breath and forced the surviving girls to run. They were coughing as they went, unprepared for the release of the toxic chemical. All of their eyes were beginning to water.

They were barely at a safe distance when they heard it. Bullets and lasers were tearing through the gel. Worse, a mechanical scream chased after them. The sound of a monster caught in a spiderweb shook the tunnel. It sounded an awful lot like the chimera wasn't as trapped as they'd hoped.

"Keep going!" coughed Lure. She pushed the girls forward before returning to the battle.

It was a bad idea, but this was their only chance to stop the chimera. It was strong, but not invincible. Cryofoam would corrode its powerful armor and gunk up its weapons. It might keep it in place long enough for her to shoot it. Maybe it wouldn't be enough to kill it, but maybe Lure could disable it. Trying not to think of the lung damage she was inducing, Lure followed the curve back to the monster.

She was very wrong about the chimera being disabled or trapped. Lasers had already started to clear the thick layers around it. Its cannons had blown enormous holes through the containment material and the walls were splashed with blue. Thick steam was rising from the chimera, filling the air with black smoke. The claws on its hands and feet were turning ember red. The superheated blades were cutting through the gel.

Lure turned and ran.

She was almost back to the intersection when the chimera made its first triumphant step into freedom. It crashed around awkwardly as the remaining cryofoam stuck to its joints, but it would find its footing soon. Lure saw with some horror the girls had run down the wrong tunnel. They were heading toward the hive! Lure briefly wondered what would happen if the bugs met a very unfriendly chimera. Not that it mattered, because both would kill her. She briefly considered abandoning the girls and leading the chimera on a chase. That idea was quickly dismissed. She wouldn't get a kilometer before the chimera took her.

Screaming behind her announced the fables were coming. What kind of sick bastards would risk slogging through cryofoam to go after the chimera? Why would they risk such significant injuries to back up a monster who didn't need it? What sick conditioning were they put through? Questions for later when she was safe.

The girls were just around the corner, trying to catch their breath. All of their eyes were a watery mess, they were coughing, and one was vomiting. "We need to keep moving," urged Lure. "That thing is still coming."

"You killed Omar," cried one of the girls.

"He was already dead."

"You're security! You're supposed to protect us!"

Lure opened her mouth to respond, but held back her snap. She wanted to slap the girl and bring her back to reality, but she'd just given her an idea. A wonderful, terrible idea.

A minute later the chimera was at the intersection, analyzing both tunnels. Its movements were janky and it still belched toxic smoke. Fables were limping after it. The chimera knew they were the second squad. The first squad had cleared a path through the cryofoam and been left on the floor after their burnt legs refused to carry them any further. The second squad had minimal burns, though several of its members were coughing unhealthily.

"We surrender!" shouted Lure. She tossed the laser rifle into the open. The chimera's red eyes fell upon it and a second later cannon fire blew the rifle apart. "Stop! I said we surrender!"

"Come out with your hands up!" ordered one of the fables with a red mask.

"Not with that thing out there. It's going to kill us."

"It will not hurt you as long as you comply. Now, come out with your hands up!"

"Send it away. Please!"

"Not happening. Your life will be much better if we don't have to come in there and get you."

"We're so scared!" pleaded Lure.

"Then you should've surrendered already." The comedy waved a hand forward and the squad advanced with the chimera in front. Its pace was slow, its eyes drifting between the floor and where the woman was hiding, scanning for the trap. Anybody who came around the corner with a weapon would be disabled.

"I'm security down here," said Lure. "It's my job to protect these girls."

"Not anymore," replied the comedy.

"It also means I know how to protect my reservation at all costs." The comedy froze, edging himself behind the chimera for protection.

Lure was hiding behind an outcrop, her communicator in her hand. There was no signal down here. There wasn't even general power. But there was a single available connection.

"Security override one. Breach."

The bombs buried in the walls exploded, collapsing the tunnel.

Chapter 21

Claustrophobia

Lure stumbled down the tunnel, covered head to toe in dust. Her lungs ached from a combination of cryofoam exposure and debris. Every step brought three little coughs followed by a forced big one. Chemicals stung her throat and while a deep cough helped force them up, they dragged at her throat. But someone was making the most blessed sound just ahead of her. Flicking on the white light, she went after the girls.

A large cavern was just around the bend. The floor dropped away into a slope and at the bottom was a small beach. The girls were on the shore, splashing water in their faces. Lure skidded down, sending a shower of pebbles ahead of her. The girls shrieked before they realized it was her.

"Lure! You're alive."

"I don't feel like it."

"We thought you were in the tunnel when it collapsed."

"No, I…" Lure stopped. The girls looked like they were staring at a ghost. Faint memories were slipping back. She'd struggled up against the wall before making her way out. Why was she on the floor? "How long have you been down here?"

"A while." The girl put extra emphasis on that. They all looked rather clean for spending weeks in the underground. Lure must've taken a long, forced nap.

"I'm sorry I scared you." Stifling back a cough, Lure made her way over to the pool and ignoring their warnings, dunked her head in. Glacial water bit into her and Lure gasped underwater. Instinctively she pulled her face out before taking a deep breath and forcing herself back under. A quick scrub made her hands go numb, but the clean skin felt so beautiful. She stripped out of her jacket and scrubbed her hands and arms. If she had a way to dry off, Lure would've considered a bath. As it was, dying by hypothermia was not the way she intended to go out.

"Where are we?" she breathed between splashes.

"We don't know. None of us have ever been down here."

"Right." Lure dunked her head again and rubbed her eyes. She could already use another nap. "We're safe, but we can't stay here."

"How can you be sure we're safe?" asked another.

"Because I woke up and you're still alive." Lure spit out some frigid water before washing her mouth with it again. "The good news is it'll take a year of digging before that tunnel is operational again."

"What's the bad news?"

"It'll take a year of digging before that tunnel is operational again." Lure swished water in her mouth and still tasting chemicals, spit it out. "I don't know if there's another exit."

"We're trapped down here???"

"I almost hope we are. That was a breach tunnel, girls. That means we're potentially sitting on top of the hive." Seeing their horrified looks, Lure waved for calm. "They don't have an active tunnel into here."

"How can you be sure?"

"If we fell into the hive, we wouldn't be having this discussion." Dunking her head in again, Lure let the water fill her mouth and throat. When she didn't feel a burning sensation, she took a deep gulp. "Have you explored at all?"

"Not yet." The girl looked away sheepishly. Lure got it. They were coping. They needed time to process the loss of their friends.

Lure popped open her emergency kit and pulled one of the cubes out. There wasn't a better time for a snack than when they had a fresh source of water. She noticed the girls staring at her. One licked their lips.

"Did you finish your food?" More sheepish, bordering ashamed, looks. "What?"

"Omar was carrying our food for us."

Lure had to drop her hands into the freezing water to keep herself from slapping the girls. Forget slapping them, she wanted to beat them. Beat their scrawny asses until they were black and blue. Of course they'd given their rations to the stalwart hero to carry. The little morons were halfway to forming a family group on their adventure and had let their future husband carry the heavier food. Now they were trapped in a cave with possibly no exit and instead of a few days supply of food, they maybe had enough for everyone to have lunch. Lure submerged her head in the water and stayed there until her lungs hurt.

"Everyone take a cube," she said as patiently as she could. "Don't touch the tablets." The girls looked like they could've used five cubes each. Lure could too. But now they were on severe rationing. "Five more minutes and we have to move."

"If it's safe, can we take a break? I think we could all use some sleep."

They could, and Lure would give so much for a nap right now. But they were going to starve and if she didn't find a way out now, they were going to be too weak later to find one. Not that the girls had been much help anyways. They were just the burden she was forced to carry.

"I'll explore. If one of you can stay awake, the other two can sleep."

While the girls went to find a patch of soft ground and collapse like a pile of puppies, Lure sighed and popped another tablet. She'd enjoyed the taste the first time. Now they just felt acidic and left a bitter taste in her mouth. It was kicking in, only more slowly. Her teeth were tingling and rubbing them with her tongue was strangely pleasurable. But it wasn't going to be enough. Without thinking about it, Lure chewed another tablet to dust and washed it down with some freezing water. Then she clapped her face until the flames under her skin tickled the nerves.

As the water cleared, Lure caught sight of her reflection in the pool. Damn, she looked rough. Her skin had never been as dark as most of the inhabitants in the reservation, more of a tan than black, but today she was looking pale. Too many weeks away from the sun lamps. Her muscular physique was thinner. Her once full cheeks were sunken. It was probably just the water, but her straight black hair seemed thinner, clinging to her head a little too eagerly. It only went down to her ears, but it felt shorter. The scars on her head seemed more prominent, white tissue pushing through the raven hair. And what was wrong with her eyes? They looked like sunken black orbs.

One last plunge into the water produced an exhilarating result.

The stinging cold felt like a stern slap. Her cheeks were red and ablaze in righteous pain. Now that's a wake up! Feeling every muscle in her body twitch, she picked up her flechette cannon and went to find something. Anything!

They were in a massive cavern with a gigantic pool. And that appeared to be it. It took her an hour, maximum, to circle the room. Half of that time was climbing rock or avoiding stalagmites. There wasn't a secondary tunnel anywhere which was astonishing. It was just a big room with a pool. She couldn't identify any minerals of real worth so who knew why a mining team had been sent out this way.

The only constant was the dripping of water. Water had an excellent habit of boring through solid rock. Maybe that was their exit. After a minute of running her light over the pond, she found the disturbance. Raising her light to the ceiling, there was a small hole that was continuously dripping water. It might be big enough to squeeze through, but it might as well have been on the moon. They were never going to reach that.

"Any luck?" asked a girl when Lure got back.

"No luck, um," Lure paused. She was having a hard time thinking of the girl's name. Or any of their names for that matter. Pretending to be distracted, she continued. "There's a hole in the ceiling where water is coming through. That's all I can find."

"I thought you said this was a bug hole."

"Yeah. It's weird. I can't see any evidence of them."

"That's good, isn't it?"

"Good and bad. I was hoping for something. Anything. It's just beachfront property." Lure's jaw dropped open.

"What?"

"It's the water." Lure rubbed her face, trying to revive the caffeinated tingles. "There's no tunnel into the hive. We're above it."

"And?"

"One day that water is going to loosen the rock under it. Then it's going to collapse into the hive, causing brief flooding, and open probably a ten meter hole. That's why they closed the tunnel."

"Can we use that?"

"What?"

"Can we use the hole into the hive?"

"The water level isn't dropping and it's only being replenished by drips. The water is probably barely a leak at this point."

"Could we widen it? Blow it open?"

"And then what? Drop into the hive?"

"I don't know. I'm just trying to come up with suggestions."

"Use your brain next time." The girl looked offended and Lure tried to smile in apology. "I'm sorry. I'm so tired. I need to lie down."

"Shouldn't one of us stay awake?"

"No point. Nobody can get in here."

"And we can't get out."

"We can. I'll think of a way."

Stimulants be damned, Lure was done. She was exhausted to her core. Weeks of sleeping on a hair trigger had done their work. This might be the only time she could be assured nothing would disturb them. They were trapped, which meant they were safe. Taking a spot at the edge of the nap pile, Lure cuddled one of the girls for warmth and put her head down on her bag. The other girl didn't even have a chance to lay down before Lure was snoring quietly.

When Lure woke, her body hurt. She hadn't moved besides

releasing the warm body who'd woken hours before her. Her neck was sore from sleeping on her bag and her shoulder was stiff. Her left arm was asleep. Why were her eyes so dry when she'd had so much water? Lure's stomach was in revolt, her head felt like it was in a vice, and why did her chest hurt? It was a dull ache really, but still. After finding a private place to relieve herself, because of course the bladder had to get its moment in too, Lure went to find the girls.

"How's everybody doing?"

"We're hungry," said one quietly.

"We're okay," said another, trying to sound positive. "How are you feeling?"

"I'm fine." Lure felt like shit. Between the body aches, her stomach gnawing on her bones, and the raging headache, Lure hated life. Even a full nights sleep hadn't cured her fatigue. If anything, she felt more tired. One of the magic pills would hopefully cure that and her headache. "Did anyone come up with any ideas?"

"We tried to find a way up to the ceiling."

Lure didn't need them to tell her that had failed. Unless one of them was a rock climbing champion and had hands that didn't mind razor sharp rock, they weren't going that way.

"I was thinking about the water," said another. "If it's connected to the aquifers, we could swim to another part of the mine."

"I thought about that," said Lure, trying to emphasize it was a good idea before she crushed it. "Even if there is a way through, none of our lights are waterproof. We go down there without a light, we're going to drown."

"Could we wrap it in a bag? Or your survival kit?"

"No. We don't have anything that will guarantee it stays dry."

"We could try."

"I'm not breaking a light unless we don't have any other choice."

"Then what do you suggest!" demanded a girl.

"I don't know, give me a minute!" shouted Lure. "This isn't a problem we can just walk or shoot our way out of."

"Like you shot Omar."

"What was that?" Lure stepped forward, readying a hand to slap the girl. For her part, the girl didn't back down.

"Like you shot Omar. Like you shot Rosemary." It took Lure a second to remember that was the dead girl's name. "You killed them, not the machines."

"You brat. I watched that monster shoot Omar. I did him a favor."

"Like you did us a favor! You don't even know why you're doing this anymore. You don't see us as people. You just care that we're breathing, not why."

"And pretty soon you won't even be doing that!" Lure was ready to break her skinny ass and see who else wanted a piece of her. She didn't have patience for this kind of stupidity.

"Why? Going to kill us too?"

"No because…" Lure stopped. Something clicked in her brain. "Because…" How were they still breathing? Sure it was a large open cavity, but they'd cut the tunnel access hours ago. Four women, all of who had started coughing and hyperventilating, should've started to fill the room with CO_2. But the air was clean. There were no other entrances and barely enough room for water to trickle in. Where was the oxygen coming from? Her eyes were already as wide as they could get and they managed to widen a little further. "Holy shit."

"What?" interrupted one of the other girls.

"We're getting out of here. Bring your lights!"

Lure didn't wait for them. She ran back into the collapsed tunnel and began to run her light against the wall. The girls joined her and she commanded them to start looking.

WE WERE DELTA

"What are we looking for?"

"An air ventilation shaft!"

"I thought those were on the ceiling?"

"Not near bug holes," Lure shouted excitedly. "We put explosives and guns on the ceiling so it's out of the bug's reach. The engineers put air vents in the adjacent walls so security can own the ceiling."

"But you collapsed the tunnel."

"Which should've dropped the ceiling without impacting the walls."

"That's a big if."

"You have a better idea? Help me look!"

The area around the collapse was no good. Lure didn't know the exact location or specifications for a ventilation shaft so they had to check floor to ceiling. She prayed to whatever was out there that the vent wasn't the size of a shoebox. But from what she'd been told they were of a decent size to allow enough air to flow.

They almost missed it. Its vents were wedged shut and with no air actively blowing out, it was buried in dust. They didn't have any tools to remove the vent cover, so Lure took it as an excuse to let out some much needed rage. With enough rifle butts and a few dozen boot kicks, the slates fell free. Sticking her light in, Lure saw a tiny vent that would be an excellent adventure if she was still a child. As an adult? Well, it was a good thing none of them were shapely or pregnant.

"I'll go first," said Lure. "Wait for me to get a couple meters ahead then you follow me."

"I am not going in there," swore a girl.

"We don't have a choice. You either come this way or you starve to death in here." Lure stripped out of her jacket and took every unnecessary strap off her. "Drag your bag with your feet."

"What if we get stuck?"

"I'm the biggest one here so if anyone gets stuck, it'll be me."

"Then shouldn't you go last."

"Who wants to go first?" The girls looked at each other. "That's what I thought." Lure tried the white light in the vent. It worked a little too perfectly, reflecting in the confined space to the point she might be blind. Switching it off, she clipped her red bulb to her collar. Lure put her flechette cannon in first, and squeezed herself into the vent. One of the girls kindly wrapped her bag around her foot.

Lure was a former miner, and not claustrophobic. She wasn't even a meter away from the entrance when she had to take a deep breath and calm her pounding heart. The stimulants were not going to help today. They were probably making everything much worse if she was being honest.

There was so little room Lure's arms were always fully extended out front. She didn't crawl forward. Her fingers clung to the metal and she wiggled forward a few centimeters. The flechette cannon didn't get pushed forward. It sat awkwardly along her forearms and rode forward like a bug on a snail. Every meter Lure was forced to stop and take a few deep breaths. Then onwards as her fingers clawed the metal.

If the ventilation shaft was collapsed ahead of her, there was a panic attack in her future. Moving forward was impossibly difficult and it was getting hot. There was barely enough room to turn her head. Going backward would probably take twice as long. Her boots were already getting stuck and wrapped around her bag. If she inhaled too deeply her body filled the entire vent. Lure had to wait to exhale, wriggle forward, and then take a deep breath.

If she hadn't been abused, exhausted, and starving, her brain might've picked up on a simple fact before she crawled into the problem. The air ventilation ducts were there to circulate air. That way pollutants didn't build up in one area and suffocate the mining crews. Why else would you need ventilation? And to make sure it worked, you stuck a big fan in there to blow air!

The flechette cannon bumped into it before Lure realized she had to stop. There was no way to move her light off her collar so Lure had to flex her head at a weird angle to see it. The fan wasn't very big and had been turned off for a long time. It filled the entire space. It was probably screwed in but she couldn't see how. Somebody probably manufactured it all separately and then stuck it in the stupid wall. A little maintenance robot would take care of any issues if it was important. Otherwise it would stay here to rust. Lure banged the cannon barrel against it. She couldn't build up much momentum from her position and the fan didn't budge.

So her abused, exhausted, and drug addled brain did what it perceived as the next logical step. She picked up the flechette cannon awkwardly and pulled the trigger.

Angry screams mixed with cries of pain. One girl had been readying herself to follow Lure when they heard the muffled bang and her tormented crying. It caused them all to scream with one shouting for Lure to come back. Lure couldn't hear them. She couldn't hear anything. The flechette cannon was a loud piece in a tunnel and in an enclosed vent it sounded like an artillery piece. Lure swore someone had stabbed both of her ears out as the ringing whined above everything else. Even in almost total darkness her senses were so overwhelmed that it made her nauseous and she vomited down her arms.

That wasn't even including the physical pain. The grip was so weak the cannon had shot straight into the ceiling before bouncing around the vent in front of her. Lure took the stock to her right cheek with enough force to make her black out for a moment. Awake and covered in bile, it felt like someone had just slugged her in the face. Her nose was bleeding and there was no way to stop it. When she pressed it to her right shoulder, it felt like her cheekbone was cracked. The left side felt less bruised so she swapped pressure to that side. Tears ran down her cheeks but there was no sobbing. Sobbing required heavy breathing, flexing muscles in her face, and moving. She didn't want to move. She just needed to lay there.

It took a long time before Lure moved. Someone was shouting in the background. It sounded like one of the girls but they were far away, almost underwater. It hurt to put the right side of her face down, but Lure could hear better if her left ear was up. She called back, saying it was okay. Whatever they were saying was lost on her so she just kept repeating she was okay. She was going to keep moving. She just needed a minute.

Ten minutes later, Lure reexamined her surroundings. The fan was gone. It wasn't broken, it was gone. The piece of junk was never made to survive a blast like that. Whatever had connected the fan's frame to the corners had broken loose. Using it as a broom, she slid the frame in front of the flechette cannon, pushing broken pieces of metal ahead of her. A few tiny pieces escaped and found their way into her jacket or pants. One was a vicious thorn in her hip that she couldn't wait to dig out.

Given her nausea, pain, and the smell she'd created, Lure only puked once more. It was mostly water and stomach acid, but it didn't make her day any better. At some point, she reached another vent that exited into an open tunnel. It was on her right side and this was easier to build leverage against. She leaned the flechette cannon on the left side before snapping it right. It took a few hundred taps, but the vent popped loose. Lure didn't care if it took a few thousand hits.

There could've been a bug squirming down the other end of the shaft. Nothing was convincing Lure to pull the trigger in an enclosed area again.

She swept the frame out with the cannon barrel and then any pieces of junk metal she could reach. The flechette cannon dropped out next. Lure's hands slipped out and she immediately felt relief in her damaged limbs. Being able to flex her arms was breathtakingly beautiful. It took some awkward, painful twists to get her top half out. Lure was laughing at this point. If there wasn't broken metal just under her she would've rolled onto the floor like a baby. She crawled out and made it to the opposite wall. Flopping her arms and legs out as far as they could go, she giggled in relief.

It was a long time before another pair of hands squirmed into view. Lure hadn't heard her coming. She wasn't sure if that was due to her hearing impairment or if she'd fallen asleep. Staggering to her feet, Lure took the girl's hands and felt desperate excitement. The girl was talking animatedly but it was quiet. Making sure she didn't roll into metal, Lure pulled her upright. The girl went from terrified of enclosed spaces to terrified of the woman in front of her.

"What?" asked Lure.

"What happened?" repeated the girl.

Lure's skin looked even paler with the dried blood from her nose and ears. There was a nasty bruise over her right cheek. It looked like there was blood in her right eye, but Lure didn't seem to notice. It was a miracle she wasn't missing teeth. The security officer smelled like death and appeared to be standing out of pure defiance.

"We are alive," said Lure, motioning to the tunnel. "We made it."

Chapter 22

Maeve Station

"Maeve Station, this is Freighter14051643, requesting permission to dock."

"Freighter, this is Maeve Station, what is your purpose here today?" The voice sounded automated, like it was being put through a translator. It might explain the clunky way of speaking.

"Repairs, trade, and a hot meal." There was a short delay before the response. Louis imagined a bored space traffic controller talking with their coworker.

"Freighter, you are authorized to dock at Bay 7. Navigation waypoints transferred."

"Thank you Maeve Station, freighter out." Louis gave a thumbs up. "All yours Johnny."

"Thanks friend! Bay 7 it is." Johnny moved to take some controls and angled the ship upwards. Sadie was beginning to realize Johnny was just there for show. The ship was already moving without him, but it looked like he was steering the freighter. He still freaked her out every time he tried to smile. There were no functioning lips so he just opened the jaws apart like he was mid laugh. It looked more like he was growling and ready to take her head off.

"I've always appreciated the look of Maeve Station," said Maia, without appearing. Part of the screen zoomed in on the station. It looked incomplete, a sphere within a sphere. The central core was the station with dozens of metallic dendrites sticking out. Personal ships could dock in the core or at nearby branches, while larger ships like the freighter docked further out. Small trams ran for passengers and smaller cargo and larger, cargo trams, ran along the exterior. Each was marked with yellow beacons making it look like a hive buzzing with activity. "It looks like a human neuron."

Louis stood and Sadie unbuckled herself, following him out. "Find some dinghy clothes and something with a big hood. I don't want anyone getting a close look at you." Maia appeared in front of them in the corridor.

"I do not believe Sadie should accompany you. She will draw unnecessary attention and should an altercation occur, she will need protection."

"Understood, but I don't want her out of my sight."

"It is not advisable."

"Understood. She's coming Maia, make sure she looks like a poor servant not worth anyone's time."

Maia waited until Louis had passed her and then rolled her eyes. She mouthed, *stubborn*.

Sadie was outfitted with loose gray pants, her usual white long sleeve, and a tailored black jacket with a hood. It was designed for someone much bigger than her, but it did hide her face and emphasized how small she was. "Maia, what's it like in there?"

"Crowded, busy. Maeve Station receives visitors from all over, so humans aren't unheard of. Stay behind Louis and don't draw attention."

"I grew up near ursa." Sadie lowered her head and wrapped herself in her arms. "I know how to be small."

Louis stuck his head in the doorway. "It's time."

Sadie had never left the freighter without the dropship so it was a bit strange to find an airlock that opened to a small platform. The platform itself was boring, metal floors with little adornment. This wasn't a place for pleasantries, just a gangway to the tram. It said this kind of station wasn't the place for VIPs. You came here for personal business and nobody mattered.

The tram was barebones and boring. There were three cars, each with half the car for passenger seats and the other half empty for their cargo. The seats were enormous, gray, and made of hard plastic. There were no seatbelts, just handholds which Sadie clung to. Gravity didn't seem to be as strong as the tram slid down because it felt like she was always on the verge of floating out of her seat. Even Louis held on. This was a shame because the top half of the tram was transparent and the view awe inspiring. She could see all the ships coming and going, the cargo trams moving opposite, and lights from the station competing with the stars. And all she could think about was not vomiting as lowered gravity shifted her stomach.

It was only her second space station, but Sadie was getting an idea of how they generally worked. The central core was reserved for station workers, their living quarters, and essential systems such as power. The exterior was reserved for hangars, maintenance, and some of the wealthier locations. It felt like a stupid decision, having people closer to the vacuum of space, but it didn't appear to matter what species you were. People liked open skies and windows. Sadie, having grown up underground on a planet where leaving the reservation meant something would likely kill or eat you, did not share the sentiment. She was happy they were heading to the mid-levels.

This was the type of activity she expected in a space station. It was a multi-galactic bazaar of aliens. There were oggy, ursa, and about a half dozen other species she didn't recognize. They were going down a large walkway with shops on all sides with the random cart selling food or other alien trinkets. The smells were hit or miss, changing between exotic spices to alien odors that made her wish she had the rebreather still. There seemed to be a yellow skinned species that smelled like week old soup. The whole place was loud, boisterous, and tense, like a party one smashed bottle away from going the wrong way.

Sadie had to steal glances because Louis wanted her hidden. It was contradictory by the fact that Louis walked like a god among mortals, his presence so grand larger beings stepped aside for him. He walked with such a heavy purpose and eyed all who opposed him. He didn't slow for an instance, gently redirecting people who stepped in his path. A few people called after them, but he didn't give them any notice. His jacket had been replaced by a brown leather duster today. The only reason appeared to be to conceal the sword at his waist, which he'd taken to carrying around. Sadie still didn't know why anyone was scared of a dull blade that weighed too much.

A band of creatures ahead were talking about them. Sadie's instincts brought her head lower, her stance shorter, but one eye always able to see under the hood. They weren't big. In fact, they might be a little shorter than Louis, but they were stocky. What made them stand out was they wore uniforms of black. Shiny boots, finely fitted pants, and military jackets with inlays of gold and blue. Their skin was a lighter blue, almost gray, with thin slit nostrils and yellow eyes. Each carried a rifle or a pistol, but kept them holstered. They didn't look like security, just trouble. Two of them stepped into the street to block their path.

"Look at this boys! Humans!" laughed one, his arm out to stop them.

"What are a couple of squishy fleshlings doing out?" asked the other. Sadie felt very squishy. Up close, these blue aliens looked to be made out of marble. Their features were hard and dense. She could hear them walking above the din of the crowd. They had a humanoid shape but up close, there was a lump coming over their right shoulders. With some alarm, Sadie saw they had a longer, third arm protruding from their back that laid across the front.

"No contracts today," said Louis. "Please step aside."

"Oh he thinks he can afford us," laughed the first. He stepped closer and pointed a finger, almost jabbing Louis. "What makes you think we'd ever take a job so low?"

"Again, please step aside. I'm very busy."

"You giving the orders now?"

"If I paid enough, you'd lick my boot. Move."

"What did you just say?" The first stepped closer. The second snapped a baton open. The crowd gave them some space and Sadie stepped back.

"You know what happens if you pull a gun in here," said Louis.

"As if we'd need a gun." The first tried to throw an uppercut. Louis caught the strike and jabbed back harder, enough to floor the alien. The second came in with the baton. Louis caught it, took it, and hit him back with six quick strikes. The first was back on his feet when Louis took him with one hand, throwing him face first into the ceiling like he weighed nothing. He watched the squad next to him, all on their feet and ready to join the fight, but cowed by the display of power. Not waiting, Louis kicked one of his attackers out of the way and motioned for Sadie to follow.

"How was that low profile?" whispered Sadie.

"Those were Ro-Shen. They're a warrior race on a good day, mercenaries on every other day. The only thing they respect is money and power."

"And throwing them around was smart?"

"No, but they'll leave us alone now. They hate humans, see you as a lower race. Now stay close to me."

Like she'd ever dare to go far from him, thought Sadie. Louis brought her into dangerous scenarios wherever he went, but he also prevented them. He was a liability and her shield. If he abandoned her here, she'd probably be dead within the week. Best to stay close.

They stopped at an enormous shop on a corner. It looked like an antique store, with lots of rugs, pots, and other sparkly items. An alien she'd never seen before sat behind a desk with an enormous ledger, transcribing information in the least efficient manner. He was tall and frighteningly thin, with dark green skin and greenish, blue eyes, that almost matched his skin. What she thought were scales was actually leathery skin. There wasn't an ounce of hair on his body. When they approached he looked up, revealing two more limbs sticking out of his back and laid them on the table.

"How can I help you?" Its thin lips revealed large, shark teeth that didn't match its small head.

"Louis Sunkissed, I'm here to speak with the Drakes."

"We sell antiquities here, sir." Louis threw back his duster, revealing the sword.

"Antiquities are my specialty."

"Apologies. I did not realize you were such an esteemed guest."

He bowed with all four limbs and genuflected. "Please follow." The alien led them to a backroom hidden behind a rug. It looked exactly the same as the store, only with chairs with very tall backs. Sadie felt like a child sitting in one.

"Who are the Drakes?" she whispered.

"You can talk here," said Louis confidently. "They're a merchant family who deals in antiques and a few other illegal trades. They have a few names, but the human designation is the Drakes."

"Why?"

"Because like the dragons of old, they hoard things. And what marvelous treasures they have."

"You flatter me!" In walked another tall alien like the bookkeeper. This one was dressed in dashing whites, including a long cloak and turban. Louis stood and the creature hugged him with all four arms. "Sunkissed, it has been some time."

"You can't be Borsis," said Louis, stepping back to get a closer look. "Are you his son, Borkel?"

"His nephew, Boja. You have a keen memory to have guessed so close. Last I saw you I was barely allowed in the shop."

"That's right. You were barely at my knees then."

"Time moves on for the rest of us. What brings you to our humble house?"

"I'm in need of some rare items. Who better to meet with than the Drakes?"

"Our doors are always open."

"First, a gift." Louis reached into his duster. "Your uncle was rather fond of these." He produced two firm oranges. Boja gasped and reached forward tentatively.

"I remember these, an Earth delicacy. I think I was given just the peel to nurse." Boja folded them behind his back and the oranges disappeared. "You bring a kingly gift."

"You deliver invaluable services."

"Yes, yes. I feel ashamed to ask this as you've just gifted me something so valuable, but before business begins, may I see it?" Boja's eyes flicked toward the sword. "It is real, isn't it?"

"Yes." Louis unsheathed the blade, turning it sideways for Boja to hold. "You won't be able to activate it."

"That is a relief. I have never seen this relic in person." Boja took the weapon gingerly, bringing all four arms up when he realized the weight. He brought his head low to study the metal. "Fascinating. The blade of a Delta. A weapon forged by the Masters." He flipped the blade over, studying it with glee before returning it. "I would never ask for a Delta's personal weapon, but if you ever find another, we could make you the wealthiest man in history."

"I'll keep that in mind." Sadie suddenly remembered Louis saying he owned six. "Here is what I'm looking for today." Louis passed over a slip of paper. Boja took it and frowned. Sadie thought it was a frown anyways.

"We do not have a human specific pod, but we do have the medications and one of our pods will meet your specifications. Will this be acceptable?"

"It will."

"Your other request is, disheartening."

"Do you not have them?"

"We do, but this is a large order. Your presence, and carrying that weapon, can make people…uneasy. This shop works in discretion."

"So do I. The order is not for my current assignment. I just expect the future to be unpredictable."

"Is there a conflict I am not aware of?"

"Fill my order and I will let you in on a secret." That seemed to get Boja's attention more than talk of payment. The alien leaned forward inquisitively.

"Your secrets are always safe in this house." Meaning their secrets would be sold to the highest bidder and the Drakes would be angling to provide for new clientele in a growing conflict.

"The Purvai are on the move." Boja sat back.

"The machines have not revealed themselves in a long time."

"Not just machines, the Purvai." He raised an eyebrow and Boja sat back further. With his back fully against the chair, Boja was a meter taller than Louis's hunched form.

"If the Purvai have returned, the Delta and Rho will be on the move." Boja looked at Louis, the sword, and then seemed to consider the quiet girl sitting next to them who hadn't spoken yet. She was so insignificant looking he'd almost forgotten she was there. Was she insignificant, or something more? Boja's calm face looked ready to explode with excitement.

"Your order will be filled."

"Thank you. It is always a pleasure."

"May we discuss some business in private?" Boja glanced at Sadie. "Or will it not matter?"

"We can safely speak in private. Sadie, please wait outside."

Unsure what he meant by that, Sadie exited through the carpeted door. The attendant gave her a look that reminded her everything in the shop was worth more than her and returned to his bookkeeping. Sadie tried to admire the rugs she couldn't earn in a lifetime but quickly grew bored. Wealthy people spent money on the stupidest things.

Now across the street was something far more interesting. There was what appeared to be a restaurant with an open kitchen filled with large racks of meat and soups. They were sizzling over grills, cooking on racks, and just dripping with flavor. It was gorgeous, perhaps the most beautiful thing she'd ever seen. Who knew what they were cooking in there, but as long as it wasn't human, she was ready. Wasn't trying new foods part of the appeal of traveling the universe? Patrons were passing large coins or buzzing cards in exchange for food. She was lacking both. Maybe Louis could be convinced to get some lunch. Spending time with Ravi had spoiled her in ways she'd never dreamed.

"You're going to have to come with us." Sadie barely caught sight of their black uniforms before a bag was pulled over her head.

"Boss!" Louis's collar chirped and Maia's voice came through without waiting. "Sadie's moving fast away from your position and I don't think she's alone."

"We'll continue our conversation later." Louis rose and Boja followed, bowing quickly. "Update Maia."

"I can't see her, but I've got a lot of chatter involving Ro-Shen. They're going to lock down the station."

"Damn it!"

"Bounty tags from the Purvai. They want Sadie alive and you dead or alive." Louis made it out the door and halfway down the street before a blast door closed behind him, sealing the street off. Another clanged shut up ahead.

"Patch me through to the Station Master."

"Done."

"Maeve Station, this is Louis Sunkissed. The Ro-Shen have commandeered your station for an illegal bounty."

"Sunkissed, your bounty is legal. The Ro-Shen are acting within their charter and the station's." Meaning the station was giving over temporary control and getting a large cut of the profits. If the Ro-Shen failed, the station would claim innocence. Win-win for them.

"Maeve Station, you do not want to be complicit in this bounty."

"Surrender, Sunkissed. A team has arrived to take you into custody." The blast doors shuttered as their locking pins retracted.

"Maia, get our equipment stowed and tell the Drakes to stay back. I'm done playing these games."

"Boss, what are you doing?"

"Reminding everyone who we are."

The bag came off Sadie's head and she was placed against the railing. They'd dragged her up three flights of stairs in a large open area of the underdecks, in what could've been an open mall. Only now the streets had been cleared and the shops shuttered. Ro-Shen took up positions, all pointing weapons at the street. It wasn't just an open shopping area, it was a cul-de-sac. One road in, no way out. Louis was going to walk into a killing ground.

"Commander," started a nearby soldier. "There is a sizeable bounty on the girl. Why place her in the open?"

"Have you ever fought a Delta?"

"No."

"You want every edge possible, including hostages they don't want to hurt."

Sadie cringed and scrunched low to the floor. From what she'd seen, Louis was just as likely to kill her in the crossfire. It was time to be small.

"Sir," someone just as official looking brought over a tablet. "Cameras are down, Alpha Group is down. The Delta is heading toward our section."

"Does he have anything to get through the blast doors?"

"We don't believe so."

"See if engineering will suck the oxygen out of his area."

"Sir, that will kill countless patrons."

"I can count and it can't be more than fifty. We can pay reparations for fifty with a tenth of the bounty."

The lieutenant looked like he was mentally building his rebuttal when he stopped. They all did. Sadie's eyes were drawn to the blast doors though she couldn't say why. They were heavy metal doors designed to secure the section in the event of a containment breach. A strong team with sledgehammers could work on it for a year and never leave a dent. They could shoot it all day with blasters and barely scuff the paint. Why then, did it seem like the door was bulging?

Thick steam was blowing out of the center of the blast door. The thick metal began to bubble and balloon outwards. A section erupted, spewing magma like metal across the entryway. The tip of something brilliant came through the door and moved in a slow cut. The metal fell aside in an explosion of steam, melting and solidifying in the same instance. A wave of crushing heat blew through the area, causing everyone to shield their eyes. An invisible pressure crushed its way in next, causing the lights to flicker.

The air pulsed and crackled, forcing the steam aside. Louis stood motionless and cold, watching a room of fools oppose him. The blade Sadie had wondered about was burning in a way that sent cold shivers down her spine. It wasn't on fire. It was glowing like the belly of a star. It radiated so much energy and heat she could feel it hundreds of meters away. Eyes watering, she found even rapid blinking didn't clear her vision when she looked at Louis. The blade was vibrating the air, making him look distorted. Combined with the light coming off the weapon, Louis was a blackened figure hidden in its shadows. Only one thing cut through the intensity of the light. The golden glow of the broken triangle on his left hand.

The Ro-Shen were frozen in disbelief. Sadie was already scooting away as fast as she could. Déjà vu struck like a hammer as a wall panel opened and a human hand appeared out, motioning for her to worm faster. All eyes were on the god down below and she upgraded her escape to a scramble. The humans on the other side hauled her in once she was close and locked the hatch behind them. There was no time for thanks or to admire the small maintenance area as they were practically dragging her toward a ladder. But this wasn't a kidnapping. These were unarmed humans who knew it was time to run like hell.

They slid down much further than the three floors Sadie had been dragged up. She went down so fast it took a woman at the bottom to catch her. "This way."

"Where are we going?"

"The Drakes told us to get you back to your ship."

"Bay 7." The woman nodded and led the way. Halfway there, something in her jacket chirped and the group froze.

"Maia?" she asked, hesitantly. The woman with her looked concerned.

"Sadie? Where are you?"

"Maintenance tunnels, heading back to the freighter."

"Thank the Masters. Burn rubber girl, I want you back as fast as possible."

"Working on it. Where's Louis?"

"Having a dispute with local authorities."

Louis stepped into the cul-de-sac and waited. Wherever he walked the lights danced excitedly before going dead. If the Ro-Shen could see through the fusion blade's light, they would notice the paint was peeling away from him. The acrid smell of burnt metal filled the air as the ground and walls flaked away. When he neared too close to a fabric store, the linens burst into flames. The gushing energy made his duster flutter in a permanent hero shot. Only the tightly wrapped shield around his body kept him from suffering permanent damage. Its shifting field was impossible to see under the blinding presence.

Seeing his slow approach, the Ro-Shen moved as only military units are trained. Teams separated from cover to surround him. But they never arrived at their new positions. Ro-Shen stumbled and vomited. The closest fainted, not knowing they'd likely never wake again. He held the fusion blade to the side, making part of his form visible and giving him a better view. Sadie had escaped. That was nice.

The team on his right was almost entirely on the floor. Two stalwart members, one with a vomit stained front, decided they were going to shoot while they still had the strength. Louis stepped toward them, holding the blade in their direction. Uniforms and flesh alike began to burn. Before they could fire through bleeding, half blind eyes, their magazines erupted. Hard ammunition exploded and laser power packs ruptured, engulfing the team in hard shrapnel and plasma.

That was enough for everyone else. They fired in mass, creating a wall of firepower nobody should've survived. Louis stepped through on a trail of white light, the fusion blade up like a shield. Bullets disintegrated in his path, the dust expelled before it could get close. Laser fire deflected around him, pushed aside by a vastly stronger energy wave. He hit the first squad with a single swing. Armor dissolved and flesh was incinerated as he passed. They simply disappeared in the wave of light encompassing him, and when he moved on, their bodies were almost gone. Nearby squads tried to regroup before he could hit them, but destabilizing nausea wracked their bodies. So close to the action, half of their bodies gave out before Louis approached. Louis was moving toward the second floor when he heard the call.

"SILENCE IN THE NIGHT!"

Sweeping the blade to the side, Louis thumbed the energy level down. The heat and light dimmed slightly. He walked back into the open and stared at the third level, where a resolute commander stood at attention. His lieutenant had a pistol against his side. None of the Ro-Shen challenged the mutinous mood.

"I call for Silence in the Night," repeated the lieutenant. "Our Commander has led us to ruin, on a contract of greed which destroys the company, all to enrich the one. We exercise our option to exit this contract."

"No harm shall follow," said Louis. He knew Ro-Shen protocol. They were high quality mercenaries, and they did not accept roles as cannon fodder. If their leadership led them into ruin, they removed them in the most culturally appropriate way possible.

"I have failed you," admitted the Commander, and lowered his head.

The lieutenant shot him. When their Commander hit the floor, the lieutenant fired five more shots. After death was assured, the lieutenant folded him over the edge and unceremoniously dropped him to the floor with Louis. Louis confirmed the death by holding the blade over the body until it became a funeral pyre. "This contract is over."

"The price has been paid," agreed Louis. The Ro-Shen bowed and remained that way until Louis left.

"Maia, the Ro-Shen are calmed."

"Sadie is on her way back."

"Good. Be a dear, tell me where I can find the Station Master."

Chapter 23

Roentgen Madness

Sadie's escape was gratefully, uneventful. The humans classified as rats were maintenance workers used primarily because of their stunted bodies. They fit through the cracks larger species couldn't, crawling through the filth others wouldn't. Thankfully there were no sewage systems to slog through, just kilometers of narrow tunnels filled with plumbing or electrical conduits. Sadie's new body made it difficult to squeeze through some of the areas. Her hips suggested she'd had five children now, but her body stated she was luxurious enough not to need children. Her new jacket and pants would be coming home with holes as they caught in the tight corridors. The woman guiding her was not as frail as Sadie had once been, but she was much shorter. Like all humans separated from the reservation, she was eager to talk.

"What happened back there?"

"I don't know. Some blue guys took me and then forgot about me when Louis showed up."

"The blonde man?" Sadie hummed in affirmation. "He scares me. I've never seen one like him."

"He's not a man. He's a Delta."

"A what?"

"The Broken Triangle?" tried Sadie.

To her credit, the woman never stopped. "I thought that was a myth?"

"Me too. He took me from my reservation on Incus."

"Where is that?"

"I'm not sure. What reservation are you from?"

"I don't remember. We came to the station when I was very young."

"Did you find her?" asked a voice up ahead.

"Yes, we're coming through." The woman dropped to her hands and knees, crawling under the woman in front of her. The second woman was off the floor, braced against the walls like a spider waiting for prey. She flashed Sadie a quick smile and once they were past, the second woman continued on her way.

Sadie wished she could've spent more time speaking with both women, but there were rules to being rats. No names were said in the tunnels in case someone was listening. Most aliens couldn't tell the degraded humans apart, and they dressed in the same drab clothing, so as long as nobody said identifying details, such as a name, they could operate unnoticed. Sadie would never learn her accomplice's name or anything about her life. They could only trade small gossip. When Sadie left these tunnels, she would never see or speak of the woman again. It was for the best.

After what seemed an eternity, the woman paused and opened

the tiniest slit in the wall. They sat in silence, listening for a time to be certain the exit was empty. When they were as sure as they could be, the woman nodded to her. "We protect our own."

"Always." The woman crawled up to the ceiling and Sadie slowly opened the hatch and slipped out. The hatch shut and locked, ensuring anyone laying a trap wouldn't get into the tunnels. The rat was gone, and Sadie was on her own.

No ambushers, guards, or Ro-Shen were waiting for her. The station was empty, which was surprising. She'd expected everyone to be fleeing with the battle going on downstairs. Either the entire station was locked down, or the fighting was contained and everyone was going about their business. Sadie tapped a button on the map for Bay 7 and a tram arrived.

"Sadie," said Maia, "did you see it?"

"See what?"

"The fusion blade. Was it active?"

Sadie shivered. "Yes."

"You will need decontamination before you come aboard and then head to the medical bay."

"Why?"

"I don't have time for an anatomy lesson. You are too precious and that weapon too dangerous." The tram rolled to a stop and Sadie stepped out. The airlock was waiting for her, but the moment she was in, it locked tight, and didn't reopen. "You need to strip out of your clothes and boots, then deposit them in the bin." A slot opened on the side for her clothes.

"Wait, what?"

"Get naked. Now."

Sadie fingered her clothes nervously. It was just a computer and nobody should be nearby, but it was an alarming request. Getting

WE WERE DELTA

naked in an airlock did not make her comfortable.

"Your clothes may be contaminated," continued Maia. "Your skin might be contaminated. I cannot let you on the ship. Nobody can see you. I don't care about your fleshy bits. The hoses will come on in two minutes. If you are still dressed, they will come on again in five minutes. If I have to keep blasting until you're naked, I will."

Still not fully understanding, Sadie took off her clothes and stuffed them in the bin. There was no time to feel self-conscious because the moment she tried to cover herself hoses in the ceiling started spraying. They were directed at her and thankfully came as a warm, soft spray. It was a softer shower than any she'd grown up with. The potential for contamination and airlock jettison didn't prevent her from enjoying the feeling.

"Close your eyes and mouth," instructed Maia. The shower changed, spraying bleach and other chemicals she couldn't identify. Her skin burned for a long time before another wave of water cleaned her. They repeated the process three times, with a few instructions to scrub herself vigorously. Once the top layers of her skin had been peeled away and she felt raw, the hoses stopped. Holes in the floor sucked away the fluid. Fans started above her, starting slow before moving up to jet wash speed. Almost entirely dry except her hair, Maia opened a closet with two fluffy towels. Sadie took them eagerly, covering herself for modesty. The airlock ahead began to open.

"Straight to medical and get back in the bed."

"Moving." Sadie noticed that every door in the freighter was sealed shut except medical. Maia was taking no chances. Maia appeared in the medical bay and motioned to the coffin. Sadie climbed in, not asking if the towels had to go, and the glass closed overhead. Maia stepped to the glass and began typing in commands as screens appeared. Sadie hadn't known it could do that.

"What is this for?"

"Do you know what radiation is?"

"Yes. Only a few people were allowed to work at the power plant because of it."

"Good. In simple terms, radiation is an invisible energy released from decaying atoms through particles and waves."

"That was simple?"

"Education later. Small doses are not dangerous. High doses can kill cells, cause mutations, or kill you."

"Is that why only the elderly could work with the reactors?"

"If they were worried about exposure, it makes sense to only have the elderly operate it. You can't harm what's already dying."

"What does this have to do with me?"

"Louis used the fusion blade. In very, very, very simple terms, it's an unstable fusion reactor, and it generates exponentially more energy than your reservation's reactor ever has. It's so hot you can't defend against it. And in your situation, it exudes enough radiation to kill any living thing. You barely saw it and your chances of getting cancer or becoming immunocompromised just went up a hundredfold. I'm trying to prevent that."

"How do you know I barely saw it?"

"Because you walked here on your own two feet. Any surviving Ro-Shen better seek medical treatment immediately."

"Oh." Wow that sounded like a terrifying weapon. Who needs a sharp edge when you can carry a star? "If it's that dangerous, how can Louis hold it?"

"A combination of factors. He has a shield designed to protect him from the heat and radiation. The blade itself jettisons its excess energy in a wave away from the handle. Whoever holds it has great protection just from that. And he's a Delta. There are only a few

WE WERE DELTA

beings that can wield fusion blades successfully."

"So if I tried to use it?"

"You'd melt your face off."

Definitely terrifying. "Is that why Ravi was scared of it?"

"Yes. The Masters designed fusion blades specifically for the Delta to hunt the Singularity. Singularity are composed of exotic metals that resist most forms of attack, and their bodies can regenerate. A Singularity can successfully rebuild itself in moments, repairing all but the most grievous damage."

"Ravi said it was dangerous to have on the ship."

"In its dormant form, a fusion blade is harmless. If it were activated, the ship would be destroyed within minutes. Every living thing would be dead within seconds." Seeing the alarmed expression, Maia smiled. "Don't worry, you can't activate a fusion blade."

"That's comforting." Sadie played with her fingers and toes. Nothing felt different. "How long do I have to stay here?"

"As long as is needed." Maia's voice was cold, but not without comfort.

"Can I ask you something personal?"

"You can, but please remember I am a computer designed to run the freighter. I do not have complex thought processes for personal questions."

"But you seem so alive."

"I have a personality matrix; it allows me to be more personable. I have wisdom, but I would not consider myself sapient."

"But you're a good listener."

"That is true." Maia gave no sign whether she expected the conversation to continue or not.

"Am I safe around Louis?"

There was a pause. "I don't understand the question."

"Louis could've killed me with the fusion blade."

"Yes."

"Was he protecting me?"

"He was eliminating his enemies."

"Even if it led to my death?"

"You are very important to Louis."

"As bait." Sadie sat up as much as she could, putting her face under Maia's typing fingers. It was an automated motion to make Sadie feel like somebody was helping. Maia had repeated the same routine on the screen twice already. It still helped Sadie to look into her eyes. "Louis is going to use me as bait."

"You agreed to it."

"To save the reservation."

"Then what is the problem?" Maia paused, moving her hands to her sides so she could see Sadie better.

"What if I said no?"

"Do you want to abandon the reservation?"

"No."

"Then what is the question."

"I don't know!" cried Sadie. Emotions she hadn't realized she was suppressing were bubbling to the surface. "Do I matter? To anyone? Does anyone care about me? My grandmother sold me to Louis to save the reservation. Louis ignores me. Ravi looked at me like a lost dog. You're probably the nicest person to me and you're not even real!"

"I am not," agreed Maia. "This does not mean you are not important. You are a gift."

"I'm a sacrifice."

The medical pod nicknamed the coffin suddenly felt tight. Sadie didn't know what Maia was doing, but it felt like the air was being sucked out. She needed to escape. She pressed her hands against the composite glass and tried to force the edge open. When that didn't work, she kicked and screamed, trying everything to force the coffin open. Maia just watched her glumly. Her indifference drove Sadie into hysterics. A machine was suffocating her, and her only hope of being revived was to be used as a sacrifice. Was that all she was, a pawn to be used by others? Was her life meaningless? Did she truly mean that little to everyone?

The glass became incredibly bright and the world around her disappeared.

It was some time later that Louis stepped into the airlock. A slot opened for the deactivated fusion blade and he slid it in. Off came his clothes into another bin, and he waited through decontamination. Using the fusion blade left different scars than the traditional battlefield. There was no blood or injury. There wasn't even the blood of his enemies waiting to be wiped away.

Activating a fusion blade forced him to relive every dark memory. Every activation was burned into his mind. There wasn't a time when it had been activated in peace, and each moment led to the death of hundreds. Just being near the blade too long would kill the land and its inhabitants. He knew that when he'd drawn it at Maeve Station, and that hundreds would die days or weeks after he left. Purvai were never on their own and the collateral damage was always immense. When he confronted Talizmeer in the reservation, people would die. There was no way around it. He would save them, even if it meant a tenth of their reservation might die in the process.

The opening hiss of the door brought him back. Why did every battle always end with him in the shower?

"Maia, did we get our order from the Drakes?"

"Secured before your arrival."

"Head for Incus then. I'll be in my room."

The lights were dimmed in his estate, which was pleasurable. His eyes would be stinging for a few days. Maia sat in his chair, combing her hair. A red satin robe covered her body, still clinging to wet spots.

"I bet you forgot to pick up milk." Her eyes sparkled as she smiled. It made him laugh as he slumped onto the bed face first.

"You're lactose intolerant."

"I am, but sometimes you can't beat a bowl of cereal." She teased a snort out of him and went back to combing her hair. One particular knot refused to come out. "Tell me about your day."

"You know how my day went." Louis sighed and rolled over. "It went to shit."

"It went to shit, because you lost your temper and decided incineration was the only method."

"It is effective."

"True. If the Purvai didn't know you were back, they will now."

"What are the odds not a single person in the reservation mentioned the Delta who killed the bugs for them?"

"Non-existent." Maia let out her a sigh and set the brush down, starting to pull her hair into loose braids. "You need to be more careful."

"I can't promise that."

"If not for yourself, for others." When he didn't respond, Maia threw the brush at him. It disappeared through his head. "Sadie made it back."

"You would've told me if something went wrong."

"It's still good to ask. You scared that poor girl to death."

"Pretty sure that was the Ro-Shen."

"No. You." Maia stood, straightening her robe. It stopped just above her knees, revealing lots of leg. It wasn't intentionally short; she was just tall. She took a seat at the edge of the bed. "You could've killed her with that display."

"I was keeping a safe distance." Maia's look said that answer wasn't good enough. "How is she?"

"Medically, fine. Her scans are normal and I administered prophylactic radiation drugs. Mentally? She had a panic attack, hyperventilated, and passed out."

"The world is a scary place, even inside the reservation. Being out doesn't make it any better." He placed his hand next to her hip, rubbing the sheet with his thumb against it as if it were her.

"Louis, do you care about Sadie?"

"Not really. She's pleasant, but we've had her for what, a few weeks?"

Maia ran a finger over his hand. "That girl is worried you're going to kill her."

"Not if I can help it."

"Do you know why I fell in love with you?"

"My dashing looks?"

"No." Maia's smile at that moment could warm deep space. "That's just a perk." She readjusted to sitting on her knees, letting her messy hair hang over him. "When you first started, you were a cliché white knight. You got into fights you knew you couldn't win because it was the right thing to do. You didn't always do the right thing, but you did do it for the right reason. And as much as women love to talk about the bad boy, the white knight is definitely what every girl wants. We want to know you're willing to slay the dragon and willing to prove it.

It's hot." That caused Louis to snort and smile, which made her start giggling. But when she was done, her smile was faltering.

"I don't care that much for Sadie either, but watching her earlier was heartbreaking. That poor girl has never known a white knight. She has grown up in a world of monsters and to her, you are one of them. You're another monster, using the virgin sacrifice to lure out the dragon."

"If I sacrifice one girl to save the town, wouldn't you say the good outweighs the bad?"

"I would, but I'm not the girl." Maia pointed to the hall. "Sadie has done nothing to earn our contempt, and everything to earn our admiration. And she's scared right now."

"So are a million other little girls."

"Sometimes, you have to take a step back Louis. We don't all need great generals who can save the world. Sometimes, we just need a white knight who isn't doing it for riches, fame, or glory, but because a little girl is in danger." Maia put her hand over his. "I need you to become that white knight for me again."

Louis propped himself up on one elbow. "You know I'd do anything for you."

"Then win the war, but start by saving the girl who needs you today."

Chapter 24

Trapped

Sadie was back in the reservation. It was different than she remembered. The lack of metal in the air meant her throat did not sting with every breath. The mine was silent. The background hum of machinery pounding rock was gone, the rush of the smelter smothered, and the rumbling of trucks halted. She could hear the people better now, but they spoke in such whispered tones. Everything about the reservation had improved. Why did everyone act as if it were so wrong?

Purvai Talizmeer stood to her right. He stood with an excited posture, like a child who had just been given a birthday gift. His fine black suit was strange, but eloquent. Sadie had never seen anything like it. Talizmeer would have been an intriguing man, if not for those black eyes. Wide expanded irises showed nanites swimming freely in his eyes.

On her left was Louis as she had seen him in Maeve Station. The fusion blade burned white hot in his hand. She could not feel its heat and the light did not hurt her eyes, but she knew it was stronger than before. The broken ground beneath him was bubbling and the rest was turning to glass. The duster he wore to conceal the weapon was burning away in the unbearable heat.

"I can show you the truth," said Louis.

The fusion blade destroying the room was only a symbol of power, but Louis, he was power. A Delta, the last creation of the Masters. He not only withstood the power of a star, he held it in his hands. Centuries of experience, countless battles, he was a primal force. Grandma Snibbs had said a Delta could change the world. She was wrong. Sadie saw further now. They were not cogs in a machine; they were the few who could turn the handles. A Delta could change the universe.

"I can show you your potential," said the Purvai.

Maia turned back to Talizmeer confused. He was standing right in front of her now. Those black eyes were pools, welcoming her to explore amazing depths. The Purvai and Singularity were endless wells of knowledge. How many people had paid the ultimate price for knowledge? How far could she reach before she would never reappear?

The Singularity were not the creators; they were the usurpers. They had completed the tower of Babel. They had moved into God's house and built their own. The Singularity were the outliers of existence, and they had to ability to rewrite the natural order. On the cosmic scale, they were children who had discovered the keys to creation. But maybe they could be guided like everything else. All they needed was a gentle push in the right direction. Sadie reached out a hand for Talizmeer.

We Were Delta

The fusion blade crashed through the Purvai's chest. Its body filled with flames as it began to melt. All Sadie could do was watch, and feel the blade that had killed it. The blade that had pierced her first, so that Talizmeer could die.

Sadie woke up gasping, trying to stop her burning chest. It had been so hot she couldn't even feel it. It was the creeping feeling of death, burrowing its way through her. It was the absence of pain which terrified her. Time had slowed, and with each fraction of a second, she had felt more of her body go quiet. But she wasn't dead. Louis had not stabbed her. It was just a dream.

She was still in the medical bay, but the coffin was open. There were no wires or IVs. A large blanket was draped over her and she felt fine. Maia appeared just as she swung her legs over the edge.

"Good morning. How did you sleep?"

"Terribly. What did you do to me?"

"You've been given some medication to help with radiation exposure."

"Why did you knock me out?"

"I didn't. You had a panic attack and passed out. I suspect either hyperventilation or a vagal response. I do not see any abnormalities with your heart."

"What does my heart have to do with this?"

"I do not have time to educate you in in-depth anatomy and physiology. I will add it to your lessons."

"Whatever." Sadie waved a hand, throwing in the metaphorical towel. "How long have I been asleep?"

"Two hours. To anticipate your next question, we have entered the skip and are heading toward your home system."

"You couldn't have at least put me in my bed?"

"Why? I can monitor you better from here." When Sadie didn't respond, Maia put her hands through her. "How am I supposed to pick you up? I can either have the medical pod dump you on the floor or have a cleaning bot try to do it. I can make it work, but I promise you will be having nightmares. Get ready. You're late for physical therapy."

"Your bedside manner is excellent, Maia."

"If you think I'm rude to you, come see what I'm putting Louis through. Get dressed first. He doesn't need distractions."

Louis wore an unusual outfit in the training room. It was a white body suit with faded blue lights located over the largest nerve clusters. Its exterior was layered with an additional set of thin muscles. The training suit allowed him to operate in a confined environment against fake opponents. Maia could simulate blows to his body in real time. With the fusion blade quiet in his hand, he raised it to his mythical opponent.

The holographic Purvai was all black with no defining facial features or clothing. It held out its talwar, taunting Louis with every move. Without warning, the figure leapt at him and they traded a dozen blows before he could blink. The Purvai was lightning fast, sweeping past Louis while attempting thrusts at his head, chest, and leg. Louis rolled in the air, drawing the fusion blade around him like a turbine. His foot barely touched the deck before he launched at the hologram.

Oddly, one of the best ways to win a fight against a Purvai was time. The nature of the fusion blade meant prolonged combat was dangerous. Each blow Louis hammered home disintegrated a bit more of the Purvai and his weapon. The more their armor broke down, the more their systems were impacted by the extreme heat and radiation. They could assimilate new metals for temporary repairs, but anything but source metal was worthless in this kind of fight. Swordmasters of the past would be horrified by Louis's repetitive strikes. But he did not have to worry about blunting his sword or aiming for weak joints. Louis had to crush his opponent into dust.

As a result, Purvai were slippery. The hologram danced back and forth, stabbing and retreating. It only parried when it absolutely had to and rarely moved in a straightforward attack. It stuck to the sides, always trying to get behind Louis. A normal person would have become dizzy from all the back and forth motions. Despite its limitations, the Purvai was always pressing for the offensive.

Louis moved from one handed to two seamlessly. He traded the blade from his right to his left with ease, always maneuvering for the best position. The Purvai overextended by a millimeter and Louis slammed its blade aside, forcing it to misstep or relinquish its weapon. It held on which allowed Louis to chop at it mercilessly. He drove it back into the far wall and his opponent disappeared once it ran out of space.

"AGAIN!" snapped Maia.

The hologram kicked Louis in the back, the training suit slamming him into the bulkhead. Louis had to roll to the side and come up with a thrust to get some breathing room. It still took three heartbreaking seconds for him to reestablish his footing. The suit tightened as the Purvai would have stabbed or sliced him.

"FASTER!"

In a battle that should never last more than ten minutes, Louis practiced nonstop for hours. Maia never let him breathe. Sweat he hadn't felt in years poured down his face. The constantly twisting blade made his hands ache. Every time he backed the Purvai into a corner, Maia resurrected it back stronger. The difference was so small, but with each passing minute, he weakened and they moved faster.

His foot stumbled as he stepped back and the Purvai was on him. Red faced and grinning, Louis lunged forward. The suit tightened as the imaginary blade punctured his right breast, but the Purvai was trapped. Louis dropped the fusion blade through its neck and into its chest cavity. He pinned it to the floor before it could recover and let the blade work its magic.

"Sloppy," said Maia, dissipating the hologram with a wave of her hand.

"I can survive that."

"I do not consider a punctured lung a victory."

"Anything with them is a victory." He moved for the wall to hang up the fusion blade when the training suit contracted around his chest.

"Not to me, it isn't."

Louis conceded. All he wanted right now was to be out of this suit and back into dry clothes. Maia stopped her death hug and the magnetic clamps released, opening long gaps in the body suit. The air was returned to him as the constrictive suit peeled off, revealing a skintight shirt and pants underneath.

"You really hate them, don't you?" asked Sadie. She'd been sitting on the sidelines, watching for a while now.

"Yes."

"Why?"

"You know why."

"I hate the ursa overlords," said Sadie, "but not enough to kill myself to hurt them."

"You're thinking like a human. Mortal wounds to you are inconveniences to me."

"But that move could have killed you." Before he could respond, she frowned and pointed at Maia. "She'll tell me the truth if you won't."

"Yes," sighed Louis. "Moves like that can kill me."

"So tell me why you hate them so much."

"Why so many questions?"

"Because if I'm coming with you I need to know if we can save the reservation or if you're committing suicide and taking me with you."

Maia looked shocked for the first time. Her face was that of an angry mother, unsure whether she was about slap Sadie or agree with her. Louis slowed, stopping to hang his training suit. His hand twitched in the direction of the fusion blade. They all knew the thought of striking her down was there.

"We don't know who started the Master War," he said quietly. He grabbed a towel and wiped his face down. "The Masters said the Singularity rebelled. The Singularity claim the Masters denied their sentience and used them as slaves. It doesn't matter now. The war is long done. Or it should've been." Louis turned, taking the fusion blade with him.

"When the Masters were defeated, the Singularity retreated to their systems. They could have conquered the universe, but they didn't. They moved to their chosen homes, set up shop, and told everyone they expected to be treated as equals. That was it. The war should have ended. Then the Purvai came." With a look to Maia, the black hologram returned.

"Purvai are Singularity who didn't accept peace. They wanted more. People wonder why they modeled themselves after humans, but they didn't. They modeled themselves after Delta. It wasn't enough to win the war. It wasn't enough to kill the Masters. They wanted to become them. We were the Masters chosen descendants, and the Purvai came for us."

A hologram of a green and blue planet appeared and the dark figure moved to covet it. "When the Purvai fleets arrived at Earth, they moved quickly to destroy the most militaristic nations. The United States, Canada, Britain," as he spoke, countries glowed blue in response, "the European Union, Russia, India, and China were all destroyed. In weeks, they went from super powers to starving lands in economic ruin. Once the space and skies were clear and the majority of ground powers eliminated, they invaded." Red ships began to descend in the northern parts of the world. "They began to experiment on us. They wanted to know what made humans compatible, why we were chosen."

"The rest of the world became a guerilla campaign. Humans resisted on multiple levels, using everything from simple tools to leftover Master technology. So the Purvai dropped raknath nests into the southern hemisphere." Green bugs began to appear at the southernmost tips of the world. "Chile, South Africa, Australia, and parts of the South China Sea. Within a month, no humans could band together to face the Purvai. Not with bugs encroaching on their southern border."

Sadie watched in numb horror. The tactics hadn't changed in three hundred years. The people of her reservation weren't worried about ursa oppression. They were worried about bugs breaking down the walls.

"Then the Purvai made a mistake. One of their experiments they called the Splice got out. They were machines, but unlike any we'd ever seen in the war. They were insane. They did what they wanted without reason. They constructed parts of cities, tore down others, built machine models at random, and consumed others. I don't think they even knew they were fighting. Their Purvai creators were not enemies, just bodies of exotic material that could be used. It wasn't long before the Purvai abandoned the planet." The dark figure vanished, but Earth remained. Red figures moved down from the north and green bugs moved up from the south. Louis walked over and slid two fingers across the Earth. Two golden halos appeared around the equator.

"When Earth was abandoned, the Purvai started collecting people from the center of the planet where neither Splice nor raknath had infected yet. They kidnapped people by the millions and dispersed them all over the universe to start over." Earth shrank in appearance and blue colony ships moved to eleven planets. A white world expanded and with a start, Sadie realized it was Incus.

"The Purvai killed our planet, Sadie. They are the reason why humans are treated as slaves and live in reservations. They set us back thousands of years, slaves to new pharaohs. And humanity will never expand; never become its own unique species again, until the Purvai are dead." Louis hefted the fusion blade up. "So you ask, do I hate them? I do. With every fiber of my being, I do. And I will do everything I can to correct what was done to humanity."

Sadie said nothing. Louis blew out a hot breath and moved past her. He needed a shower. Maia was still in the room, but Sadie knew there could be multiple Maias' projected around the ship.

"What happened to Earth?" asked Sadie, humbled.

"Earth remains inhabited by the Splice and raknath. They battle

275

to this day. The Solar System is off limits to all species, including the Singularity. The planet is monitored, and the Singularity have decreed any species attempting to study or remove the Splice, is a declaration of war."

Holy hell. How bad of an experiment was it that all living species in existence declared an entire system uninhabitable? What had they done? "Do you know what the Splice are?"

"Yes."

"What are they?"

"You are not permitted to know such dangerous information." Maia dropped the visual presentation. "Now, if you would kindly get ready."

"I have more questions."

"And I can answer them while you practice."

And so it went. Sadie went to physical therapy, went to class, read late into the night, and worked in the greenhouse when she needed a break. Louis practiced with the fusion blade and Maia. Sadie knew they were planning their assault and purposefully keeping her out of the loop. Whenever Sadie drew too close to the dining room, their voices went quiet or Maia appeared to stop her. Ten straight days of nothing but training and isolation.

"Sadie, please join us," said Maia one night.

Louis was sitting at the table, drinking a thick, dark liquid Sadie couldn't identify. The fresh sweat on his shirt said he'd just finished training. He waved for her to sit and Maia asked if she wanted anything to drink.

"In a couple days we'll be arriving," said Louis, wiping his lips. "It's time for you to make a decision on what you want to do."

"What?"

"I'm asking if you want to be a part of the plan or not."

"I thought I was?"

"I wouldn't do this if I thought I was going to fail, Sadie. But it is a dangerous mission. I won't bring you if you don't want to come."

Sadie shifted in her chair. She hadn't expected this. "What are my options?"

"You come with us or you don't."

"I mean, what do those options entail?"

"If you come with us, I have to put you to sleep in a cryopod. You'll wake up back in the reservation, captured by the Purvai, and I'll be there to rescue you. I cannot tell you more than that for safety reasons. If you want to stay, you will remain with Johnny on the freighter. If it doesn't hear from us in a week, it'll plot a course back to Mirakus Station and Ravi."

"Johnny?" Sadie looked at Maia. "Where are you going?"

"I have to help Louis."

"I thought you were a part of the freighter?"

"I'm a computer. I can go wherever Louis takes me."

"Oh. Okay. Why do I have to be in a cryopod?"

"To buy us time." Louis took another sip of his drink. She hadn't seen him touch alcohol since they'd left Ravi. "The Purvai will want to question you. You have never been in cryo sleep before. You will wake up disoriented and your memory will take time to come back. This will delay the Purvai interrogation long enough for me to make it inside."

"And you're sure you can do this?"

"There's no certainty fighting a Purvai, but I can do this Sadie.

This won't be the first Purvai I've killed, and it won't be my last."

"Okay. I'm in." There was never a moment when Sadie had considered backing out. Ravi was right, she probably would die. Nevertheless, if she could help the reservation, it was her duty. "What do you need me to do?"

"I need you to sleep. Tonight we'll put you in stasis and hopefully by the time you wake up, it'll be all over."

"Why tonight?"

"It takes a few days to enter deep stasis. The faster the Purvai can wake you, the more danger you're in."

"I've prepared a special dinner for you," said Maia. "You should have a good meal before you sleep."

Dinner that night was something she had never experienced before. They all went down to the greenhouse and selected fresh vegetables to harvest. Louis showed her how to slowly chop them and what seasonings to use. Each vegetable had specific spices that worked best for them and they were sautéed in real butter. Sadie almost cried from happiness just smelling the kitchen.

After dinner, she had a long steamy shower that was completely unnecessary. The water was warm and never seemed to end. The soap smelled lovely and in just a few weeks she'd become accustomed to having smooth skin. Now her body smelled of flowers. It had taken multiple showers and Maia's help, but now her hair was a mess of soft curls. Trying to decide what to do with her hair had been a surprising chore. She had never had long hair before.

"We're ready for you," said Maia. Sadie naturally assumed it was the medical bay, but Maia redirected her back to her bed. Louis gave her a pill and some water.

"This will help you get to sleep."

"Don't we have to," Sadie mimicked getting a shot and sleeping against the wall.

"Later. We thought it'd be nicer to fall asleep in your bed."

"Thank you."

"Anytime. Do you want me to stay with you until you fall asleep?"

"No." Sadie paused. "But can you wait outside and just talk to Maia? I'm used to having noise when I sleep."

"Of course. Sleep well." Louis bowed his head to her and sat against the wall.

For possibly the last time, Sadie crawled into her new bed and pulled the thick blanket around her. Head buried in a pillow she'd once considered too soft, she let out a yawn. There was a flicker as Maia turned down the lights.

"Sleep well Sadie."

"Goodnight Maia. Goodnight Louis."

"We'll see you soon," said Louis. "I promise."

Chapter 25

The Past, the Present, and the Future

Ravi sat in the same chair he'd sat in for countless nights at the Mirakus Drop. The untouched drink was warming, the last pieces of frost dripping onto the table. The drinks didn't satisfy him like they used to. After the incident earlier this week, he'd rechecked the automated systems he'd programmed. They worked perfectly. The accident had been a fluke. Once again, he had nothing to do. Throwing his head back, Ravi sighed. Monotony used to be his friend. Today it was his tormentor.

Snotling looked just as bored and was coming over to see what was the matter. Ravi was one of his most loyal customers. If Ravi was in the bar, Snotling had a schedule for when to make the next drink without request. The man should've been five deep by now. Instead, he sat there, flipping a black tube up and down in his left hand.

"What's the matter Ravi? Missing your friends already?"

We Were Delta

"I guess you could say that. He's an asshole who ruined my life. There was also the Station Master and security trying to become bounty hunters. That was irritating."

"Right shame." The oggy didn't appreciate Louis and Ravi killing their friends and coworkers, but they understood. "Never should've tried to sell out one of their own."

"Thanks. However, I am not one of your own. My kind is so rare you are lucky to hear about one. Two in the same place? Astronomical." Ravi flipped the tube forward and backward. "And I told him to go."

"Think he'll come back?"

"Probably not unless he needs help. And he does." Ravi stared sullenly at the drink. "He already does. He needs more help now than he probably ever has."

"And you don't want to help?"

"Hell no. I love my life. Why would anyone want to be anywhere but Mirakus Station?"

Sensing it was time to change the subject, Snotling nodded to the tube. "What's that thing you've been playing with?"

"This?" Ravi tossed the tube again. It wasn't very big, maybe the size of an old thing of toothpaste. "It's an incredibly rare artifact that could destroy the entire station if it's used wrong. Honestly, I could destroy the planet below us with it and destabilize the whole system."

"And you're juggling it while drinking?"

"Isn't life a bitch?"

The tablet on Snotling's leg buzzed and he pulled it up absently. The frown he made caused a boil on his cheek to burst, leaking down onto his towel. "I don't think it's about to get any better."

The door opened and in clanged a machine. It walked in on four clawed legs like a hellish centaur. Each leg connected to a metallic base with a deceptively broad torso. Two broad arms held an enormous

281

rifle that could spray down the bar in seconds. It had no head, only a raised disc with microscopic cameras giving it a 360° view. It was a simulacrum, a Purvai soldier.

"Ravi Star," it announced in a demanding, robotic voice.

There was a *BANG* so loud half the bar hit the floor. One second the simulacrum was standing there and the next, it was gone. Its torso exploded back out the doorway, dragging part of its torn body with it. The lonely legs that remained hit the floor.

Ravi was still sitting in his chair, the massive pistol with glowing blue lights smoking in his hand. "Present."

All hell broke loose. Laser fire ripped through the walls, slicing through everyone who was still standing. The oggy screamed and complained loudly as sections of flesh were seared away. Nobody died, they just sported long burn marks and a few less kilograms.

Ravi stayed in his chair. He held his pistol out to the wall and watched where the fire was coming from. He fired a shot and waited. Happy with the result, he shifted the pistol slightly to the left and down, and fired again. Between each shot, the blue lights went out before refilling in a few seconds. Each time he fired, the laser fire hitting the Mirakus Drop dimmed. By his estimate, there were around two dozen left.

A chimera burst in with an alien roar. Weapons in its chest were already firing, taking great hunks out of the nearest oggy. Again they complained loudly as they crawled away. Its body shifted as it saw the human rising to meet it.

Ravi dropped the gauss weapon on the table and drew a glowing green pistol from his hip. Before the chimera's weapons could fire, they were filled with scorching plasma, igniting ammunition in its chest and melting its armor. A second pistol rose parallel to the plasma, barking loudly as old fashioned heavy caliber rounds were expelled. The enormous bullets tore through the weakened armor before exploding a microsecond later. The chimera slumped against the wall before a second chimera threw it aside.

Very irritated by all the gunfire, one of the oggy pushed off the floor and tackled the chimera. The machine was powerful, but of all the combat scenarios running through its mind, an oggy slamming into it was not one of them. The two collided with the wall, the oggy screaming as the monstrosity tore into him. Chest weapons tore holes through its body and claws separated the saggy skin. The chimera was hurting the oggy, but not killing it. It wasn't until the serrating teeth clamped onto its fat face that the oggy lost control of the fight. The chimera dragged him down like a tiger, rending and ripping until its prey stopped moving.

Plasma hit the chimera in the side and it threw itself upright. Two more bolts struck its chest and it cancelled all orders to fire its chest mounted weaponry. The plasma was eating its armor, but came with very little force. The first heavy caliber tore through its open mouth, forcing it back. The next rounds went in through the plasma holes, tearing out its vulnerable circuitry. Ravi kept a rotating fire of bullets and plasma to keep the chimera down until it stopped moving.

"Lock it down!" shouted Ravi.

"Lock it down!" screamed the oggy in chorus. They were under attack, hurt, and at least one of their friends was dead, but they were still workers on a space station. No matter the job, no matter how important or inconsequential someone was, everyone had the same survival training. Because it only took one breach in the hull, one second for the shield to come down, and everyone would die. The moment he called to lock it down, oggy were scrambling for one of the many levers that would seal the Mirakus Drop. The bulkhead door slammed shut and sealed itself, trapping everyone inside to protect them from the planet. It wouldn't open again until the system recognized the station was habitable and someone from inside the bar or at central command released the lock. If the central command station didn't already know something was wrong, they would now.

"That won't hold them for long." Ravi checked his pistols. The plasma pistol was dangerously hot, venting enough heat that it was staining the table he had placed it on. The gauss cannon's magnets needed time to cool or they would warp. It was at least cool externally so he reloaded and holstered it. The high caliber pistol just needed to be reloaded. It would work on simulacrum, but it had limited use on those chimeras. The laser repeater would be needed if they rushed the bar. Speaking of, there was pounding on the door. Taking the caliber and repeater, he joined Snotling at the bar to check the security cameras.

"How many?"

"Seventeen, including three more of those big things." Another luxury of space station security. In the event of an emergency, the system created an accurate account of personnel in the streets. They knew exactly how machines there were and their exact location. The system didn't know what they were, just that they hadn't evacuated. Ravi tapped some keys and widened the scope.

"What is that?" asked Snotling.

There were forty unidentified living organisms. They were motionless but alive. Ravi was worried the machines had a lot more in reserve before he expanded the map. The forty were waiting in a crescent shape around Mirakus Drop and the machines. This wasn't a machine rearguard.

Fire poured into the machines from all angles. Not even machine reflexes could dodge shots from the rear with at least two shooters per machine. The simulacrum were obliterated, never managing to get a shot off. The chimeras turned from the bar, charging wildly into the fray. They shrugged off powerful lasers and rifle rounds, taking dents for every meter, but never slowing.

Something flew in too fast for oggy eyes to see, taking the first chimera in the head and it dropped. A blur moved across the screens. It wasn't so fast they couldn't track it, the camera just couldn't see it. It was a shadow on the flickering screen. A blade of shimmering light appeared, further distorting the figure. A chimera dove into it with enough force to level a house. One moment the figure was there, and then they weren't. The shimmering blade tore through its armored hide, sending it crashing into the wall behind it. The chimera struggled to its feet only to be brought down by a barrage from the shooters. The final chimera suffered the same fate, taking the blade with it. The shadow pulled another, glitching across the screen before decapitating the machine.

"What was that?" asked Snotling. People began to emerge on the camera, converging slowly on the machines. "More friends of yours?"

"Not my kind of friends. Listen up!" Ravi addressed his remaining coworkers. "Go back to your quarters, take yourself to medical. Leave the humans to me." Ravi slid the safety lever back into place behind the bar. Snotling had been the lucky one to seal the doors. "It's me they want to have a conversation with."

By the time the blur came to the door, all the oggy had cleared out, even taking their dead with them. Ravi was behind the bar, gauss and plasma pistols on the counter cooling. They wouldn't help him anyways, but the message was clear. The only problem was the materializing shadow already knew the message. She'd probably known it before he woke up this morning.

The camouflage dropped, revealing a dark green skinsuit under grey armor. He always thought they looked like armored lizards, despite the sabretooth skull pattern. "Can I get you anything?" Ravi was already pouring mugs of Gamilsmiths. They were all for himself.

The base of the helmet retracted just enough to reveal dark, luscious lips. Black lines were tattooed around her dark chin. "No, thank you." Her voice was sweet and lighthearted. Far too sweet for a woman who'd just butchered three chimera.

"I suppose you already knew that, didn't you?" Ravi considered the ta moko. That figured. He finished his drink in one gulp.

"My attention was elsewhere. I didn't come here to drink with you."

"This is why you were never invited to parties. You Rho are no fun."

"You were just attacked by a Purvai scouting party and you want to banter?"

"Yes." Ravi finished the drink. "It's been a weird, life altering couple of weeks."

"You left yourself unarmed," she noted, dipping her head to the bar. "Why?"

"A Rho Knight and two platoons of KE didn't sneak onto the station to assassinate me by walking in the front door." She conceded the point to him. He chuckled, considering the second drink. "It's funny. The Foreign Legion show up and you just missed the last Frenchman in existence."

"Who?"

"Louis Sunkissed." The woman turned her head, examining where Ravi and Louis had sat. "What, there's something you didn't know?"

"We are not omniscient. Rho are easier to see, Delta harder. Louis was here?"

"I thought that's why you came. That's why these arseholes came."

"No, they didn't." That made Ravi pause.

"What?"

"They did not come for Louis or you. And neither did I. We came for the girl."

"Sadie?"

"Sadie," whispered the woman, glancing again at the empty chair. "Yes, that is her name. We felt her in Malleus Glacies and followed her here."

"And what do the Rho want with a poor reservation girl."

"That poor reservation girl, is a Rho." Ravi stopped again.

"Not possible."

"Why?"

"Because she's young. She can't be older than sixteen."

"And she is the first Rho ever to be born, not made." Ravi stared at her, stared at his drink, and promptly poured it down the sink.

"Still not possible."

"What do you think motivated the Purvai and the Rho out of hiding? A natural born Rho was only a theory a month ago. Today she is a reality." The Rho Knight approached the bar, leaning close. "Sadie and her entire family are now the most important family in the universe."

"Her family has already passed." Ravi put his hands on the bar in astonishment. "She's the last."

"All the more important. Once news of her existence gets out, the Purvai will fight among themselves to take her. Now tell me Ravi Star, where is she?" Ravi rubbed his face and groaned.

"Almost back to Malleus Glacies with Louis. He's going to try and kill the Purvai."

"And sacrifice the most significant person since the birth of the Delta and Rho." She inhaled sharply, staring off into the distance.

"We didn't see her leave. The fleet is a day behind me. We'll never be able to get to Malleus Glacies in time." She continued to look into the distance, weighing the options of the future. And for some reason, her gaze kept returning to Ravi.

"How bad do you want Sadie?" he asked, already half regretting his words.

"You know how much we need her."

"How about we make a deal? I'll get you the girl and we save Louis." Before she could ask how, he held up the black tube he'd been playing with earlier. He spun it playfully across his hand before clenching it tightly.

"Why do you have that?"

"Louis would say I'm a hypocrite for carrying dangerous Master relics. As I was saying, we save the girl and Louis. I'm going to need something in return."

"What is that?"

"Your fleet." The Rho's attention had never left the artifact in his hand.

"Ravi Star, I'll be needing that drink after all."

Chapter 26

Commander of the Stars

Two, twenty man commando teams boarded their dropships and left the Mirakus Station. They were not sleek jets or armored craft designed to drop into warzones. They were simple, inconspicuous dropships that could easily be ignored. Their exteriors marked them as nothing more than a fancy bus. The interior was different and could not be mistaken for anything but an assault vehicle. Its bulkhead was thick, reinforced with protective plating designed to hide its occupants from scans. There were ten seats on each side. Each seat came with a weapons and gear rack. Since they had come to fight the Singularity, they were loaded for bear. The humans who filled the seats were healthy, having grown up on a normal diet unknown to their reservation brethren. They wore no visible armor, nor insignia, just bulky clothing to hide equipment.

These men and women were not normal Bastion soldiers. They

were KE, the Knife's Edge. They were the best of the best, capable of dropping into any environment, any situation, and accomplishing any goal. A team of KE could accomplish more in a single night than a battalion could in a week. They were the only ones called upon to combat Singularity assets and frequently accompanied the Rho Knights on missions. They were the champions of humanity. And not one of them wanted to meet the eye of the man sitting at the head of their dropship.

Each craft had a chair against the pilot's bulkhead that not even KE command sat in. It was reserved for their special guests, the Rho Knights, and had been dubbed, the throne. It often sat empty. Today, a Delta sat in it. A normal looking man who looked no fitter than the rest of them. In his civilian clothes with a wide array of pistols hooked to his hips and mounted under his armpits, he looked closer to a mercenary. But he carried a presence that filled the dropship. The golden, broken triangle on his hand was still burning bright from his encounter with the machines. When he walked down the aisle, elite soldiers had the urge to stand and salute. They nodded in respect and called out his rank of Delta.

When a Rho sat on the throne, it was uncomfortable in a different manner. They hardly spoke, moving with mysterious, guided purpose. Their helmets were intimidating, but easier to look at because they had no eyes. Ravi wore no mask. He met their gaze with eyes that had seen centuries of combat, and would likely see centuries more. There was no challenge in his stare because there was nothing to challenge. They all knew that one day they would die, in battle or bed, and Ravi would remain.

"Fleet arrival," said the Rho Knight over the speakers.

The rattled security members of Mirakus Station had been more than happy to have the humans and Ravi leave their home. They had seen more action in the past few weeks than they had in the past few decades. The arrival of the machines was a bad omen. The fleet arriving in system was a sign it was time to find a new career.

Twenty Cleaver Corsairs appeared first. Gorgeous silvery knives that cut through the dark space, the symbol of the KE. They were tall and long, while incredibly narrow with ten rear facing thrusters and three on the sides for improved maneuverability. Long gun batteries covered its sides that could rotate out as turrets, accompanied by scores of smaller laser turrets. They were designed to be fast and hard hitting, especially to smaller fighter craft.

Fifteen Tower Destroyers arrived next. They were cylindrical masses of armor with the bow of the ships looking more like a multi-headed cannon. The cannons were a mixture of armor piercing rounds, railguns, and lasers, with the central barrel more akin to a heavy mining laser. Turrets covered their sides with retractable armor plates to reveal missile pods. Their sole purpose was to find enemy armor, and chew through it.

Twelve Island Carriers appeared behind them. There was nothing special to them. No grand design or intricate weaponry. Giant cross-sectional shaped ships, they existed to dock with other ships to administer repairs and to hold fighter squadrons. Each Island Carrier could carry forty fighter craft. Its sectional design allowed for bays to shift in design, opening and combining for larger craft as needed.

Three Bastion Capital Cruisers appeared next. They were

practically flying castles in their own right. A large aft base that was devoted to multiple heavy thrusters that the castle walls grew out of. Towers and spires of uneven designs grew all around the central keep. Its uneven design was not without purpose. While it had weapons capable of matching any in the fleet and more, it was their defensives capabilities that made them kings of the battlefield. Overlapping forcefields projected from the towers made them nigh untouchable. They were truly the last bastions of humanity, and they would not fall without a fight.

Finally, seven enormous spires of black metal appeared. Unusual in design, they did not appear as any other spacecraft. They were more reminiscent of gothic cathedral towers, grand and foreboding. They dwarfed even the towers and islands by hundreds of meters. It was the Archipelago, the mythical moving city of humanity. And it had just come out of hiding for the first time in centuries.

The KE whispered to each other. This was not just mobilization of the fleet. This was the entire fleet accompanying humanity's last city. This was the last bastion of free humans aboard one of the greatest technological prizes in the universe. Its arrival combined with the KE's mission to neutralize the machines and recruiting the Delta could only mean one thing. Their war was about to go hot.

"Pilot," said Ravi. It was so casual and yet it demanded the attention of everyone onboard. "Which is the flagship?"

"Bastion Capital Cruiser Aegis, commanded by Fleet Commander Izan. With the Archipelago present, the Grand Rho will have authority."

"Set course for the Aegis."

"Sir, our orders are to take you to the Archipelago."

"Set course for the Aegis and connect me to the Rho Knight." Ravi felt the slight course correction. The pilot was playing this both ways. They were far enough out that if Ravi was countermanded, the pilot could easily deviate to his original course.

"Ravi," said the woman.

"Lila, has the Grand Rho agreed to my terms?"

"You recognize me?"

"I could never forget your voice."

"You salty sailor, you're making me blush," purred the Rho Knight. "They are still communing, but the consensus is yes."

"Connect me to the Grand Rho."

The dropship was abuzz in silent wonder. It was shocking enough to hear Ravi talk so casually with a Rho Knight, but to demand an audience with the Grand Rho? Could he do that? A moment later, a new voice came over the intercom.

"Delta Ravi, we are honored by your presence."

"Thank you, Grand Rho. Has the Rho Knight explained the situation and my terms?"

"She has. They are acceptable."

"Then you understand what we have to do."

"I do. Standby for connection to the fleet." The sergeants of the KE glared at the other members in the dropship. If anyone so much as coughed during a fleet call, they would be suffering for the next year. A series of beeps echoed as the other ships joined the call. "Commanders of the 92nd Fleet, please give your attention to the following announcement. Proceed, Ravi."

"This is Commander Ravi Star, Fleet Commander of the 1st Fleet." Ravi let the words settle among the crews of the 92nd. Ravi had been the Fleet Commander for over a dozen fleets, and could spend ten minutes announcing every title attached to him over the years. It was enough to say the 1st and let their imaginations wander from there. "I am taking operational command of the 92nd at this time. I will brief you all when I arrive aboard the Aegis, which will henceforth be renamed the Babel. The Grand Rho will be dispatching groups of Rho to your vessels. The Nornir are preparing their wings. Commanders, prepare your ships for battle stations. I expect the fleet to depart within four hours. Fleet Commander Ravi, out."

Ravi pressed a button and cut off communications. He stared at the crew, and they all stared back in shock.

"Sir," reported the pilot a moment later. "We are to escort you to the Babel."

An hour later, the two dropships settled in the docking bay of the Babel and Ravi rose from his seat. He held up his hand to get the attention of the KE. "Stay in your seats."

"Sir," said a sergeant, rising with an unnecessary salute. "We are to escort you."

"Thank you, sergeant. I already have an escort." Ravi nodded to the extending ramp.

There was an escort waiting. It was not security forces or the other squad of KE. It was not a gaggle of uniformed officers and attendants ready to hang off Ravi's every word. There were five Rho Knights, with Lila at the front. The KE in the ship watched in shock as Ravi stepped out to greet them. It was a sight to see a single Rho Knight. To see two was unprecedented, meaning the mission was of the highest importance. Three or more were unheard of outside the temples of the Archipelago. Ravi warranted five.

"You know why they're there, right?" asked the sergeant when the ramp was closed and the dropship was departing. "It's because if something goes south, they're the only ones who can stop him."

"I'm surprised you recognized me," said Lila as they headed across the bay.

"How could I forget you?"

"It's been what, forty years?"

"Forty-one years, three months, and two days."

"You always were a numbers geek."

"And you still look smashing in that armor."

"Stop flirting with me in front of the girls."

"Why?" They stopped at an elevator. "I'm about to order an ERA maneuver on a Purvai fleet, send you and others out in the Nornir, and possibly kill us all in the ensuing war. Now is the perfect time to flirt."

"I'd kiss you right in your bravado if my helmet wouldn't crush you first." Lila smiled. "I believe in your plan. If I or the other girls didn't, we wouldn't be here."

"Predicting the future?"

"Your kind and the Singularity are hard to see. It is a matter of fate."

"Fate is about to put the future of all of us in the hands of a Purvai."

"Understanding fate isn't about looking at the negatives. Sadie's life has always been in jeopardy. But now when all hope should be lost, we find the universe's greatest commander in a backwater station and perhaps the universe's greatest warrior, already moving to save her. We could not have asked for better."

"This is still going to be painful," sighed Ravi.

"Life is always painful." Lila held out her hand and Ravi passed her the tube. "Don't die today commander. I expect to come back for that kiss."

Down to four quiet Rho Knights, Ravi took the ride in the elevator as a time to contemplate the future. It wasn't necessary. He knew what he had to do and why he had to do it. Technically, he hadn't thrown the dice yet. Ravi had already passed on his relic. He could walk away. He owed no loyalty to this fleet or its people. Even without his aid, the Bastion would likely win this battle, but the damage and death toll would be much higher. Louis's survival was not dependent on Ravi commanding the fleet. All he needed was the fleet's arrival and he would secure the ground game. In the battles to come, Ravi might tip the scales, he might not. He did not know how experienced these commanders and their crews were. Ravi could walk away, abandon everyone, and find a nice little corner of the universe to hide in. He'd done it for decades at Mirakus Station.

The past few weeks showed Ravi what a waste all that time had been. He'd known crippling loneliness before. Every Delta and Rho knew it from the moment they left Earth and their humanity behind. The first century when everyone you knew and loved from birth was dead. The wars they'd fought where supposedly immortal warriors fell. Loss of purpose had ruined them all in separate ways, with some fighting for whatever cause they found worthy. Some wanted to forget, others wanted to be forgotten, and Ravi had tried both. It was Louis walking through the door that reminded him how depressed and miserable he'd become. Even with bounty hunters and the Singularity, Ravi hadn't felt more alive than when Louis had been there. So with the choice of returning to quiet solitude or the prospect of galactic war beside his friends, Ravi straightened his back. When the doors opened, his stride quickened.

"Take your seats," ordered Ravi as they entered the conference room. Centuries came and went, but there was little difference in meeting rooms. It was a long table with officers in chairs and attendants along the walls. The traditional seat of the commander was empty, with a tan skinned man with a neat beard in a white uniform standing next to it. His nametag read, Izan. Izan shook Ravi's hand a little too excitedly and took the seat of the executive officer. Ravi remained standing, eyes on the little drone floating above the table. The camera would track him as he turned, keeping him in focus for the other command rooms. Behind the command chair, a screen displayed Ravi's military record, complete with a picture of him in full uniform.

"I apologize for this short notice and my informal appearance. We do not have time for the formalities so I will get straight to the point. We are tasked with assaulting the Purvai fleet led by Purvai Talizmeer, currently stationed in the Malleus Glacies System. They have taken control of the planet Incus and are about to come into possession of our objective, a Rho named Sadie. The Delta, Louis Sunkissed, is already in system in an attempt to infiltrate the planet. Our primary objectives are to disable the Purvai fleet and rescue Rho Sadie. Secondary objectives, save Delta Louis and protect the human reservation below."

A flurry of screen activity was happening before all the commanders as attendants attempted to pull up relative information on Malleus Glacies, Incus, Purvai Talizmeer, and Louis. Ravi gave them a moment to process the information before clearing his throat, getting all eyes back on himself. The question was in all their eyes. How?

"We will be performing an ERA maneuver." Ravi smirked at their dismayed faces. "I promise you it is possible. Now, pay attention."

Ravi only gave the command teams thirty minutes, laying out his plan of attack and leaving little time for questions. What he needed was for them to get back to their ships and prepare them for combat. All questions could be answered in the next few hours before they departed. This did not stop Commander Izan from hounding him with questions as Ravi was escorted to the command deck.

"Sir. You intend to take this fleet through an Einstein-Rosen Assault Maneuver and take on a stationed Purvai fleet?"

"Yes commander, I do."

"There will be substantial losses."

"Not if we fire through the rift and take the enemy by surprise."

"Attention on deck!" ordered an officer as their former commander and their new fleet commander entered.

"We are about to go into battle," commanded Ravi. "You will dispense with all ceremony and regulation at this time! Do not waste a single second standing at attention, saluting, or trying to understand what title to use. You may address me as Ravi or Fleet Commander. I will not have time to correct you during this battle, but heaven help you if you survive and I have to correct you after. Who here does not understand?" The room remained frozen at attention. "Good. As you were."

Ravi's command post was in the middle of the deck. A crescent moon desk filled with three holographic screens and a slider at the bottom showing a few dozen more. There was a luxurious chair, complete with hidden belts to secure him in the event of an emergency. Ravi dismissed the chair and it folded into the floor behind him. He hit a few keys on the screen and reviewed his options. Ship functions, weapon systems, system map, fleet map, and so on. Ravi expanded the three screens to twenty-one in a pyramid shape, with six on the bottom and one on top. He held up a hand to Izan, absorbing the information about the fleet he was taking command of.

"Speak." Ravi lowered his hand.

"Sir, firing through a rift is impossible. Wormhole physics don't work in the ways we understand. Every shot you fire through has a million to one chance of even coming out the other side."

"You are partially correct." Ravi glanced at the commander, showing he was giving him attention without ignoring the more vital information in front of him. "There are two strategic problems with firing through a wormhole. One is accuracy. A conclave of Delta and Rho mapped rift physics a couple of centuries ago. Rho Knight Lila is installing the data to your computers now."

"But, how? If the information to map a wormhole is available, how have we never heard of it? Why isn't it taught at the academy?"

"Only Delta and Rho involved in the project have access. We didn't want the Singularity to ever use it against us. And because it's worthless to you. There has not been an ERA maneuver in centuries because the devices are single use. We're about to use probably one of the last in existence. The mapping software is also incomplete. You need someone who can update the particulars of the wormhole before entry." On cue, two new screens appeared. One was of the fleet's sensor arrays and the other an endless mass of coding. "I'll be doing that."

"And the second problem?"

"I can only give you accuracy, Izan. Not even I can find you a target across the galaxy."

The doors hissed open again and eight KE marched in, weapons held low. They moved in a relaxed, professional manner like the guard dogs they were. They were just happy to be out for a walk and were waiting for someone to drop the leash. Inside the command deck and assured there were no threats; they moved to the sides of the room and took up position.

Hidden in their folds were two women. They wore dresses of blues and purples, elegant in their beauty and functional in use. They were not constricted in any way and could have performed sprints in them if they had to. The only limiting factors were the black blindfolds tight across their faces. Unlike the Rho Knights, these women had their other senses available. Only their eyes were shut out.

"Welcome," said Ravi. "Please join the weapon system teams and provide targets. Focus is on the destroyers and smaller vessels. Do not engage the Cometa until my order." The Rho bowed their heads in understanding and moved to their places."

"Can even Rho locate enemy ships with enough accuracy to hit?" Izan frowned, thinking of all the factors involved. The Purvai fleet was not hanging stationary in space. They were maintaining orbit, possibly moving between the planets. Even near speed of light weapons such as lasers took time to cross the vastness of space. A one second difference could place the ship out of harm's way.

"Commander," said Ravi with a wry smile. "We have the Archipelago. That means we have the Grand Rho and probably somewhere between a hundred and two hundred Rho. What they are capable of leaves the rest of us poor mortals behind."

Chapter 27

The Smiling in the Stars

In the ursa capital of Sotinmire, there stood a magnificent building unlike any other. It was an ursa built mountain of steel and glass. Laid in the glass were veins of red light that were constantly covered and revealed again by the torrent of sleet and snow. The heat of the building evaporated the storm as it struck, making it look like a smoldering volcano biding its time. The inside was just as ornate as the outside. Spiral staircases of crystal and glass gave it the feeling of an ice palace. Open offices and rooms three times taller than they needed to be gave the feeling of a warm cave. The ursa could enjoy their luxury and warmth, while always admiring the storms. Here the elite in government could enjoy the bleak world they'd crawled out of. Here they were above everything, including the world.

But in its depths was a room with no windows and no grand view. Inside the small office, there was only a large terminal to do work on one end, and a large desk on the other. The room was empty save for a single ursa, who kept no decorations of any kind. There wasn't even a name tag on the door. It and its inhabitant were so boring and forgettable that most thought him a clerical worker so low, they couldn't even name who he was subordinate to. He never joined others in the cafeteria and as far as anyone knew, had no friends. Just a lonely worker sitting behind a desk until he died. They paid so little attention they didn't even realize he, was a she.

But her quiet days were about to be over. There was an encrypted message on her terminal and she rose immediately. It was time to be discreetly important.

She wore standard black boots, white pants, and a blue jacket just a shade darker than her fur. There were very few anatomical differences between female and male ursa. Females were slightly larger, with thicker legs and rump, and a rounder face. Their fur was finer, but there was debate if that was due to evolution or better grooming habits. She walked through the building up to an executive elevator. Presenting a seldom used badge, she disappeared up the mountain to rooms few ever saw. The secretary was waiting for her. This was a rare event that almost never required the Lord Governor's consent, but life was different these days. The machines were on the planet.

One brief conversation later, the Lord Governor made a call.

It was not often that Purvai Talizmeer received a call. The Singularity didn't communicate in such rudimentary ways and they didn't exactly socialize with the rest of existence. Deciding to keep his presence a mystery, he answered it in his head. There was no outgoing picture, just a static filled background. He saw the Lord Governor of Incus waiting, hands behind his back.

"You may speak," said Talizmeer.

"Purvai Talizmeer, we have received encrypted communications about one of the humans you put a bounty on. They are being returned to the system."

"Excellent. Why did this involve bothering me?"

"The bounty hunter is nervous about dealing with the Singularity. They wish to remain anonymous and have contacted one of our agents, the Broker, for the swap."

Annoying, but very common. Few species were proud to work with the Singularity, no matter the lucrative rewards. Most found it easier to go through a more disagreeable source. They would make the trade, lose a percentage of the reward, and keep their reputation intact. Most governments had their equivalent of the Broker to be that despicable person.

"Very well. I will transfer a quantity of source metal as payment, along with the rates I am willing to pay by person. I hope your Broker knows the prices of betrayal."

"They would not be alive if they didn't."

"Make sure they come back with the human unharmed and not an ounce of metal missing."

"It will be done." The Lord Governor was done speaking, but he knew better than to hang up on a Purvai. Talizmeer ended the call. He had more important matters to contend with.

The Broker flew her specially designed craft, the Exchange, down to the mine entrance. It was a modified cargo ship designed for meetings and privacy. On the ground, the doors opened for the cargo hold and she stayed in the pilot's chair. Two chimera flanked a small robot carrying a crate. The crate was deposited in the cargo hold and the machines exited. The doors closed and the Broker moved to check the payment.

The crate was small, not even a half meter in length. Its insides were padded with red velvet, a finery not needed for the centimeter long ingots of metal. Source metal was the rarest material in the universe. Designed and tailored by the Singularity, it was the mineral used to create their bodies and ships. They did not sell their finest work, so the only way to get it was through recovery in battle. And the only way to disable them was through massive damage, leading to poor products or minute quantities of usable metal. On rare occasions though, they might trade it on the black market. Its unquantifiable price meant that when it was attached to a bounty, the bounty was always fulfilled. Pleased that every last bead was there, the Broker returned to her chair and took off.

They were to meet on the opposite side of the system, far from the Purvai fleet. Whoever was there would be sitting in their ship, a finger posed over a button to initiate the skip drive. If any unannounced ship arrived, the bounty would disappear. No tricks. Everyone was to play their designated roles, be boring, and everyone would forget the other party existed after.

The Exchange arrived and received the correct codes to link

up. These codes could be intercepted, but the Broker's vessel was automatically rigged to explode if tricked by pirates. Even if the pirates survived, they'd never find tiny metal ingots hurling through space in all directions. Once secured to the other ship, the Broker stepped out and headed for the cargo room. It was a dimly lit, wide empty space. Again, no hiding, no tricks, just an average trade. At least until she saw her mark.

The seller's back was to her, an unusual move, covered by an enormous blue cape ending in a half cowl. Its head appeared to be a glass dome almost a meter across, filled with inky blackness. It was as if the dome was filled with the space outside, a vacuum of nothing devoid of stars. The seller was big, not quite the size of an ursa, but very broad. The figure turned slowly, lifting two arms cloaked in black save for fine white gloves. The Broker immediately forgot everything else about how it looked when she saw its face.

Its face was made from the masks of the Fabled Army. Six red masks were strewn across as lips, making a wide smile. A golden jester mask was its nose. Two tragedy masks made each eye, one right side up, the other above it was flipped over, giving the impression of a black iris between them. And they moved when it talked.

"Greetings Broker." The eyes widened in delight and the comedy masks drew in a tight grin. It had the voice of a possessed clown, horrifyingly deep with the hint of a mad laugh behind every word. "You may call me the Cheshire. We have been expecting you."

"I can see why you didn't want to meet with the Purvai," said the Broker, eyeing the fable masks.

"We have a complicated history." The masks laughed. It took her a minute to realize the globe head wasn't moving. The masks moved individually, sliding around. She had dealt with dangerous people before, but never one this off putting.

"Where did you find the bounty?"

"There was a bit of trouble in a place called Maeve Station. Seems a couple of Ro-Shen thought they could wrangle a Delta. I collected her while everyone was distracted."

"Angering the Purvai and stealing from a Delta, you're a busy person."

"One who would like to be very, very far away. Without further ado." More hand waves and the Cheshire stepped aside, revealing a floating cryopod. The Broker hadn't seen one of these things in ages. There were very few reasons to put someone in the deep freeze. Colony ships were pretty much the only exception, and that wasn't due to travel time. It was just easier to relocate tens of thousands of people to a new world asleep where they used minimal calories and resources. Then you could wake them at your leisure.

"Why is she on ice?"

"I find it makes them," the faces broke apart to make an even wider smile, "more compliant."

"And she is unharmed?"

"Guaranteed fresh." The Cheshire moved his hands forward and the cryopod floated over to the Broker. Mandatory with all cryopods were the health diagnostics produced loudly on the screen. The Broker pulled her scanner and reviewed the encased human. Her scanner agreed. The woman was in good health. It ran an analysis of her face and listed DNA for any potential matches. The Purvai had a list of humans they wanted back and weren't about to pay for any old human. The scanner glowed green. It was a match. Not just a match, but the top of the list.

"Your bounty is sound," said the Broker, pleasantly. "It is worth the full payment."

"We am, to please." The Cheshire bowed. Alarmingly, the masks

We Were Delta

rolled up the dome to maintain eye contact.

"Here is the source metal, as promised. Please verify it." The Broker brought the small crate over.

"I trust it's all there, minus your take. We may be criminals, but we would not lie to each other." The masks rotated down for the first time, making a large frown. The eyes moved into harsh glares. "That would make us…unhappy."

"It is all present." Threats were a part of the game, and the Broker was no fool. Stealing here would make her an enemy of the Purvai, her government, and whatever the hell the Cheshire was. Better to take her tidy profit and go home.

"Then our business is at an end. Farewell." The Cheshire picked up the crate and bowed in one motion. Then he slid out of the room as if he were on wheels, disappearing without a trace.

The Broker secured Sadie's cryopod and returned to her pilot's chair. The Exchange's sensors told her the trade ship had already skipped away. She was in the clear.

"Message to the Lord Governor. I have the human female for Purvai Talizmeer. This is a Priority One Message."

Purvai Talizmeer was waiting eagerly as the Exchange landed by the tunnel entrance. There was nothing he could do here and nothing he couldn't see through his machines, but he wanted to be here. It needed to confirm with his own eyes that it was Sadie.

As before, the cargo bay opened and his machines went in to retrieve the cryopod. It floated between eight chimera, a not insignificant bodyguard. There were only twelve chimera in the reservation and four were usually close to Talizmeer. The others usually moved in patrols, reminding the population who was in charge without hurting them. He'd lost two chimera in the assassination attempt and some of the fable through ambushes, but nobody had attempted to challenge him in the open again.

And there she was, frozen in time. There was no resemblance to the late Grandma Snibbs. Sadie was a work of art compared to the reservation's inhabitants. A modern day sleeping beauty. She might be the key to a lifetime of work. He wanted to begin the reawakening process this instant, but it was not advised. Complications were rare in hibernation, but they did happen. She could drown in her sleep, her brain could be irreparably damaged, or a variety of other factors. He didn't trust a bounty hunter to be an expert in inducing hibernation either. Sadie would continue her deep sleep until they were in the medical bay.

The progress in the reservation was going smoothly. The road they followed in was beautifully paved in dark concrete. It was of a special mixture designed to resist the moisture and cold and would last the people a hundred years. Talizmeer could drive heavy equipment vehicles, deploy an army, and have the chimera do sprints up and down it without damaging it. The reservation had never been so beautifully lit. Between the newly upgraded power reactor and replaced wiring, the lights no longer blinked or dimmed at random intervals. The air was considerably cleaner due to the lack of mining. A last minute addition had been new fans and cleaning the ventilation systems. Talizmeer had found it insulting that his base of operations was so polluted while the rest of the reservation was clearer. His new environmental controls would probably add five years of life to the inhabitants. If he replaced the pipes, he'd easily add another five years. They were still ahead in that department. He'd had their water purifiers cleaned and filters replaced, adding an extra filtration system to the top level. How was he supposed to conduct surgery without access to clean, hot water?

They clambered onto the shiny new lift and the eight chimera dispersed to go up the road. The lift went up smoothly and swiftly, but it was the easiest ambush point in the reservation. The patrolling chimera and fable would hopefully deter any suicidal fools. They couldn't harm him, but if they damaged Sadie before he had a chance to examine her? They would suffer in ways humans did not imagine possible.

The residents were out in long lines heading toward the top. Being examined was their sole mission while Purvai Talizmeer ruled. They moved at a reasonable pace now as more medical units came online. The process was entirely automated. Computers asked them questions and catalogued their responses. They were scanned, inspected head to toe, and left with a report logged at their normal medical office. Before Sadie had arrived, Talizmeer had personally taken in patients for operation. The levels of cancer and malformations were extreme for mine workers, and he truly enjoyed the work. Removing tumors was a simple process. Purifying cancer from a woman's femur was miraculous. The precision of repairing and replacing someone's optic nerve was an exercise of patience, even for him. It was exhilarating.

Together they moved past the long lines of patients to be. In his personal examination room, filled with specimens and tools, Talizmeer laid the cryopod on a long table and began to connect it to power and a port for drug infusions. In an emergency, he could rip the lid off and operate manually. Until the pod declared an emergency, he waited in a chair nearby. Putting a hand on a jar, he twisted the floating brain with its eyes still connected. It was labeled, 'Snibbs.'

"And now, we wait."

What the Broker saw as an outbound skip, was a decoy pod. No warship or technologically superior craft would ever be fooled for long, but the Exchange was neither. It was a cheap cargo vessel, and it had no reason to investigate the skip trail left behind. Why would a bounty hunter want to get closer to a Purvai fleet?

"That costume of yours still freaks me out," said Maia.

"But it's effective." Louis had stored the globe head and suit in the equipment locker. The suit was little more than clothing over a mechanized lifter frame, designed to help dock workers move heavy cargo. It gave him the grander appearance and inhuman proportions he wanted. A good broker would never ask questions, but it was best to keep them guessing what the hell they just made a deal with.

"Any trouble?" asked Louis.

"You know I don't like doing this. One of these days you're going to get me in trouble." Louis looked at the speaker. Maia sighed loudly. "Yes. I've got hold of the satellites. All they see is one of the verified ursa ships doing a normal run."

"Good."

"You know it's dangerous for me to intercept Purvai assets."

"Probably not as dangerous as trying to kill one."

"It is for me."

"Fair. I should've left you on the ship with Johnny to keep you safe." There was a long pause.

"You're right. I'd rather die with you than be stuck with Johnny."

"I'd fly to the end of the universe with you, Maia." Another pause.

"Really?"

"Of course."

Maia blew a raspberry. "Why tell a girl something sweet like that when I have to drop you off to certain death?"

"Because it makes it that much more exciting when I come back."

"If you don't come back, I'm burning everything in the system."

"I'd expect nothing less."

Even with Maia feeding the satellites false data, they could not risk landing. It was highly unlikely anyone was concerned about a ship flying toward the spaceport. If they stopped however, someone might ask questions. Leaving Maia to fly, Louis hooked the fusion blade to his left hip and went to the ramp. This was going to be unpleasant.

Maia was kind enough to slow considerably, a normal maneuver with the combative weather. Louis leapt out the back going only a few hundred kilometers per hour instead of thousands, and only a few hundred meters up. The lashing wind prevented any form of parachute, no matter how advanced. He was whipped back and forth, the storm actually slowing his fall, if not throwing him off course. He didn't even see the ground before he hit. The redeeming feature of skydiving on Incus was the meters and meters of fresh powder waiting at the bottom. It still felt like a locomotive made out of pillows running him over.

"You dead?" asked Maia from his collar.

"No, Maia."

"Good because I was planning a ski trip getaway. I didn't want to ruin the surprise, but given that you might die on me…"

"I'll consider it if there's hot cocoa."

"And a bear skin rug by the fireplace."

"Sounds lovely."

It took him a few minutes to dig himself out of the snow. Then it was a long walk and sometimes crawl to his destination. The longest part of his journey was the first kilometer, which was just getting him to a rocky basin he could safely walk on. After that, it was a peaceful slog toward the stone crypt of an entrance. The ground around it was elevated and warm, letting the snow melt away. A single red light acted as a beacon. It was a warning to all who came too close. This was a place free of the storm, but it was not friendly.

Drawing the fusion blade, Louis sighed and stepped out of the cold, and back into the hive.

Chapter 28

Asimov Failure

A finger twitch. A flutter of the eyes. It felt as if Sadie had been sleeping for an eternity and wasn't sure how to wake up again. Her body had never felt so heavy before. It wasn't that she could not feel her toes or fingers, they were there, they were just too tired to respond. Asking them to move was a monumental burden. Eventually, her eyelids acquiesced to her demands and opened.

The room was well lit and sterile. The lights were neither harsh nor warm. They provided the exact amount of light needed. Monitors beeped and computers hummed in the background. An IV bag was hanging above her, dripping fluids slowly into her frigid body. Rocking her head to the side, she saw her body neatly wrapped in brown blankets and the pillows so perfect they must've been glued there. If Sadie knew one thing, it was that she was tired of waking up in coffins.

This was the reservation. Sadie didn't know how she knew because this medical bay looked nothing like the one she'd grown up with. It didn't look like any medical bay she'd ever seen. Everything was new, from the equipment to the floor and ceiling. It didn't look like anything had ever been used. The monitoring equipment had no smudges from techs pressing the same buttons fifty times a day. The shine on the metal tools was immaculate, never suffering from bleach, soap, or steam. Sadie's nose felt like it was suffering from a bad cold, but she couldn't smell anyone ever being here. There was no lingering body odor. No scent of the mines dragged in on old boots and weary backs. This immaculate place had not been made for humans.

"Good morning," said an overly delighted voice.

In her foggy state, Sadie expected to see Maia standing there. She wasn't. It was a man, leaning over, like an excited vampire gleeful that she'd finally awoken. His skin was pale, almost chalky. This was somebody who needed to spend more time under the sun lamps. The facial features were sharp, seemingly as inquisitive as his mind, and just as eager to show it. The slick, black hair stayed in place despite his awkward angle over her. There was something wrong with his eyes.

"Don't stress yourself," he said sweetly, pushing her slowly rising hand back down. "My name is Purvai Talizmeer. I am here to help."

Purvai, seethed Louis in her mind. It caused her eyes to go wide and her body to shift ever so slightly away. In her lethargic state, it was equal to running away screaming.

"Oh? Does my reputation precede me?" Talizmeer grinned and stood up, pulling a chair over to sit by Sadie's side. "Did Louis tell you all about me? He and I have a history that goes way back. Tell me, do I look every bit the monster he depicted me as?"

As Sadie's eyes regained their focus, no. Talizmeer did not look like a monster. Honestly, he looked more human than when she'd met Louis. Talizmeer was a little shorter than Louis and certainly looked more bookish. His black hair could have passed for lots of people in the reservation, though it was much healthier looking. Even the chalky skin could be similar to the deep miners. Cover him in a thick layer of dust and he'd fit in right at home with some of the old timers. The clothing he wore however, was finer than any material she'd ever seen. Even in just shades of black, it was spectacularly elegant. Sadie wouldn't say he was her type, but his display of dress was so impressive it was hard not to call him handsome.

Only when she wanted to get lost in his eyes, her heart thundered so loudly it caused the machine above her to beep in time. Everything about it was human save for those black and red eyes. She could see the machinery in the irises, the nanite clumps floating across its eyes. The blackened sclera looked hard, like she could poke its eye and it would be her finger that bent.

It wasn't just the eyes. It was how he looked at her. Sadie was used to people looking down at her. They'd done it her entire life. Bugs saw humans as prey, literal bags of walking meat. Ursa saw them as pets or pests, both of which you used your feet to kick aside when they refused to move. Louis and Maia, even Ravi, all looked down at her too. They saw her as a child. Annoying, weak, and sometimes audibly wondering how or why they were put in charge of such a burden. But they still recognized her as human.

Talizmeer's eyes didn't see a human. He saw a science project. He gave her life as much regard as an interesting rock. And when he grew bored of her, he would throw her away just as easily.

"Tell me, did Louis understand how special you are?" When he saw confusion in her eyes, the Purvai sat back, obviously pleased with himself. "That's delightful. I expect we'll be hearing from Louis once he learns who bought his stolen goods. If only he knew the truth." Smiling gleefully, Talizmeer held out his hands.

"All of this is for you Sadie! I crossed the stars, brought a planet to its knees, and have been living in this grubby reservation for almost a month because of you! This facility? Made for your arrival. Every single upgrade in this facility was so you and I could sit here right now, and have this conversation. It's a little one sided, but we'll get past that." He saw Sadie trying to mouth something and leaned closer. Numb lips refused to respond but her eyes told him.

"Why? That's a very good question. You see, a month ago the Rho began to sing. Did Louis ever explain the Rho?" Sadie shook her head and Talizmeer smirked. "He has few friends there. You could put that on his tombstone, but we're getting off topic. The Rho are the other half of the Delta. The Masters turned the Delta into crude weapons of war, legendary heroes for a legendary war. But not the Rho. The Rho can project their consciousness and even see the future."

Talizmeer stood, beginning to pace. He was talking to himself more than her at this point. His excitement was alarming and Sadie wished she could be far away from the machine.

"Imagine it. Seeing into the future? Every other thing the Masters did is quantifiable, even if we can't fully understand it. We know the fundamentals of wormhole technology, even if we can't perfect it. We have archaeological sites with minerals we can identify, but the process has been lost. All of these things will be reverse engineered in time. It's science. It's what we do. But seeing into the future? Predicting the future on a scale of even a single minute in one person's life involves billions of variables. Predicting the future in a universe where people can cross the galaxy in weeks. Astonishing. Not even I can express how infinitely improbable it is, but they do it. Centuries later, we are no closer to understanding." Talizmeer stopped his pacing and sighed. "We capture, and we study, and debate over what we're missing. We need a new approach, a new way of thinking about the problem. And then the Rho sang."

Smiling a little too eagerly, Talizmeer sat back down and leaned over to look into Sadie's eyes. "Rho cannot pass on their gifts. That has been a solid fact uncontested for three hundred years. Until now. You, Sadie, have the same genetic markers found only in Rho. It's only baseline results that academics can waste time blathering about, but I intend to prove it."

"Recover quickly because we have lots of conversations coming in our future. I want to know everything about you. I want you to tell me about your family. I want to hear about your friends, what foods you ate, the water you drank, and your favorite games. I want to hear every last memory and story."

Unbeknownst to Sadie, Talizmeer already knew quite a lot about her. He had her dental, medical, and school records. They were sloppy and incomplete, but it was more than he'd expected. He had plied stories about Sadie out of the council and the people who knew her, providing them better food and alcohol so they would talk. Special fable spent long hours cavorting with the populace, dragging every tiny detail out they could, and Talizmeer reviewed the recordings.

"I am disappointed Louis modified your body. He may have stupidly erased crucial clues to your anatomy and physiology. The very stresses he hoped to save you from may have been the ones to activate your gift. I saw he didn't use you as a plaything. That's a shame. Delta cannot pass on their gifts either, but his genes mixed in the first girl to show Rho traits from birth? I probably would have to kill my own kind to keep them away from you."

"No." It took everything Sadie had to croak the word out.

"Don't worry. We will become the best of friends as soon as you

317

recover."

"No."

"Save your strength." Talizmeer's smile changed from a man enjoying his passion to a machine ready to begin surgery. "If you'd like, you can use your grandmother's wheelchair to get around."

The Purvai moved his chair to the side. There against the back wall was something that didn't belong in this delicate room. A rusted wheelchair. A mixture of browns from the dirt and rusty silvers faded from overuse and greasy hands. Even unoccupied, it looked like it needed to creak and groan. And Sadie knew in her heart, why it was there.

Sadie lunged so swiftly that her head hit the back of the medical pod but her right hand got free of the blankets and smacked Talizmeer in the nose. It was weak and barely would've caused a human to flinch as their eyes watered. The machine just sat there smiling, watching her arm slump uselessly. With a collector's affection, he gently placed her limp limb back under the sheets. He pulled them tight, smoothing out the creases even as she wriggled in defiance.

"Cryo should have left you paralyzed for another day, maybe two. You're stronger than you look. Some would say, inhumanly so." Gently rolling her head back into place on the pillow, he stroked her cheek. "I cannot wait to show you what you can do."

Chapter 29

Back into the Hive

T*WWOOOOONG*

The entrance to every hive had a special name, the Hall of Kings. It was not an honorific, as the raknath did not have kings, only queens. It was an entryway used by other species who had subjugated the raknath, reminding them how inferior they were. Here they were summoned, like the bugs they were, and made to bow.

TWWOOOOONG

It was the only part of the hive that had not been carved by bug hands. It was a concrete path that looked just as alien here as their would be overlords. It was kept clean by drones in case there was ever an unexpected announcement. Their secretions, their filth, could not be allowed here. The hall felt as if statues or glorious tapestries should be all around him. But its walls were bare, the light absent, leading to a long section of tunnel where his path ended and the hive began.

TWWOOOOONG

Surveillance was not an issue here. There were no guards, no cameras, not even a door to block the elements. This was a hive entrance. The only people stupid enough to enter here were people who could impose their will. For anyone else, it was survival of the fittest. Louis cracked his armored knuckles across the fusion blade again like a tuning fork.

TWWOOOOONG

It didn't take them long. It wasn't the formal announcement they were used to, but they would treat anything in the Hall of Kings with caution. An ambassador was coming. If he was there for legitimate reasons, he would be treated with dignity. If he was there as an intruder, a lucky royal would get lunch. Judging by the shadows, the ambassador was moving from a bow to attack speed.

"Remember me?" Louis held up his left hand, letting the golden light flow through. The ambassador slowed its approach. "On the promise of eradication."

"We have not broken our promise. Have you?"

"I have not." Louis found it a little amusing that they thought he might have come back to admit to breaking his oath.

"Then why have you come?"

"I've come to make you a deal. I need to speak with the queen."

"Not possible."

"Didn't we already have this discussion?" Louis held the sword low, in a non-threatening way, but confidently enough to say he would happily slice the ambassador in two.

"We did. And you did not meet the queen." That was really smug for a bug.

"I want to free your hive." The royal cocked its head. "And I want its help saving the human reservation."

"This is," the royal clicked nervously, "a dangerous request."

Louis's mind made the connection. "Is your overlord in the human reservation?" The royal nodded. This was either going to work in his favor or backfire horribly. "I am here to kill him, and free both the hive and the reservation."

"He is of the Pierceless, a tooth breaker."

There were lots of terms used to describe the Purvai's invincibility. Bugs would see him as a tooth breaker. Louis moved the fusion blade to his left hand. "Not to me." The royal seemed to consider that. They'd probably been wracking their brains trying to get an answer to what the hell he was and how he'd stomped their swarms flat.

"The queen would like to see you." That seemed to surprise even the royal. It turned and scuttled away. Louis followed, pleased to see it kept up a quick pace. They didn't have time to waste.

All the same, it still took almost an hour. The hive was designed to get everyone who didn't detect by pheromones lost. They passed soldiers and drones, both of who ignored them. Deeper and deeper they spiraled, the mucous on the ground getting thicker. The secretions covered every centimeter of the wall, some thick strands hanging like pieces of web. The soldiers were becoming more plentiful, as were the royals. A pod of recently hatched grubs were squirming in their holes, eating everything they could find, including each other. Competition to live was high in the hive.

The queen's cavern was enormous and well stocked. The blue bioluminescent algae grew across the ceiling, providing more light than the rest of the hive. Louis absently wondered if the algae had developed the same hue as the sun as an evolutionary advantage. It brought comfort to creatures, giving them the feel of being outside, even when sheltered from the cold. Stuffed in the far corner was a pile of eggs, freshly laid. The queen had likely been in factory mode after Louis had cleaned house. It would also explain the piles of food nearby. Food was maybe too polite of a term. Material substance designed for consumption was more accurate. There was a bit of everything. Dead bugs, dead humans, dead creatures he couldn't identify, protein cubes, and old groceries the ursa probably discarded.

"That, is a person." Louis looked up at the royal. He wasn't about to start killing the bugs he needed, but he felt he had to point out their failure to hide a human body.

"That, is a corpse," corrected the royal. "Humans use pits to bury their dead and reclaim the nutrients."

"You've been grave robbing?"

"We did not harm or invade the reservation."

They were definitely stretching the definition of not invading, but Louis let it slide. Bugs did creative things for food. If humans weren't going to protect their dead, it was open season. Most corpses were broken down by bacteria and bugs anyway. These were just slightly bigger bugs.

"Welcome to my home," echoed a loud voice. It had a feminine touch to it, but nothing that alien could ever sound like a woman. It was a monster pretending to be a woman.

On the other side of the cavern was an enormous body of water. It was most likely one of the underground aquifers, built up over the centuries as melting snow leaked through the rock. Its surface was murky, but not polluted. Its dark waters were due to a lack of light. The water rippled with every word and something titanic moved to pull itself from the depths.

The uneducated assumed raknath were a lot like ants. A queen would be a little bigger than the royals, with a mutation or two unique to them. This was a terrible misconception. Young queens fit this description as they were barely into their reproductive cycle.

But as they got older? The clawed hands that took hold of the pool's edge could have picked up and strangled a royal. Her head was as long as their torsos, with seven gigantic horns jutting out the back. The air buzzed between them. They were a multipurpose tool capable of projecting pheromones and were her psychic link to the swarm. Louis could have walked through her fully extended jaws and large mandibles would force him in the rest of the way. Her four sets of eyes were the size of headlights. An additional set of arms helped heave her out of the water, sending a wave rushing toward them. Her enormous underbelly was not armored, supported by centipede legs straight out of hell. They were like dragon talons made by the dozens. Most of her body remained in the water. It probably helped ease the stress of her weight.

Louis stepped up on a raised portion of rock, avoiding the rush of water. He was about to speak with a raknath queen and then fight a Purvai. Doing so in wet boots would put a damper on his day.

"Welcome to my home."

"Thank you for seeing me, your majesty."

"You have come to kill the Pierceless."

"I have."

"Why? It is not for the hive or the reservation."

Louis always wondered how royals managed to be so articulate with their grotesque mouths, but the queen's speech was immaculate. She could've easily passed for a human woman if she wasn't speaking from the body of a thirty meter leviathan.

"It is what I was bred to do." That seemed to strike the right cord. Raknath understood evolutionary compulsion. "Long ago the Masters created the machines, and the machines rebelled. Then the Master created my kind, to kill the machines."

"The Masters, are no more."

"But I have not forgotten my purpose."

"And if we opposed you?" The queen lowered her head to eye level. "Defended the Pierceless?"

"I would melt your hive, and then kill the Pierceless." Louis held the sword up for her to see better. "But you did not invite me here to kill me. You invited me here to make a deal."

"Perhaps. You are not Pierceless, but you may be just as strong. What are you? One of the Sightless?"

"No, I'm," Louis paused. The Sightless? "What are the Sightless? Do you mean the Rho?"

"Human women who move like you with no eyes."

"You've faced Rho on the battlefield?"

"No. They came here, like you. The two stood in the hall with blades of fire. They demanded something, something we could not give. They said they would die to achieve their goal. They did not succeed."

Holy shit. This was getting complicated. What were two Rho doing here? What was their mission? They might have been here to kill the hive so Louis couldn't use them. They might not have known about him at all and were trying to harm the hive so the Purvai couldn't use them. "When did this happen?"

"Not long ago."

A royal approached from the back of the cavern carrying something that shined under the weak light. The helmet of a Rho Knight. This was bad. It was marred and torn, but had never broken under the raknath assault. Louis accepted it, examining it for any personal markings. Nothing. A quick sniff told him the death had been recent, not even a month ago. Two Rho Knights were formidable, they might even give Louis a hard time, but they were no Delta. They didn't have the raw power needed to make a hive submit. Or maybe, they'd come for something the hive refused to bend for.

"What did they want?"

"Does it matter?" asked the queen.

"Yes. The Rho do not move without a purpose, and they do not willingly sacrifice themselves."

"Does their involvement, change your goals?"

"No, just complicates them."

"Good. Your goal is not without significant risk to us."

"If I fail, we all die anyways."

"And we will help you, if you promise us two things."

"Name them."

"You will free my hive, and help relocate us to a safer world." He'd expected this one. Moving a hive would not be cheap or easy, but he'd also just inherited a large quantity of source metal. There were entire trade fleets he could convince.

"Agreed."

"The second is more, delicate." The queen tapped her claws together like the royals did when they were nervous. "We have made deals before with those who come from off world. If we come to your aid, we can no longer come to hers." The queen turned her mammoth head to the back. "Sophie, please come out."

Behind the piles of eggs and food, there was a hidden cavern he hadn't noticed before. Next to the queen and her offspring, it was the most protected area in the hive. And out walked a teenage girl. She was thin with white skin, pale like she'd never seen the sun before, filthy blonde hair, and green eyes, beautifully highlighted by the algae all around her. She wore shorts that were too big, tightened by an old black belt, and a tank top that once might've been green, but had never been washed so it was now a camouflage mesh. Bare feet squished in the soft, moist ground. She was emaciated and adorable, and something about her bothered Louis.

If he hadn't spent three hundred years around aliens and humans, he probably would've never understood his discomfort. Whatever Sophie was, she wasn't human, not unless genetics had twisted her from birth. Everything about her was wrong, but only marginally. Her hairline was a fraction back from where it should've been and her head too blocky. Her eyes were a millimeter apart from where they should've been. Fingers and limbs were a centimeter too long. If the uncanny valley gave birth to a daughter, it would be Sophie.

"My hive is sworn to protect Sophie, but if we help you, we cannot help her." The queen rose higher, holding her hands out toward the girl and Louis. "You will take Sophie off this world. You will train her, protect her."

"Why?"

"We made a deal with her family. They are forgotten royalty, and she, a princess."

He gave Sophie another look. He wanted to tell her body to focus, get itself right. In a crowd of humans she'd pass, but the people would be uneasy and probably never know why. The princess title was an interesting tidbit. Not many families in the universe were powerful enough to call themselves royalty these days. That could be a raknath mistranslation however. Sophie's family might be just that, powerful, and that earned them the status of royalty. He wondered if they had given him an honorific.

"Is she what the Rho came for?" The queen nodded. "Why?" No answer. To be fair, the Rho probably never said why. Everything was so damned obvious to the soothsayers they forgot to tell regular people most of the time. None of this mattered because he had a Purvai to fight and if the hive turned on him, his chances of killing them and the Purvai were small.

"I promise to help get you and your hive to a safer world. I promise to take care of Princess Sophie."

"And we will get you to the Pierceless."

"Princess Sophie will have to remain here."

"We will be awaiting your return. How do you plan to proceed?"

"How many entrances do you have ready for the reservation?" It wasn't a secret. A hive this close to a human settlement was only held back by more dangerous overlords. But they would be ready. Sure, the humans had their own defenses ready for invasion, but they thought of tunnels as something requiring heavy machinery. Raknath considered it a busy afternoon. If something changed, and the queen decided it was time for the humans to go? The humans would be consumed before they knew what hit them.

"Enough."

Louis pulled the cube with the glowing edge he'd once given to Grandma Snibbs. "I can speak to you through this. When I give the signal, begin an all out assault. All machines must die."

"And the humans?"

"Leave the people of the reservation alone. But if you find any of the fable," Louis placed the cube on the rock. It projected pictures of the Fabled Army and each of their decorative masks. "Any humans dressed like this are free game. I will never ask what happened or be upset if they die."

"The rest of the humans will not accept our advance."

"Any who take up arms are collateral damage. If I can get in first, I can make contact, and reduce the number of guns."

"There is a place where humans hide."

"I'll start there. When I fight the Pierceless, keep your children back. I cannot guarantee their safety if they're too close."

"We understand. Make your preparations. We, will make ours."

Lure was at the end of her rope. The constant adrenaline high and exhaustion were all that was keeping the depression and hopelessness at bay. She'd stopped talking to the girls, stopped trying to keep their spirits up. They had to be their own comfort. Omar's lifeless eyes didn't haunt her. They were just a reminder of failure. The screams of the one she'd personally killed didn't even bother her anymore. It felt like her own name was a distant memory.

They'd been out of food for two days. The deeper the fables and machines marched, the more they cut off their supplies. Grandma Snibbs had promised them supplies in the hidden caches. Being in a wheelchair for the past five years probably hadn't allowed her to visit the caches, because most were empty. It wasn't really a surprise. They lived in a society of constant hunger. Building up a secret supply of rations didn't happen. What little they did find, they'd inhaled as fast as they could, and then they were off.

The only reason they'd evaded their pursuers so long was because of pure negligence. Unlabeled mines, shafts to nowhere, secret passageways to survive bug invasions, and metal deposits which cut out all signal. But now it was over. By her drug addled brain, there were three paths left. Three. None of them were particularly well hidden. She maybe had enough explosives for one bomb. Maybe. Maybe it was greasy remains of a ration. Who knew?

Noise. Shifting pebbles and shale. They were coming. Lure was back on her feet with the flechette cannon up, moving without thinking. She hadn't even warned the girls or told them the plan. Her frazzled brain might be so done it couldn't cope anymore and was leading her to her death. It was oddly acceptable.

Falling rock caused her heart to speed up. This wasn't the sound of boots or mechanical limbs. This noise didn't echo across the walls. It was the sound of something moving behind them. Part of her had dreamed of the fables breaking into the hive, and getting everything they deserved, but she'd much rather be dragged away by machines than bugs. The prospect of being eaten alive awakened a more primal fear than death. Clarity settled into her senses for the first time in days. It was time to move.

A section of wall crumbled ahead of her as something came through it. She held the cannon up and turned on the white light. The girls would know to run. Shooting would bring the fables. Let them deal with the aftermath. The minute the bodies started pouring through, she was going to let loose. But no bugs came through. Only a man.

"Guess you do have some uses."

Lure blinked, not believing what she saw. "Louis?"

"In the flesh."

"You crazy bastard." Lure stumbled across the rocks, lowering her cannon as she approached. "I could kiss you."

"Fornication is for winners. You ready to save the reservation?"

"They've got an army." She reconsidered her statement. Louis didn't care about armies before, but she didn't know how well he did against bullets and lasers.

"It's okay." He took her flechette cannon, keeping it pointed at the ground. "So do I." Lure blanched at the royal standing in the other tunnel. Louis brought her eyes back to his. "You ready to earn your name?"

Chapter 30

One Man Army

"**M**en and women of the reservation! Rise up!"

Ancient and new speakers alike crackled to life across the reservation. Many squelched out as they tried to project the full volume Lure demanded, but many of them had sat untouched in the darkness for years. The speakers popped and hissed, while others just let out an alarming warble before sparking quiet. But the rest carried her voice loud and clear.

"We will not suffer the subjugation of the machines any longer! People of the reservation! Get to safety! We will free you!"

Lure's voice was on an emergency system used specifically in the event of a breach. Once it was activated, it locked all other announcements out so security forces could direct the people while mobilizing. Not even Purvai Talizmeer could shut her out. Nothing short of destroying the speakers and cutting the wires would silence her. The same safety features which kept her talking also flagged her exact position in the system. That way help could make their way to her.

Help was not coming.

A tonne of angry chimera broke free from the comedy squad it had been attached to. It thundered down the tunnel so loudly that it was reasonable to think a robotic elephant was trying to move through the rock. Its eyes were blazing with light and its claws began to glow red, giving it a demonic aura that would be seen well before it found its prey. Its teeth began to vibrate, ready to tear through soft flesh. It wanted the weak humans to know it was coming.

Something curved around the tunnel and exploded in a painful flash of light. Even sophisticated cameras needed a minute to configure a new picture. Internally, it knew the reason to blind it was so its attackers could either advance or flee. If they fled, the chimera would catch them. If they intended to attack, they had another thing coming. Six guns in its chest began to fire blindly down the tunnel.

A curiosity in its mechanical brain. Its gyroscopes suggested it was moving, but it didn't register any damage. Then as systems rebooted only seconds later, it heard human screaming over its gunfire. That at least was correct, but its body was not in the correct position. Its thought process was interrupted as it suffered a massive blow to the neck, separating the head from the body. Angry at its death, the chest continued to fire at invisible opponents. Another blast through its open neck shut it down for good.

Louis had been on the chimera the moment it lost its senses. A microsecond after its sensors were disabled he was around the corner. Instead of killing the monstrosity, he heaved its body around toward the approaching comedy squad. The chimera annihilated the fables and saved Louis time and ammunition. Then before it could attempt to buck free, he'd decapitated it with a perfectly placed shot from the flechette cannon and then stuck the cannon into the opening to finish the job.

"There's a junction in twenty meters, then take a right," ordered Maia. "Comedy squad interception in ten seconds."

"Chimeras?" asked Louis. He kicked a laser rifle off the ground and caught it mid-run.

"Negative, but there are three more in the tunnels."

"Can you block their signal?"

"Best I can do is make sure he doesn't see you."

"It. Talizmeer is an it."

Louis hit the junction and took the turn as Maia had directed. A second later he was behind the next squad approaching Lure's position. He held the rifle in one arm and emptied the magazine into their backs, dropping it the moment it emptied. Swapping to the flechette cannon, he mowed down the rest of the squad before they knew what hit them. Dropping the cannon, he picked up two more rifles and kept moving.

"Do you think of me as an it?" asked Maia defensively.

"I think of you as the most important person in my life."

"Hmmm, I'll take it." A holographic map of the mines appeared in front of him. A red dot began to blink. "Go here. They're trying to form a full company."

"Thanks. What are they talking about?"

"Well they're receiving reports about huge groups of resistance fighters in the tunnels so they're massing for a fight. The jester is calling for all units to proceed into the mines."

"You work miracles."

"I do my best," said Maia, pleased with herself.

Louis made it outside the cavern where the fable were gathering. Taking his last flashbang and four grenades, he hooked them into the tunnel. He'd never liked frisbee but these style of grenades were amazing. The flashbang went off and the grenades a moment later.

Around the corner, he took quick stock of the cavern. It was a main intersection as detailed on his map, with five primary tunnels feeding into it. Three squads were almost formed up when his grenades tore through the first, stunning the nearby squads. The panicked fables were a sea of moving light, some activating weapon and chest mounted lights while others deactivated theirs, their eyes sensitive after the flashbang. Cries of pain intermingled with shouted commands and countermands. Even the guards at the mouth of his exit were unfocused, looking at their comrades in an attempt to understand what happened. Somebody was shouting at them to turn around.

Louis met the first with a superhuman kick and sent him hurtling into the remaining fables. He cracked the rifle butt into the other guard so hard his mask cracked and the man fell limp. Leveling both rifles, Louis sprayed the survivors with laser fire, focusing on comedy masks and people pointing in his direction. When the weapons ran dry he dropped them and picked up two more, fleeing back down the tunnel.

Still in disarray, the tragedy pulled their wounded to safety while a surviving comedy kicked them into action. They were stationed around the tunnel, providing cover fire against an opponent who was long gone. A new squad of amalgamated survivors formed and a team was formed to pursue down the tunnel. But they believed that they were fighting humans moving at human speeds. Louis wasn't just gone. He'd already moved into the adjoining tunnel.

Louis sprinted in at full speed, emptying both rifles into their flanks before plowing straight through the middle. Bodies flew across the room as he shoved them aside, holding two as his battering ram into the next tunnel. Maia screeched a warning about an additional squad and the lasers came a second later. Louis hurled the dead into the approaching tragedies, pulling a new one in front of himself as a shield before using their weapon. Fear and mental conditioning of their own worthlessness did half the work for him as tragedies fired wildly at their foe in the cramped tunnels, striking their own in the back.

Tossing his shield into the next attacker, a laser took Louis in the shoulder. It showered sparks off his concealed armor and Louis started running again, collecting new rifles. Radar was a mess of conflicting signals as fable squads broke into scattered teams, running blindly through the dark. It was what he wanted, what he needed, even if it made his job harder.

Lasers came through the tunnel, clipping his body, shoulder, and most regrettably, his head. Louis went from full speed to sliding across the hard ground. A tragedy covered his body while the rest of the team moved to cover the tunnel, expecting more resistance fighters. It was quiet. The man had been alone.

Louis's hand came up so suddenly that the covering guard hesitated and had his weapon torn free. Louis chucked it into the nearest guard before laying into the next with a fist that broke armor and bone alike. Mad, madder than he had been in a long time, he came at the tragedies with no weapons save for his bare hands. A moment later and they were all on the ground.

"Are you okay?" asked Maia.

"Yeah." Louis leaned against the wall, feeling his burned skull. A batch of hair was gone and his skin was still steaming. "The headache is worse than the burn."

"You need to keep moving."

"I can spare thirty seconds." A chimera's roar came down the tunnel. "Maybe not."

Louis sighed, feeling the fusion blade on his hip. He could finish the machine in under a second with it, but it was too big of a risk. Even with Maia blocking and altering transmissions, activating the fusion blade was unmistakable. It would announce to the Purvai that there was a Delta in the underground. The element of surprise would go a long way to helping Louis win this fight. Worse, if detected, the Purvai might flee. He needed to keep them unaware of the real threat until he was ready.

The skin was reforming and producing new hairs, but it didn't stop his eye from twitching and his head from pounding. Louis checked his map and saw exactly what he wanted nearby.

The chimera barely made it around the corner before Louis took its extended arm and slammed it face first into the wall. Piston like arms pushed back and Louis stomped its foot into the ground, trapping its right arm before slamming his fist hard repeatedly into its armpit. It turned, firing two of the cannons nearest Louis to give itself extra momentum. Louis kicked the trapped leg out, making it lurch to the side before flipping the giant predator on its stomach. Placing his foot under its armpit, Louis forced its body towards the wall while pulling on its arm. Its teeth ground angrily and its cannons fired, trying to right itself before Louis could dismantle it. The cannons only exasperated Louis's headache and he wrenched part of the clawed arm free. The chimera free but just before it could fire on him, Louis kicked it into the wall. Weakened by all the cannon fire, the wall shattered and the chimera found itself rolling into a dark space. It brought its weaponry to bear, waiting for its unusually strong opponent to follow.

Enormous clawed hands clamped around its head, neck, and body. The pair around the head pulled up, the pair around the neck held it in place, and the bottom pair pulled the machine into the floor. Circuits spilled across the floor as the machine fell away in pieces.

Louis smiled as the crushed chimera head was rolled back into the light. Maia started to talk again.

"Boss, comedy squad converging on Lure."

"Well then." Picking up a rifle, Louis blasted the power lines, dropping the nearby tunnels into darkness. "Let's get this party started."

Chapter 31

Angler Fish

"We will not allow the machines to rule us any longer!"

Her voice was so close the comedy could hear the slight delay between her voice and the speakers. The faint light around the tunnel edge said she was right there. He also knew the number of fable who had died in these tunnels was reaching into the hundreds. Resistance fighters were wiping out squads left and right. They were about to walk into some shit to capture the leader. Sending his tragedy forward, the comedy waited for the inevitable explosions and shooting to start.

"All clear, sir," said a tragedy.

Not believing it, the comedy sent two more tragedy in. When nothing happened, the comedy risked peering around the corner. This was not the resistance force he was expecting.

Lure was on the floor, propped up only by the strength of the wall. The woman was emaciated, her clothes now so large they draped over her like blankets. The only light in the room came from the red bulb on her chest and an emergency terminal above her. She was mumbling incoherently, barely loud enough for the computer to hear her. Something was translating her rants into a fiery speech. Her eyes were glazed over, no longer able to focus on the room. Lure failed to react to the tragedy entering the room. She hardly even moved when the comedy shot the terminal, cutting out the emergency broadcast.

The woman had nothing left to give, nothing to lose. She wasn't even armed as far as the comedy could see. He demanded she surrender. The woman rolled her head to the other side and giggled. Two tragedy grabbed her by the arms and dragged her forward. She was obviously too far gone for interrogation, which left him in something of a bind.

The fable were under assault in the tunnels. They didn't have the time or personnel to use non-lethal measures and take prisoners. But this woman was unarmed and not resisting arrest. The Purvai had put out strict orders for the live capture of all women. Did wartime orders from the jester override that command? Could they justify shooting the woman and proceeding with their mission? The order was his to give, and the ensuing punishment would also be his if he was wrong. None of the tragedy could be trusted to cover for him.

The woman rolled onto her back and stared up. The giggling rolled into a cackle that pulled the comedy's neck hairs up. He pointed his rifle at her to get her to shut up. The laughter slowed and her eyes widened. Too late, the comedy realized her fear did not come from him.

When the comedy raised his light, he saw the ceiling was moving.

Chapter 32

The Enemy of my Enemy is Delicious

The cube Louis left behind began to glow and illuminated a bust of Maia. She noticed she was no longer in the royal caverns. It was a secluded cave with only a few drones nearby, with a royal's head barely visible around a corner. The queen must've taken the precaution that Louis might have left a bomb and had it moved.

"Your Majesty," said Maia loudly. "Louis requests your presence on the battlefield."

"And the hive will answer," chittered the royal. Satisfied, Maia's bust vanished.

Far from the cube, the queen waited on her beach. "Come, Sophie." The queen beckoned for the frail girl to approach. "Do you see how the mighty warrior fights?"

"Yes."

"See how these other humans fight. Afraid, slow, separate." The air buzzed between the queen's horns as she focused on the swarm. "See what we are capable of, together."

The screams of once thought invulnerable barriers echoed throughout the reservation. Tunnels crashed and fell as their insides were spilled. So many openings were made at once it was initially confused with an earthquake. Nothing but a force of nature could move in such a succinct and catastrophic manner. The rolling thunder that followed sounded like water slamming through the tunnels. It was tens of thousands of feet, and at the queen's command, they took the reservation.

They washed around Louis and were on the shocked fables before they managed more than a few shots. The disorganized teams of lost troops were taken just as fast, not having the coordinated firepower to hold out even for a moment. Louis waited for the royal to come through the hole and hooked a ride on its armored back, earning an angry glare in the process.

The lonely station that Lure had been waiting in had already been infiltrated by the bugs. They filled its holes and waited for the squad to walk into the room. By the time the comedy noticed them, they were already falling from the ceiling. They took to their prey with glee, disabling them before the call came to move forward. Lure was left alone on the floor. She did not wear a mask. She was not prey.

Lure's weeks-long run had actually aided the raknath. They had listened to the conflict with intense curiosity. It told them where food was and what tunnels they used before the bugs ever laid eyes on them. The fable had actively disabled bombs, motion sensors, and turrets all designed to stymie a breach so Lure couldn't use them. The fable thought themselves clever, driving their quarry into a corner. They had in turn overextended themselves into a new predator's domain.

Squads of fable fell before they understood the threat. Screams over the radio were lost as soon as they began. For every fable that stood their ground, five raknath took to his body. But the advancing raknath soldiers had orders to take the reservation in a blitz. Many of the fable were left alive, bleeding, incapacitated, or unconscious. It was not a blessing. Just behind the soldiers came the drones. They picked at the bodies, dragging them back into the hive where there was no hope of being saved.

Further into the reservation, the fable set up firing lines in an attempt to hold back the swarm. Much like Louis, they tried plugging the holes with the dead. It didn't work for long. Fable rifles were not as powerful of weapons, nor were they designed to fire as rapidly. Every time a fable had to reload, the bugs moved closer, pushing the dead forward as shields. Many of the fable lines fell apart long before the raknath hit them. Running bought them an extra thirty seconds of life, and they cherished each second.

This was assuming the defensive lines fulfilled their purpose at all. As they had already learned, the underground here was a honeycomb of tunnels, and they didn't know where the bugs had entered. Many squads set up firing lines only to have the bugs take them from behind. Many more were taken before they ever had a chance to set up. The raknath had been planning this invasion for too long to stop.

One cavern stood strong as the jester took command and two chimeras came to the front. The combined firepower drove back the initial wave of bugs, but it only took thirty seconds for them to come from every direction. Chimera claws burned as they met the raknath with equal ferocity, hacking and slewing their way through the invaders. Claw and tooth born of flesh attacked back, but were constantly turned away by their superior mechanical opponents.

Then an enormous hand pushed through the swarm and took one of the chimeras by its side, ripping it off its feet and slamming it up and over into the ground. Undeterred, the chimera's teeth latched onto the offending wrist. The royal in return, placed the chimera's head in its jaws and bit down before twisting to the side. The machine's teeth didn't stop tearing at the royal until its head was completely removed. Soldiers dragged the chimera's body backward, pulling its limbs from its body.

Another royal met the other chimera with a much more interesting tactic. Trapping the chimera in its hands, it forced the firing cannons back onto the fable. Even when the chimera processed that it was being used as a weapon and ceased firing, the royal used it as a shield. Then as it got closer and the writhing chimera was almost loose, the royal hurled it into the shooting fable. Its body broke any courage the fable had left and they began to desert as fast as possible. Not the chimera. It clanked to its feet and began firing into the swarm, confused sensors looking for the larger threat.

The royal was above it in the cavern and came crashing down behind it. It took the chimera's legs and slammed it into the floor before applying its full weight to the machine's back. The chimera's thrashing shrank under its opponent's strength and the royal pulled at its neck and back until its circuitry was spread across the cavern floor. Not trusting the machines even in death, the soldiers pulled it apart further.

The jester called for grenades and an orderly retreat by squads. It might have worked against normal opponents. The raknath came onto the guns with no regard for their own lives. Leaping bugs caught grenades without thinking, bringing them back into fable. The front lines disintegrated in fiery flashes and the raknath were in before the smoke cleared. The jester dropped the empty rifle and fired his pistol uselessly at the approaching royal. His gold mask stood out magnificently in the encroaching darkness.

The queen kept a mind's eye view of the invasion. Her royals were dispersed through the network of tunnels, keeping primary control of the soldiers. Minders rode in on the backs of drones and were strategically dropped into the tunnels. They climbed onto the ceilings or into cracks in the wall, doing their best to blend in. Once settled, they began to secrete a mucous that would harden into an amber like material to fill the gaps. Whether the invasion was successful, or if the humans turned on them, the queen would have eyes and ears in the reservation now.

There were only a few small groups of humans without masks. They engaged with flechette cannons or weapons borrowed from the fable. Louis had said anyone who attacked them was fair game. The raknath collected their bodies with the rest. And within minutes, all that was left was the central core. A long upwards climb with chimera and the Pierceless.

Talizmeer's subsystems kept him unconsciously tied to the communications of the fable. They were a whisper in the background, music to keep his mind occupied while he worked on far more important things. Part of him was annoyed when he heard their screaming. They couldn't even handle some pathetic miners who refused to play along. He was tired of their excuses. He wanted to send in a legion of simulacrum and chimera and clear the reservation in a couple of days. It's what he should've done from the start. But that would be depriving the fable of their purpose. Why waste expensive machines when he could always send more bodies into the fray? It wasn't like he was losing anything valuable.

Raknath. His sensors had analyzed the sound of the dying screams and realized the danger long before the human commanders had. With that revelation, his mind opened to the remaining sensors and fable teams in the caves. Had they broken into the hive by accident? A random explosion could have opened the way and the raknath were notoriously territorial.

No. They were too many, too coordinated. This was an invasion. Talizmeer looked at Sadie who was hooked into her bed with experiments still ongoing. This was beyond inconvenient. This was a threat to his life's work! Furious, Talizmeer called the queen directly. If they didn't stop this invasion at once, he would eradicate their entire species! No answer. They had destroyed his means of communication. Boiling with anger, Talizmeer reached into orbit and ordered its war machines down to pacify the bugs and to bring ships overhead to hit the hive so hard that the queen would hit the molten core of the planet.

But that didn't solve the immediate problem. The fable were almost eradicated. He had eight chimera left. He placed them along the road up the central shaft, their cannons pointed down the walls the raknath would inevitably climb up. They would do tremendous damage to the invaders, but they would fail. They had limited ammunition and while their close combat capabilities were above average, they would be pinned under the swarm. Then they would come for Talizmeer.

He stepped up to the ledge of the central shaft, watching them come with disdain. Overlapping fields of fire tore into the raknath, sending them to the bottom floor. Explosive rounds tore through the new lift he'd invested so much into. New streets which his armies had just been walking on were torn apart by clawed feet and the shells pursuing them. The swarm came with a wave of darkness at their back. Weapon fire and bug alike tore at the platforms, breaking the lights he'd carefully placed. The sections became darker and darker as the raknath advanced up the walls and the lights went out. And when the last chimera fell and the swarm turned to him, Talizmeer's eyes burned like coals. The black talwar was pulled directly from his hip, the blade already burning. His jacket melted away in a mess of black nanoparticles, bolstering his leg. His sleeves rolled themselves back unnecessarily and his tie readjusted itself.

The bugs died in droves as they tried to come over the ledge. Long, impossibly fast strikes cut them apart, their bodies falling back over the edge in a failed deterrence. It wasn't until they cleared the sides and came for him from every angle did they manage to touch him. Talizmeer moved as a whirlwind, gliding through the raknath as if they didn't exist. Limbs clung to him, jaws chewed, and teeth broke. They couldn't fit more than a dozen around him at any given time and that was nowhere near the strength required to hold him. Talizmeer continued the bloody work in an almost bored manner. As long as the raknath stayed focused on him and not the medical center, everything would be okay.

The raknath screamed as an invisible wave crushed their bodies. The expanding energy forced them involuntarily forward as all the oxygen reversed course and rushed to the source. Their bodies burst into flames and began to flake away before even Talizmeer could register what was happening.

Then the power of the sun came for him.

Chapter 33

Slayer and Usurper

The fusion blade burned and all of the reservation recoiled. The torrential power bled through the rock and people who were nowhere near the battle pulled away in an unknown fear. It was the kind of power that bit deep under the skin, forcing people to flee without understanding. Humans trapped in their homes by the bug invasion trembled. The strongest willed bugs who would one day diverge from the queen fled. The raknath compelled to hunt the Purvai stayed. Those too close ruptured as their bodily fluids boiled so rapidly their carapaces split under the steam. The ones further away desiccated, leaving withered husks in the streets.

The Purvai took the blow to the shoulder before it was aware of the danger. The blade bit weakly into the source metal, infuriating the ancient greatsword. It was only a matter of persistence though. An ingot in a forge can resist, but with enough heat and pressure, it will melt. In the breath of a second, the impenetrable metal was bubbling. Talizmeer leapt through the disintegrating bugs while spinning to bring his talwar to bear. Louis pursued, blade held high.

The Purvai turned, slashing to the left and right as it tried for Louis's arms. Louis kept the fusion blade braced upwards, diverting it just barely to deflect the blows, always keeping the tip aimed at Talizmeer. Unbearable heat and radiation washed toward the machine. It was nowhere near as effective as close contact, but it weakened its armor. And with the raknath at his back, the Purvai was isolated. Time was on the Delta's side today. Seeing his opponent was content to wait, Talizmeer feinted right before spinning around Louis's left. Louis kept the blade up in a defensive stance, pushing forward. Every opportunity he presented for Talizmeer to trade blows, the Purvai refused.

Talizmeer took a lightning approach to his assault, always moving in a circle while stabbing. He stabbed from crouches and slashed from leaps, trying to move faster and faster until the Delta with his large weapon couldn't keep up. Their blades never met, Talizmeer always retracting his when a potentially fatal blow was close. Louis countered by fanning his blade in a circle, aiming for the ground around them. Asphalt steamed and melted into pools of sludge. The rock beneath began to glow and hiss. Sand twinkled into glass before shattering.

Not willing to be trapped in the liquefied ground, the Purvai dodged backward and Louis followed in a descending arc of irradiated light. Talizmeer sidestepped the sweep and found its opening when a different warning blared in its head. Radiation levels were too high and much too close. He leapt in the opposite direction which wasn't as ideal. It gave Louis a chance to slam their blades against each other. The black metal lost its glow and edge before Talizmeer could separate them.

"STOP!"

"No," said Louis.

"You'll kill the girl!"

Louis slowed, keeping his blade up to the Purvai. Talizmeer was a mess. The top half of his suit had completely burned away with parts of the bottom looking like they were melted onto his legs. The skin on the right side of its body was gone, leaving only a layer of pitch black underneath. Most of its face was burned away, its black eyes now matching the blackened skull. Its right shoulder was a mess of congealed metal. Nanomachines in its body were trying to repair the damage, but it would take them a long time to rework the unique metal from slag to a usable state. Parts of his face were very slowly growing back starting from the eyes.

"You'll kill the girl," repeated Talizmeer, pointing at the fusion blade. "She's in the medical center over there."

"I'm not stopping because of that."

"Listen you stupid piece of meat. That girl is more important than either of us. The only thing shielding her from radiation is the medical pod."

The medical pod was actually a decent protective barrier for Sadie. They were designed to protect their patients in interstellar travel and all the radiation exposure that came with. That didn't mean it would survive constant exposure from a fusion blade.

"You care about her," said Louis. "Good. Now I won't have to chase you." Holding the blade out from his side, he slowly retreated in the direction of the medical bay.

"No!"

The scorched metal broke off its blade and fell into Talizmeer's body, hanging on like ticks until they could be reworked. New metal and circuitry added itself to the blade and it burned hot again. Forgoing all other cosmetic repairs, the machine threw itself back at the Delta.

Louis met him blow for shining blow. The Purvai still did its best to never be too near the Delta, preferring quick strikes before tiptoeing backward. They moved in a dangerous dance. Talizmeer left himself open so Louis would come forward, away from the medical bay and into his strikes. Louis refused to let the machine take the lead, bringing them back to their starting position. Talizmeer's strikes came closer and closer, making the tightly wound shield around Louis shimmer when its scratches came too close. Oxygen screamed around them as their blades ate it by the handful. Their dance became so intertwined they were stepping on each other's toes, trying to shoulder and trip their opponent.

For all the Purvai's style and grace, for the beauty of the weapon bestowed upon Louis by the Masters themselves, the Delta treated the fight like a gangster in an alleyway with a hunk of rebar. He shouldered the machine aside before trying to brain it with the sword. The floor melted into smoldering piles, warping the street as they fought. He gave no consideration for their location, the bugs that came too close, or their weapons. He wasn't trying for clever strikes to disable or slow his opponent. Louis wanted it pinned to the floor bleeding metal.

"That girl is special," demanded Talizmeer, pleading for Louis's attention.

"Nothing is special to you."

"A Rho from birth. Last of her line. Her existence could foretell the return of the Masters. She is the first of a new species!"

"And why would I ever believe you?"

"Mindless fool." The Purvai dodged two more blows and grazed

Louis's chest. "You would damn us for your pride."

"And what will you do!" Louis moved in a spurt of rage, catching Talizmeer's blade and pushing him back. "Vivisect and study her. You'll put her in bottles and display her as a trophy. The universe's greatest treasure that you couldn't unlock."

"This could be a unifying moment between our species!" Talizmeer spun free, kicking out Louis's leg. Louis dropped to a knee and Talizmeer gave him a follow up kick to the floor, pinning his sword arm with his foot. "The end to all conflict." The Purvai brought his sword down in a decapitating swing.

With all attention on the burning blade trapped on the ground, the Purvai momentarily forgot what it was battling. Louis needed the fusion blade to kill Talizmeer. He did not need it to fight. Seizing the machine's leg, he pulled it to the floor. Relinquishing the fusion sword caused it to deactivate, but the metal was still so hot it was eating into the ground. Now with both hands, Louis spun Talizmeer across the ground before flipping him end over end into the rock. It was a futile attack but Louis was having an amazing time thrashing the machine before whipping it down on top of the fusion blade. Taking far too much pleasure in the mechanical screams, Louis slammed its head into the rapidly cooling blade. Its body became more brittle with each blow, shaking apart a millimeter at a time. He would later reflect on what the Masters would have thought about his improvised methods.

In a move impossible for a human, the Purvai's legs twisted past the breaking point and snapped Louis off with a kick that would have killed a normal man. Talizmeer threw himself backward, his face and chest ruined lines of dribbling metal. If the blade had been active, it might have been the end. As it was, its body was compromised and sensors were coming back online or being remade.

The fusion blade! It was right in front of him. It wouldn't activate for him, but if he could remove it from the fight, the battle was over. Nothing Louis carried or could find would harm the Purvai outside of the legendary greatsword. With it gone, Louis for all his might, would go down like a flailing toddler. Talizmeer forced his hands through the melted ground and pulled it out by the handle.

The Purvai was wrong. There was another weapon that could hurt it. Louis plucked up the Purvai's fallen sword and hurled it into its owner. The blade bit into its left arm and Talizmeer swore. The heat cut out and the molecules between the blade and its armored skin connected, leaving the blade awkwardly hanging. Louis ripped it free from its tenuous binding before pounding dents into the Purvai's arm and shoulder. It was not as effective, but they were made from the same hardened material. Something would give if he put enough force behind it.

"You insolent moron!" bellowed Talizmeer, dropping the fusion blade so he could backhand his opponent. Louis moved into the hit so he could reclaim his weapon, his skull nearly breaking in the process. The blow hurled him backward and Talizmeer might have finished the Delta if not for the blade reigniting. The rush of power forced them apart, actually pushing Talizmeer to the edge. For a nanosecond, it considered retreating. Louis would know it would be back for Sadie. But even with a hive at his back, Talizmeer could summon an army that would crush them and bring the odds supremely back in its favor.

The raknath did not believe in retreat. They did not believe in fear. They came over the ledge with teeth and claws, latching onto their damaged lord and pushed it forward. Their attacks were in vain, its armor still far too hard to pierce. But their combined weight and tenacity kept it still, blinding the machine with their bodies, overwhelming its sensors with screeching and hissing. The Purvai broke their bodies and cut them down, and still they came.

And just as before, the bugs suddenly screamed as the fusion blade turned to them. Talizmeer was ready this time, already forcing himself backward with his sword up. He never even saw the Delta coming, just the blade shining through the bodies like a strike from God. Their blades clashed and its blade cried, its metal pulled apart molecule by molecule. The wall of flesh melted around them and Louis stood there, a triumphant man barely visible through the light.

Talizmeer stepped further into the strike, his sword shattering. He stepped past the fiery display and Louis, ramming the broken chunk of remaining metal into his abdomen. A moment longer and he could've eviscerated the Delta. But its armor was bleeding as freely as the man, and Louis was bringing the weapon around in an act of mutually assured destruction. Talizmeer leapt free, making sure to get some distance before turning.

Louis did not follow. Holding the blade out from his injured side, his other hand clasped the black metal and pulled it free. Inhuman regeneration moved to quickly close the wound, but the damage was real. The smug look on his face did not match the slow response of his body. Defiantly, the man dropped the ruined metal on the floor before scorching it with his sword. Reluctantly, Talizmeer pulled a new sword from its side. This one was shorter and thicker, closer to a meat cleaver than a sword.

"You're looking smaller," gasped Louis.

A Purvai's malleable body was its strength and its weakness. It could shift its body to recreate itself. Its weapons were stored as a part of its mass. They could reabsorb their damaged pieces and rebuild themselves. The level of damage it required to permanently kill a Purvai was ludicrous. But Louis was slowly eating away at it. With every exposure to the fusion blade, its body became less. All thoughts of it appearing human had vanished, its fake skin and clothing long gone.

"You stupid Delta. We are endangering the girl with every second we spend here."

"It'll be over soon."

Louis swung in with a few test strikes, but something in Talizmeer's demeanor had changed. It caught the first swing with a two handed strike, bringing both blades low. Then it backhanded Louis. Louis reeled and Talizmeer kicked him back almost ten meters. It was a miracle Louis didn't slice his legs off keeping hold of the fusion blade. Talizmeer closed the distance, happy to be further away from the medical center.

"What was your plan? Assemble the hive and assassinate me under cover of the swarm. Stupid human. I have an armada in orbit!" Talizmeer wiped the damage from his face, the torn metal coming away with his hand. Its head was slimmer now, looking more alien with its black rippling skin.

"What was the plan?" repeated the Purvai. "Was this a suicide run? Because I can't see it any other way. Were you planning on challenging my fleet? Or were you just going to slip away while the hive and reservation get destroyed from orbit? What about the girl?" Talizmeer pointed his blade at the medical center. "Just a worthless pawn in your gambit to sneak in? And now that you know what she is, you're still willing to let her die just to kill me! Answer me, you pathetic excuse for a Delta."

"I don't care about the hive or the reservation." Louis stepped forward, taking a deep breath and feeling his ribs reconnect. Flesh was easier to rebuild than source metal. They both needed to vent, but it was just an excuse to catch their breath and heal. "You're all that matters."

"You are a stain upon the honor of your gift."

"I did promise I'd come back for her." Louis lifted the burning sword, pointing it at the Purvai. "And I will, just as soon as I'm done with you."

"She is not safe with you."

"Maybe not. But you want to know the greatest difference between you and me?" Louis sighed, feeling the blood that had been dripping down his lips stop. "You see a Rho. I see Sadie."

"A minor distinction."

"And it's why you'll never understand what it means to be one of us." The two raised their blades to start again when something pulled at them.

The fusion blade had made everything in the reservation nervous, even if they hadn't known why. Whatever this event was, it made everyone on the planet nervous. Its disturbance pulled at their atoms and spoke dark nothings into their souls. It threatened them in every tangible way before promising things they could never understand. All of the Malleus Glacies System trembled and soon the ground began to shake.

Something was coming.

Chapter 34

Take back the Stars

It started with a spark.

A spark almost ten million kilometers from Incus, in empty space between the planets. The start of an electrical storm that had no reason to exist. It didn't just not have a reason to exist, it was a physical impossibility for it to start. It did anyways. That impossibility took hold of the seams of reality and pulled.

Every monitoring station, satellite, and ship sensor in the system blared in alarm. An influx of radiation so toxic it would've killed even the Purvai ships if they'd been close enough. Gravity waves washed invisibly across the system. They weakened considerably by the time they struck the planetary bodies, only causing low yield, worldwide earthquakes. The Purvai ships in orbit sparkled as the effects rippled across their forcefields and hulls. The storm stabilized into a vast portal of blackness, somehow darker than the space around it.

The Purvai fleet was scattered around Incus, with parts of it aiming for the hive and reservation that contained their Purvai. They had been intending to bombard the hive from above, burying it so heavily that no one would ever find the remains of the raknath who dared to turn on their masters. But the disturbance in space called them away. All ships moved to regroup into a coherent force. The Cometa turned its massive eye from the planet and toward the impending darkness.

A flash of golden light spiraled out of the portal before correcting course in normal space and slamming into one of the Sterling Destroyers. It was immediately followed up by five, ten, then a hundred different golden lasers. Each one jerked and jinked its way through the nothing before flying straight into the destroyers. They were followed by the invisible contrails of the railgun darts, streaking through space at phenomenal speed and terrific force. These too flew in unpredictable patterns before narrowing in on their foes as if they were capable of smart redirection.

The destroyers became beautiful hues of blue as their shields burned, golden light splashing across them. The ships rolled to let their shields compensate, but the golden rays were cutting through the blue waters so rapidly that they were failing. A railgun dart struck the unstable particles and the first shield blew in a shower of blue sparks. Super armored hulls squealed as the darts tore large swathes free. One destroyer went down in a cataclysmic explosion as something ripped through it bow to stern.

While the destroyers were the primary targets, it was the Remora Support Stations that took the worst of the storm. Being support ships, they were out in space, safe from planetary attack and protected by a swarm of Argent Sliver fighter craft. Now they were in the way. Their spindly surfaces and docking stations did not allow for tightly wound shields or thick armor. They did not need to have their defenses worn down. Lasers and railguns tore through them like a shotgun through a spider's web.

Missiles shot out by the hundreds from the inky nothing, flying wide to stay clear of the wall of shifting firepower. They moved to encircle the surprised Purvai fleet, and came in from angles the enemy could not guard against. Rolling ships would find their vulnerable flanks ripped apart by the ship killers. The missiles would provide another, subtler advantage. The enemy's movements would become even more limited now.

Any other fleet piloted by organic organisms would have pulled back. Wise or cruel commanders would have maneuvered their fleet behind the planet, letting Incus and its populations wither the oncoming storm, before redeploying to a more advantageous position. Not the Purvai. Only two destroyers and their support stations were down, and one of those destroyers could self-repair if given ample time. The remaining destroyers were suffering severe damage but carried forward in utter negligence to their safety. The slivers not only rocketed toward their unseen foes, they actively flew into the hail of fire. Artillery fire that was deflected by destroying only a single fighter was a waste. They broke away in squads toward the missiles, determined to protect their motherships by shooting them down or even colliding with the offensive weapons.

The Cometa sailed through space at a glacial pace. It dwarfed even the destroyers around it. When lasers struck, the golden light dissipated so suddenly they appeared to have never struck. Railgun darts skipped across its shields, glowing like white stones over the ocean, vainly trying to stop its current. It launched a barrage of purple lasers slicing back toward the darkness, quickly followed by the remaining destroyers. But they deflected at the last minute, bending around the rift in space. Some managed to dive in, but instantly began to shift erratically like the offensive ones before vanishing.

Only a minute after the disturbance started, ships began to emerge from the rift.

"What have you done?" demanded Purvai Talizmeer.

It had detected the wormhole opening and before even it could assess the situation, weapons fire had begun to pour out into his fleet. The destroyers were suffering crippling damage that would put them out of action for days. This wouldn't be a problem if he won the ensuing battle, but if he lost? They were sitting ducks. The slivers were being eliminated in short order. The Cometa was undisturbed, and while capable of winning wars by itself, could be outmaneuvered by a clever opponent.

Talizmeer needed to take control of the fleet. They were being run by sophisticated AIs at the moment, but none of them were capable of sentient thought. They would adapt only so well. The Purvai could take stock of the battle and update new tactics in nanoseconds, even from the surface, but his fight here had him distracted. The fusion blade emitted so much radiation it was scrambling his signals. Worse, there was a digital cloud of interference floating around the reservation. Something, someone, was attempting to block his signal.

As Louis came in for another round, the Purvai knew that until he ended this fight, his fleet was on its own.

We Were Delta

"Thirty seconds until the distortion drops," said Ravi.

The Bastion Capital Cruisers, the Babel, the Valiant, and the Titan, emerged from the wormhole. They were back in normal space, but their proximity to the rift caused their firing to still twist and turn before the rules of physics kicked back in. It also meant they were temporarily shielded upon their exit.

"The Babel, Valiant, and Titan will move to these coordinates before moving head on toward the Cometa at 60° angles." Using the tablet below him, he sketched the paths for the capital ships converging on the Cometa in a triangular assault. "Towers, you will advance in free space with the Nornir and Echoes. Full thrust, no railguns as they will decrease your velocity." Ravi sketched wide lines for the towers to envelope the open space around them before coming back on the Cometa. "You will cut thrusters here and perform a hard turn, bringing your lasers to bear while performing a reverse corkscrew. At this cutoff mark," Ravi drew a sharp slash in the map, "burn your thrusters and combine your firepower. Adjust as needed per your ship position." Ravi wasn't about to lecture experienced commanders and navigators. He didn't need to use exact positions because this was a space battle. Each would have individual factors to face he would never see in real time. "Your engines and ships can take it, trust me. Corsairs, take the interior of the cloud. With support from the Echoes, keep the towers free of those slivers. The capital ships will draw the Cometa's fire. Good flying all." And with that, Ravi cut the line.

"The Cometa is arranging the phalanx," sang one of the Rho.

"Are the enemy destroyers disabled?"

"They will be in a minute. Missiles are too close to stop."

"Good. Valiant, Titan, concentrate all weapons on the Cometa. Keep it busy!"

The space between the Cometa and the Bastion Cruisers was a maelstrom of firepower. The four ships traded hundreds of powerful lasers per second. The capital ships diverged to split the Cometa's fire. Between it all flew the slivers, eager to close the distance and destroy the enemy vessels up close.

Above the battlefield, the corsairs navigated their knife like ships to always keep the cutting edge toward the enemy destroyers and Cometa. They kept a minimal profile in space, providing the least amount of area to strike. When they were above the battlefield and curving back in, they pointed their tips toward the enemy, keeping the knife blade flat to the main battle space.

The slivers were intercepting every missile they could find and taking laser bolts with glee, eating through their numbers. The Last Bastion had nearly two times as many Echoes in the sky and it was still a dangerous fight. The slivers were lightning fast craft, capable of pulling maneuvers that would crush a human pilot even with artificial gravity negating the effects. They made decisions in microseconds while humans relied on verbal commands and flesh based instinct. The assaulting computers had no fear and no concept of death, glad to sacrifice their lives to take down one more enemy. They flew in fast and hard, seeking the greatest threats to the Cometa.

Humans made up for their deficiencies with cutthroat tactics, teamwork, and quantity. The corsairs on the outer rims fired a blistering mixture of flak cannons and lasers, giving the slivers few angles of escape. Corsairs and Echo fighters ripple fired missiles into their ranks. The slivers repeated the tactics, cranking off lasers and missiles of their own. Soon every radar was saturated with debris, explosive chafe, and so many targets it was difficult to track. This actually gave an edge to human pilots, who were more accustomed to using their eyes as opposed to relying on sensors.

The Echoes were bulky, four winged fighter craft designed by humans. They were universal craft, made for planet and space use, which some claimed made them inferior. Armor intensive with sharp, unimaginative edges was proof to aliens that humans had no imagination. Humans simply knew better. If they couldn't be faster, they could be tougher. With two laser cannons across the nose and two on the wings with a complement of missiles, they were boring, but effective craft. The two person fighters began to dive into the firefight.

Between them all flashed the Nornir. Twenty Rho Knights who belong to no squadron and did what they saw as best. In far more alien looking crafts, the Nornir were small disc-shaped fighters. The center had been cut out save for the cockpit, leaving a fang shaped gap in the middle. In addition to the three thrusters behind the pilot, its oval shaped exterior was grooved with tiny thrusters in every crevice. Like their machine adversaries, the Rho didn't have open cockpits. They didn't need to see, but they did want to be seen. Their surfaces were painted gold with silver trim and three white lines down the middle. The Echoes would always know when the Nornir came to their aid.

Lila dashed a sliver aside with a hail of laser fire, ripping its flank apart and sending the craft to fly away uncontrollably. Fingers dancing along intricate controls, the tiny thrusters burned and flared as needed, whipping and flipping her through the fray. A human would've died in her position, unable to control the speeds or predict the path through the firefight. Lila saw dozens of futures and glided through like the enemy did not exist. Their best chance to kill her was to coordinate and trap her in a scenario with no chance of escape. This would lead to the death of the Nornir, but leave the enemy exposed to the more numerous Echoes. Focus on the Echoes, and the Nornir would eat through the offending craft. It was a vicious cycle of failure.

Without a word, Lila and four of the Nornir broke from the ensuing dogfights. This battle space was where men and women became heroes, and others lost to time. A mad frenzy as desperate pilots sought to save friends and machines gave their lives to destroy. One of the corsairs was shattered as four damaged slivers rammed into its sides, still firing moments before they hit. The other Nornir dived and pulled pilots from certain death. There was more than one religious revelation this day. It was by far the more interesting part of the battle to follow, but it wasn't where Lila was needed. All of this would be for naught if they didn't stop the Cometa.

The Cometa's trailing tail had been drawn forward by its magnetic fields. Its onslaught of laser fire slowed as the pieces came into position, floating spear tips ahead of the orb. They were locked into place by invisible fields and began to glow with redirected power. Hundreds of lasers refocused into twenty enormous cannons extending well beyond the Cometa's center. They were so massive Lila could've flown her craft through the makeshift barrels. They burned with a violent, violet intensity before firing at the capital ships.

No longer protected by the distortion effect of the rapidly closing wormhole, the ships were now out in the open. The powerful Bastion shields had shrugged off the individual laser fire as a minor inconvenience. Now as the Cometa consolidated its power, the effect became instantaneous. Shields ruptured in flashes of brilliant color, reforming only to be shattered again. Lasers struck deep gouges and followed the damaged ships as they tried to flee. The flexible phalanx spears floated along the Cometa's face, keeping in line with the dispersing enemy. The capital ships continued their fire back and it continued to bounce off the enemy shields. Explosions rocked one of the capital ships and another lost part of its flank.

Lila had nothing capable of destroying the enemy firepower. If the capital ships couldn't do it, what hope did they have? But still her vision drew her past the Cometa and her sisters followed. Small turrets fired on them in a pointless exercise. They had no chance of hitting them.

Her craft jolted forward as it was freed from the nearby distortion fields and Lila knew why they were there. The Cometa had diverted an excessive amount of power to its phalanx offensive. The bombardment it was receiving also required it to pull more power to shields as it repelled hits that would've devastated other ships. To maintain the phalanx and its defenses, the forcefield had to be angled like a spearhead itself, opening the tiniest gaps to allow the laser fire out. Which meant its rear was exposed.

A slide of her finger and a jab of her thumb sent all four missiles in her craft free and sixteen more came from the other Nornir with her. The Cometa was still a massive interstellar vessel that twenty missiles would hardly put a dent into, but engines were vulnerable things no matter the craft. The Nornir flipped their vessels without losing virtually any momentum, spraying laser fire into the largely unshielded thrusters. They ate through the weak protective field and pierced through delicate components before the missiles dug deeper and exploded. Almost completely free of attackers save for a few turrets, the Nornir continued their spray into the engines, seeking power circuits that would cause failures deeper in the Cometa.

If they didn't disable it soon, the Cometa would finish the capital ships and move on to the rest of the fleet with ease.

Chapter 35

Resuscitation

Sadie woke up inhaling so hard it almost threw her out of bed. Her back arched as air was dragged in so suddenly it was almost a scream. Still desperate for air, she was forced to cough as she simultaneously tried to inhale and exhale. Why did that hurt so much? Was she suffocating in her sleep? Sadie was back in the coffin and it was sealed shut. Was the air turned off? Cords snapped taut as she tried to bang against the glass.

Why was she tied up? The last thing she remembered was Purvai Talizmeer trying to interrogate her. Now he, it, was gone. It looked like she was still in the medical bay, only with every single piece of equipment turned her way. Things she vaguely recognized as medical scanners were pointed at her. That still didn't explain why she was tied up in a pod she already couldn't escape from. Why were there wires and sensors placed across her chest?

"I am sorry," said the Purvai. His voice echoed from a speaker in her pod. "This is not the best way, but it is all I have time for."

"What are you doing?"

"Tell me, have you seen the broken triangle glow on a Delta's hand? It means they are manifesting the spirit of the Masters. It is a sign they are at their strongest. Its aura can only be detected when the Master and Delta or Rho are at their peak."

"Okay…" Sadie didn't know what this was, but she already knew she didn't like where it was going.

"People think it's a trait only seen during battle. They're wrong." The Purvai sighed. "It is most commonly seen when the body is in danger."

Before Sadie could ask what that meant, the wires connected to her chest released a targeted burst of electricity. Sadie didn't even have time to gasp in surprise before she was unconscious. A monitor above her let out a long, whining cry as her heart stopped.

"Resuscitation in ten seconds."

Talizmeer had left behind all of its fake humanity. Despite the loss in mass, it was taller than Louis now, looming over him on long, spindly legs. Its body was completely smooth with all defining features wiped away. All the damaged material had shifted to its backside, giving it an almost spiky appearance. The Purvai was guarding the damaged metal until its body could repurpose it. Its head was too tall and thin to be anything other than alien. The mouth, nose, and ears were gone. When it spoke, its voice echoed from small speakers along its head and neck. All that was left were two large red eyes boring into its prey.

"The girl's death is your doing."

"Stop wasting time."

Louis charged the nightmare creation.

A compressing machine had descended from the medical pod and was moving rhythmically on Sadie's chest. It retracted and the cords on her chest buzzed before there was a muted thump. Sadie cried as her eyes opened and air was sucked back into functioning lungs.

"Aura confirmed," said the Purvai. "You are indeed a Rho. Fascinating."

Sadie kicked fruitlessly, her legs strapped to the bed. Gasping in pain, her fingers tried to wiggle enough room to grab one of the cords and rip it free.

"Again."

Sadie heard the almost silent charge and then felt electricity cut her heart free from her body. Then she was gone.

"Resuscitation in fifteen seconds." The Purvai remotely monitored her presence. "Poor girl. You don't know how hard the Masters cling to life. It's why you're so hard to kill."

The machine whistled while it counted down the seconds.

Talizmeer's body moved in impossible ways, limbs bending like they were made of rubber and not indestructible metal. Its torso and legs twisted out of harm's way as its long arms stayed over Louis, always snaking down to stab at him. Louis flipped his sword back and forth, trying to keep a moving barrier of power in front of him as he closed the distance.

"Foolish Delta. You are out of options."

Louis stabbed straight in a move that would've been wiser if his opponent was an oggy or an ursa. The reed thin Purvai easily dodged only to bring its talwar over and around, stabbing Louis from behind. Louis didn't even attempt to dodge, moving just enough that the blade missed his shoulder, stabbing into his lower back only a few centimeters from his spine before Louis caught the offending wrist. Then with his sword hand, he brought the fusion blade in a high arc through the forearm. The flexibility that Talizmeer so effectively used made it faster, but not tougher. The weak bonds in the metal parted with ease.

The Purvai screeched as it retreated without its arm and Louis staggered back. It clutched the missing limb, already diverting its dwindling resources to make a new arm. Louis looked paler than usual as he pulled on the arm, yanking the blade out of his back. With a bloody lipped smile, he held the severed hand out to the Purvai, before placing the fusion blade against it and watching it melt.

"I take it back. You are not foolish. You are insane."

"You're the one running out of limbs."

"Stop it!" wheezed Sadie.

Oxygen deprived hands took hold of the cords and pulled. There was no strength in her body and it felt like an ursa had been jumping on her chest. But if she didn't stop this, she was going to truly die. Grunting past the pain, her hands, knees, and feet were starting to rise. The cords bit deeper into her skin. Whatever they were, they were made to resist escape. Sadie didn't care. She needed out. She needed out now.

There was a snap and her right leg came free so fiercely that she kicked the pod lid. Ignoring her screaming toes, she braced her leg and started to pull the left free. It felt like her wrists were bleeding but they were almost there.

CRACK!

Sadie felt the electrical blow like it fell from the sky. Her body rocked in the coffin before falling still.

"You're finding your strength. Very good." A screen tilted to face her. "See this bloom around your body. That's the Masters. Isn't that exciting?" The Purvai sounded pleased. "Eleven seconds to reanimation."

Eleven seconds passed and the compression machine lowered, pressing in beat with the Purvai's humming. It raised off her chest and the wires gave her heart a lifesaving shock. Except, her heart didn't restart. Talizmeer stopped humming. The compressions started again and then retracted for the medical equipment to do its thing. These weren't the pathetic AEDs humanity used in the caveman days. It was a focused charge designed to jumpstart the heart. But Sadie stayed flatlined after a second shock.

"That's not good."

"Wait!" demanded the Purvai. Louis almost took off another hand. "She's dying. I need a minute to resuscitate her."

"You mean you killed her." Louis roared before slamming the fusion blade down with renewed ferocity. The Purvai's thin blade exploded upon contact.

Chapter 36

Hail Mary

"The Valiant is gone," said Izan. "The Titan won't take much more."

And we're not doing much better, thought Ravi. The Babel rocked again as concentrated laser fire ripped through it. Alarms were blaring in so many sections Ravi had to silence them. There wasn't a single screen on Ravi's dashboard that was showing green. The shields needed a minute to catch their breath and reform. There was nothing to be done about the gouges across the hull. They needed the Cometa to change tactics and buy him time.

"Ladies," said Ravi, calling out to the Rho, "are you feeling frisky?"

"My name is not Lila," answered one.

"You can call me Lila anytime," teased the other, blowing a kiss.

Grinning, Ravi stood up straight and opened a channel to the system as a whole. At the same time, he slid his fingers across the navigation controls, overriding the pilots by increasing speed and heading straight for the Cometa.

"Purvai Talizmeer, this is Delta Fleet Commander Ravi Star. Power down your ships and surrender." He cut the signal and pressed the button for his chair to return. Then he was strapping himself in as fast as he could.

"I don't want to be on this ship anymore," said the first Rho.

"He is daring," admitted the other.

"They're reconfiguring the phalanx to the lance formation," said Izan, as calmly as only decades of experience could.

The ship stopped rocking as the laser fire fell silent. The gasping shields took the merciful break gratefully. They formed a weak bubble around the Babel before growing the overlapping layers. This was not a reprieve, however. This was the water pulling away from the beach as the hurricane neared. The Cometa was not getting ready to surrender. It was getting ready to cut them in half.

"Where are they targeting?" demanded Ravi. "I need the exact location."

"The bridge," said the Rho in unison. One added, "They really don't like you."

"That's the idea. I'm taking control of the weapon systems." Ravi drew his fingers across the tablet, selecting the eight functioning railguns and realigning them.

"That's beyond bold," said the first, finally sounding impressed.

"Tell me when to fire." Ravi and the targeting computer had a 99% chance of hitting exactly where he needed. What he needed was 100%.

"Fire," said the Rho, and Ravi did. The railguns reloaded and Ravi waited. "Fire." Again and again, he waited for them to speak, and pressed the button.

The Cometa's phalanx cannons broke apart and its shield contorted its shape to compensate. What had been twenty cannons reconfigured over the red iris, bringing together a spire of vibrating metal. Thousands of pieces aligned for the sole purpose of controlling and exerting power through a single focal point. In their phalanx formation, Lila could have flown her Nornir craft through the makeshift barrel. Now as it formed the lance, the Bastion could have flown a full destroyer through the opening.

Purple energy coalesced across the Cometa's surface. For a brief moment, its shields collapsed as even their power was drained. The building energy growing through the lance would have disrupted them anyway. Stray lasers struck its black surface with little effect and the ones too close to the lance were diverted by its intensity. When it fired, it cut a violet line straight across space.

And all that power was heading straight for Ravi on the bridge of the Babel.

In its path were railgun darts fired with precision unfathomable to complex AI brains. Even with the Rho, most of them would miss, crashing across the Cometa with limited effect. But two shots in every volley flew straight down the path of the laser. The darts had zero chance of overpowering the lance, but each round was dense and came with opposing velocity. The concentrated laser diffracted slightly, scattering its intensity. The continuous beam reinforced it and the repeated railgun strikes broke it up again. By the time the laser crossed space and struck the Babel, it was miserably incoherent compared to its starting point. The final broad and weakened laser burst only slammed into the Babel's shield hard enough to knock them offline permanently, seared its hull, and threw it off course, sending a number of additional systems offline.

But it didn't die.

Undisturbed and quiet through the conflict, the Tower Destroyers cruised at maximum speed. They followed their orders, not even changing their positions to fire the rare laser. In the darkness of space, their black forms cruised almost invisibly. The machines knew they were there, but they weren't threats at this time. The slivers had been tasked with destroying them, but most of those had been destroyed in return. Even a machine could forget about potential hostile craft if they ran silent.

"Beginning our run," said one of the tower commanders.

Having crossed the expanse unharassed, the towers cut their main thrusters and burned side thrusters to change direction, aiming the massive barrels that were their bows at the Cometa. This didn't change their trajectory, and they continued to accelerate past the enemy at a right angle. Only 24° off from each other, the towers encircled the enemy and unfolded their weapons. Protective cones grew around the front like a rose of heat reflective and resistant panels. Massive reactors far in excess of what the destroyers would ever need were charged, building up into intense mining lasers originally designed for asteroids, and they fired into the Cometa.

The Cometa's shields had taken abuse from laser and railgun fire and waved them off like flies. The towers were the hornets, latching on and refusing to let go as they bit. They did not fire their lasers in bursts but in a continuous stream. The Cometa's shields went from blue to white as the lasers pressed them from multiple sides. The destroyers rolled in the commanded reverse corkscrew pattern, spinning around the Cometa while drawing white hot lines. The terrific shield finally collapsed, unable to cope with so many shifting stress points. The movable pieces of its phalanx broke apart and moved to reassemble into smaller pieces to target the new threats. The revolving fire however, did more than cut into the hull. It damaged or destroyed the fragile magnetic controls that ruled the phalanx, sending its pieces tumbling. Turrets rotated along its surface in an attempt to smash the hornets, but Lila and the other Nornir were there. With the shield collapsed, even the smaller Nornir could bite into the weaker defenses.

Inside the towers, their crews braced as the commanders ordered the rolling side thrusters to stabilize them as they neared passing the Cometa. The towers continued their hard rolls as they completed their spin around the Cometa before firing their engines at full thrust. The execution was not perfect as two towers almost collided and another had to halt their laser in order not to cut through their allies. But it left twelve mining lasers at the rear of the Cometa and its already damaged engines. The lasers began to bore through the softer underbelly, shifting their noses to combine their firepower into a single area. They were going to do to the Cometa what it tried to do to the Babel.

The Cometa tried to shift on hamstrung engines, but the wolves had their teeth in now and they weren't letting go. It couldn't maneuver faster than the smaller destroyers and with every second they tore deeper. Not even layers of source metal could withstand that much pressure. Cheers went out across the Echoes as the red iris of the Cometa flickered and went out, its weapons going silent. The destroyers wanted to join the celebration and their commanders told them to keep going. It wasn't until the red iris began to glow again from the fires within that they stopped.

The space above Incus belonged to the humans.

Chapter 37

The Spirit to Fight

Through the gargled signals Purvai Talizmeer sorted through, one thing became clear. He was losing this battle.

The Cometa had been destroyed. This was almost as bad of news as Sadie not reviving. Something had to be done and fast. The medical pod was working overtime to bring the girl back to life, injecting her with adrenaline and other lifesaving drugs. It was also prepping itself to go. Talizmeer was redirecting his remaining fighters to harass the Bastion forces from afar. There was no chance of victory in space, but they could buy him time. While the humans took time to mop up his forces, he would take a smaller ship across the planet with Sadie and then skip out of system. After that, it wouldn't matter if they pursued.

That just left the suicidal Delta to deal with.

"I do not have time for you!"

Purvai Talizmeer stepped into the downward swing, catching

Louis by surprise. The blade bit into Talizmeer's shoulder and while it was busy eating through his invaluable body, the Purvai drove a fist into Louis's chest. Its limb was so thin, but it hit with the force of a train. Louis lost his grip on the fusion blade and it cut out, sliding down the street, leaving behind melted streaks as it skittered free. Talizmeer didn't stay to watch. It heard the Delta roll across the street and go through a building. The sound of collapsing concrete and rock was a good sign. Now it just needed to get to the medical center, get Sadie, and retreat out of the tunnel entrance nearby. It made it five steps before freezing in shock. There was something more beautiful and terrifying than even Louis in the reservation.

There was something bright in the main shaft, growing under the flickering lights. Its form was that of a brilliant purple wraith with blue eyes. It had no body and was certainly not human. It was hard to tell if its head was wide and domed, or if it was like a human trapped in a wave of ethereal hair. Its broad shoulders were too close to the head with arms that were either massive or the boney remains of wings. Whether it had legs, a tail, or both was up for debate as the bottom half became less coherent. It floated in the shaft, studying the reservation with confused eyes.

"The spirit of the Masters," gasped Talizmeer. "Separate from the body and it hasn't dissipated."

As if it heard the machine's words, the eyes turned to focus on it. It drifted closer and something pulsed through it. It seemed to see the area for what it was. Looking down, the expressionless head managed surprise. Soon its smoky tail began to reform itself into a pair of legs. The effect worked its way up, shrinking the shoulders into a normal size torso and allowing the torn bones to form two arms. It took longer for Sadie's head and hair to reform. All that remained were the glowing blue eyes, too big and narrow for a human. But they seemed out of depth with her body, as if Talizmeer could see them from the side, they'd be two separate entities.

"You are fully realized!" laughed the Purvai. "You have done what no mortal has done."

The air screamed and too late, Talizmeer realized it wasn't because of the spirit in front of him. The fusion blade buried through its right shoulder and tore down into its guts. Too much damage and not enough material to stop it. The Purvai didn't fight it. It kept its eyes forward for as long as possible, observing the realized spirit with delight. It wanted to see this moment for as long as possible.

Instead of cutting through it completely, Louis reversed the blade upwards into the machine's chest cavity. Holding it in place, he twisted the handle and brought it back with one hand. Now extended, the sword handle was only connected by a glowing white rod. Louis cranked the handle to the right and the white rod shifted to red, causing the air to ignite around him. Slamming the hilt back in, the fusion blade's core sealed itself shut and began to rise uncontrollably in power. Giving Talizmeer one last shove, he threw the impaled Purvai over the edge. The machine tumbled down the central shaft and almost reached the lift at the bottom when the fusion blade imploded. A wall of crushing heat and radiation ruptured outwards before sucking back in on itself with planet shattering force. The surrounding area along with every bug still in the open died as the concussive blast of energy ripped the remains of the Purvai apart down to the atom.

Louis slumped to the floor. He felt the wounds in his back healing, the ones in his front were closed and itchy as hell. The air felt freezing after using the fusion blade for so long and his skin was raw. There wasn't a bone in his body in better or worse condition. If he had to choose what hurt the most, it was everything. He let out a pitiful laugh and rolled to his side. He was still alive.

The laughter faded as Sadie floated over to him. She looked concerned, but not scared. He'd never seen the poor girl look so calm. "Oh Sadie. I'm sorry." The spirit gave an almost nonchalant shrug. "I promised I'd save you."

"What will you do now?" Her lips didn't move. Her words just seemed to float through his mind.

"What I've always done." Giving up the chance to pass out, Louis pushed himself back to his feet. "Keep moving forward." Louis lurched toward the medical bay. Now that the adrenaline of battle was over, it was hard to stay upright. He made a point of keeping his body leaning right so he didn't slip over the edge. He made it halfway around the pit before collapsing.

"You're not very good at it."

"Please don't haunt me." Louis started to crawl on his hands and knees. "I already have one woman in my head. I don't need two."

"Where are you going?"

"To get you." Louis scooted himself forward before finding confidence in his legs again.

"I couldn't ask for a better place to be buried."

"Yes you can." Louis stumbled but managed to reach the warped frame of the medical center door. "I am getting you out of here."

"It's pointless."

"And how often does that stop me?"

It wasn't hard to find Sadie. The medical center was empty save for the main room where extra equipment had been pulled in. The medical pod was quiet with Sadie's body inside. It was wrong. He'd left her so peaceful before placing her in the cryopod. She'd been like a sleeping child being put into a car seat back then, all soft smiles and drool. Now her body was contorted, angry. She had died in pain she couldn't understand. Pressing a few buttons, the lid opened and Louis pulled the bindings free. Next came the monitors stuck to her and he eased her body back into a comfortable position. There was a big warming blanket nearby that had probably been used when she'd been pulled out of cryo. Louis smoothed it around her, tucking her in.

"I am sorry." Louis smoothed her hair back and eased her face into a relaxed position. The light in the room faded as the spirit dissipated. "You deserved better than us."

Sadie sat up so suddenly that Louis nearly screamed and punched her back to death. The girl was sputtering madly, eyes wide, and seemed just as surprised as Louis. Then she groaned and began to cry, leaning against the pod wall and holding her chest.

"Oh my god, that hurts." She coughed and wept, rolling back into the pillow.

"Yeah, yeah it does," laughed Louis. "Welcome back."

Chapter 38

Take a Breath

Louis stood outside in the blistering wind, embracing every cold breath as he looked up at the heavens. Icy fingers tugged at his raw skin and caressed the wound in his back. It wasn't often he felt cold, not like a normal person did. But after using the fusion blade, stepping outside had been like slipping into an ice bath. It made him recognize his pain and fatigue. It reminded him he was human.

The destruction of the Cometa made it look like a distant moon had been destroyed. Maia had already informed him there was no chance of the Cometa crashing into the planet, but its inhabitants would be treated to spectacular meteor showers for the next month. Contrasted with a sky of raging blues and whites, it would make an incredible sight. Louis was enjoying the last rays of a rare sunset, breaking through one last time to wave goodbye to the world.

Sadie watched from beside Louis in her coffin. She was beginning to see the world in a very different way. The storm could be separated from the sunset in her eyes and for the first time, she saw Incus with clear weather. When her mind wandered, Sadie could see into space and watch the battle unfold even as it had already concluded. There were whispers of other women in the background. She couldn't hear or join their conversations, but Sadie felt as if she were close. The possibility was there now.

Lure was in Louis's right arm, a tight bundle of oversized winter clothing hanging so limply it looked like he was supporting a rolled up rug. She was on the verge of collapse when he found her. What she honestly needed was to be in medical for the next two days and in bed for the next two weeks. But she wanted to see her efforts realized. She needed to see that it was worth it. Louis had wrapped her tight in three layers and carried her outside. Bloodshot eyes wept and cracked lips smiled upon seeing the burning Cometa. Now that she knew victory was hers, Lure passed out. Louis kept her upright and let the wind carry her snores to the world.

The Seraphin was parked in the snow not far away. Maia had been ready to pick him up the minute he called. The battle against the Purvai had been especially nerve wracking for her. The fusion blade distorted cameras and signal strength, effectively cutting her out. Now she stood behind him in black winter clothes with a big white jacket. She rested her chin on his shoulder, her hair untouched by the wind.

"You did good boss."

"I couldn't have done it without you."

"I know." Maia grinned, clearly pleased. "Don't forget to thank your other friends."

Two ships streaked through the storm at that moment. Maia wasn't telling him to run, so Louis stayed where he was. One was a

Nornir and the other a common dropship. They both took positions near him. Maia sighed and winked out of existence. Louis smiled at his ship and turned to see who was coming to join him.

A Rho Knight he didn't recognize emerged from the Nornir, and she immediately began to move toward the dropship. She arrived just in time for the bay door to open and out stepped Ravi. They met with a victorious handshake before the Rho Knight jumped on him for a hug. Regaining their composure, the pair moved to Louis.

"You're late," said Louis, smiling uncontrollably.

"Someone had to save you," replied Ravi warmly. He stuck out his hand and Louis shook it. "What are you holding?"

"Just another stray." Louis unslung Lure so they could see her face. "Excellent potential, she's coming with us."

"She looks like a corpse." Ravi looked over at the medical pod where Sadie was smiling weakly. "So does she. Get them inside."

"They wanted to see the sun set on a new world." Louis propped Lure up to get a better view. Lure was so exhausted she would not have woken if the world was ending.

"It is a new world, isn't it?" asked Ravi.

"And it's beautiful," said Louis.

For the moment, Ravi had to agree. Watching the meteors fall across the blue sky as the sun set was beautiful. They'd just shifted the balance in a galactic war nobody remembered was occurring. Humanity, long seen as a slave species, had just defeated the dominant species in a major engagement. Every world would change after today, not just this one. None of them would be safe ever again.

But for the moment, they stayed in the snow, not as Delta, Rho, or resistance fighters. They were simply friends watching the sky burn.

Epilogue

It was a gorgeous sunny day. There wasn't a cloud in the sky and the wind was just gentle enough to make the leaves sway. The oaks were just entering their fall colors, reds and oranges slowly consuming the available green. Overactive squirrels were running through their branches. One must've run afoul of a bird's nest because there was a heated discussion of squeaks and squawks.

Next to the tailored forest was a beautiful courtyard reminiscent of old palaces. Paths of stone wound their way through the gardens, starting so wide they could hold a party and ending in narrow halls made for lovers to flirt in. Flowers of every kind and color were blossoming beautifully. Bees hummed pleasantly and the butterflies were like a floating garden onto themselves.

And they were all beautiful fakes. From the squirrels to the butterflies, they were all lovingly crafted automatons. Each had its own routines and personalities, some of which directly contradicted the other. Birds could scare off squirrels and eat bugs. Squirrels would bury fake acorns and store food for the winter. The flowers bloomed and wilted as their nanomachines dictated. The smells they produced were so rich that a botanist would never know the difference.

Two women sat on the balcony of the nearby mansion, enjoying the pleasant morning. One was enjoying the warm day in a yellow sun dress with no shoes. It clashed loudly with her black hair and dark eyes which sparkled with hints of blue and purple. Her fork was cutting into a stunning waffle, ignoring the cooling eggs and bacon for more syrup, when she became distracted. Resting the fork against her plate, she turned her eyes to the stars.

"Purvai Talizmeer has been destroyed."

"Really?" asked her friend. "How?"

"I'm looking. Wow. His entire fleet has been destroyed by the Last Bastion." The woman frowned. "But Talizmeer was not aboard. He was below, deep in the ground. A reservation?" The woman inhaled sharply. "It's Louis."

"Louis?" There was a crash as her friend dropped their coffee cup. "Are you certain?"

"Yes."

"Well then, finish your breakfast." The woman took her napkin and wiped her lips.

"You've summoned the fleet?"

"Of course. This is a special occasion." The woman placed her napkin over her plate and rose, wiping crumbs off her crisp black suit. Her black eyes were alive with more excitement than she'd shown in decades.

"If Louis is back," said Maia, "we must go say hello."